I0655747

Earl's Retreat

John E. Woodbery

Perelandra Press
Monroe, Washington
2004

also the author of

Hidden

Two Tomb Covers

Copyright © 2017 by John Woodbery
TXu 1-207-109
Published by Perelandra Publishing, Inc.

All rights reserved. No part of this publication may be reproduced or transmitted in any form by any means, electronic or mechanical, including photo copy, recording, or any information storage retrieval system, without permission in writing from the publisher and John E. Woodbery, author. Requests for permission to make copies of any part of the work should be mailed to 23324-171st Ave. SE, Monroe, Washington 98272.

Library of Congress Cataloging-in-Publication Data

Woodbery, John
Earl's Retreat / John E. Woodbery
ISBN 978-0-9860924-2-8

Manufactured in the United States of America
First printing

For more information on the author and upcoming books, visit **www.johnwoodbery.com**.

Cover and contents layout by Joff Huerth, Zing HQ
www.zinghq.com

Author photo by Kimberly Jackson

Cover artwork by Amber Jackson

DEDICATION

My friend and college fraternity brother, the Honorable Judge Michael J. Carter (Ret.) whose contributions to my recall of the southern culture of my youth and the way the language was spoken back then has been priceless in my writing.

ACKNOWLEDGMENTS

The author acknowledges with much appreciation the contributions of Amber Jackson for the cover art, Kimberly Jackson for the author's cover photograph and his wife Dee's tireless and thorough editing assistance. Also, many thanks to Jeff Hoerth at Zing HQ for his layout and cover design.

Contents

PREFACE

In the northern part of Florida, beneath the skies so blue, stands an old abandoned still house, known as Earl's Lagoon.

Earl Bryant was a moonshiner, buried so to speak, in the Florida backwoods so deep that no Federal Agent with sense enough to scramble eggs on Sunday morning would be caught dead trying to find it. Death is precisely what one of them found one early morning in 1933 at the Bryant homestead deep in Liberty County. It was a good name for this part of the county, filled with wildcats, wild hogs and wild men fiercely devoted to the proposition that all men, especially free white ones, were created equal and free to do just exactly what they dammed well pleased.

What some of this hardy breed of men particularly pleased to do, and had been doing since the end of the Civil War, among other pursuits, was to make moonshine whiskey and sell the stuff to customers in the surrounding counties at a time when alcohol of any kind had been prohibited by an amendment to the United States Constitution back in 1919 but produced and consumed nonetheless under a banner of freedom. These men largely made this possible.

The story of Earl Bryant is typical of such men in one sense but quite different in another in that the upbringing that developed the cunning and tenacity to outwit determined Federal Revenue Agents brought him to a crisis in his life that would determine whether the rationale that stood behind his life style would allow him to survive the consequences of his own choices in it.

John E. Woodbery
Monroe, WA

STILL

As related to Hail a 1930-1940 Vir.

Bluff

55 GAL. MESH WORKING BARRELS TOP CUT OUT

SHORTS OR BRAN CAP

1 Gal. WOOD KEG

PER BARREL MIXTURE
50 LBS. WHITE SUGAR
3 GAL. CORN MEAL
WATER to FILL & YEAST
CAP WITH SHORTS OR BRAN
APROX 3 DAY WORKING TIME
to PRODUCE BEER.

YEILD 5 GAL. MOONSHINE
PER BARREL

60 G.
COPPE
COOK

Bryant By
-ge moonshiner STILL

10 GAL.
WOOD
THUMPER

SPRING
DAM

COPPER LINE

7/8" COPPER LINE

NOTCH

DOUGH SEAL

25-1-3/4"
COPPER
WORM

moonshine
Sold for
2.00 Gal

AL-
A-ER
ER

FRUIT JAR

55 GAL cooling
BARREL

COOLING WATER
RUN OFF

1. Line of sight

The floors creaked ever so softly as the two men tiptoed around the bare office in the early morning predawn hours, not wanting to disturb the other men sleeping in the cots braced against the outside walls. They were silently gathering their guns and ammunition for the long trek out of the Tallahassee office of the Federal Revenue Service, and into the blackness of the night and the mystery of the north Florida pine woods. The Special Agent in Charge of the Federal Bureau of Investigation, Tallahassee Office, who had tactical control over these operations, had secretly handed this assignment to them. Congress had passed the twenty-first Amendment in February, 1933, repealing Prohibition following President Roosevelt's re-election in 1932 and the states were bound to ratify it before the end of the year. Fourteen years without a legal drink of whiskey was about all the nation could stand and that meant that the run of selling illegal whiskey had to be stopped. The government couldn't tax what wasn't supposed to be sold and once the gate was open to sell legal whiskey, the Feds could not allow the illegal stuff to compete with taxable sales. It was simply a matter of incentive. Before, there wasn't any real reason to enforce the law other than those few agents who saw a duty in spite of the generally accepted view that the people had to drink something, prohibited by law or not. But now it was different and the Service had been given its mission to allow only the revenue generating legal whiskey to be sold and it was up to the Revenue Agents to carry it out. And because this was one of the early search and destroy missions to wipe out the now illegal whiskey trade in that pursuit, it was better kept as their secret in the inimitable way of bureaucratic decision-making, just in case something did not go according to plan.

They were Federal agents, these courageous paladins of perspicacity, now dedicated to the capture and elimination of the illegal whiskey element of their society fueled and fostered by the elusive moonshiners scattered around the wild undeveloped areas surrounding Tallahassee, the State Capital. These wild and daring entrepreneurs had fulfilled a necessary function underneath the appearance of legality during Prohibition in a society that pretended it wanted to do the right thing but acted otherwise. But the impact of Prohibition had been seen and felt by nearly everyone in the community, some things for good and some for bad. It was a religious movement in practical effect, pure and simple, that had legally throttled man's natural tendency to drink whiskey and beer or anything else that would lift the dreary tedium of life with that marvelous intoxication that came from just enough of the spirits. Too much was a bad thing even then, but just the right amount was inspiration swirling up into ecstasy like wood smoke rising up the currents of a chimney.

The Churches had celebrated in 1919 when the last required state had ratified the 18th Amendment to the Constitution giving the Federal Government and the States the authority to enforce Prohibition, but most of their congregations only gave lip service to the morality of the law. However, many of them gave practical "lip" service to the edge of the whiskey jug or cup in its consumption in their private pursuits. After all, if whiskey production in the dark of the night or the deep of the woods was in full swing as it had been since those dismal days of reconstruction following the end of the lost War for Southern Independence, as the locals were fond of describing it, somebody had to be buying and drinking the whiskey being produced. Since everybody who was anybody in town attended one Church or the other most Sundays, then it stood to reason that some Church members, if not most of them, must be hypocritical on the whiskey question.

The Federal Government was the keenest enforcer of the statutes prohibiting the sale or consumption of whiskey spirits. Because even though the 16th Amendment permitting the levying and collection of income taxes had been ratified in 1913 (some to this day dispute whether it was ever legally ratified), the primary source of Federal Revenue was from excise taxes in general. It was the job of the Federal Revenue Agents to keep the revenue flowing. It was against the law, dammit, and their job was to enforce it, whether it had been uniformly done during the last fourteen years or not.

Frank Stiller was the senior man in the special unit recently organized to put an end to the recently made illegal, substitute liquor business in north Florida. He was tall, lanky and iron hard from an upbringing of hard work and moderate appetites. He was pushing sixty and by all accounts should have by his age, left the field work to younger men like his partner Clyde Browning. He was a veritable boy of the age of twenty-five and counting. Frank should have by then moved on to the bureaucratic bookwork or management of some of the teams. But the truth was he loved the field work and the excitement that the flowing adrenalin brought in the hunt for his prey and it could not be replaced in his way of seeing things by more money or less strenuous pursuits.

Even if he had left the Service, he was the kind of law officer of folk legend you hear about who would hang around the station listening to the stories of the action of the other men and absorbing as much excitement as he could by vicarious absorption. But he wasn't ready for that just yet since he had as much strength and energy as the next man and this morning was too important for him to be anywhere else but in the Model 1932 Ford truck barreling out of Tallahassee's downtown brick-paved streets and out west into the hinterlands on the way to Liberty County.

Frank was one of those rare dedicated men who had believed that if it was against the law to make and sell moonshine whiskey, taxable or not, it was his job to enforce it. He had been working on the Bryant case for years with his legendary network of informants of whiskey still operations and devoted and loyal employees who would follow his lead in the Service. However, the tip the Service was working on this time was just too tempting to pass up. Besides, the substantial pressure from the FBI on the Revenue Service to force these still operators out of business was ever present now that legal whiskey would generate tax revenue again.

Their inside source had disclosed to the Service at great risk to his own longevity in the liquor business, not to mention his own life and safety, that Earl Bryant had assembled a ready shipment of liquor mostly by mule and wagon to a secret assembly point from the far-flung moonshine still locations of his empire in Liberty County. From that assembly point, a truck would take it far away from the reach, hopefully, of the federal revenue agents.

He was planning an unusual large scale delivery by truck from the assembly point within a few miles of his homestead for a shipment out of Liberty County and up into Georgia or somewhere for the broader market for the stuff. Now that the "Feds" were gearing up to shut him down in Florida, due to an aggressive Special Agent in Charge in that region, a large shipment into neighboring Georgia was a risk Earl thought worth taking.

The Service in Georgia was run out of the Atlanta Office and operations in Decatur County in South Georgia were too far away from command central to have any power behind its enforcement. Earl was a good enough businessman to see that and his sense of timing was impeccable on such matters. Now was the time to move his inventory if he was ever going to do so. The word was out, by the country rumor mill, that a change of some magnitude was coming in the enforcement business. Earl wasn't about to be caught with his substantial whiskey inventory caught up in some federal law man trap.

The secret word from the snitch or mole in the Bryant system was that Earl would be having breakfast at home that morning just before meeting the assembled trucks back deep down into the pine wood forests surrounding his place. Frank intended to interview him and at least interrupt the flow of the stuff, slow it down or just possibly nab Bryant with the illegal whiskey on him in the process. If they got lucky, they might stumble on part of the shipment and find enough evidence to make an arrest.

It had never worked before but hope springs eternal as the saying goes and Frank thought it was at least worth a try. Bryant was a clever man and had eluded such attempts many times before but the information this time seemed just secure enough that the man most likely did not know they were coming. The element of surprise was the key, for if Bryant or any of his operatives got wind of the arrival, the loads would disappear as fast as they had been assembled. Bryant was so well known in this illegal business, Frank didn't think he would dare risk using force, so Frank felt reasonably safe in making the investigative raid without much fear for his personal safety.

The truck bounced and jolted its way southwest of Tallahassee that early December morning on December 5, 1933, after turning off Highway 20 just west of the Ochlocknee River about six or seven miles on some of the most miserable dirt roads known to man. Clyde held on to the armrest under the window of the truck and gripped the back of the bench seat for dear life as Frank Stiller pointed the Ford straight toward his goal in Liberty County.

The engine rattled and clanked, as those early Ford Models were known to do, which made conversation difficult. Clyde tried anyway.

"Do you think he'll really be there, Mr. Stiller?" Clyde asked.

"Clyde, I been chasing Earl Bryant for, what was it, twenty years ever since he broke free from that worthless piece of shit his old man was and struck out on his own, or more accurately, took over for him. As an individual operator and polecat moonshiner, Terrell Bryant was just as dangerous as his son Earl came to be, but not near as deadly and not half as smart. We could contain Terrell before 1913, I think it was, until Earl got old enough to begin to make an impact. Terrell had no sense of vision; it was as simple as that. He couldn't manage much more whiskey than he could brew and drip on his own. That Earl is a snake with a different twist on him. He must a been in his mid-thirties by then and the old man was getting tired and sloppy. That's how we finally got him, just wasn't watching out like he did in the early days. Sprung a trap on him, I did, and he didn't even see it coming."

Frank Stiller confirmed his explanations to his young assistant with a repeat of what he would have said to Earl's father if he could have done: "So sorry, Terrell, couldn't have happened to a more deserving snake of a man unless it's Earl on the same plate."

"After Earl took over there was vision and systems. He showed us he had both. He gradually turned that polecat single still operation of his old man into a network that could truly produce the stuff in quantity. Earl was pushing the old man before then, our sources said, you know, to modernize, expand, really pump out the stuff but old man Terrell was stubborn. He hung on to the old ways, which was, you know, comfortable. And then in a few years with Prohibition in full swing, there was no end to the market and Earl's succession to the old man's operation came just at the right time.

"By that time it was full stride. If you produce it, the folks will buy it. It's man's nature to want to get high or even drunk and no law is going to stop it, but that doesn't mean we can't try. His people are loyal or scared and for whatever reason they ain't talking. That's why we got lucky this time, I'm thinking."

The truck going practically full speed on these roads, hit an especially deep chuckhole in the road and Frank had to wrestle the steering wheel with both hands to keep the thing on track.

"Hold on, Clyde, or I'll bounce you out of this thing. He'll be there all right or my name's not Frank Stiller," he explained.

"Pardon me for asking, Sir, but what is the plan exactly, for this morning I mean?" Clyde assertively stated.

"We drive down to the bridge at Salty's at the Ochlocknee River on 20 and turn south on 65 in Hosford until we get to Taylor's Crossing and head into Bryant Country. When we get close to the homestead, we stop the truck and hike into there to arrive about six o'clock, around breakfast time. By then Earl will have checked everything out to coordinate the combined shipments and be back home for breakfast. If we're not expected, maybe we'll invite ourselves to breakfast. Wouldn't that be a turn for you? You got that search warrant Judge Ben Parker issued for us?" Frank asked.

"Yessir, it's right here and I'm anxious to serve it on that feller," Clyde said.

"Well don't get ahead of yourself, Clyde, we have to find him first, and no matter how good the tip was that justified probable cause to Judge Ben's satisfaction, there's just as good a chance that old Earl won't show up this morning," Frank explained to his over-eager companion.

The truck made the bridge at Salty's by five o'clock. Then they headed from the other side so they could find their way down Highway 65 to the crossroads at Taylor's Crossing and turn southeast into Bryant Country. The heavy pine wood canopy encased the Ford in a dark depressing gloom-like feeling even though in the early dawn light the surroundings would have been visible by now out in the open. Frank pulled the truck over to the side of the two rut sandy road and came to a stop. He set the hand brake and he and Clyde busied themselves getting their handguns with sufficient ammunition in place and headed down the dirt road on foot seeing only by the narrow flashlight beam that Clyde pointed ahead for safe walking.

Pretty soon and by first light, the two men came upon the sight they had been expecting. The Bryant homestead was a large single story clapboard house with a tin roof, with screen porches encircling practically the whole house. The front entrance, as best they could determine it, was centered on the northern exposure to the house and marked by a screen door. Frank and Clyde walked resolutely up to the door and Clyde rapped on it with the back of his hand to gain the attention of the occupants, and hopefully Earl Bryant would be one of them.

A couple of red bone hounds came boiling out from under the porch with their voices baying ready to defend the place from the invasion of these strangers or anyone else who happened to show up this deep in the piney woods.

"At ease, boys," Frank stated authoritatively, as if he were talking to a junior agent or an obedient soldier from the ranks, a command that the dogs did not appreciate, much less understand or obey.

"Hush, Blue, shut up, Red, git down, dogs," came a high-pitched female voice from inside the screen porch. How you would name a red, red bone hound "blue' was a mystery if one had time to think about incongruous things like that. But this morning that was beyond thinking about. "Mrs. Bryant, that you?" Frank Stiller boomed out hoping the attacking dogs would listen and they did, obediently backing down at the command of the mistress of the house.

"Yes, Sir, that's me and would you gentlemen please state your business, this is private property if you didn't know it and I hope to God you ain't lost," Mrs. Bryant said.

"We came to see Mr. Earl, Ma'am, we're Federal men and we have some business with him, is he here?" Frank asked politely, without disclosing that they had a search warrant from Judge Parker to check the place out for any whiskey business.

"No, Sir, he ain't and if you fellers had any sense, you'd turn round and beat it back down that road that brought you here. I hope to God you ain't walked all the way from Tallahassee, cause you'd had to have been at it all night," Mrs. Bryant stated sarcastically.

"No, Ma'am, we got a truck up the road a piece, but we need to speak to Earl and we have a search warrant from Judge Ben Parker to check the place over. Show it to Mrs. Bryant, Clyde," Frank Stiller explained.

As Clyde reached inside his coat pocket to grab the edge of the warrant, Frank Stiller lunged forward and fell across the top of the porch steps. Only then did the younger man hear the sharp flat report of the rifle that seemed to lag behind the blow that felled his partner. Clyde quickly turned with his upper body to survey the scene behind them where the rifle shot had undoubtedly come from and quickly seeing nothing, turned back to see what he could do for Frank. He quickly concluded that Frank was dead and that if he didn't get the hell out of there in a big hurry, he would be next.

It was one of those cases where discretion was the better part of valor. He turned on a dime and bolted across the yard and on up the road toward where the truck was parked. Realizing quickly as young men with all the brain cells they had ever been given can do, that the keys to the truck were with Frank; he spun around once again and raced to the corpse. Without a word to Mrs. Bryant who stood dumbstruck inside the porch, he retrieved the keys from the very dead Frank Stiller before racing with reckless abandon away from that obvious place of danger.

He had drawn his handgun but it was as useless at that moment as a fishing rod at a bull fight. Remarkably, he thought later on when there was time for such thinking, he had not been killed along with or in place of Frank Stiller. As he regained the truck, he fumbled his way into starting it, by a process that seemed in his panicked state of mind to take hours, when in fact it was only seconds.

He slipped the clutch, pulled the hand throttle down as full as he dared for the rough sandy road's condition and roared his way into the now sunlit escape to safety. He would make it home somehow and raise the hue and cry and let the US Army, if necessary, go back and get Frank's body and arrest Earl Bryant. He had had enough of Bryant Country for one day and maybe forever.

2. The Escape

On his arrival in Tallahassee, and slowing down to more safely navigate the city streets, Clyde gripped the steering wheel of the Ford truck with grim determination. He roared up Tennessee Street and turned south on Monroe Street on his way into the parking lot in back of the frame structure housing the Still Buster Unit of the Federal Revenue Service.

On the long trip back to Tallahassee, he had had time to collect his thoughts after the fear and panic had subsided somewhat. *Damn, that son of a bitch could have shot me just as easy as Mr. Stiller! I'm too young to get shot by some moonshine crazy man in Liberty County.*

It had occurred to Clyde that the rest of the team may not be impressed with the way he had run for his life without even checking to see if Frank was actually dead as he assumed. *Hell, I never even drew my damn gun until it was way too late! The word coward just might get thrown in my direction. No matter now, too late to think about that, what's done is done. Just turn in the truck, make my report and let the chips fall. I may quit this job anyhow. Not nearly as glorious as it all sounded back last year but I sure needed a job and the pay is good. Come to think of it, it sure beats the hell out of plowing and baling hay back on the farm.*

Clyde sat for a final few seconds in the parking lot to recall all the details of the raid, the conversation with Mrs. Bryant, the shot, and his escape. He climbed out of the pickup and ran up the stairs into the office to face the music. He could almost imagine he heard the strains of a funeral dirge, his funeral, possibly, as he opened the office door and rapped on the door of the Special Agent in Charge, known among those on the inside and around the criminal justice system, or the "Court House Ring" as it were, as the SAC. *No panic now,* he told himself, *but hell, there was a shooting, I have a right to be excited, don't I?*

"Come in," commanded the SAC. "You might as well give it to me straight Clyde, but make it quick, I don't have all day. What'd you two find down there at Bryant's place? Wait a minute, Clyde, where's Frank Stiller, he was in charge of this team, wasn't he?"

"Sir, there's been a shooting down there, Mr. Stiller, he's, he's , he's….," Clyde stuttered and stumbled, getting red in the face with fear or embarrassment, unable to get out what had happened on the raid.

"What are you trying to say, Clyde? Where is Frank Stiller? Spit it out, son!" the SAC said. He could see the young agent was excited, frightened and maybe worse so he tried a different approach. "Now calm down, son, have a seat over here by me and tell me about it, you can tell me, son," the SAC said. Clyde found his way to the seat and slumped down next to Buford Gregory and began to tell his story.

"We left the truck back up the road a piece and walked into the front yard of the Bryant place where we engaged Mrs. Bryant in some conversation, accompanied by her two hounds. She no sooner shut up the dogs and told us Earl Bryant wasn't there when it happened!"

Clyde said, expecting Mr. Gregory to understand what he knew and had not said yet.

"What happened, for God's sake, son, would you explain this thing?" the SAC said with exasperation in his voice.

"Oh, right, Sir, I guess I assumed, of course you couldn't have, no way you could have known, well, you see, Sir, a rifle cracked---, no, that's not how it seemed, I didn't hear anything immediately, he just fell full across the steps in front of me and then I heard it, the shot, Sir!" Clyde explained, as he saw it anyway, though the SAC was totally confused by now.

"Exactly where is Frank Stiller, Clyde?"

"Dead, Sir, or at least that's what I think, Sir. I left, got the hell out of there before he shot me next," Clyde desperately explained.

"You mean to tell me, son, that Frank Stiller, the most experienced agent on this team managed to get himself shot in Liberty County this morning and you don't know whether he is actually dead? You left him there?"

"Walton, get in here, NOW! Walton, not next week, YOU HEAR?," the SAC yelled out into the outer office and before many ticks on the old clock in the office had sounded, Fred Walton came running into George's office.

"Here, Sir, what's up?" Fred asked as he ran into the office on the wave of excitement from the SAC's loud command having spread through the Still Buster Team office like a whirlwind.

"Clyde here says Frank Stiller has gone and got himself shot down there in Liberty County on the Bryant raid and is still down there, dead probably, so you get a team together and go back down there, take Clyde with you. You up to it, son?" the SAC asked, pausing only briefly to catch the nod of Clyde's head. "And make sure you have enough people, Fred, to get him out of there and find that damn Earl Bryant and bring him out on the same trip," Buford Gregory barked.

"Yes, Sir, right away, Sir, but Sir, how did it happen and what evidence do we have that it's Bryant, did you see him do it Clyde?" Fred asked sensibly.

"No, Sir, Mr. Walton, Sir, I only saw him fall, Mr. Stiller I mean, and then heard the shot. I didn't see anything before I skedaddled, figuring I was next, if you know what I mean, Sir?" Clyde explained.

"Well then, that raises an interesting point, Sir," Walton said enigmatically.

"What point is that, exactly Walton, and if you don't mind, Stiller just may still be alive down there and we're wasting valuable time with "points" aren't we, Walton?" the SAC sarcastically said.

"Yes, Sir, I'll get going immediately, Sir, but the point I'm thinking of is the old probable cause problem with no evidence to support an arrest. We really need an arrest warrant, don't we, Sir, before we pick up Bryant on this evidence, Sir?" Walton explained, sticking to his guns.

"Now that's good thinking, Walton, but the only man in Liberty or Leon County for that matter, with balls enough to assassinate a Federal Revenue Agent on Bryant's front doorstep is Bryant himself. Don't we have a snitch in this deal? This shooting and a potential arrest of Earl Bryant puts a different light on things with a liquor empire up for grabs, somebody is bound to want to talk, but your "point" is well taken, Walton. Send a team to recover Stiller, another to mine the snitch vein and report back to me. I'll go see the U.S. Attorney to work out the legal strategy, and by the time you have some information, then we'll go see Judge Parker. Then we make the arrest. Bryant's not going anywhere and that much is for certain. But for now, get cracking!," the SAC commanded.

"Yes, Sir," Walton responded and bounded out of the SAC's office to carry out his orders, with Clyde Browning right behind him. There would be no more thought of returning to work at the farm for him until this business was over. He owed Mr. Stiller's memory that much.

3. Scrambled eggs

Earl Bryant made his way casually from the truck assembly point up to the house and entered it from the rear just in time for breakfast. Ellie was sitting slumped over the kitchen table with her head down and trembling. The rear screen door slammed shut as Earl entered the kitchen and found her there. "Ellie, woman, what in the hell is wrong with you? Where's my breakfast," he said in his demanding style. "We have a shipment to get out of here this morning and not much time to get it done in, you hear me woman?" Ellie slowly raised her head, turning to look at Earl and spoke through tear blurred eyes, her whole body trembling with fear, shock and anger.

"You son of a bitch, Earl Bryant, we got a dead Federal agent on my front steps and you want to talk about breakfast?" Ellie blurted out at her husband, shaking in rage and indignation.

"What Federal agent dead and on your, my, front step to boot, are you crazy, woman?" Earl said with apparent incredulity. *There now, better to check this out before going off halfcocked,* he thought.

"Go see for yourself, Earl Bryant, he's right out front on the steps like I said, if the police ain't come and got him and you yet but I can see they ain't got you as yet," Ellie veritably shouted at her husband who wasn't five feet away and he was not deaf by any means. Earl said nothing to the accusation and ran through the house as though genuinely surprised, knocking over a couple of chairs in the kitchen and the front room just as a startled man ought to on his way pell mell out to the front steps on such an occasion. He pushed open the screen door and stared unbelieving, or at least a rational observer would have thought so, at the lifeless body of Frank Stiller lying where he had fallen across the top step. Earl looked carefully at the body and saw that the dead man was just that, dead and cold by now, but the face was turned sideways revealing the cut of his profile, a profile Earl had seen many times in his encounters and near misses with the oldest and shrewdest Federal Revenue Agent in the District of North Florida. He paused just a minute as Ellie Bryant came shuffling up behind him in her bedroom slippers and peered carefully over his shoulder, as Earl had bent over to get a closer look at the dead man.

"I better get out of here, Ellie, the Feds will be a coming' soon, they'll never leave one of their own down here to rot, even though that's what the bastard deserves for all the grief he's caused me and my family over the years. Pack me some clothes and food, Ellie, I better be scarce around these parts for a few days. The Feds will send a team down here for this stiff and I'll be down in the swamp at one of the stills. They'll never find me down there. I'm not telling even you where I'm at so they can't sweat it out you," Earl explained.

"If you had nothing to do with this, Earl, what have you got to hide for?" Ellie asked naively.

"Don't be a fool, Ellie, it will take that Still Buster team about five minutes to pin this rap on me, who else could have done it, they'll think," Earl said, not exactly denying it, and turned back into the house to grab a few bits of clothing. He sat at the dressing chair and removed the work shoes he normally wore and replaced them with his hunting boots. The boots were the lace up kind with leather laces. Earl's feet were odd in appearance with the big toe on each foot flanked by a sort of mass for where most people had the other four toes. There was a kind of crude nail like appendage on the combined toes that gave the appearance of a cloven hoof of a calf or pig. Almost no one except Ellie had ever seen this odd formation on his feet.

The boots had been worn long enough to accommodate the abnormality by stretching to the shape of his feet.

After he finished lacing up the boots, he got up and Ellie followed him through the house until she veered into the kitchen to put together some corn bread, cold sausage, and a small jug of buttermilk to hold him until some of the men could resupply him at the hidden location. He had not told her where he was headed but it did not take a genius with her knowledge of her man, to pick his destination. He was headed for the lagoon. Nobody would find him there, not for a few days anyway.

Earl grabbed the food and banged his way out the back porch and headed down one of the innumerable hog trails that crisscrossed his dominions that he and only a few others knew how to navigate without getting totally lost in five minutes. But he would never get lost on these trails, not in a million years.

4. The search

Fred Walton, Clyde Browning and a team of sharp shooters and crime scene investigators in three trucks full of men and equipment, roared out of Tallahassee headed west toward the Ochlocknee River bridge crossing and into the Liberty County heartland where Bryant Country was the epicenter for this morning's mission. They turned south at Highway 65 in Hosford to Taylor's Crossing where they turned into Bryant Country and made their way down the narrow sand-rutted roads headed toward the Bryant place where the the dead body of Frank Stiller hopefully remained undisturbed.

There was no need for stealth this time as every man on the team fully expected Earl to be deep into the river swamp country by now and Mrs. Bryant and her dogs were not a threat worth worrying about.

Fred questioned Clyde over and over again about every step of their approach that morning, hoping with each re-telling of the story some new fact just might come out. Frankly, after seven or eight tellings, Clyde and Fred were sick of it and Fred was convinced he had mined that vein for all it was worth.

The motorcade pulled up into the clearing that comprised the Bryant front yard and came to a screeching halt. The sharp shooters bounded out of the third truck and fanned out like an infantry assault team Surrounding the house as though they really expected Earl Bryant to be stupidly holed up inside or worse yet armed and ready to do battle. Bryant was probably armed all right wherever he was and clearly not inside the Bryant house as they quickly found out.

Frank's body lay prone across the top step just where Clyde Browning had reported at least ten times that morning it had fallen the moment before he heard the shot. Sound carries funny that way in that a high-powered rifle bullet would always arrive at the target before the sound of it if you were in the direction of the target as Frank had been. Rigor mortis had clearly already set in as Frank's body seemed stiff and unmoving to the casual eye.

Fred Walton boldly strides up to the front porch of the wood frame house, climbed the short front steps being careful to step over Frank's corps without disturbing the evidence, walked across the front screened porch and rapped on the door announcing loudly that Federal law enforcement agents had arrived, demanding that whoever was in the place better come out without weapons. Some of the crime scene men attended to a close inspection of the body and others fanned out to cover the entire yard for any signs of evidence that might provide a clue as to the perpetrator's identity.

Every member of the team was convinced beyond any doubt who that was but that state of being convinced, however strongly held the conviction, was not worth two cents to a jury in Judge Parker's Federal Court where a jury would have to decide Earl's guilt beyond and to the exclusion of a reasonable doubt. One thing was certain, that no matter what evidence could be found in scouring the yard and grounds surrounding Earl Bryant's house, that if it were left up to a vote of the Still Buster Team in Tallahassee and those at the Bryant homestead that morning there would be an arrest of Earl Bryant and a trial for murder and the vote would have been unanimous.

Ellie Bryant finally came cautiously up and opened the front door just before Fred was preparing to bust in the door and said: "Yes, Sir, what can I do for you this morning? You don't have to yell and rap so loud on that door. We're not deaf down here."

"Excuse me, Ma'am but I'm Fred Walton with the Federal Revenue Service and in case you haven't noticed, that's one of my oldest and best men lying dead on your front steps right where he got shot by somebody down here about six o'clock this very morning," Fred said.

"Course I noticed Mr. Federal Service man cause he managed to get himself shot right in front of me this here morning and in case you are asking me, I have no idea who or what done it to him," Ellie bravely said not yielding an inch of ground to this stranger down here with all his team of investigators and sharpshooters.

Ellie Bryant was a diminutive little woman a bit younger than Earl but displaying a kind of wiry toughness in her almost five foot tall one hundred pound body. If she had one ounce of fear inside the tough exterior she portrayed, the Federal Agent could not detect it. Fred expected her to say nothing and her lack of intimidation was a total surprise. He had halfway expected her to be the hell out of there altogether by now and hide in the swamps or piney woods with her renegade lawbreaking husband and seeing her stand up to him and give him a measure of lip back was even more surprising.

"Where exactly is that husband of yours, Mrs. Bryant? We have a few questions for him if you don't mind." Fred asked with a purposely-faked politeness that had a sarcastic ring to it if it had anything. Sincerity and southern politeness was definitely not the approach he was prepared in his view of the matter to give to the wife of a cold-blooded killer.

"I ain't got no idea where Earl's at for this moment, nor any other time this here day either, Sir and if you must, go ahead and search the house and do what I know you will do anyway. You did bring one of those warrant papers with you, didn't you Mr. Federal man, like you said you had before?" Ellie replied equally sarcastically and caught Fred Walton off guard because he did not have one of those "warrant papers" as she called them, course she didn't know that at the time, but Ellie felt she had nothing to lose to call his bluff. It worked too, for he had no legal right to search anything and if he was so fortunate to find some evidence of Earl's guilt it would be embarrassing in front of the Judge so he had to switch gears and try to talk his way into searching the house and grounds.

"Now, Mrs. Bryant," Fred explained suddenly sweet as corn syrup at a Fourth of July picnic, "we're down here to retrieve our man's body and the warrant paper as you call it is a little, you know, out of order at this stage of the investigation, but it's such a long way down here it would sure help us save some time for you and us to go ahead and let us look around a little bit, if it's not too much trouble, Ma'am. If Earl's not here now and it sounds like he hasn't been here all morning anyway, he couldn't have been the one who done it anyhow so just looking around a little bit on this trip would save us all a lot of time and keep us from bothering you for that second trip, you know, the one with the warrant paper. We would have to go see old Judge Ben Parker up in the Federal Court House and explain to him just what seems to have happened down here and sure as shootin' he would send us back down here with a warrant and we would have to tear this place apart looking for evidence that's probably not here anyway and a little search on a purely voluntary basis, you understand, Mrs. Bryant, just might satisfy the Judge that the official warrant with all the digging and ripping apart of things around here just might prove unnecessary."

"Well go ahead, Mr. whatever your name is, if we can keep a Federal Judge out of this by you making your little search about the place, then go ahead if you must but I'll give no consent to any damn damage you might have been planning on doing this morning and if that's your true intention then go get that Federal Judge or whoever else you think you need, including the whole damn United States Army if you think you need them and leave me in peace for now at least. So which is it going to be Mr. Federal Man?" Ellie blurted out with a force emanating that seemed incongruous with her wiry tough little body.

"Now hold on there, Mrs. Bryant, you don't have to get excited about this, we just want to look around the house and the grounds a bit. There will be no damage to the place I can assure you, Ma'am, so if you will excuse us now, we'll take a quick look through the house and my other men will search the grounds," Fred explained and walked past Ellie Bryant into the rather plain but well-constructed wood frame homestead and began with Clyde Browning in tow to make a method-ical search of every room in the house, being extremely careful not to damage any personal effects but to look carefully for any evidence that might point to Earl Bryant's guilt.

He did not expect to find any but George Gregory, the SAC, would be satisfied with nothing less than a careful room-to-room search of the premises. This they accomplished and as expected found absolutely nothing useful toward their objective, the proof of what everybody on the team accepted as gospel that Earl Bryant and Earl Bryant alone was the guilty party.

The crime scene investigators on the other hand were more professional in their examination. It was true that no footprints could be found in the yard on the side of the house that the shooting took place in but they were able to find the point of entry and exit of the single rifle shot that had passed through Frank Stiller's body and buried itself into the wood frame supporting the screen door on the front porch entrance. A quick calculation of the height of the entry point and a rough approximation of the angle that the path of the bullet had taken, gave them a fairly close approximation of where the fatal shot had originated. It was a flat angle if not slightly inclined which showed the investigators that the shooter had been roughly at ground level and either shot from a slightly crouched position or made by a fairly short shooter.

Since Earl Bryant was known to be about five foot three in height, notwithstanding his rather tall and tough reputation, the rough geometry of the analysis did not prove anything one way or the other but it did not rule out Earl as the perpetrator. Since this was what they wanted to find anyway, the excitement of the calculation spurred the team of investigators on to greater efforts. Since the clearing was only so big and the range of most non-military hunting rifles produced in those days was fairly limited, it didn't take a genius to figure out about from where the shot had come.

The likely spot of the shot did have some scuffmarks and a possible knee print but no foot prints of any use could be detected. Consequently the plaster cast impression of prints at the scene of the shot or leading to it or away for that matter, they were prepared to make, went unused. The rifle ball dug out of the wood frame was preserved in a little cloth bag brought for such purposes for the return to Tallahassee and examination in the state crime lab or the FBI lab in Washington DC, if necessary, to see if there was any rifling left on the projectile smashed almost into a tight little wad. This analysis would be made just in case they were lucky enough later to find the murder weapon and pin this crime on whomever the unlucky gun owner happened to be. If it turned out to be Earl Bryant who owned the gun that did it, then, well, that would be justice, wouldn't it?

These were Federal Revenue agents and not murder investigators but if they could put Earl Bryant away with a murder rap and break up the biggest and smartest still operator in the region in the same fell swoop then that would be a doubly delicious accomplishment. It was still a long shot at this point but the objective was clear and highly motivating for the team.

After finishing with a meticulous inspection of every nook and cranny in and under the old house, Fred and Clyde joined the others out in the front yard area. The investigators were finishing up wrapping Frank Stiller in a body bag and gently placed it in the back of one of the trucks for the return trip to Tallahassee.

"Where did he make the shot from, boys?" Fred asked the team of investigators, assuming that by now they had figured out that elementary and preliminary conclusion from the evidence.

Bill Staley, the lead of the team, turned from his close inspection of the bullet's impact in the porch doorframe to answer, "It's over yonder, Sir," Bill said as he headed hurriedly that way pointing out west of the front yard to a patch in the nearby thickets that by now was beaten down by the over-eager investigators searching in vain for the shell casing or a previously overlooked print.

Clyde had reported only one shot and no evidence was found to the contrary so it stood to reason there had to have been only one shot. One had been enough to snuff out the remaining years of the dearly loved Revenue Agent. There had been no sign of a struggle after the shot which seemed to have felled Frank right in his tracks. Clyde had confirmed this with his consistent and fairly detailed reports of the incident though he had undoubtedly been scared out of his wits by the episode.

Fred walked over and joined Bill and the other team members at the scene.

"It had to have been about here, Mr. Walton," young Elliot Nash said from his involvement in the scouring of the crime scene in search of evidence or at least clues. "See the scuff marks right there by that stump and the imprint of something, probably a knee where he kneeled down to make the shot. I figure he rested the gun on that cut off pine stump and kneeled behind it to steady his aim. Otherwise it was a risky shot from this distance of about one hundred fifty yards, as I make it," Elliot explained from his youthful overconfidence being the veteran of only a few crime scene investigations but not even one murder investigation.

Notwithstanding the speculative nature of his conclusion, most of the team agreed, with the nodding of their heads, that the young man had it about right.

"Make a plaster cast of the knee print and dust that old stump for the fingerprints you are not going to find but do it anyway. I'll not have the FBI people second guessing my team in this, you hear?" Fred ordered.

"Yes, Sir!" they all answered with enthusiasm and jumped to the task to get everything wrapped up in a hurry. It went without saying that as long as they were in Bryant Country, no Federal Officer felt safe with these woods surrounding them and Earl Bryant and his whiskey still people running loose and armed.

The task of investigating and searching being about done, Fred walked back to the house and sought out Ellie Bryant for one final encounter before leaving. "Respects, Ma'am," Fred Walton spoke courteously as he tipped the brim of his hat in the typical southern greeting or leaving ritual.

"Well Mr. Federal man, have you done with your searching and

stuff so you can get the hell out of my house and off my property,"
Ellie said defiantly, ignoring Walton's poor attempt at courtesy under
the circumstances. In her view, this whole episode was an invasion
of her privacy by the government she and Earl hated, not to mention
the peace and normal tranquility that pervaded Bryant Country. The
fact that the Federal agent had been shot dead on her front step and
her husband had appeared shortly thereafter without one word of
explanation and then hurriedly left for the safety of the piney woods
or river swamp didn't seem to have made much of an impression on
her sense of justice or for that matter, curiosity.

"Yes, ma'am, we're done and we're out of here. I know you didn't like
it but we do appreciate you voluntarily permitting the search without
the warrant paper as you call it and believe me it just saves everybody
a lot of time and you a lot of bother. Your Government thanks you
whether you accept that as kindly as I mean it or not," Fred politely and
carefully explained making sure that other team members were sight
and hearing witnesses to the fact of the voluntary search. Young Nash
hurriedly scribbled notes of the exchange to preserve the consent for
the record and prepared then a paper for Mrs. Bryant to sign, which
he handed up to Mr. Walton at the front of the group.

"If you don't mind, Mrs. Bryant, would you sign this paper that
acknowledges that you consented voluntarily to the search? It won't
matter none because of these witnesses here but it makes it clear what
we're doing and Earl will want to know that you cooperated just in
case the law boys want to come down here and talk to him and that's
likely, I'm thinking," Fred said hopefully, handing her the paper and
not having a clue whether she could read or not or whether she would
just drop the thing or worse yet tear it up and spit in their faces with
that mouthful of tobacco juice all of them could clearly see she was
working up to full, just in case.

"Ain't signin' nothing, Mr. Federal man, so if you don't mind why don't you and these boys climb back in them trucks with that stiff in it and get the hell out of here like I asked you to the first time?" Ellie glowered at the group not being intimidated in the least by the numbers or, as she saw it, false attempt at politeness. As far as Ellie Bryant was concerned, these Federal men were the enemy to her husband and all he stood for and she didn't give a damn what anybody including these very men thought about it.

Among many other qualities, Fred Walton was a realist and no further jawing with this female hellion was worth the effort. They had recovered their man's dead body, pinned down approximately from where the shot had been made and recovered the spent bullet that had killed him. They had accomplished all George Gregory had asked and more. It was time to leave Bryant Country and the team was for that one hundred percent. They quickly mounted the trucks like steeds in the old west and gracefully and manfully as they could, turned around and drove defiantly, or so it seemed to them, out of the yard and back down the lonely and dangerous road back to civilization.

Ellie watched the three trucks leave her yard headed into the woods and up the road toward Tallahassee and gloated in her anger that had not subsided even a little that she had stood up to the Federal bastards at least this one time whether her husband had been there to back her up or not. There would be time to deal with him and the consequences of his actions in this thing but for now peace had returned for the time to Bryant Country and she remained as the ruler of the roost for this day at least.

5. Discussions

The road opposite the return to Tallahassee meandered more or less southerly from the Bryant homestead following the convenient up but mostly down folds of the hillsides on the way to the river. The stalwart long needle pines with bush grass, wild crepe myrtle and palmetto underbrush gradually faded into a heavy canopy of evergreen live oak and deciduous hickory and bay trees, with a thick carpet of rotted leaves smothering the ground as the road approached its destination in the area of the river swamp known to the locals brave enough to ever go there as "Bryant's Lagoon." It was actually a chainlink series of sloughs and isolated water bodies left by a change in the Ochlocknee River's course over the centuries. The water in each little pond as it were was smooth and black as pitch from the concentrated tannic acid extruded from its decaying leaf and muck bottom. But because the hill country where the Bryant family lived was considerably higher in elevation than the bottom of the river, hills and valleys were the typical terrain on the way down the access road to the river in this region.

That cold and frosty morning in December, as Earl Bryant joined the river road from his trek cross country from the back side of his house to avoid the front yard where the dead body still lay at that time, was peaceful as far as nature was concerned, if not for everyone such as the victim formerly living in it.

Florida is known across the country as a warm, hospitable state for vacationers and residents alike and for most of the year this is true. But due to the humidity, when it turns cold in extreme north Florida, it is cold indeed. This was one of just such mornings. But the cold rarely lasts very long into the day as the rising sun melts the frost and warms the heart in due course, no later than usually by lunch time. As it turned out, if Earl had been able to see through the woods clearly that morning, which no human was able to do in these thickets, he wasn't the only one making his way to the Lagoon by way of wild hog trails that morning.

It was far from peaceful in the mind of Earl Bryant. If the Feds had finally built up the courage to do what no other law men had done during his tenure as master of Bryant Country, and actually come knocking on his front door, a raid on his whiskey still operations was undoubtedly not far behind. He had lived relatively free from interference in his business operations since Prohibition was passed in 1919.

Any fool could see that Federal Agents, or anyone else, didn't care if people drank illegal whiskey as there was no way to tax it anyway. The Speakeasies in the cities, not too cleverly disguised as places to get a drink, and jugs passed around in the county at almost any gathering of country folk, was proof enough of that. People were going to drink one way or the other, and it had been Earl's mission in life that most of the whiskey drunk in that part of the country came from him.

Earl's stills were isolated in the heart of Liberty County, in a territory most white folks and no Negroes with any sense and not working there would dare invade. His reputation for absolute control of his dominions and his tough-minded willingness to enforce his own trespass- sign restrictions were legendary. It doesn't take much to create legend where desperate conduct is concerned.

For example, there was a story about a State Legislator driving from west Florida one year on the way to the State Legislature in Tallahassee, for its annual session, who missed his turn in Hosford and mistakenly went south on Highway 65 rather than east on Highway 20. Well, as the story went, his car ran out of gas at Taylor's Crossing. The Legislator happened to have a gas can with him it seems and made the mistake of turning southeast down the road into Bryant Country to look for a station or a generous farmer. Well, he found neither and after compounding his mistake by walking past one of Earl's "No Trespass No Hunting and we shoot fools" signs to look for a gas station in that Godforsaken part of the world, he had to run for his life when he found Earl Bryant with a shotgun barring the access to the non-existing gasoline supply. How he managed to get back to Tallahassee was not ever explained.

It is told that the Doctor in Tallahassee, who had to pick the bird shot out of the Legislator's rear end after a painful and embarrassing retreat from "Bryant Country" couldn't help himself against the telling of it even in violation of medical ethics and the Doctor Patient privilege and the story had gotten out. In a few days, it was all over Tallahassee and even the State Legislature growing bigger and better with each telling.

Finally, the full blown version of the legend of Earl Bryant shooting the State Legislator in the ass after stopping his car from driving through Taylor's Crossing in full daylight and chasing him all the way to the bridge crossing of the Ochlocknee River, was considered by every resident of Tallahassee and the Surrounding counties as the gospel truth. That story permanently enshrined Earl Bryant in the "tough man" hall of fame. As a consequence, nobody would mess with this man in his "Country" thereafter, or so conventional wisdom had it.

Earl made his way on foot down the last little stretch of the access road to Bryant's Lagoon and found most of the crew reported for duty as on any normal day. If word of the shooting had made its way to the hamlets, campsites and villages his crew walked from each morning on the way to work, it was not apparent.

Earl employed a crew of ten reliable men who came and went during the day as needed to keep the mash barrels full, bottle the whiskey that came out of the cooling barrels, receive the regular arriving deliveries of white sugar, corn meal, yeast, bran and jugs and handle the capping and delivery of the finished product.

The whiskey still operation at Earl's Lagoon was large by north Florida country standards where the usual moonshine still operation was a one-man show. Earl's operation had a dozen fifty-five gallon mesh working mash barrels, six sixty gallon copper cooking kettles and a matching set of six gallon thumper kegs and a corresponding number of cooling barrels fed by a nearby spring constantly flowing clear spring water through the cooling barrels with a specially made copper coil or "worm" in each barrel.

Earl had a separate department at a location closer to civilization to organize the surreptitious methods necessary to buy supplies without it looking like it and the transportation system to bring them into the still and to distribute the finished product.

It was hard to disguise the purchase of that much white sugar but Earl was a master of deception, and capitalism worked anytime there was something to sell with a ready source of cash to pay for it. The off-site location was called "the office" by anyone involved in the large efficient whiskey production and distribution operation.

The whole "factory" was an area about the size of the floor of a good sized tobacco barn up in Gadsden County, covered by a canopy made of two by fours supported by tree poles with a tin roof but covered over the top with earth so as to be not visible from above. A chimney over each of the six separate copper cooking kettles allowed the exhaust from the hickory fires to escape into the river bottom air. Hickory wood makes a good fire for this kind of thing because it is a hard and tough wood that gives off little smoke if properly dried before use.

Earl had some of his men constantly working in the fuel preparation department of the operation so that the ready supply of fuel never ran out. The roof had been there so long the grass and small trees growing out of it looked like an incongruous flat area of the undulating and tree-covered river bottom. It wouldn't be visible from the air, anyway, even in the winter since the tree canopy of evergreens and Spanish moss was so thick down here in the river swamp. Radar, if there had been such a thing in 1933, wouldn't have penetrated it either but no chances were taken. The main security for the place was Earl Bryant's reputation, which kept most lawmen away.

"Morning' boys," Earl said to the crew as he hung his war surplus Model 1917, 30-06 Enfield bolt-action rifle on one of a row of pegs mounted on a board against the inside wall to his left as he entered the factory floor. "Good mornin,' Suh, to you, Suh" was the typical reply or with a nod of the head if not made audibly from the all-Negro crew assembled for the start of the Bryant workday. Hub, the most dependable of the black men working for Earl, came up and said to Earl, "Everything ready for the delivery this mornin' as planned and we have has assembled and crated the heavy glass jugs for the product and were waitin for instructions."

"Hub, did you make a count of the sacks of sugar needed this week and check the hickory supply for the kettles, like I told you to yesterday?" Earl said. "Naw, Suh, we ain't done it yet, but I go finish it now, jes' like you say, Suh," Hub said and turned to leave by a side exit.

Ten minutes later, as if scheduled to coincide with the start of the work day or by chance, or for other purposes yet unknown, George Drucker entered the factory with his own Enfield 30-06 slung across his shoulder, lifted it off and hung it carefully on the peg rack next to Earl's, along with his coat and gloves. He came alongside the boss with the men who were gathered across the back side of the sheltered area just in time for the job assignments about to be announced.

Earl did not seem surprised at the time at George's presence down here at the factory although he normally spent his time at the office where he managed the supply and distribution portion of the operation for Earl. Hub returned shortly thereafter and resumed his work in the still, moving around the premises here and there, checking on sugar and fuel supplies, saying nothing to the other men, which they thought was odd at the time. Only one man in the Negro crew happened to notice the timing of his departure and return.

George Drucker was a contemporary of Earl Bryant and a close confidant on business matters, though only an employee and not a partner or part owner in any sense. His father, Abner Drucker, had been one of the typical small time operators of whiskey stills up and down the Ochlocknee River valley, since those difficult days following the Civil War, when there wasn't much work for white men to do on more honest and law abiding employer jobs to earn a living.

George had learned the whiskey-making trade from his father, and for a few years after trying his hand at sawmill and railroad construction jobs, had tried a life of petty crime, the other principal occupations of unemployed White and Negro men in the region at the time. He didn't turn to crime because he couldn't get work, because the young George Drucker had always been able to impress a jack leg sawmill operator, or a railroad construction crew supervisor, that he was worth the pay available for labor work. He turned to crime because he was not the type to work full time at anything, especially where hard manual labor was concerned. He was too smart to ruin his health for low wages, no matter how honorable that was to white society. He had ambitions to be somebody although he wasn't sure what kind of somebody he wanted to be just yet.

As a consequence, after numerous episodes of petty theft, he had made a working acquaintance with the labor skills taught by Sheriff's Deputies in control of forced labor road construction, otherwise known throughout the South as "the chain gang." Fortunately, for him at least, he had avoided making the leap into the big time life of crime, which would have landed him in prison for a longer stretch. That would mean on getting out, even after serving your time and getting a decent job thereafter was made problematic by the fact of having been a prison inmate in those years.

George was smarter than the average petty criminal and had learned his lesson rather quickly after only a few stints on the "chain gang" that there was a better way to be a criminal. That decision sent him to Liberty County and Bryant Country. His background as the child of a whiskey man, his intelligence and toughness made him a natural for Earl Bryant's operations. So far the relationship had developed to the position of mutual trust. Earl respected George's experience, smarts and his believed reliability and George found Earl's operation a natural haven to satisfy his present needs. He had ambitions of making his own mark in the business world and would bide his time until the opportunity for that presented it. In fact he had been working on that "opportunity" for the past few months, but for obvious reasons, so far known only to him and one special agent of the Federal Revenue Service, he could not discuss this with Earl.

Earl nodded his acknowledgment of George's presence at the factory and commenced his orders for the day to the crew standing ready for work. The shooting had disrupted the plan for the day because the giant shipment of "product' scheduled for that morning would have occupied the whole crew in assembly, loading and restocking the inventory of supplies rather than the normal routine of tending the production process. He notified the men that the scheduled large shipment had been delayed so they must resume the normal production activities. The crew nodded their recognition of the change in orders without question and turned to their respective assignments for a normal day's operation, which needed no special instructions from the boss.

Earl then beckoned to George to join him over in a quiet corner in the other side of the Still, away from the hearing of the other men and asked, "What did you do with them trucks, George?"

"I spec they had sense enough to lay low when the shipments didn't come and make their own way out of here. I've been making my way down here since early this mornin' and ain't seen nobody yet," George said, seemingly oblivious to the specific problem to which Earl was referring.

"You hear the shot, George, or see anything up by the house this mornin?" Earl asked, feeling George out to how much he knew or was willing to say about the shooting.

"No, Sir, I come by the Back River Road, myself to get here."

Earl thought that strange to some extent since anybody on the Back River Road could have heard the rifle shot coming from the direction of his house, it wasn't that far away and it was a quiet morning at that time. "Yore hearin' alright, George, any problems like that?"

"No problem Sir, or.... yeah, it's alright, why'd you ask, Mr. Bryant?" That was a strange reply for George for whatever he was to Earl Bryant, formal addressing to a man roughly his own age was not the style of George Drucker.

"Just wonderin', George, for you see there was a shootin this mornin' up at the house and one of them Federal men got himself shot dead on my front door stoop," Earl said, watching George carefully for any sign that he had known all along, in spite of his denial about hearing anything on the way down here on the Back River Road, if he was on the way down here on the Back River Road or by some other route.

"No kidding, Sir, shot at the house, on the front damn steps and dead, Sir, damn that?" George asked seemingly incredulously.

"Yeah, George, somebody shot the bastard. I got a good look at him before I come down here and it was that Stiller fella, you know the one, the old bastard in the Federal Service, the one that's been a burr under my saddle for years, and them Federal boys are damn sure to think I done it, don't you figure, George?" Earl said looking again carefully at the poker face he saw on George Drucker, with just the right amount of surprise but not shock, which could have meant anything or nothing or everything. His own face was about the same and George could get no reading from him, the suspicions were mutually distrustful at that moment and at the same time inquisitive.

"That's a fair conclusion, Sir. The whole north part of the State knows you're the kingpin in the illegal whiskey business and the meanest son of a bitch around here to boot. I mean that as a compliment, Sir, don't get me wrong. What are you going to do about it, Sir?" George said taking the safe line in such things, not asking too much or telling anything.

Any neutral observer to this scene would have thought this exchange was most like a game of chess, but moving much faster with the need to decide on the next move being instinctive not tactical or strategic.

"Lay low, what else did you expect?" Earl said and turned to other business with George by discussing the white sugar supply and a reschedule of the whiskey shipment as though to say, without saying anything, really, get on with business and let me handle this. George didn't need to be encouraged and he too turned to the other business almost with an eagerness that went beyond his more methodical and laid back methods.

Something for nothing was what each man expected and got that morning. Life resumed as normal and would remain that way too until the inevitable insertion of Federal authority yet to come, that was bound to come like a hammer blow when it fell. There was nothing to do for now but to put your head down and keep charging ahead. George turned to walk out of the factory and lifted a rifle, as expected, from the rack and passed out into the swamp to make his way back to the office back up country, as was his custom. Later that day, he returned to the rented rooms he had up in Telogia.

6. Undercover

The area around the bridge crossing on the Ochlocknee had a community feeling all its own. It was a gathering place of sorts for fishermen, travelers and even idlers from the countryside interested in the gossip that was passed along from travelers on their way to and from Tallahassee. The peak season, so to speak, was the spring of the year when the Legislature was in session and the month or so before and after where expectations and results were measured, discounted or embellished as the need arose in varying levels of hyperbole, positive or negative.

Mid-December was a wee bit early for the upcoming 1933 Legislative Session but not by much and the collection of travelers and hangers-on was considerable by now. It was popular enough for old man Ed Salter, also known as "Salty," gossip mongerer extraordinaire, to set up his little crude café under a makeshift shed of tin supported by tree poles where he would rustle up some grub on occasion as the need arose.

On most days this meant lunch only, unless the catfish were biting and enough night fishermen would gather at dusk to talk and compare fishing hole tips before shoving off in the few boats Salty kept handy just in case somebody with a couple of dollars might come along and want to rent one for the night. Salty was no puritan by any means and during Prohibition he always kept a jug of Earl's finest around, just in case the boys wanted to drink a snort or two with dinner or before shoving off to fish for catfish on the river.

George Drucker managed to put in some of his off duty time at Salty's Place just to keep his finger on the news of importance to him and Earl, of course. But George was the kind of guy who was always figuring an angle on things that might benefit himself, and if he could help out Earl with a tip now and then, so much the better. It was Friday afternoon, a day or so after the shooting down in Bryant Country, and by this time the news of the event had spread across Liberty and Leon counties and become common knowledge, as the men liked to say, when they wanted their friends to think they were in the loop on some things or avoid it altogether when it suited them.

This was one of those former times because every white man in Liberty and Leon counties, if not Gadsden, too, knew it as a fact that old man Earl Bryant had shot the Federal man right on his front door step and had gotten away with it. The conventional wisdom on the thing was that the United States Attorney had been bought off by Earl or he didn't have the courage to bring him to justice; and it had taken about two days for that consensus to become common knowledge in the region. Common knowledge was golden, everyone assumed, not because it was necessarily truth, but because it was common to most who believed it.

George noticed that since it was Friday night and that even though the catfish had been biting as they usually did this time of year that the unusual crowd could not be explained by the good fishing rumors. Most likely, he thought, the crowd was here to discuss and spread the news about the shooting. This did not surprise him in the least. He took a seat in a hard back, crude wooden chair, with hand-woven cane bottom positioned on the back side of Salty's little pavilion, as he liked to call it, and helped himself to the jug hidden not too well under the boxes accumulated in that corner.

Salty never charged George for the few drinks he took because George managed to keep him supplied with Earl's finest at reasonable prices and accessible supply. The other men gathered in the pavilion were caught up in their private conversations and didn't notice the tall stranger that made his way into the pavilion and took a seat next to George.

"Evenin', George, have you got it?," the stranger asked enigmatically after helping himself to a pull on the jug sitting under the little table between he and George.

"Got what?" George replied equally ambiguously with a question of his own, and since both men knew exactly what the other meant, the stranger knowing he couldn't ask what he wanted out right, and George knowing he couldn't answer anyway, the two danced around the subject for a time without revealing anything.

Any uninformed listener would have thought the two men were either complete strangers to each other or talking nonsense. This is exactly what the two men intended by the manner of the exchange, hiding their true business to any prying eyes, or more importantly, curious ears.

"The business I asked you about last week when you got the money, George," the man said.

"I ain't gone in business yet," George said, indicating that the time wasn't ripe yet to conclude their business transaction.

"What we want to know, George, my business partners that is, did he make the right deposit two days ago when the delivery was to be made, or did somebody else make it? What can you help us with that will settle the matter, George? We have to have direct stuff this time, no more rumors and such like that big delivery we paid you to tell us about the other day, an eye witness or maybe an admission on the QT, to you or somebody believable?" the stranger said, lowering his voice conspiratorially, looking George square in the eyes and leaving no wiggle room for a response.

George looked away from the stranger and took his time before responding, weighing, it would seem, the gravity of the matter before responding. Fate, his fate, that is, was hanging in the balance for he was smart enough to know that if Earl didn't go down over this, he would have to clear out of the country and be quick about it.

"What I needs to know, Mr. Under-Cover Man," George said, all pretense and clever language having been abruptly abandoned, since this was deadly serious now, "Can I count on you fellers to keep that bastard off me during this business and what can you do for me in case he don't go down over this?" George asked more seriously and directly than he had ever talked to these people before.

"You tell us he done it, George, and help us prove it, and we will step out of the way for a time and you can take over most of his operations. We can't promise to give you free rein forever, but we can agree to back off for a spell to get you started. After that, you are on your own. You do most of it anyway and depending on what you tell us, you know, how much help you can offer us to get that bastard, he'll be picked up and won't see the light of day until this is over, if you know what I mean. And if for some reason that guy skates on this thing, and there's little chance of that, we will move you out of the territory and set you up in a job somewhere so Earl Bryant won't be able to get at you, and that's certain," the undercover man said.

George considered the offer for quite a while, wanting to be damn sure he had thought it all through first. The agent knew his man and gave him all the time he wanted to think it over. The noise in the pavilion was a perfect cover anyway. Not a soul could hear their conversation or understand it if they could. George was pretty sure that if Earl Bryant was arrested and that was certain to come based on what he was prepared to tell the Under-Cover Man this evening, the Feds would undoubtedly put him in a hole somewhere and sweat it out of him.

Earl was tough and he could stand a lot, but sooner or later he would fold or the fear of hanging would cause him to "cop" a plea and take a few years in one of those Federal prisons they were constructing all over the state, most likely the new one being built right there in Tallahassee, rather than risk taking the hangman's noose.

The State prison at Raiford was a hellhole, all right, but the word was the Federal prisons weren't half bad, if you had to do time somewhere, that is. By the time Earl got out, George would have made his money and could clear out to Kentucky or somewhere else safe from the revenge of Earl Bryant. In the meantime, George thought, somebody would have to take over the supply of Earl's customers and who better for that but him. He was born to whiskey making and for years had done all the important stuff for Earl that made the operation run successfully as a business. It was an opportunity he could not pass up.

The only question was how much and what to tell them. He believed from what Earl had told him, or more accurately what Earl had done immediately after the shooting, that it looked like Earl was the one who did it. The Feds believed that anyway and all he had to do was point them in the right direction, with enough circumstantial evidence to make them believe what they already wanted desperately to believe and go there. Earl had been in the immediate area at the time of the shooting and had the perfect motive for the crime.

Frank Stiller had been a thorn in Earl's side for many years. Hadn't Earl admitted that much the morning right after the shooting, when he met him down at the Lagoon? Not many people knew it, but he knew there was much more to Earl's dislike of Stiller. In fact he knew from very reliable sources, that Earl had a personal reason to kill the Federal Revenue Agent and motive went a long way to turn circumstantial evidence into proof beyond a reasonable doubt.

He would hold this little but significant part of the story until the right time. George was no lawyer, but he understood proof in a criminal case from his own experience in trying to beat the rap for charges from time to time. He had beaten it a few times, but not in most. He had come to the opinion that if the prosecutor wanted to convict you and had any evidence of guilt, a jury in Leon County would cooperate and find the way to vote for a unanimous conviction. This would be a Federal Court case but the jurors would be the same kind of local folk.

George concluded his thinking about the question and finally said to the Under-Cover Man who had been patiently waiting, "Earl was in the area that morning and showed up at home right after the shooting. He couldn't have been far away from the way he told it to me. He went out to the front steps where the agent was dead and stayed long enough to make him out as Frank Stiller, his old nemesis. He admitted that much to me and confessed that Stiller had been a burr under his saddle for a long time. He was the oldest agent in the Federal Service and had been on Bryant's case for years.

"Now I didn't see the shot, Mister, but Earl came straight to the Lagoon right afterwards and had his rifle with him. I managed to check the chamber later in the morning and one shell was missing from the magazine. When you find him and it better be quick, you'll see I'm talking turkey on this thing. Earl has always carried a full clip as long as I've known him. There was only one shot taken as I heard it, am I wrong? Besides that, he as much as admitted he shot Stiller, when he said and I quote, 'That Federal Agent has had it in for me for years and I ain't forgot what he done to me and my family way back then, and its only fitin' that he got his comeuppance this time. I would do it myself if nobody else would and who else has the brass balls to do this, George, on my own damn front steps to boot. The nerve of them fellers to come knockin' on my front door in Bryant Country and expect to get away with it, can you figure it, George?'

"I swear he said it Mr. Under-Cover Man and he had that self-satisfied look that he gets when he sets out to do something and damn near always does it. He done it all right Mr. Under-Cover Man, and I'm willing to swear to what I told you, and that's no lie," George concluded his explanation having made up his mind and doing the deed all in the same fell swoop, as country people were fond of saying.

"Are you prepared to tell what you just told me to a Federal Marshall and Lawyer in Tallahassee, and if so, will you go with me right now and do it?" the Agent said, not willing to give George a chance to get scared and change his mind.

"Yes, Sir, I am that. If you're ready, then let's get in your truck out front of the bridge and make tracks to Tallahassee. I don't trust spending the night in Liberty County with Earl Bryant on the loose and folks around here knowing I'm headed to Tallahassee tomorrow with a stranger, so let's get at it. Unless I'm badly fooled, Earl Bryant will know before daylight tomorrow mornin' that we left Salty's before supper and you fellers had better agree to keep me safe or I'm not doing it at all, you hear?" George said convincingly.

"Relax George, from this moment on you are in protective custody and won't be going back to Liberty County until you feel it's safe, so shall we go?" the Agent said.

"Sure, let's do it before I get scared and change my mind," George said as they left the pavilion without even so much as a glance at any of the other patrons in the place.

But the lack of attention of some of the other patrons was not uniform, as an old fisherman and petty thief on occasion who was sitting on the other side of the pavilion had watched the entire episode with serious interest. He knew George Drucker alright however the other man was a stranger to him but there is something about a policeman that other lawbreakers can always spot. Whether it is the way they hold themselves or a certain look about them that nobody can describe in words, but never miss in perception, country people could always tell. This stranger was a cop all right and Johnny Caldwell was certain about it. He knew George was Earl Bryant's man and being with a cop was not good news for Earl no matter what they were doing together.

His sympathies were with the local men and against the government, especially if they were his friends, so as soon as the two had left the pavilion, he drew himself up from the barrel hoop seat in the corner and shuffled out back where his mule was tethered. It would take him a spell to make it by mule to Bryant Country, but make it before dawn that was certain. Sleep would be upon the Bryant household by the time he got there but no matter about inconvenience, he was certain Earl would thank him for the interruption.

"Git up mule, haw now, and make tracks!" Johnny said, as he hauled the reins to the left to turn the mule back west to make his way toward Taylor's Crossing, and slapped his flat hard palm a time or two across the mule's haunches to spur him into action. This would be an eventful night for several folks and the consequences of those events yet to come were hard to predict at this point.

7. Wake him up

The Federal prosecutor's office was all-dark and closed by the time George and the Under- Cover man made their way back into Tallahassee. That didn't bother Ed Smalley for in his business office hours were the figment of the imagination of those who didn't have important things to do. In his mind, an office was a place to put off doing today what should have been done yesterday and making it look like it was just on time. The real business of life took place at night or in the morning when fateful decisions and most mistakes were made. He lived on the mistakes of others, turning one of a kind into two of a kind and back again if it suited his purposes. He understood that most of society was crooked, even those who worked at regular jobs for a living but they, most of them anyway, were just too cautious or scared to take risks and do what they really wanted to do in the first place.

But the criminal element which Ed Smalley dealt with was not limited to men on the run, bootleggers or illegal whiskey men, but he was quite prepared to set up those people for the fall if he was paid his price. He was a kind of bounty man in reverse, taking pay to put people in jail by deceptively gaining their trust rather than returning them when they skipped bail. He was tough, devious and smooth, able to talk his way in or out of most any situation imaginable. He was "good at this business" he was fond of saying with a sense of pride in his ability to trick just about anyone except those who paid his fee.

The United States Attorney for the Northern District of Florida, Dan Fernell, had made his appointment as all such men did in those days by being on the right side of the political fence. He was a fine criminal trial lawyer in his own right but that was not the reason he had been appointed. Florida had been a Democratic State ever since the end of the war for Southern Independence and no Republican would dare run for local office or Congress for that matter with any chance of success.

But Herbert Hoover had had the misfortune to be elected as Republican President in 1928 at a time when the world's economy was about to go into the tank starting with the "Black Tuesday" stock market crash. Fernell had supported Mr. Hoover in the nomination and election process utilizing his political contacts in northern states. Consequently, when Mr. Hoover took office, he exchanged Republican US Attorneys for loyal men of his own party in the manner of Presidents from time immemorial.

Dan had an able staff of younger attorneys and entrusted them with much of the day-to-day work of the office. The Earl Bryant investigation was no different than any other and the young man he had selected to advise the Federal Agents in the arrest and to try the case once the man was charged fell to none other than Houston Gilchrist, one of the junior men on Dan Fernell's team.

Although junior in age, he was by no means inexperienced, having probably fifty criminal jury trials under his belt in a combination of private practice and government service. His last job had been in the criminal fraud section of the State Attorney General's office, no slum of a place to try cases. Criminal Fraud cases were hard to try and win because there were so many elements of the case to prove and the failure of even one element would allow the defendant to walk. Houston had been watched by Dan's upper echelon team for a year or two before he was asked to make the leap over to the Federal side and he had proved his mettle once he was over there by being able to make his charges stick, time and again.

Ed took one look at the shuttered and dark US Attorney's office, glanced with disdain at his watch under the pale light of the street lamp by the corner where he and George Drucker stood, and beckoned to George to follow him back to their truck. In a few minutes they were parked in the Meyer's Park area of Tallahassee in front of the brownstone rambler where Houston Gilchrist and family lived.

"Wait here, George, I'll only be a minute until I can rouse somebody in that house over yonder," pointing to the quiet but totally dark neighborhood immediately across the street, Ed Smalley said. He was true to his prediction for in a few minutes after Ed rapped loud enough on the kitchen door on the alley side of the darkened house to wake the dead, as it seemed to George, anyway.

A light appeared deep in the house and before long a young man in a sleeping night shirt stuck his head out the kitchen window, took one quick look at Smalley, unshaven and rumpled in his dirty country clothes and turned to make his way to the outside entrance for a conference.

The street light cast an eerie glow about the grounds that made the two men seem more like silhouettes rather than real figures. But they were real all right and it didn't take Houston long to determine that the rather rude waking he had received was well worth his time and inconvenience.

"He said what?" Houston said as the Under-Cover Man outlined the story of the evidence Smalley had accumulated. Ed mumbled his version of the snitch's story about the shooting and the ambiguous confession he claimed to have heard from the most notorious whiskey man in the District.

Houston was generally familiar with the case and had already reviewed the evidence that had been accumulated by the team of crime investigators so far, which wasn't much. The part that interested Houston was the story about the rifle magazine that had one shell missing, however briefly that condition might last. The investigating team had the bullet that had passed through Frank Stiller's body and killed him and matching that bullet with Earl Bryant's rifle was enough probable cause to convince Judge Parker to issue an arrest warrant.

A more thorough interview with the snitch was critical, but time was of the essence for the evidence they did have would quickly evaporate into the swamp with Earl Bryant unless the arrest was made sooner rather than later. Bryant had his own sources it was believed and this was one case where believing and suspicions were about one and the same.

"Meet me in the office in ten minutes," Houston commanded and turned back into his house to dress while Ed and George climbed back in their truck and headed back toward town.

"Tell me that part again when Bryant said no one other than him had the guts to do it," Houston asked once again having gone over the so called confession about a dozen times hoping against hope that the snitch would think of something new or trip himself up if it was a lie.

Houston had tried enough criminal cases to know that snitches were historically unreliable and a good defense lawyer could pick holes in a made up story faster than a cat can skin a mouse. This story though sounded plausible to Houston and he could not see any holes in it yet, that is until an arrest was made and the physical evidence was compared to the story part.

"So you say Earl Bryant had it in for Frank Stiller not just because he was Federal Revenue Service Agent but for something personal?" Houston asked his witness deliberately.

"Yes, Sir, he said, "That man has been a burr under my saddle ever since I was a kid," the snitch said.

"Wait a minute here, George, was it? You say this man Earl Bryant would shoot a Federal Officer on his own front door step, right where everybody could see it? Why would the man do that? Is he a bigger fool than I think he is and not what his reputation says he is? What about your motive George, you run parts of his whiskey operation don't you? Why not tell on the old man and take over his set up? Why shouldn't a jury expect you to do that, George, and believe Bryant was set up and therefore innocent?" Houston asked.

George had to be careful here for not letting Bryant get off the hook because if he got nervous and played it that way, it was a fast way that he would have to find a ticket out of the country. If Earl got wind that he, George Drucker, had turned on him, his life wouldn't be worth two cents in Florida, Georgia or Alabama, if not even Kentucky. He thought it was about time to play his hold card if he was ever going to play it on this round.

"I get your meaning Sir, but consider this, Earl had a better reason than inconvenience to shoot that Stiller feller, a personal reason," George said ambiguously, waiting like a good fisherman for the bait to be taken before setting the hook.

"A personal reason you say, George?" the lawyer had finally become comfortable enough with the identity of George Drucker to remember his name.

"Yes, Sir, very personal," George said letting the lawyer take one more tug on the bait.

"George, if you have a motive beyond what you've said then spit it out, I'm getting tired of this game and it is a game you're playing isn't it George?" the lawyer asked.

"No, Sir, it's no game, Sir, it's the truth I'm worried about with my ass on the line, so to speak, if Earl Bryant gets a hold on to me after he learns, and he will, probably already knows it by now that I'm talking to you fellers. Earl Bryant shot Stiller because Stiller shot Bryant's pappy on a still raid back in ought two before package whiskey was illegal. Earl was younger then but he seen it all and ain't never forgot. You ask anybody in Liberty County or check your damn Federal records here or up in Washington City, if you don't believe me, but he had a reason, a damn personal reason, if you ask me," George said convincingly.

Houston Gilchrist was overwhelmed with the logic of the revelation. It all seemed to fit, opportunity, confession, well almost anyway and the gun. All they had to do was go get that warrant, arrest the man and seize the gun before he lit out for Texas or somewhere. It was getting daylight by now and Judge Parker wouldn't mind being wakened early for this emergency, especially if Houston was right. But of course he wouldn't know that for sure for quite a while but from his experience, this was probable cause sufficient for an arrest. The proving it would come later.

"Let's go men, we got to go see a Judge about a man," Houston said and they left the office and headed for Alice's breakfast spot to grab coffee and roll or something quick before heading over past Tennessee street to see Judge Parker at his residence near the Governor's mansion.

8. Friend for life

The Bryant household was deep in slumber that same Saturday morning, in those long hours before dawn when sleep is at its most precious if unrecognizable time, secure in the belief that although strange winds had blown through their domain in recent days, that there was nothing much to fear from the dead Federal Agent episode.

Bryant Country was still the place none but the brave, lawman or lawbreaker, were apt to risk approaching the Bryant house this hour of the night. It was pretty much true any other time, but never at night, especially now that a man had been shot dead there, giving life to the legend that this was the fate of anyone down here unless you were on Earl's business. Events might prove that sense of security to be erroneous but for now all was peaceful.

The crickets' high pitch but almost rhythmic screeching, made a steady chorus of percussion against the more melodious if slightly discordant treble sounds of the tree frogs and the base notes of the bullfrog sounding out his mating call from the nearby still water pond bordering the yard to the Bryant house in a nighttime serenade to the peaceful slumber going on in the Bryant home. Earl really did sleep that night having none of the post episode jitters that might spook a weaker man.

The moon wasn't quite full that night but it lit up the place well enough for Johnny Caldwell to find his way on mule back heading south of Taylor's Crossing toward Earl's place. When he got close, the redbone hounds camping out under the screen porch on the front entrance side of the house detected the smell of the old mule or heard it long before anyone in the house had been aroused from their sleep. Red and Blue opened up a chorus of their own that soon drowned out the cricket and frog orchestra announcing the arrival of Johnny and his mule like a ward heeler on election night.

Earl was instantly awake, as was Ellie, as they lay there in bed for a moment or two listening to the hounds baying their outcry of welcome or more accurately of warning that someone, foolishly or not, had invaded their secure space in the dead of the night.

This will never do, No, Sir, not at all, I'm thinking, Earl thought before saying anything to Ellie and before rolling his legs out of bed onto the floor with his hand reaching for his rifle that he kept within reach by bedside.

"Earl, what'd you suppose would wake up them dogs, company at this here hour?" Ellie said.

"Hush Ellie, if you don't mind woman, I'm listenin'," Earl said trying to get his bearings or trying desperately to figure out what fool would come to his house at oh-dark thirty or earlier in the morning and expect to live through the experience. He raised himself from the old four poster bed and reached for and put on his trousers and a shirt hanging on a chair nearby where he had left it the night before. He then walked out of the bedroom to the front of the house and peered out through the moonlit yard just in time to see old man, Johnny Caldwell on his black as coal mule ambling up to the front door without so much as a hail, how are you, or some such greeting, to warn the folks he was there so as not to get himself shot in the process.

"Must be important," Earl said to nobody in particular or Johnny would never be here before daylight like this. He was a friend all right and safe from being shot on a daylight approach, but even friends knew better than to risk the same approach in the dark. "Hey Johnny, Johnny Caldwell, that you out there?" Earl yelled out from the darkened area of the screen porch where Caldwell could not see him.

"Yes, Sir, Earl, it's me all right," Johnny said, relieved to hear Earl greeting him rather than shooting at him as he approached the front steps. Just the day or so before, the dead Federal Revenue Service

Agent had been there long enough to almost start adverse possession proceedings on the top step before a team of agents finally came and got the body. But that was then and this was now and Earl was mighty curious just why his old friend, Johnny, would ride his good black mule all the way down here into Bryant Country.

"If you don't mind me saying so, this was a damn fool thing for you to do this hour of the damn morning, Johnny." Earl said in a friendly mocking sort of way.

"Well, Earl, I decided I had no choice but to come, after last night at Salty's," Johnny said.

"Well Johnny, why don't you tie that mule up yonder," pointing to an old itching rail still standing like a sentinel at the side of the front steps, although almost nobody used it anymore with automobiles and trucks having become the prime transportation for even these country people. "Ellie is making up some coffee by now so come on in and tell me what it was that was so all fired important to bring you down here on that mule," Earl said and waived his old friend into the house.

Ellie did have the coffee pot boiling on the iron stove back in the kitchen where all-important Bryant discussions were held, family or otherwise.

"Sit down here Johnny and tell me about Salty's last night, you hear something, did you?" said Earl as he grabbed one chair across from the one offered to Johnny and leaned on his elbows with his full attention fixed on his early morning visitor. When Earl Bryant looked at you like that, you knew you had his full attention and this was one of those times. Johnny took a sip of the steaming hot coffee Ellie had poured into his cup and thought a minute before answering.

How exactly do I tell him that I seen his own man Drucker "cheek by jowl" with a policeman at Salty's and I ain't got one clue as to what them two fellers was talking about. He'll think I'm slam crazy for haulin' my ass way down here on something as slim as this. Hell, it's damn near invisible, but necessary, I'm thinking'. He looked up at Earl, took another sip of the coffee and began to speak.

"Well you see Earl, I was sitin' there at Salty's Pavilion Friday night mindin' my own business, sipin' on one a yore jugs and I happened to notice your man Drucker across the room locked up in conversation with a stranger." He paused a minute half way expecting Earl to understand immediately the importance of the revelation, and Earl did have a way of seeing clear through a subject but not this time apparently because he said nothing with a "Well?" question all over his Early morning unshaven face.

"Oh!" Johnny said, realizing he had not given him much to go on and proceeded, "have you ever noticed how the po'lice looks, Earl? With that ramrod straight look like somebody shoved a rod up him when he weren't lookin' and forgot about it years later after he quit it on a regular basis? They just don't look the same as regular people, they're, well, different, don't you know?"

"Are you trying' to tell me, Johnny, that my man George Drucker was collaborating' with the po'lice right there under my nose, so to speak at Salty's?" Earl said with exasperation as though that would have the nerve to take such a chance unless the stakes in such a game were right. The more he thought about it with the shooting, George's unusual appearance at the Lagoon right afterwards, his foolish explanation to him about the shooting and how he detested the man Stiller for personal reasons, it became clear what George and the ram-rod man were discussing and it was bound to be him, Earl Bryant, soon to be, he thought, murder suspect, with an arrest warrant being served before the week was out.

Ellie took all this in from her respectful woman's place over behind the kitchen stove and said nothing, which was her role to play anyway up to now, but her man's liberty was at risk if she could read the tea leaves like they were turning up and she was trying to sort out the events of the last several days.

She began to think on it. *Earl came into my house right after that damn Federal Agent got shot on the front steps and didn't seem to know anything about it. But Earl is a sly one when it comes to appearances and he could fool a Sunday Preacher at a Vestry meetin' if he had a good enough reason. Come to think on it that would be a good reason, to try to fool me! Damn that Earl, had to go and let his hatred for that Stiller feller get up front of his good sense and my interest. What am I going' to do about this? Stand by yore man is my thinking.*

"Earl, you want breakfast now or later, you and Johnny better eat somethin', no telling what this day will bring?" Ellie said prophetically and began dishing up the grits, eggs and bacon she had been fixing all the time the men were working things out.

"Yeah, dish up, Ellie. Johnny, did you hear anything they said?" Earl asked.

"No, Sir, too far away and too crowded but they left together and two cents will get you a dollar, they was headed to Tallahassee when they left Salty's Place and made the bridge east. Now why else would George Drucker and a stranger go to Tallahassee in the middle of the night if not to get somebody in trouble and I figured it was you?" Johnny said.

Earl and Johnny said nothing further and began to eat, each occupied with his own thoughts.

I kin tell he's glad I came down here thought Johnny, *he pitched into that food without sayin' grace. His mind must be burnt clear up tryin' to solve this thing and it shore is a puzzler. Should I stay or should I go,* thought Earl, *those Federal men will be down here with cuffs and leg irons before sunset tonight or my name is not Earl Bryant. But where would I run to anyhow? Texas? Cuba? Alabama or Georgia is no damn good, can't hide a snake in the states from Hoover's men and they'll be in on this if I run and who would take over my still operation either way? Lost it I reckon, with George in on it or lost it if I run, same difference and I ain't never been any good with them Spanish talking folks, makes no sense to go there. Better stay and take my lickin'. They can't prove nothing no how with no witnesses. Beat it out of me? I'll just have to tough it out, its only pain as they say. Had plenty of that anyway. Heh' heh', heh'* he laughed as it were, deeply to himself at the irony of the dilemma he faced. *Damned if I do or dammed if I don't. How's that for choices? Only old Hobson could equal that with one of them sorry ass horses to pick between.*

"Good grub, Ellie, wouldn't you say so Johnny?" Earl said with equanimity on the Surface that belied a cauldron of emotion moiling underneath, but he would never let them see him sweat, not now, not even then, when the heat was really on and sure to come. He was a proud man and it would take all the pride his lifetime of controlling his emotions and his circumstances could muster to beat this thing, but beat it he would for there was really not much of a choice for the Master of Bryant Country anyway.

"Yeah, sure is, Ellie, you're the best cook this side of the Ochlocknee and that's saying somethin'," Johnny said, not quite sure how to make out Earl's reaction to his terrible news but he was a good enough friend to play along until the game plan was put in place. He didn't yet know his part in it, but he would be ready when the man said he should play.

"Thanky, Johnny, you boys want seconds?" Ellie offered, refilling the coffee mugs as the first crack of light from the dawn broke out in the eastern sky, reminding her once again that the demands of the day must trump the worrying about what might come, no matter how much of a storm was headed her way.

9. Show him the papers

Judge Benjamin Parker, Jr., had been appointed to the United States District Court for the Northern District of Florida after President William Howard Taft came into office in 1909. The Senate confirmed him on October 12, 1911, following his non-controversial appointment in 1910. The appointment was not controversial primarily because he had been a Federal Prosecutor for a number of years and had earned a fine reputation as a trial lawyer after he left the U.S. Attorney's office and went into private practice in Tallahassee.

He had taken on all the tough criminal and civil cases that had come along all across the panhandle of the State from Pensacola to Jacksonville and had earned the reputation not only for toughness. He was so persuasive in his summations that juries were known to weep uncontrollably in some cases out of sympathy for the injury or injustice done to his clients. They would often deliver favorable verdicts so quickly the bailiffs hardly had time to get a decent cup of coffee before the cry went through the Federal Court House, "Jury's back,." The court house ring of reporters and other hangers-on would scramble back into court to hear about another spectacular verdict from Ben's Jury, as they were frequently called by some of his clients.

Judge Ben, as the locals called him, had a fine legal pedigree, too, since his father the Honorable Benjamin Parker, Sr., had been the youngest judge appointed to the Circuit Bench in Florida History, by then Governor Milton, before the Civil war, and had served honorably and capably until his untimely death in 1903 at age 78. A Federal Judge, like Judge Ben, Jr., unlike his father of the state Circuit Bench, in those days was the closest thing to a god-like position since they were appointed for life and had total control of their courtrooms and the people in them.

Judge Ben heard the rap-tap-tap on the kitchen door of his stately antebellum style mansion on North Adams Street just north of the Governor's Mansion that same early Saturday morning. It was too early for a social call, but not too early for business, since he was the only Federal Judge in the Northern District Court. He was on call, so to speak, for any emergency requests for writs and especially arrest warrants, no matter what time the emergency arose.

Most Federal Prosecutors, including Houston Gilchrist, however, had enough respect for the demands on the Judge that they would plan even their emergency requests to minimize the Judge's inconvenience just as a common courtesy. This emergency with the Earl Bryant arrest warrant request was no different, but by the time Houston's Secretary had typed up the probable cause affidavit and Houston, Ed Smalley and George Drucker had had breakfast at Alice's Spot and made their way over to North Adams Street, it was full daylight and the Judge was by then full awake and having his morning coffee in the kitchen on the back side of the mansion.

The door was pushed open from the inside and Judge Ben looked out at the three men in the Early morning sunlight and said, "Well men, good morning to you and what pray tell brings you out this early, a man that needs an arrest, a disturbance at the capital, a prison riot, or do you just like to make my morning coffee time less private than it usually is?" Judges from time immemorial have a knack of making it seem like what they are required to do by law is a great personal sacrifice and make the lawyers feel guilty for even asking. It just kept things in their proper perspective because in his courtroom, a Federal Judge was the closest thing to having the aura of Jesus Christ in His spiritual kingdom and usually about the same power and respect in the Judge's judicial kingdom.

"We have a request for an arrest and search warrant, Judge, one of our Revenue Officers got shot down in Liberty County and we need to move quickly to pick the man up before he lights out to Texas or someplace," Houston said as George and Ed stood by silent somewhat in awe that they were in the presence of the almighty or at least his earthly representative.

Harrumph," Judge Ben said and turned without so much as a come on in or get lost, why don't you, leaving doubt in the mind of George at least, as to whether they should go or stay.

Houston, however, though young in years, had had enough experience with this kind of thing not to be intimidated by the Judge and followed him into the kitchen signaling with a toss of his head for the other men to follow him. Marilyn, the Judges beautiful wife, busy with breakfast preparations, saw that some business was needed to be done in her kitchen so she left the room with not so much as a how are you or good morning, as if she had to tend to some pressing domestic business.

As they approached the kitchen table, Judge Ben was already seated and had poured coffee all around, beckoned the men to be seated as he quickly read and grasped the essence of the probable cause affidavit.

"You don't have any eye witnesses it seems; but you have a near confession, the bullet, opportunity and motive. I'm satisfied you've shown probable cause Houston, but that confession is damn weak, if I've ever heard one, is this your inside man here?" Judge Ben asked looking at George.

"Yes, Sir," Houston said, "Tell the Judge what the real reason Earl Bryant had for shooting our man Stiller, George," Houston said.

"Well you see Sir, Your Honor, that is, Earl witnessed the killing of his father way back in ought two on a whiskey still raid and this agent, Stiller, I think his name was or is, which way is it said Sir when someone's dead, is he a was or an is?" George asked somewhat stupidly, out of nervousness mostly.

68

"Never mind that Son, it don't matter anyhow, and how exactly do you know this about Earl Bryant?" Judge Ben asked, getting to the nub of the matter.

"He always talked about it your Honor, Sir, and yesterday, he brought it up again. Everybody in Liberty County knows about his Pappy getting killed but not everyone knowed it was this here Stller feller that done it, exceptin' me and a few of the black folks, they know everything anyhow, don't you know, Sir?" George said confidently.

"Where is the gun George, at his house or someplace else," Judge Ben asked.

"It was at the Lagoon where the kettles are at Sir, least wise it was yesterday mornin' but he most likely took it with him and its where ever he's at right now, if I'm figuring' it right, Sir," George said.

Judge Ben considered the matter for a minute and having already previously issued a search warrant for the house only based on the indisputable evidence presented that a whiskey operation was going on in Bryant Country, he pulled a blank arrest and search warrant form from his brief case, that had somehow mysteriously appeared from underneath the kitchen table, and began to write it out in his beautiful long-hand cursive style, identifying the places for the search to include the entire real estate owned by Earl Bryant in Liberty County.

"You have your warrants," Judge Ben said as he signed the parchment and handed the documents over to Houston who thanked the Judge, corralled the two men and headed out of the back door of the Judge's mansion and out to the street.

Houston drove the car over to the United States Attorney's Office and the three entered the office where teams of lawyers and staff were beginning the day. An arrest team from the US Marshall's Office was organized and on its way and before the morning coffee among Ellie, Earl and Johnny was over in Bryant Country. By noon they had cleared the Ochlocknee and headed south toward Earl Bryant's home to do their duty.

10. Lest we forget

The heat and humidity during that long ago summer of 1913 had been atrocious if not unbearable deep in the forests of Liberty County, where Terrell Bryant had his still. It was hidden all right, deep in the river swamps where you could get lost trying to find it, but not unknown generally to the fledgling Federal Revenue Department, by then operating out of Tallahassee assigned the job to keep a lid on the flow of the illegal and dangerous homemade whiskey called moonshine.

The lapse in enforcement that would arrive with Prohibition after 1919 when sellers, not having anything to sell on which a Federal excise tax would be imposed had not yet given its reprieve to illegal moonshiners, due to bureaucratic laziness, so the Federal agents made somewhat of an effort to keep the lid on the more well-known moonshiners like Terrell Bryant.

The agents knew he had the still and saw the evidence of his products in the drunk tanks in the various local jails in the area every weekend, but nobody in law enforcement had found the precise location of Terrell's still as yet. He was careful and limited his production to what he and his family could make and distribute by word-of-mouth, bell trees and bootlegging.

For example, a farmer could drive his wagon and team of mules into a much younger Ed Salter's place on the river crossing to buy fish bait, ground corn meal or whatever else he wanted and tell the boy at the drive through approach what he wanted, including a half pint or pint of Terrell's finest, if he had just made his crop and had the cash for it.

While the farmer went inside to pick up the other goods, the boy would hide the bottle somewhere unnoticeable in the wagon. No money changed hands for the liquor in those days before cash registers because the marked up price of the goods would pay for the whiskey. The clerks were sharp enough to know or had some tell-tale hand signals or nods from the boys at the front approach that the price for the groceries was miraculously adjusted to cover the cost of the moonshine container sold and safely hidden in the farmer's wagon.

The farmer would load and drive on, turn around and head back to Liberty County or go on to cross the river by bridge returning back wherever he had come from. The whiskey then was on its way and before sundown, the farmer would be tying one on.

The local Sheriff certainly was aware of the practice but he had to stand for election every few years and his constituents wouldn't take kindly to interrupting their nocturnal pleasures from the stuff. So the local boys in the Sheriff's Department took their regular "gifts" from bootleggers like Ed Salter and kept their mouths' shut until after election time.

Occasionally there would be a raid on the bootlegger's place, carefully selected so as to not put too much of a burden on any particular constituency, especially if the "gifts" were lighter than usual around election time and a big story in the local paper would satisfy the Churches and WCTU crowd that their Sheriff was on his toes trying to stop the moonshine liquor trade. The system worked well for moonshiner, bootlegger and law enforcement alike, especially in really rural places like Liberty County, well named for its libertarian tendencies. The Federal men who weren't running for anything except theoretically justice, however, were a different story.

The stuff was illegal because it was made and sold without paying any Federal excise taxes and dangerous because it was made all over the place without regulations as to quality or purity and the alcohol content was high compared to regular packaged and other regulated alcoholic goods. Most regular customers and the moonshiners themselves rarely made it to sixty years of age from the cumulative damage to their bodies from drinking the stuff, but the smarter still operators never touched it themselves, only touching the money they got from selling it.

The social cost of the use of their products was never even considered by the moonshiner men, just like a modern day casino operator never thinks about the money spent in gambling that should be paying for food and medical care or other essentials. The casino customers are so preoccupied with the chance at some big prize that comes just often enough to some to keep hope alive and the damage continuing to mount especially for those addicted to the practice. The casino operator, like the moonshiner, was quite content to let destructive habits continue so long as a sufficient profit was made.

The main objection of the government to moonshiners was that the cost of government had risen to pay for the Civil War debt and later the enforced reconstruction of the South, which had been financed largely by excise taxes, including a heavy tax on whiskey. By 1894 Congress had raised the direct tax on whiskey to as high as $1.10 per gallon and that was before the modern effects of inflation. It was serious money in that day and is still high as a so called "sin tax" which people are willing to pay, even though they don't like it because they won't give up the particular sin. Although during the Civil war, an income tax had been used temporarily and was later declared unconstitutional because it was a direct tax and not apportioned among the states by census or population as required in the Constitution. The practice was abandoned immediately after the fiscal crisis of the war was over. The ratification of the Sixteenth Amendment on February 3, 1913, creating an income tax, quickly took care of that little problem, but it took the Supreme Court in 1916 to sort out the objections related to retroactivity and apportionment which settled the matter for everyone except for tax protesters, who claimed the amendment was not properly ratified and therefore not lawful. Those diehards have been relegated to the outer limits of rationality and have made no progress in the courts. The income tax, as a practical matter, was here to stay after 1916, but the battle over whiskey was just getting heated up in 1913 with Prohibition just around the corner. However, it would take a few years for the Congress to find the limits of the voters' tolerance for this new income tax, so the excise battles on whiskey, as far as the government was concerned, was dead level serious in 1913.

The practice of fermenting sugar and grain, primarily obtained from readily available corn, and cooking off the alcohol generated in the fermentation process had been around Northern Florida in one form or another at least since the end of the Civil War and possibly as long as memory cannot forget.

A single still operator like Terrell Bryant could produce about five gallons of moonshine from a fifty-five gallon working barrel; and it only took three days of working time to produce the so called "beer" to make the stuff, so a single operator would only have a couple of mash barrels to support his usually single sixty gallon copper cooker and one fifty-five gallon cooling barrel with the tightly wound copper "worm" down the middle to condense the gaseous alcohol out into a jug or jar as a clear liquid called "white lightning."

The real limit for a single kettle operator like Terrell was the distribution system. There were only so many stations like Salty's in the immediate area and trust was the only security a still operator had. The further his customers got away from the source in Liberty County, the more they freely talked and the riskier the increased sales would become. Alcohol did funny things to people's loyalty, and the loose lips that clever Federal Agents could find in any drunk tank in the area on Saturday night would sink the ship of a single still operator like Terrell. As a consequence, the old man kept his still to a one-kettle size and had managed to avoid arrest or worse in his many years as a whiskey man in Liberty County.

Earl Bryant, son of Terrell, was raised in the back woods and had spent more time helping run his father's still than he had spent in school. This was a perfectly normal thing to see in family traditions just like any other skilled trade where a son would follow in his father's footsteps. Making whiskey was easy once you had the kettle and worm apparatuses in place but the key to making good whiskey was the recipe. These were highly guarded secrets in moonshiner families in the South and Terrell would not reveal his formula to Earl until Earl was at least old enough to be trusted to keep it secret.

But long before then, however, Earl, who wasn't stupid, had figured it out for himself. He was the best in the region at making the worm which required that the twenty-five foot long, 3/4 inch diameter copper tubing be bent into a coil without a crimp and fit inside the cooling barrel, which was no small task.

As soon as Earl reached manhood, which for whiskey families this meant by sixteen at the latest he was expected to learn things about his father's business. Although Terrell wouldn't listen to any boy until he was more of a man which meant around twenty, Earl had, before then, discovered that the bottlenecks in the business were supply and distribution.

It wasn't easy to find a source to sell them the fifty pounds of white sugar per mash barrel to go with the yeast and corn, which were more readily available. But expanding beyond that was risky. There were enterprising dealers in white sugar who thought more of the profits

from the sales than they worried about the risk that some enterprising Federal Agent would notice an occasional uptake in the sales
volume of the wholesale dealer in flour, sugar and rice might show on
an occasional tax audit. Audits would be hard to plan and carry out
because that old problem of establishing probable cause was necessary
to convince Judge Parker that a search warrant be issued. As a result,
men like Terrell Bryant were generally safe on the supply side if they
kept their production more limited.

However, Earl could see the profit potential and like all young men,
his testosterone out produced his fear hormones, so he pulled and
pushed Terrell into expanding his operations. The second still had
not been up and running long before bad luck landed on the Bryant's.
Several other single still men had done the same thing and the sales
of raw sugar had climbed to the level of justifying an audit to support
a probable cause affidavit.

The audit that followed quickly showed the various points of the
spiked demand coming from Liberty County. Frank Stiller had also
wormed his way with an undercover man into the bootleg community
and had identified the increased traffic at Salty's and other Liberty
County bootleg outlets.

It didn't take too smart of an agent, which Frank Stiller was a prime
example, to put the finger on Terrell Bryant as one of the expanding
capitalists in the whiskey trade. He set up a stakeout at Salty's and
before long one of the undercover men had found the source of the
bootlegger's main supply coming from the South into Taylor's Crossing
, up Highway 65 to state road 20 and on East to Salty's, was none other
than his old target Terrell Bryant.

The arrest warrant was easily obtained on this information and the
teams set out one early morning to locate the still. One team left Salty's
by boat down the Ochlocknee and the other set off cross-country in

a classic military search and destroy operation. The plan was to cover the area west of the river until they found the hidden still, probably deep in the Swamp of Liberty County and close on the place, make the arrest, hopefully of the whole family involved in production, and bust up the still in the same operation once and for all.

As luck would have it that morning, Earl was not at the still having been sent on a delivery and collection trip up river into Gadsden County. Some of the bootleggers had a habit of financing their inventory by not paying the suppliers, including moonshiners, not quite as regular as the moonshiners would like it. Earl had been up in Gadsden County convincing his wholesalers of the foolishness of such practices and having completed the mission by teaching one particular wholesaler that Earl Bryant was not to be played with that way, was on his way home.

The river team struck pay dirt first by finding a trail where somebody deep in the swamp, too deep to be evidence of a fishing hole you might find alongside the main road, had beaten a path to and from somewhere in the interior and concluded that this was a trail from a still to access the river for water, fishing or swimming, to give the younger members of the family some tension relief from the long tedious hours of minding the kettle and refilling the mash barrels.

It was a long shot at best but there was no other purpose for a trail this deep in the woods. The team tied up by the bank and sent a couple of scouts to follow the trail with careful instructions to not get too close to alert the Bryant's, see where it led and report back to Fred Barnes, the team leader. In anticipation that his hunch was right, Fred marked the coordinates on one the topographical field maps they carried and sent the map by a man on foot, cross country with the map and a compass to the contact point with Frank Stiller.

They had agreed that Stiller would keep one man at the coordinates at the point, which shifted south a few clicks every hour at prearranged intervals and to frequently check back so that the two teams could stay in rough touch with each other. This meant that a runner would have to be shifted every hour but the inland team, under Frank's tutelage was large enough for that contingency.

This was in those days long before field radios or walkie-talkies, as they were later to be called, and these cumbersome methods were all that was then available to coordinate a complicated maneuver like this over rough terrain and under densely covered forests.

The twins, Johnny and Tommy Myers, were selected for the river team because they were raised in the woods and the hunting and fishing they thrived on as boys plus some experience in the army as trackers or scouts had made them essential contributors of the river team. The Meyers boys followed the trail for a few hundred yards and Johnny in the lead held up his hand in the standard halt signal as he began to notice the smell of wood smoke and hear the low murmur of voices ahead in one of the ravines in the river swamp. These were a tell-tale signs of a still in the deep woods, for why else would there be smoke and talk this far into the woods in the summer? Smoke in the woods in July was a sure sign of somebody up to no good for it was too hot in July for a fire for any other purpose.

The twins dropped to the ground and by careful hand signals spread out and crawled to within sight distance to confirm the target. sure enough, it was a still all right and in operation too. Johnny could make out the older Bryant from the pictures the team had been furnished, but the younger son, Earl, was not on site. Tommy made a quick survey of the surrounding territory and made mental notes careful to locate indelibly in his memory the topography of the site. Johnny caught Tommy's eye and being a twin, he could almost read his mind that his survey was finished and signaled to his brother that they should carefully withdraw to avoid detection and report back to Mr. Barnes, the team leader.

When the twins returned and made their reports, Fred left instructions that the rest of the team was to move the boat up river from the trail entrance. He left his senior man, Isaac Bradford, in charge with clear instruction that he be ready on a moment's notice to move out and surround the still; but that if they were spotted, he was to do the best he could and make the arrest anyway. The plan he devised was for the team to block the natural avenue of retreat, for all country men who thought they were safe to get across or in the river in an emergency. It wasn't necessarily true, but conventional wisdom drives conduct in a tight spot. Fred certainly hoped that the Bryant's were soon to be in such a tight spot; and if the land side push by Frank Stiller's team flushed the Bryant's toward the river, his river team could pull the drawstring on hopefully a full sack of Bryant's.

Fred shoved off cross-country and soon achieved, with that fast striding gait a woodsman can reach when he needs to get somewhere fast and doesn't particularly care who hears him. This was one of those times because the dead reckoning he had done to the hourly contact point told him precisely what setting on his hand held compass he must follow, and he was familiar enough with cross country hiking in terrain like this to know pretty close to the quarter hour how long it would take him to make it to the desired point.

Unlike when he would be hunting or sneaking up on a target where stealth was critical, he could throw caution to the winds and charge ahead noisily full steam this time. The only risk was rattle snakes this time of year, but usually the diamond backs would sing out their attack rattles well before you stumbled on them. Fred had to get there fast this time so he would just have to risk not stepping on a sleeping rattler in the afternoon sun.

As luck would have it, by the time Fred Barnes reached the designated contact point, Frank Stiller was there having given one of the younger men a breather because the multiple trips to the rendezvous points had just about worn the whole team out.

"Frank, that you?" Fred yelled out excitedly as soon as he spotted the familiar figure standing by an old pine stump.

"Yeah, Fred, it's me! "Frank yelled back and was really excited now that his team leader himself was coming.

This could only mean one thing: pay dirt, for Fred to make the cross country trek. The two men quickly closed the distance and Fred spread out his map and pinpointed the still's location. Frank Sirveyed the map for a few seconds and a plan began to formulate in his mind.

"Your team, Fred, will guard the back porch and place flankers on either side (pointing to two different coordinates on the map) just in case any of the Bryant's makes it out of the kitchen, if you get my meaning. We'll close from the north and west putting a cork in the jug on the front porch side. The high sign will be a signal up in the air from one of them newfangled flare things, red I think, anyways bright. When you see the sucker, everybody closes and I make the hands up, you're under arrest bit, loud and clear. If they surrender being sensible criminals, who no criminal ever is, we'll take them into custody. If not, you'll know what to do; you have some cuffs don't you?" Frank explained the plan.

"Yeah, sure Frank, we've got cuffs and weapons too, if we need to use them," Fred said.

"Shotguns will work best at close range and in that brush. I would use buckshot loads for the best stun effect. Don't try for kills but if it happens in a firefight, so be it," Frank Stiller said noticing Fred's acknowledgment to the suggestion. "You took how long getting up here?" Frank asked, checking his watch for estimating a kick off time.

"It's quite a hike Frank, but I make it thirty minutes to the river and judging by the map coordinates, you should need about the same to get into position," Fred said, boldly suggesting to the boss a plan of attack. Frank nodded his agreement and the two men shook hands and shoved off to their respective points of debarkation.

Frank arrived back with his team and laid out the game plan, checking his watch to be sure he allowed enough time for Fred to return to the river, deploy into position on the river side and have two flanks covered of the still site and gave the command for the men to move into position. They hiked on down river for a ways checking the map coordinates to pull up short of the pre-planned positions around the now located still site.

The still was hidden deep in a narrow ravine that ran roughly east and west, pointing at the river like a long finger. The trail Fred's team had found that located the still was at the other end of the ravine. The hills west of the start of the ravine formed a ridge across it like the cap of a letter T. The sharpshooters spread out and began to crawl military style along the ridge being careful not to make a sound that would alert the prey down below. When they got into position, they checked their watches and waited.

Fred found his men anxiously waiting at the river bank and they quickly got on board their boats and drifted silently downstream and landed just short of the river access trail at the eastern end of the same ravine. On Fred's hand signal, his men spread out and took up a flanking position on either side of the ravine and moved stealthily west as close as they dared to take up positions as the back door of the trap.

Unbeknownst to any of the two teams of stalkers, Earl Bryant happened to have returned to the area from his successful mission to re-educate a Gadsden County bootlegger just before the attack began.

As an experienced woodsman himself, having lived in these river swamps all his life, he noticed immediately that somebody who didn't belong here was in the woods today. The bird cries, usual for the summer season, were strangely silent. He noticed no gray or fox squirrels chattering away in the upper reach of the forest canopy as usual and that the ground had ominous signs of heavy foot traffic. A man who could tell you how long ago a deer track had been made by the freshness or staleness of the track would have no difficulty spotting foot prints in the roads and trails by men who did not expect to be detected so cared little for hiding their tracks.

He paused at the signs and pondered to himself. *Damn, tracks, lots of them! Woods are too damn quiet; must be something up. I wonder? Raid on the still? Most likely. Better get on down there but careful Earl, no need to be stupid about all this!* Earl cautiously approached the area knowing full well the lay of the ground before him and where the still was situated. The still had seemed peacefully so far this morning down in that ravine when it had been deemed so secure before and now to Earl at least seemed more like a trap.

When he got close, he saw right away the men spread out across the hill overlooking the still in the ravine. The ravine was like a bottle or jug and the Federal men were about to cork it, he thought. He felt helpless watching events unfold and could only fret over what his Pappy was about to face and him not able to do a damn thing about it but watch.

Earl crawled as close as he dared to be able to see the most, but not be detected. He didn't have long to wait before the action started. The flash of the flare as it streaked up into the sky startled Earl for he had never seen such a thing. Its red fire showed like a miniature beacon across the sky before it settled back to earth under a silly little parachute. Then the next thing he saw or more accurately heard was the booming voice of Frank Stiller, a man he would come to know by reputation and worse over the next twenty years.

"Terrell Bryant, you are under arrest for moonshining, come out with your hands up and your guns left behind, Sir!" He emphatically commanded in the formal way of that day even though the term of address was wholly inappropriate to the circumstances.

Terrell heard him loud and clear and had no intention of going down without a fight. With Earl gone and his younger son Edward hardly much help in a fight, the old man had only a few Negro hands left and they had no use for a scrap, cowering in the corners of the ravine, too scared to fight or run. Terrell, seeing he was going to have no help in this fight ordered his young son to lay low, grabbed his rifle and slipped out a side trail out of the ravine that he thought was a safe exit to the north, avoiding the obvious escape trail to the river on the hunch that the Federal men would not leave that way open. They would not expect him to head north, he thought. He was wrong as it turned out for precisely in front of him was his old nemesis, Frank Stiller, armed only with his handgun and barring the escape route.

"Stop right there Terrell, you are NOW under arrest!" Frank commanded forcefully not ten feet in front of and full view of Terrell Bryant, holding his service revolver in front of him pointed squarely at Terrell's chest. Terrell had been so Surprised that anybody would think of his private escape route and have even that covered; he was unable to get his gun up in time.

"I suppose you think you got me Frank Stiller, well I got news for you Mr. Federal man, I ain't going to no prison so you better go ahead and use that damn pop gun while you got a chance, cause I'm coming out of this hole whether you think so or not, dead or alive, dammit." Terrell bellowed harmlessly.

Frank pulled back the hammer and raised it up so that Terrell could look right down the barrel of the service revolver and his courage failed him for his bellicosity had not shaken Frank Stiller. He dropped his gun and fell to his knees, dejected with despair. He looked up at Frank with the fight all gone from him and pleaded with the Federal Agent to spare the life of his young son Edward Bryant. However, by this time the order having already been given to rush the ravine. The assault force rushed into the still and shot dead the young boy Edward and the Negro hands cowering in the edges of the site. From his vantage point up on the ridge, Earl watched all this in abject horror. And then when it seemed nothing worse in the world could ever happen to his family, Frank Stiller spoke or shouted so loudly that Earl could hear every word up on the hill where he was hidden from view.

"Terrell Bryant, I'm going to save the people of this country the trouble of hanging you and the people of this county from a slow death from your rot gut whiskey. Terrell Bryant, in the name of humanity, I sentence you to the only kind of death you deserve, good day Sir," Frank lectured at full volume and deliberately fired his pistol into Terrell Bryant's face, killing him with one pistol shot.

Terrell never knew what had it him and fell dead in a heap at the feet of his nemesis of twenty years. Earl stood to his feet, raising his rifle to his shoulder with the full intention of exacting revenge on his Pappy's killer right then and there but he saw out of the corner of his eye, the other Federal men coming at a run to the sound of the shot.

Earl Bryant would never be accused of cowardice or weakness but he was too smart or wise to exact revenge at this moment no matter how sweet it seemed at the moment. His Pappy was dead and he couldn't change that and there was the future to think of. The one site still was either gone or would be in a few minutes but as long as there was a thirst for whiskey there were always more barrels and copper kettles. After all, he did know this business and how to rebuild it, that he could do. He took one more look at Frank Stiller standing there triumphantly below him in full view and thought to himself: *Well now, Frank Stiller, you think you've won don't you? You're sitting there like a cock of the walk crowing to the morning sky and don't realize your life ain't worth two cents if I chose to end it. Maybe not now Mr. Federal man, but for sure you'll get yours later, or I'm not Earl Bryant, and that's for damn sure!*

He lowered his rifle slowly, savoring the final moments of the temptation to take sweet revenge, and backed away from the ridge before turning back up river to make his escape into the deep green forest under a blistering summer sun up there somewhere. He would never forget this day and someday he would make Frank Stiller remember it differently and that, by God was a promise you could take to the bank.

Frank Stiller faced the rest of his team including Fred Barnes, Isaac Bradford and the Myers twins, from the river team, at the body of the fallen moonshiner.

"Tried to bring up his gun, he did!," Frank explained, looking frantically from side to side searching for legal cover and nobody in the group much cared or ever told it differently. That's the way it was in those days, the object, not the method, was the thing that mattered. The Bryant still operation and the man Terrell himself were finished. They may later have to deal with the son who survived him, but that was fight for a later day.

11. Memories are made of this

"Ellie girl, wash them dirty clothes and thangs and git back here from the river quick like, you hear?" Eunice Griffin said by way of command to her teenage daughter who was still hanging around the slat board house she and her drunken husband Floyd Griffin called home. Floyd worked at one of the lumber mills in the area and drunk up most of his wages he earned leaving the family in poverty like most of the victims of the mean spirits. Ellie would have been gone by now since she was old enough and filled out enough in the right places to draw attention from any number of young men known to hang around that neck of the woods. But the right guy hadn't come along yet and taken her out of this mess although she had her eye on at least one of them.

"She ain't doing it because you yell at her Eunice, it's that Earl Bryant, Terrell's boy that meets her down there," Floyd said enjoying the challenge to his wife who normally had full control of things at the Griffin household because he was usually too drunk to fight with words or care for that matter.

He fought only with his abusive fists when he got mad enough, which was often. By then, Ellie was gone anyway, and even if she had heard her parents sniping remarks about her or each other as she had heard many times before, it would have made no difference to her.

She had about had enough of that mess anyway and as soon as she could talk Earl into taking her away from there she would be gone. She believed deep within her being that the young man, Earl Bryant, who came calling around there from time to time was to be her husband and she knew exactly how to bring him to the decision to ask her and take her away from all this.

Ellie was what they called a strong willed girl; soon to be an even stronger willed woman, who was not afraid to talk back to anybody and take the whipping she often got from whomever dished it out. But she knew what she wanted and usually found a way to get it.

It was not that she didn't find Earl Bryant attractive but she saw something else in the young man that strangely drew her to him. He was tough as shoe leather but lacked all of the social graces young women would like to see in their men but seldom got, especially from this country variety; but he had an unshakeable stay with it quality she didn't see in the other young men who came courting. He had been raised in the woods by a moonshiner Daddy who taught his boys that the world was a place where only the toughest survived and they had been trained well, especially Earl.

The river made a long sweeping curve at the end of the trail down from the Griffin place, and due to the speed of the current at that location it made a deep pool of relatively clear river water spreading out from the river's edge of the bank about five feet or so beneath a grass covered off bank with a bottom, deep enough for both swimmers and divers. Ellie skipped along the trail that morning glad to be free for a spell from the dreary conflicts at home and out into the free air of the river country. She whistled some unrecognizable tune making a kind of melody that spoke more of a free spirit than music. When she got to the river, she threw the sack of dirty clothes to the side and stripped off her one piece cotton dress in a single motion over the top of her auburn colored hair, and without a moment's hesitation, dove with a beautiful and graceful arc into the deep clear pool.

As she came to the surface and turned back toward the bank, Earl Bryant appeared from nowhere holding the flimsy cotton dress in his left hand and stretched out his right hand as if to offer her a hand out of the river. "Earl, you were watchin' me undress all that time, weren't you?" Ellie said with a coy smile that showed she was not at all displeased with his arrival.

"It didn't take long Ellie; you were out of that dress and into that river buck naked in a flash. Girl, I hardly saw anything, damn it" Earl said in the tone of one familiar with her reaction and not embarrassed in the least.

"I'm coming out of here, Earl Bryant and you better help me and no looking, you hear?" Ellie said with a smile across her face that said yes to whatever question he had on his mind. And for young men his age, Earl had only one question ever on his mind. Will she or won't she this morning?

He kneeled down on one knee, reached his right hand down to Ellie in the water grasping hers and pulled her out in one fluid motion and rush of excitement, pulling her young nubile body dripping with water up against his in one smooth as if practiced motion and embraced her lovingly right there with each hand caressing a shapely buttock in full view of nature, caring nothing for who might be looking.

He gently lowered her down into the tall grass growing lushly at this spot on the riverbank where the sunlight splashed across it making a meadow like appearance. As they rolled in the lush grass together they frantically stripped his clothing away until he ended up naked astride her where her body was slightly recessed in the lush grass. It was like her body was being held in a large comforting hand cradling her with his weight held off her by his strong young arms. He looked down into her hazel eyes asking without words, *"are you ready for this?"* not willing to force his way into her and with an answer also without words, her hips heaved upward as if in invitation, and he entered her gently.

The seepage of virginal blood from the parted hymen was hardly noticed by either of them. After a brief stab of pain that caused her to flinch away reflectively, she instinctively welcomed the full extent of him in her body. He rocked in and out, again and again, faster and faster with her body responding eagerly to meet each plunge and withdrawal to their mutual climax, erupting like an impacted volcano exploding in a phantasmagoric fantasia of pleasure that lifted them like sky rockets in flight to unknown destinations.

It was one of those rare first sexual encounters that lovers generally don't experience until the passage of time and experimentation develop delicious combinations of mutually physical stimulations in enjoyable and satisfying encouragements. As he continued again and again and all the while gently stroking her slender but blossoming young body with his not yet hardened or calloused hands, feeling with additional pleasure her firm breasts whose nipples were at this moment peaked and seemingly expanded in an expression of unbridled pleasure.

As this continued in a rhythmical extension of the last physical and emotional reserve left to them, they held each other in a warm and satisfying embrace. He held her and she responded holding him as well, as they passed unnoticed into sleep until the afternoon sun faded into shadow.

When he awoke he noticed she was already awake looking at him smiling contentedly reflecting on this first sexual encounter for both of them.

"Well, you've gone and done it Earl Bryant," Ellie cooed contentedly.

"Done what?" Earl asked, really curious exactly what she meant by that remark.

"Gave me a baby I reckon," Ellie said. Frankly the thought of a baby had not entered Earl's head, although as he thought about it he had been a damn fool for taking this chance with her.

Why didn't I think to pull out before it, oh hell, who am I kidding, my pecker was doing my thinking back then. No man would a done different. So what do I do now if she has got a young one? He thought, not sure what to say to Ellie. He loved this young girl and did want to marry her someday but how and when?

"I guess we did take a big chance Ellie and if you got one from me, I'll do the right thing, cause you see, I do love you girl," Earl said with a sincere expression of his true feelings. She turned her back to him and snuggled closer hanging on to the last dregs of the experience.

But as luck would have it, there was to be no child this time cause it wasn't at the right time of the month, or God knew he wasn't ready, being only sixteen years old and not able to set up a place all his own yet, but that would come. He had found the right girl though and he wasn't about to let her get away from him and she was in full agreement.

In her view, it was a mission accomplished and as to the rest, it was only a matter of timing.

12. Back to the future

Timing was the thing on another afternoon many years later deep in the heart of Bryant Country. Ellie and Earl had spent the early morning after breakfast and after Johnny Caldwell had left, discussing what they would do. Earl figured he had no choice but to stay put and after he explained it all to Ellie, she pretty much agreed. Of course she did for most things anyway.

They calmly moved from the kitchen to the front room and took up their position in their favorite chairs where the early evening napping was done before bedtime. The room was dark even though the sun was bright outside, because the shades were drawn the way Earl liked it. Besides it wouldn't do any good to sit there with an open window and make an easy target for Federal Revenue or US Marshall sharpshooters.

It made no sense to trust these people to refrain from an outright assassination because Earl had seen the compassion and respect for law they had demonstrated with his Pappy. No matter what his prospects were with an arrest, possible conviction and sentence, he was not ready to hand himself over and make it easy for these folks.

It was a cold blustery December day as the arrest team arrived just short of the Bryant residence to wait for Tom Boyle, United States Marshall for the Northern District of Florida, to give out the assignments for the arrest of Earl Bryant.

"He's not likely to be holed up at the house but it's the logical first place to start men," Tom said. Boyle was a veteran of the American Expeditionary Force having served in France with General Black-Jack

Pershing and somehow, with the General and others, managed to Sir-
vive the Meuse-Argonne Offensive in 1918. He was wounded in the
battle and received the Purple Heart commendation and was never
tired of telling of the experience, unlike most combat veterans who
found combat to be too painful an experience to re-live it by telling.

He had parlayed his war record to gain the prestigious if not generally dangerous post of United States Marshall. US marshals may
have had a legendary and heroic reputation against the bad guys of
the wild west; but in the relatively peaceful environs of rural north
Florida, there was little opportunity or need for heroics. It never
bothered Tom, however, for he reveled in the vicarious exploits of
his more exposed colleagues out west and to hear him tell it, no US
Marshall ever faced more danger and lived to tell it than him, Tom
Boyles of Tallahassee, Florida.

His tales of personal exploits were legendary in north Florida, if not
generally believed to be true. He brought to the job the aura of one
full of himself and that aura affected every member of his team with
a determination to make this thing go down right. With the charge
he had from Dan Fernell's office, through the direct orders of lawyer
Houston Gilchrist, his assignment was explicit and by damn, he was
determined to carry it out to the letter.

"Elliot, what we have here is a renegade possibly holed up in that
homestead with six guns, shot guns, rifles and God knows what other
kind of armament in there. It goes without saying, he's armed and
dangerous as a stirred up pole cat," Tom Boyle said, standing feet apart
with his hands on each hip splayed side to side atop the with leather
pistol and cartridge belt, as though he was king of the roost.

"You know the plan Elliot, we spread out the special ops men under
Ruben Smokes, you and me, left, right and center with a team headed
by Clyde Browning covering the back door," Tom said.

"Clyde's a bit green for this ain't he, Tom?" Elliot asked daring to question the leadership of "The Great One."

"Not so, Elliot, Clyde earned his stripes against fear when he survived that Stiller shooting to fight another day. He was standing right next to him it was as I hear it told, and he never flinched. That boy has the makings of a Marshall, Elliot, and I aim to see that he gets the chance. And besides Elliot, he's the only one who knows the lay of the land, the set up. That's why I asked that he be assigned to us for this mission," Tom said.

He had stood his ground against the challenge of his authority and looking Elliot down with a look of concentration of his will so that Elliot had no doubts that he had pushed the limits a bit too far this time.

Elliot pondered all this, but just for a moment. *Stood his ground did he?, I hear he skedaddled out of there without so much as a check the dead feller's pulse or pull his pistol. But "The Great One" has spoken it seems and mine is not to reason why, goes that old saying. I hope it's not my ass that does the dying, however.*

"Yes, Sir, Mr. Boyle, I see your point. You've got your finger on this one all right. He'll do fine, you just wait and see," Elliot said running for cover in the obsequious role of the fawning subordinate, Assistant US Marshall.

Elliot thought some more before responding. *Course if it goes wrong and Earl Bryant and who knows who else is holed up in that house runs slap over that boy, it will be Hell to pay with me at the gate saying, "It was my idea all the time Sir." Shall I bend over right here or would you prefer over yonder? Stuff runs downhill I always say, but just wait till I get in the cat bird seat, if ever, it'll be different then for sure!*

The teams spread out silently taking up their positions so that all expected approaches, or worse yet, escapes were covered all around the Bryant homestead. On "The Great One's signal, they advanced with guns at the ready.

Tom assumed the position of a field general slightly behind Elliot's team, but in a position to see everything in the field of fire. Elliot's team covered the northern approach and Ruben's covered the southern. That left Clyde to close the loop and stop up the jug with a cork in the rear escape route.

The teams closed the gap slowly until they were situated around the yard of the frame house that housed the man himself, but they didn't know that yet. Tom gave the hold sign and he had been careful to instruct Clyde to come no closer to the rear than to where he could not possibly be seen from the house. Tom's plan was for Clyde not to make the arrest, but to be there in case Earl made a break for it. Clyde had reached that point and he signaled his men to hold position.

Tom walked through the ranks of Elliot's arrest team to within a stone's throw and in hailing distance of the front steps of the Bryant household. He raised himself to his full height and shouted out with stentorian authority, "Earl Bryant, this is Tom Boyle, United States Marshall. We know you're in there. Come out with your hands up where I can see em!" Silence was all that greeted "The Great One's command.

Elliot Erikson looked on Tom's face to see if he could guess what he would do next. None of them particularly wanted to go stand on the very front steps where Frank Stiller had got himself shot just days ago, knock on the door and try to summon up the courage to bust in the door, and risking being shot from the inside, too, just to serve an arrest warrant.

Why won't the bastard just come on out of there and get cuffed like the criminal he is and deserves or thoughts to that effect Ruben, Elliot and most of the other men wondered or wished was more like it.

"We're coming in Earl Bryant, whether or not you resist it. This is your last chance to come get arrested, peaceful like, or I won't be held responsible for what is about to happen, Sir!" Tom said this as if he

92

really expected the man to come out and face the music just like that because he, Tom Boyle, "The Great One," commanded it so.

Silence continued to be the theme to the music that reverberated in the souls of every member of the arrest team, as they looked anxiously at each other, as if those looks would find some solace for the fear that gripped each one of them.

Clyde Browning's mind was churning with confusion. *What if he runs out of that house and right into my lap? Should I shoot him, grapple the sucker to the ground if he don't shoot me, or just stop? Damn, Clyde Browning, yeah it's you, me that is, I'm talking or is it thinkin' at? Why I didn't head straight back to that farm and the hay bale machine, like I knew I should have instead of volunteering for this mess. My Daddy was right, I ain't got any sense yet,* Clyde thought to himself trying to maintain an outer calm so that his team of sharpshooters would not lose heart. They were like him, scared out of their wits, but nobody wanted to admit it yet.

The time for true confessions might come later on, while some of them would beat their breasts and brag about how brave they were, after it was all over and the danger past and Earl Bryant was dead or cuffed and leg ironed. Not now anyway; nothing to do but wait it out and hope they shot him or cuffed him first up front before the rear door team had to act. Clyde's hands were getting sweaty, as he gripped his Government Issue twelve-gauge shotgun.

"Elliot, cover me, I'm goin' in," Tom whispered with full authority so as not to alert Earl that a change was about to take place in the game plan. He signaled to two men to follow him in and walked out into the open straight up to the same step where the rifle shot had felled Frank Stiller. He pounded his fist on Earl's screen door, "Earl Bryant, we know you are in there, come out Sir or this door's coming down right NOW!" Tom shouted with full volume.

Inside the house Earl and Ellie rose from their seats and moved toward each other across the room to make a long neglected embrace, which might be the last opportunity for a long time. The intimacy and lovemaking that had started their history together had faded in frequency and intensity over time, as Earl particularly had so concentrated on the business of whiskey making, empire building, and territorial protection. He had lost that soft part of his nature that had appealed to her from beneath the rough exterior he presented to the world.

She had grown to accept this change in him and stoically focused her attention to household duties and took her pleasures whenever she could make the opportunity pay. She knew he loved her; and the children they had raised and sent out into the world were the evidence of it. None of the children had taken to the whiskey business and because of the shame of knowing somehow it was wrong, though they were never taught that in the rearing process. They had one after another moved on to other pursuits in other parts of the country, with little contact, except on the occasional holiday get together. Occasionally when Ellie, with much difficulty could persuade Earl to leave the County to make a train trip to Atlanta , Nashville, and Charlotte, she would get to see her kids.

The only one in the immediate area was their baby daughter, Emily, who had married a Bainbridge, Georgia, Doctor, who absolutely refused to allow either parent come to their home. This was fine by Emily, because she had seen enough of the illegal whiskey business growing up, and wanted nothing to do with it affecting her life and her husband's reputation.

The kids, including Emily, had never come back to Bryant Country once they got old enough to get out of there and get on with their lives. Even though there was little formal schooling available, and not much inspiration in that way coming from either parent, somehow the children had managed to get an education, in spite of their parents' faults and disinterest in the matter, and were quite content without them.

Earl held her tightly and looked into her eyes with an old softness he had not shown for many years, and said to her softly, "Ellie, girl, it's time, I'm thinkin'. No need to get anybody else hurt over this, and it's inevitable that I'm in the hands of them Federal fellers, whether I like it or not. If I go quiet like, there'll be no trouble. You get on in to Tallahassee after I'm gone and look up a lawyer for me. They'll have to let me talk to a lawyer sometime, I'm thinking," Earl said quietly, almost with a surreal calm, in the contrast to the pounding fist style of Tom Boyle, US Marshall. He was pounding his fist into the screen porch door frame, as if to break it down if Earl didn't come out soon.

Ellie looked back into his eyes leaving behind, so to speak, the defiant nature her temperament would normally demonstrate about now and said, "Which un should I see about it, Earl? That Lawyer Martin at the Capital or Jones who's got an office up on Monroe Street?"

"Roland Martin knows everybody who counts in the whole state and a hard man to beat, I hear. You see him. He'll know what to do," Earl said, hugging her one final time before pulling loose from her embrace to walk slowly across the room and out the front door to Surrender.

"Hold on there Mr. United States Marshall, or whoever in Hell you think you are, I'm comin' out so take it easy on my door frame, would you?" Earl said sarcastically, in a voice that even Clyde Browning could hear out back.

Tom was so startled by this unexpected event that he stopped pounding and stood there waiting to see what would happen next, half way expecting a trick up the sleeve of Earl Bryant, the notorious moonshiner, and in his mind, murderer to boot.

Earl emerged peacefully without weapons from the interior of the house and said, "What can I do for you?"

"You are under arrest, Earl Bryant, for investigation of the pre-meditated murder of Frank Stiller, Federal Revenue Officer, right here in Liberty County, Florida, by the authority of me, The United States Marshall for the Northern Federal District Court of Florida in Tallahassee. This here paper is an arrest and search warrant signed by the Honorable Benjamin T. Parker, Jr., United States Federal District Court Judge just yesterday, do you surrender peacefully Sir?" Tom asked. He grabbed Earl's right wrist with one hand and in the same motion, reached behind his back and removed his handcuffs with the other hand and snapped the open cuff across Earl's right wrist.

He quickly whirled Earl around, with the right arm pulled behind his back, and cuffed the other cuff to Earl's left wrist. The two back up men quickly brought in the leg irons, and before the clock in the front room of the Bryant house had struck fifteen seconds later, Earl Bryant, notorious moonshiner and now accused murderer, was in the Federal custody of "The Great One", Tom Boyle, himself.

With all his talk, and the obvious suspicion that talk was about all there was to it, in the minds of many in Tallahassee, he had pulled it off without a hitch. Legends would grow out of this successful arrest, if not everywhere, certainly in the mind and telling of Tom Boyle. Tallahassee, and all its social snobbery, would just have to get used to it, if he had any say in the matter. As far as he was concerned in the saying business, he would have plenty to say.

Just watch him, he thought. This was better than the exaggerated Wild West and the terrible Meuse-Argonne all rolled up into one. Tom ordered his team to search the Bryant House for any evidence and turned up the Model 1917, 30-06 Enfield bolt-action rifle, and an assorted collection of other weapons. The 30-06 was the one the search team was looking for as the suspected murder weapon. They did not really expect that Earl Bryant would actually have the murder weapon in the house at the time of the arrest, but they took it anyway, as authorized by the warrant signed by Judge Parker, being careful not to smudge any fingerprints on it.

Tom pulled a stoical Earl Bryant stumbling along in cuffs and leg irons out front into the yard and yelled out to Elliot to call in the team to leave. There would be celebration in the old town tonight, and he for one, could hardly wait for it to start. In a few minutes, the trucks arrived and the arrest team and sharpshooters loaded up their equipment. Earl and his team headed north for home, with a mission accomplished feeling permeating the air. Earl sat glum and silent in his chains, as the men in a celebratory mood joked and laughed at everything and nothing, as men will do in such a time of success. The two moods were stark in their contrast and for Earl Bryant, at least, it was a time of despair and hopelessness he would never forget, however long he had for a time of remembering.

It was dark and lonely inside the Bryant home for Ellie Bryant, and no time since she was a frustrated young girl in her terrible upbringing was she as sad as she was now. Her husband and lover for life had just been taken to jail; and for what she thought she knew about his hatred for the dead man Frank Stiller; she fully thought Earl was guilty and may just be gone for good.

How he expected to get out of this and stay so calm in the middle of it was a mystery to Ellie. She walked out to the front of her house and called her dogs in for some companionship at least, even though they could not possibly understand how hopeless it all seemed to her at this moment.

There was nothing else to do but keep at it, she was thinking it all over. *There was nothing she could do tonight anyway and tomorrow was Sunday. Didn't all lawyers have families; go to church or something other than see the wives of accused criminals? But Earl was in the jail tonight and it would never do, wait that is. I'll see if on Monday I can remember how to drive that truck and head on into Tallahassee and see that lawyer, Martin, was that his name?*

Monday morning, as soon as breakfast was over, she dressed, brushed her tangled still auburn colored hair, grabbed her purse and coat and headed out to the barn to see if she could remember how to get the pickup started. It was easier than she thought, having seen Earl do it so many times and having actually driven it herself a few times over the years. She backed it out of the barn and drove the thing slowly out across her yard and headed north to Taylor's Crossing and beyond to find Earl the lawyer he wanted.

13. Greetings

The convoy of black Model 1932 Ford vehicles (was there any other color than black in those days?) with Earl Bryant in custody, rolled up in front of the Leon County Jail on Adams Street late that Saturday evening. The County Jail provided detention space for those arrested by the various Federal law enforcement agencies to be held in custody until bail was granted and the conditions met, or who were bound over until trial in Judge Parker's Court.

There was no Federal Jail as such in 1932 in Tallahassee and prisoner custody came under the supervision of the Leon County Sheriff, Eldon Strickland, who had been in office since 1923. Erik or Dickey Tooms, as he was popularly called, was the Sheriff's man in charge of the detention center.

Detention center sounded a little too polite or refined a name for the single story sweatbox, tin roofed, temporary structure, circled by barbed wire fencing and known to the inmates as "The Hell Hole." It had been built around the turn of the century as a temporary structure with the intent to build a permanent facility someday, but that well-meant intention had somehow been postponed probably indefinitely.

The night when Earl Bryant was delivered in handcuffs and leg irons he was about to be indoctrinated into the rigors of local jail hospitality. The prevailing attitude in the corrections system at the time was that prisoners were required to make an economic contribution to the State of Florida during their confinement. This meant each prisoner had to provide a valuable service while in custody, in exchange for his keep, as it were, even though forced to be there. Anyway, that was the policy advocated by the Director of Corrections for the State Prison at Raiford, and that attitude had trickled down to the local jails, especially those within the same geographical area as the State Prison. In effect, this made Leon County a part of a sort of prisoner feeder system for area projects requiring hard hand labor that nobody else wanted to do.

Tom Boyle proudly exited the lead vehicle of the parade and walked triumphantly back to where Earl was gloomily sitting in the back seat of one of the cars with his head bent over in dejection. "Well Mr. Bryant," The US Marshall said with an emphasis on the "Mr.", as if to exaggerate the shame Earl was experiencing at this moment with a false, if not sarcastic address of respect not earned.

Earl was ashamed not because he had been making moonshine whiskey and gotten caught, every moonshiner expected that someday; but because he was in custody for something he hadn't done. They had not arrested him for making whiskey, and under these circumstances he was, in his mind, unjustly detained in this God awful place. Freedom, which was a precious commodity to him, had been something he had never been without in his lifetime, until now.

"Welcome to the Leon County Jail, Sir, this is going to be your home for a few weeks minimum since Judge Parker is not too inclined to grant bail to the likes a you.," Dickey Tooms said, wanting to establish his authority right from the start.

Earl said nothing as he stood there waiting for the inevitable humiliating strip search, interrogation, or Lord knows what else the system had in store for him. He had gone over this moment in his mind on the trip up to Tallahassee and was as prepared, as anyone could be, for he expected unpleasant experiences yet to come. While expectations were for most folks the greater part of life in the positive sense, the same worked in reverse for the negative. A person in Earl's shoes would naturally expect the worst and build it in his mind well past reality in that direction by the time it came. A lesser man might be scared out of his wits. Earl Bryant was no lesser man in that sense. But little did Earl know at that point that the future held far more than he ever expected in his wildest and most despairing imagination.

Never been in a damn jail house before; can't be too bad can it? What can they do? Isolate me, deprive me of food, beat me into submission? Well they got another think comin' if they think I will give into this shit! Its only pain ain't it? I've had plenty of that. Isolation, deprive me of my lawyer, stack the damn Jury agin me? Well I got news for them bastards, I ain't confessing to nothing! Beat me if they will; won't work cause they can't leave evidence of it, for even a bought and paid for jury wouldn't go for that. All I got to do is tough it out and say nothin', period till they get tired of this shit! That's my plan and I'm sticking to it! But can I stand it? These bastards will have no pity, Earl thought ambivalently, almost arguing with himself as he rode in the procession on the way to what could be his doom. However, he remained calm in the face of the inevitable punishments that Dickey Tooms was about to hand out.

"Bring him in this way boys," Dickey said pointing toward the entrance to the old jail facility opening like the jaw of an alligator waiting to crush and tear his prey as the handlers brought the dejected, but defiant, moonshiner shuffling uncomfortably forward in his shackles and leg irons. They stopped inside the building at the entrance way where prisoners were introduced to the new rules of their lives for the foreseeable future.

It was a stark humorless room with only rugged wooden benches for furniture. "Put him over there," Dickey commanded to the two burly officers holding each arm of the prisoner, pointing to a special bench where the prisoner would be relieved of the handcuffs and leg irons that had held him uncomfortably for several hours. They moved him in that direction and turned him so that he could sit on the bench when shoved down, and pushed him down without opposition to the seated position. One man removed the handcuffs from the hands held behind his back and the other unlocked and removed the leg irons, and together they piled the restraint equipment over behind the rough but sturdy examination bench.

In the brief respite the releasing action had taken, Earl moved both hands to the front and predictably rubbed the wrists of each hand alternatively where the unforgiving handcuffs had created what seemed to be a permanent groove in each wrist.

"Strip him," Dickey commanded without hesitation, and the two officers proceeded to roughly and unceremoniously remove the country clothing consisting of overalls, long sleeve woolen shirt, long underwear socks, and brogan work shoes. His clothing was shoved over into the corner of the room where they would be saved for the return to the prisoner should he be so fortunate to be released on bail.

Although undisputed kingpin in the world of moonshiners and bootleggers, Bryant had no ostentatious manner of dressing or showing the wealth he was gradually accumulating from his years of operating his illegal whiskey business. His wealth was socked away primarily in a growing inventory of land in Liberty and Leon County where long needle and slash pine grew year by year while investments of a more traditional kind continued to shrink in stocks and other liquid securities, with the advent of the great depression gripping the rest of America in 1933.

Earl sat there exposed, naked as a jay bird with the typical stomach paunch of a man in his mid-fifties, revealing the lily-white skin of an authentic white person whose body below his red neck and above his hands were never exposed to the sun.

President Abraham Lincoln in an earlier era had said, "The Lord sure must have loved the common people, because he made so many of them" and the corollary to that pithy comment, for which the President was made into a legend of wit and wisdom, was that the human body after age twenty-five or so was covered up by clothing for good reason beyond modesty, because it was embarrassingly common, undesirable to the perceiving eye and better left hidden by clothing.

Earl Bryant, though unusually tough and hardened from a life of hard work for a man his age, was no exception and the stripping and searching process for new jail inmates served a dual function. One, it made sure no weapons were secreted in his clothing; and two, it started the demoralization process that was necessary to break down the will to resist the inevitable, a determination of guilt and the concomitant punishment that would surely follow.

For most ignorant and scared prisoners the jailers ever encountered, they knew the jig was about up and it didn't take much to soften them up for the interrogation process to generally bring out a confession, one way or the other. Earl Bryant was a horse of a different color, as the immortal wizard would say in the movie to be released later in 1939, and presented more of an obstacle than Dickey Tooms and the expert handlers in the Leon County jail expected. But they were an egalitarian lot, plying their trade to all inmates the same without regard to preconceptions for toughness or reputation.

"Bring him to his feet," Dickey Tooms commanded and the burly handlers quickly complied with minimal resistance from Earl. "Assume the position," Dickey commanded this time directly to Bryant, as if the prisoner had the slightest idea that his jailer intended him to bend over for a rude and painful examination of his anal body cavity.

"Say what? You do speak the English language don't you, Sir?," Bryant spoke out for the first time in a defiant tone, not having the foggiest idea of what the man was talking about, though he had commanded it as if he expected to be obeyed, and said it in a manner as though he expected he would be understood.

Dickey Tooms, not used to surly behavior from prisoners this early in the process, looked with amazement at the prisoner who had the audacity to question his commands, much less his methods, and condescendingly told his handlers, "I can see this feller is going to make things hard on himself, so show the "gentleman" the "position" we want him to take," Dickey said and his assistants pulled Earl backwards over the rough cut board bench, and before the fall had done serious damage to the older man, rolled him over on his stomach with his head and arms down so that Dickey, who seemed to particularly relish this particular part of his job, pulled out and put on his good hand, a tight fitting and well used rubber glove, and quickly and painfully examined the lower body cavity of the prisoner.

Now it was highly unlikely that a prisoner would have anything hidden in the cavity inside his rectum in those days, but it served the dual purpose of inflicting pain and instilling additional humiliation to the already emotionally painful exposure of his naked body to strangers. Finding nothing as expected, Dickey Tooms roughly withdrew his index finger and disgustedly pulled off the rubber glove and tossed it over into the corner where a Negro orderly would clean it up for the next incoming prisoner's examination.

"Stand him up!" Dickey commanded and the two men rolled Bryant over and brought him defiantly to his feet. He glowered with unmitigated hatred at his adversaries, having never been violated in his person that way before. Dickey Tooms took the look head on and shrugged it off, seeing that Bryant had won the first round. *No matter, Mr. Smart Ass, we'll see how you take to the hoses when the time comes. You'll break, you Son of a Bitch, or my name is not Dickey, by God Tooms*, he thought with a smile of confidence in eventual victory, matching by contrast the scowl of defiance on the prisoner's face.

"To the showers and then clothe him," Tooms commanded, realizing that Bryant was unaware of what was coming, a disinfecting shower applied to all incoming prisoners to remove the vermin that often lived in the clothing and on the bodies of the criminal class, followed by dressing in the standard prison coveralls marked with the further identifying and humiliating "P"; as if the prisoners really needed to be reminded that their pride, freedom, and humanity was about to be taken away and in his case maybe for good.

The disinfectant shower was unpleasant enough and the pastel pink colored coveralls, adding an insulting feminine air to the male prisoners forced to wear them, was even worse, but nothing was to equal the most intimidating force of all, the loneliness of isolation of a jail cell.

Because he was a murder suspect and on trial for his life, regulations were clear that he must be isolated from other inmates, theoretically to protect the other inmates from this "killer", but in reality, depriving him of the one comfort left to man in this situation, companionship for the lonely.

He would find himself alone in dark isolation, aware only of his own existence away from the companionship of other prisoners, who could at least share each other's misery and the gossip of experiences to anticipate even if to dread. Soon the misery of loneliness and fear would feed on the prisoner's imagination a thousand shapes of woe which he would not be able to control, direct, or even distinguish from real events soon to come and made worse in the process. Feeling abandoned, spared the visitation of loved ones, at least for the present, he would be ripened for the interrogation process designed to achieve one objective and one alone, the confession.

Earl was thrust into the narrow, dark, single prisoner cell and before he could turn to face his tormentors, the heavy iron bar door slammed shut behind him, forcefully punctuating the sentence of his dramatic induction to prisoner life with an exclamation point, possibly a double one. The two strong handlers who had brought him there, left without a word of instruction or explanation and Earl Bryant, kingpin of Bryant Country, and master of his beloved emerging timberland empire, found himself a prisoner, almost a slave, subjected to who knew what kind of treatment that lay ahead.

No Negro slave on the worst plantation in the antebellum south ever felt as helpless and abandoned as he did at this moment. Time alone to think he would have nothing else to do it seemed, and think about things he would. Somehow he would reach deep within his strength of purpose and find a way to make it through this ordeal; and hope against hope that Ellie would find Roland Martin soon and get him out of this hell hole. But for now, all he could do was wait and try to make the best of this hopeless situation.

14. Good cop bad cop

Before Earl had time to adjust to his dismal Surroundings, he was about to be confronted by the first round of interrogation. That job had been assigned to Ruben Smokes, special operations officer, who had headed one of the arrest squads earlier that day. In those days, before Miranda and other constitutional protections later imposed by the US Supreme Court, a prisoner was not advised of anything remotely concerning his rights. He did have the right to be represented by a lawyer of his choice, and that selection process was underway at this very minute, as Ellie headed purposefully toward Tallahassee in Earl's pick-up truck to find one.

Once counsel was hired, he would beat it over to the jail and quickly tell Earl to keep his mouth shut, but Marshall Boyle understood very well that this present opportunity to question the suspect without that warning was fleeting by the minute. It was a race of sorts for protection and justice, depending on what side you were on and the law of proximity. Opportunity gave the edge to the opportunist in the race at this point to justice.

Tom Boyle had remained at the jail while Earl had been given the benefit of the indoctrination to the life of confinement, to soften the man up for what was coming next. "Ruben, you know what to do; take Clyde here with you as the sympathetic figure and you lean on Bryant until you get that confession, you hear?" Tom ordered.

Clyde spoke up bravely in the face of this momentous opportunity, which sounded like asking a lot of him but put him right in the middle of the investigation, "Sir, just a question, Sir, I have never done this kind of thing before; isn't that risking a lot?"

"Now boy," Tom said sympathetically, "I can understand your hesitation but this isn't that hard to do. All you have to do is put in a word now and then, as though you were sympathetic to what Bryant is going through, as you have a tendency to do anyway, speak up I mean. It's a time-tested model, Son; believe me, it'll work and you don't need to understand it," Tom said looking condescendingly at the young Federal Revenue Service officer, who like it or not, was being drawn into the business of law enforcement as it was really done by the Marshall's office.

"But, Sir, I just thought I'd mention it, but he must know by now that I was at the scene of the crime and wouldn't I be a witness to the shooting, for Court later, I mean, Sir?" Clyde asked, sticking to his guns from a sense of hesitation, based partly on the fear of the unknown and partly on his rather uncommon dose of common sense for a law man this young and inexperienced.

"Humm," Tom muttered, though only to himself, which would have been an embarrassing moment for "The Great One." He had never thought of that. There was no opportunity to get legal advice from the Prosecutor's office; and besides, Tom would never admit he didn't know something as important as that, especially to this rookie policeman.

"Don't you concern yourself about that Clyde, leave the legal points to me and you do just what you are told," Tom said. Clyde mulled this over in his mind for a second, and realized what good was it for him to object, he was just a greenhorn in all this, so he just shrugged and tilted his head a bit reflecting his remaining hesitation and said, "Well you know best, Sir, when do we start?"

"Right now! Time's a wasting, that lawyer will be here any minute, so get at it Ruben," Tom said and watched as Ruben nodded and gave Clyde the follow-me sign and they headed into the bowels of the Leon County Jail.

Earl saw the two men walking down the dimly lit corridor in the isolation section of the jail and thought, *well, here they come! Don't see the hoses yet, must be they gone to try to talk it out a' me. Fat chance of that, but they get to try it anyways. We'll see about that.*

Earl sat on a short bench in the dark corner of the windowless isolation cell waiting for the inevitable. He didn't know anything about legal rights and had barely ever heard there was a document called the

Constitution and knew nothing about what it meant to him in this situation, even if he had so he simply stood his ground and applied his own sense of what he should do.

The jail guard put the heavy key in the jail door and allowed Ruben and Clyde to enter, bringing two stools with them, before closing it behind them with a slam and a turn of the heavy key in the door lock. Every prisoner in every jail would never forget when he heard "the slammer" close for the first time. It was part of the jail motif, where everything was designed for the inconvenience of the inmate.

"Good evening Mr. Bryant, I'm Ruben Smokes and this here is Clyde Browning. We're officers under the leadership of the Honorable Tom Boyle, United States Marshall, and we have a few questions for you about the murder of Frank Stiller, Federal Revenue Service Officer, who you shot to death on your front door steps day before yesterday.

"Says who?" Earl challenged the accusation defiantly, revealing at least that no inmate or sympathetic guard had passed the word to Bryant that he had the right to remain silent; or if they had, that he was going to talk anyway.

"Why don't you come clean Earl, we got the gun you shot him with, we got proof of your motive, we got the bullet for God's sake, dug out of the door post after it went through the man. It's over for you fella, come clean while there's time for somebody to put in a good word for you," Ruben said, offering up the first round of the attack designed to break down Earl's resistance. Clyde sat silent.

"You ain't got nothing, Mr. Marshall man or whatever in the hell you say you are," Earl said continuing his tough stance.

"We'll see about that Earl Bryant. You know we got you dead to rights with a witness, who placed you right in the vicinity, and a confession to boot," Ruben said bringing up the heavy load into the chamber of his investigative shotgun and waiting for the right moment to fire. This latest threat caused Earl to stop and think. He looked Reuben Smokes squarely in the eyes while he mulled this new information over in his mind.

Damn that! I ain't confessed to nobody, not even Ellie and she'd soon as die as tell anyways and she don't know nothin'. Who'd I talk to about this shit? Certainly not the fellows at the Lagoon and Drucker? Wait a minute, that bastard did get into this that morning. I wondered at the time why he showed up just then and had no idea about the shot. What did I say to that fella. Damn, can't remember. But he could say anything he wanted to. The wanting to is the hard part to figure. Earl finished his internal debate with himself and said, "If you think you got something on me from some lying son of a bitch, it don't make no difference to me. I ain't confessing to nothin'! You ain't got nothin,' unless it's some scared feller tryin' to beat some moonshine rap at the bust up of my still. I know you fellers done that, you wouldn't be the assholes you are if you let that opportunity pass you by," Earl said, taking up the challenge to the next level.

Ruben took the shot and just smiled before responding, "Well now Earl, we know you had it in for Frank Stiller cause of your Daddy who Stiller shot way back when, and you had the motive to pull this thing off, didn't you? Well, didn't you?" Earl's head sagged a little, almost unnoticeably, except to an experienced interrogator like Reuben Smokes who picked up on the body language immediately, and felt a small sense of satisfaction as to how the interrogation was going.

How in hell do you suppose they know that? Wait a minute, course they know Stiller shot Pappy, it was a Federal raid wasn't it? But do they know that I knew it? He shot back at Ruben with all he had, "Well, well, well," Earl said enigmatically, "I always wondered which one of you bastards shot my Pappy, was he the one that done it?" Clyde didn't know if this was his cue or not, but lacking experience of when to speak his part, he shot from the hip the best he could.

"Mr. Smokes, pardon me for interrupting, Sir, but a man's father being shot is a cruel thing to spring on him like this, is that really fair?" He looked sympathetically at Earl, as if he was really supposed to care for a murder suspect at this personal level. Earl ignored the young man's comments, being deep in thought himself, remembering as if he were re-living that day when Frank Stiller had shot his Pappy right in the face, after his pitiful father was on his knees begging for mercy. The thought of it just rekindled the hatred he had for the man, almost to the point of forgetting that it was his ass that was on the line right now, not his long dead father.

"Nice try Earl, but that dog won't hunt, we got evidence that you confessed to having a personal grudge against Frank Stiller for years, reason well enough to kill the man. And it didn't come from some whiskey still Negro hand. That spells m-o-t-i-v-e, m-o-t-i-v-e!"

Earl pondered that for a full minute and they let him, too, hoping the ploy was working. *That could only mean Drucker. I think I told that bastard that I had a grudge against that man Stiller. Why'd I go and do a damn fool thing like that? No matter now. It's done. Can't change that. So, what to do? Can't confess, they'll hang me for sure that way. Take my chance with a jury, that'll be my only chance, and might as well take it,* Earl thought deeply, and then turned and faced his tormentor.

"Tell you what, Mr. Federal Marshall, or whoever the hell you think you are, I got one thing to say about this, and then I'm done. I didn't shoot your damn Federal, Agent Frank Stiller, no matter how much he deserved to be shot. I can't say, I'm sorry he's dead for what he did to my Pappy, but that's got nothin' to do with this business. You do what you think you have to do, but I ain't helping you to hang me in the process. I guess I'm done talking, and if you don't like it, then put that in your pipe and smoke on it. It's all you're getting' out a me. Not now, not never!"

"Looks like he means it, Sir," Clyde chimed in as almost an after-thought, but clearly the truth in the situation as was obvious to even Ruben Smokes.

And with that, Earl shut up, and no amount of interrogating or sympathy was going to change it. In later years, the Miranda warning might avoid this kind of interrogation, but for now. Earl Bryant's good sense and caution had saved his bacon. He had made no damaging admissions, but had to face the rest of what the jail experience had to offer. Ruben Smokes was an experienced enough investigator to con-clude that he meant it for now. There was no face-saving way to extract himself from the scene, so he abruptly rose with Clyde following suit and yelled out, "Jailer, get us out of here!" Within minutes, they were headed out to report the failure of the interrogation to "The Great One" himself.

15. Call the lawyer

The prospect of driving Earl's pickup truck out of the garage shelter in the side yard was frightening enough to Ellie Bryant, considering her inexperience with driving anything, mule driven or otherwise, much less one of those infernal trucks. This was the only means for her to go hurriedly to Tallahassee and hire a lawyer quick as Earl had instructed. Driving out of the shed and up their own private road, out to the highway, was one thing, but driving it across country in the presence of other automobiles on the highway was quite another.

Both paled into insignificance with the terror she experienced on reaching civilization. She had never driven this thing in traffic, and the thought that the oncoming truck or car would not run right into her was beyond her imagination. After the first car or two passed her rapidly on the city streets without collision, she began to watch the approaching vehicle to the last minute, and then grip the steering wheel fiercely with both hands, close her eyes and hope for the best. She drove as slowly as possible to still keep the thing moving, looking desperately for the street name Earl had told her about, where Lawyer Martin had his office.

Unfortunately the office of Martin & Martin was located near the State Capitol where the heaviest traffic occurred, especially in December with the Christmas season in full swing and the preparations for the legislative session next year were somewhat underway.

She had made an early start on Monday morning. By the time she got to Tallahassee and looked for Martin's office, the business traffic on Monroe Street was heavy. Ellie stopped her truck several times, to get her bearings and with great difficulty. She finally found a local citizen who mercifully directed her down Monroe Street toward the Capitol buildings, where the Martin firm was located. She was fortunate enough to find a parking spot on the street close to the front entrance to the building where Roland Martin and Son had their law offices. Luckily there was enough space for her to drive the truck into it and out of the street traffic even though the two or three attempts she had to make was a challenging experience for her in a driving way.

Ellie walked up the front steps into the building down to the hall to the back offices on the ground floor, where a glass door with the gold letters Martin & Martin, Lawyers, was displayed across it, and was surrounded by etched glass in an ornate design. The wood of the door and the panel within which it was framed, was a rich mahogany that signaled to any approaching client the image of quality.

Inside the door was a spacious reception area with hardwood floors and a Persian rug laid out in front of the desk of the receptionist. Comfortable, but not ostentatious, leather chairs were placed around the outer office, with a small table here and there containing either the daily newspaper or various magazines to entertain the clients while they waited for their appointments.

Several men were busily engaged in hopefully patiently waiting their turns with their lawyer, when Ellie uncomfortably approached the receptionist, Anna Devlin, whose name plate was displayed on a small triangular shaped wooden stand, so that everyone would know who she was, and relieve that natural tendency of people to forget names of people they have no reason to remember, but need to do so for a polite greeting. Anna looked up from her work as Ellie approached tentatively and pleasantly asked, "May I help you Ma'am?" Ellie came up close to Anna's desk and bent over to speak, so as to avoid the embarrassment of the reason for her visit, especially with strangers in the office.

"I'm Ellie Bryant and I need to speak to Mr. Martin about an important legal matter," Ellie said.

"Which Mr. Martin do you wish to see? I don't remember setting an appointment Ma'am?" Anna said looking hurriedly at the book in front of her.

"No, I don't have no appointment today; I guess it's Mr. Roland Martin, my husband said I should see, and it is terribly important. If you don't mind asking him now," Ellie said with a note of impatience in her voice as if she didn't need an appointment or that the young woman must know already what she assumed everybody in Tallahassee was talking about by now concerning her husband and would have figured that out already.

As with most assumptions, people are always surprised when the other person is not on the same page and Anna had no idea to what she was referring.

"Mr. Martin is busy with another appointment right now; who did you say you were, Miss?" Anna asked, again politely as she had been instructed to do by Mr. Martin. *Never forget, we depend on our clients to think we care about their case, which to them is the most important thing in their lives, or they would not be seeing Martin & Martin, now would they?"* Anna was thinking, as she greeted this new potential client of the firm. Roland Martin seemed to never tire of reminding Anna and the other staff people who ran the office to think and act this way.

"Would you like to take a seat over there, and I'll ask Mr. Martin if he can speak with you for a moment if it's really that important. What may I say this matter of urgency concerns?" Anna said.

Ellie leaned over close to the uncomfortable Anna Devlin and whispered into her ear so that no one else in the reception area could over hear her, "Now look here Miss Devlin, my husband has been arrested for murder, and right this here minute is in the jail somewhere in Tallahassee having the tar beat out of him or worse, and you wan't to talk about appointments? My husband is Earl Bryant from Liberty County and he said to me, "Ellie, you go find Roland Martin, the best lawyer in these here parts and hire him for my case, and hurry! Now would you please go interrupt that lawyer and tell him we have an emergency we're dealing with here!"

Anna got Ellie's point and the name Earl Bryant finally registered in her memory as one of the most well-known, if not notorious, characters in north Florida. She excused herself and hurriedly went into the back of the office where she ran into Aaron Martin, the younger partner of Martin & Martin, just ending a client conference out in the hallway as she approached. The client excused himself and left Aaron to talk to Anna.

"Hey Anna, what's up?" Aaron said. Aaron Martin was the only son of his father Roland Martin but a well experienced trial lawyer in his own right. In fact, Roland Martin was getting up in age and hardly ever went to Court anymore, so Aaron did, or supervised most, if not all, of the firm's trial practice, civil and criminal, with his father confining his practice to political and economic deals that flourished in and around the State Capitol.

"Did you hear about the shooting death of that senior Federal Revenue Agent, Stiller, I think his name was? Well Earl Bryant's wife, Ellie is her name, is in the outer office saying she wants to see your Father because he, Mr. Bryant that is, has been arrested for murder. It must be the Stiller case," Anna explained.

"Bryant, Earl Bryant! Is he the notorious Moonshiner over in Liberty County? I think I've heard of that guy," Aaron said. "Anna, go interrupt Father and tell him we have to see Mrs. Bryant immediately. She asked for Father so we have to honor that request, but since it will come to me anyhow, I'll sit in from the start. Go see to it, Anna. If he's in custody, I'll need to see him before the heat gets up. Did she say where he's confined?"

"I believe she didn't know but that it was in Tallahassee she felt sure," Anna said, trying to remember everything Ellie had told her just minutes before.

"Makes sense. No Federal holding jail around here just yet, and if it's a Federal Agent murdered, that's a Federal offense, otherwise he wouldn't be in Tallahassee. Go now girl, hurry," Aaron commanded and she hurried on down the corridor to gently knock on Mr. Martin's office door and enter to explain the emergency by whispering the essentials into his ear. He politely excused himself from his client, and explained that there was an emergency he had to tend to, and would he please come back later in the day. The client left with Anna.

Roland sat back in his leather chair and waited for the emergency about to enter his world. In his younger days, he would have relished a bang up controversial murder trial case but he was too old for that now, and thanked God once again that Aaron had decided to join him in his practice after law school. Returning quickly to the outer office, Anna fetched Ellie Bryant and brought her into Roland Martin's office and seated her in a comfortable chair in front of Mr. Martin who sat behind his large antique desk. Aaron was already seated by his side, off to Ellie's left.

"Now Mrs. Bryant, let me introduce my Partner and Son, Aaron Martin. Now Mrs. Bryant, please tell my partner and I what this is all about," Roland said in his best calm self-confident baritone voice, that had resonated in court rooms all over north Florida and South Georgia, and always put his clients at ease, giving them that confidence that they were in good hands, if not in the presence of greatness.

"Thank you for seeing me without no appointment, but you see Sir, my husband, Earl Bryant, has been arrested for the murder of Frank Stiller, one of them Revenuers. It happened last Friday morning on my front door step." Ellie went on to explain the officers' arrival, the gunshot, death of the agent, and her husband's later arrest. She explained that he was in custody somewhere in Tallahassee and that Earl had told her to come see Mr. Martin, the best lawyer in these parts.

"I appreciate that compliment, Mrs. Bryant, but my partner, Aaron Martin, right here, also is my son, and he does all the trial work for this firm now, so I've asked Aaron to sit in with us," Roland Martin said.

"You say the man was shot on your front door step. Where was your husband at the time of the shooting?" Aaron asked, taking over the natural role of the lawyer probing for the facts, as one who would have to try the case.

"Before you get into that Aaron, we must make our financial arrangements, since murder defenses are expensive. There is the bail hearing, the Grand jury, and of course the trial, and possibly even an appeal. The fee for the case will be $1,750.00, Mrs. Bryant, and if the trial runs over three days, we will need a refresher of $100.00 per day. Can you afford that Mrs. Bryant?" Roland Martin asked, careful to make the firm's position clear on that point.

Ellie gulped, never having dealt with lawyers before, or amounts of cash in this magnitude either, but her husband's freedom was at stake. She replied, "My husband has done well with his business interests, and by the way, am I free to tell you lawyers everything about us, even if its bad stuff?" Ellie asked the question sensibly, before divulging that Earl was a moonshiner even though everybody in north Florida, who was anybody, knew it already.

"I'll take that one Dad, you and your husband are our clients, Mrs. Bryant, and everything you tell us is protected. Not even a judge can make us divulge what you say and you can count on it."

"I see," Ellie said, and went on, "We don't have that much cash money, Mr. Martin, maybe $1,500 in our bank in Bristol now, with the rest comin' a little later, and will you accept a check drawn on the Bristol State Bank for the $1,500 and the rest within a week? We're good for it." Ellie said, hopefully. Roland nodded in the affirmative.

"But what I want to know is can you get my husband off from this thing?" Ellie asked.

'That's hard to say Mrs. Bryant until we see all the evidence and interview your husband," Aaron said.

"Speaking of that interview," Roland Martin said, as he picked up the receiver of his telephone and waited for a few seconds for the operator to come on the line.

"Number please," the pleasant sounding voice said into the earpiece of Roland Martin. Aaron and Mrs. Bryant sat silent while he talked. "Miss Eddie, is that you? This is Roland Martin, connect me with 356 please over at Marshall Boyle's office, would you please, Ma'am?"

"Yes, Sir, here's your connection," Miss Eddie said, and the phone rang in the office of Tom Boyle, United States Marshall. Roland introduced himself to the receptionist and asked to speak to Marshall Boyle, who came on the line momentarily.

"Marshall, this is Roland Martin, over at Martin & Martin Lawyers, we represent Mr. Earl Bryant, who we understand is in your custody. I wanted to confirm that and arrange to see him right away; would that be all right, Tom?" Roland Martin said in that familiar and confident way he had in dealing with people, making them feel important, with an air of both formality and familiarity that engendered cooperation, which was precisely why he had developed that skill to perfection.

"Yes, Sir, we have Mr. Bryant in custody over in the Leon County Jail, and you can see him anytime you want to, Sir," Marshall Boyle said in a spirit of cooperation.

"My Partner Aaron Martin will be handling the case, Tom, and I expect he'll be right on over there today, if it's all right with you, Tom?" Roland asked in that same tone no law officer could refuse.

"Fine, Sir, if there is anything we can do, please call us," Tom Boyle said, engaging in the ritual of professional politeness he always used when dealing with defense lawyers, even though he personally disliked the whole lot of them, because of who they represented. Especially was this true in Boyle's opinion when it came to Earl Bryant.

Roland Martin hung up the phone and nodded to Aaron to get on over to the jail before the pump and hose brigade could be used effectively, as local lawyers liked to call the methods utilized in the Leon County Jail in those days,. He and Aaron understood that by now, Earl Bryant would have been interrogated if not roughed up a bit, to try to get a quick and easy confession out of him. The Sheriff's office investigators, the local prosecutor's investigators, and especially the United States Marshall's interrogators, always got the full cooperation of the County Jail men and the treatment Earl Bryant had received on his induction into custody. This was just typical for all these agencies.

"I'll visit with Mrs. Bryant a bit further, Aaron, while you get on over to the jail to see Earl. Aaron excused himself and left the office and stopped by his own office to grab his brief case, leaving by car to the jail.

"We will try to arrange bail, Mrs. Bryant, but because it's a capital murder charge, and the Federal Grand Jury isn't meeting yet, it's not likely he will be released just yet or even later today, but we'll try. We get two shots at it really. Once we are before Stillman Henry, Magistrate, he is almost certain to deny bail, just on general principles. Then the second chance is at the arraignment and that could be a different story. Judge Parker is a fair man, I knew his father the Circuit Judge well. I used to run fox hounds with him, but he has to consider that a man charged with murder might be tempted to run to Mexico or Cuba, so he is not likely to grant bail. But we'll wait and see about that, Mrs. Bryant. May I call you Ellie?" Roland said, oozing charm that he had used to persuade jurors all over the state in his career as a trial lawyer.

"You mean he will have to stay in that hell hole till the trial is over? My husband won't run, or he would have already been gone," Ellie said desperately, knowing deep down what lawyer Martin was saying was true, but she had to ask anyway.

"The Judge has the responsibility to be sure Earl stands trial and gets a fair trial, so if he has to err, he will do so on the side of assuring he will be there when the case is ready. Does that make sense, Ellie?" Roland Martin asked.

"I guess it does, Mr. Martin, even though there is no chance in hell Earl would go anywhere but back home," Ellie said, accepting the inevitable. She reached into her purse and brought out a checkbook on the bank of Bristol and wrote out the retainer check and handed it to Mr. Martin. He thanked her and offered to let her wait in the reception area, or leave and return in a couple of hours when Aaron would report back with the results of his interview.

16. Just the facts

Aaron walked into the interview room at the Leon County Jail and waited a few minutes until the jailer brought Earl into the room, where Earl took a chair at the table in front of Aaron Martin and the jailer left them alone. Earl's handcuffs and leg irons, like all other jail prisoners in that day, had been removed so he was permitted to walk to and from his holding cell.

"Who are you Sir?" Earl asked impertinently, having been roughed up several times by now, and didn't know or trust this man or anyone else at that point, as far as he could throw him.

"Relax, Mr. Bryant, I'm Aaron Martin, your wife hired our firm to represent you in this case, would you like to see some identification?" Aaron said.

Earl looked at the lawyer suspiciously, but sensed that the man was not lying to him. "I asked Ellie to hire Roland Martin, don't remember no Aaron Martin?' Earl said, standing his ground.

"That's my father, Mr. Bryant; I do all the trial cases now for the firm. It's either me or some other law firm, I'm afraid that's just the way it is, Sir," Aaron said, just as firmly, looking Earl Bryant squarely in the eyes.

Earl blinked, thought a minute, realizing he had not much choice in the matter, because he needed to talk to a lawyer today, whoever he was, and said, "Well, I guess you'll do, Mr. Martin, where do we go from here, Sir?" Earl asked, and waited patiently for the lawyer to make the first move.

"All right, Earl, May I call you Earl?" Aaron asked, noticing the nod of approval and continued, "You've been arrested on suspicion of the murder of Frank Stiller, Federal Revenue Service Agent, shot dead on your own front steps, down in Liberty County. What happens next, procedurally that is, you will be brought before a Magistrate to determine whether you are to be released on bail. That will probably happen today or tomorrow. We will try to get you out on bail, but don't get your hopes up. So far, you are arrested only for investigation of the murder of Frank Stiller.

Aaron continued to explain where they stood procedurally in the case. "Murder is a capital offense and the Constitution requires an indictment by a grand jury, before you can be formally charged with the crime. Now, we won't allow you to testify before the grand jury because you'll take the Fifth Amendment, which is your privilege under the Constitution, not to testify against yourself. But that won't matter much, because a Federal grand jury in Tallahassee can indict a ham sandwich if it wants to, as we lawyers are fond of saying, or do nothing if it wants to do that. In fact, they can do any damn thing they want to, but in my opinion they'll indict you in the end. A human being is dead, and the only evidence they'll hear will make it look like you're guilty. There will be no defense or contrary evidence presented unless the jurors themselves take control. But don't count on it; that rarely happens, Earl."

Aaron continued, "After the indictment, they will bring you before old Judge Ben Parker where you'll enter a plea of not guilty. That will be our second opportunity to request bail, but at that point it's about as likely in a murder case as a snowball in hell, but we'll take a shot at it anyway. The Feds will have to give us what they have on you after that. That's called "discovery" and then we go to trial. So far I don't know much about what they have so we have to wait to see what they have. But for now, I find out from you what you know or don't know, and we will take it from there. Before we go any further, you are not to say one word to anybody without me present, is that clear? I hope you haven't done that already, Earl," Aaron concluded and waited for Earl to speak.

"No, Sir, I ain't said nothing to those bastards, exceptin to tell them to go to hell, even though they enjoyed pushing me around!" Earl said defiantly, which wasn't exactly the whole truth, but it was the truth as Earl considered it. He failed to tell Aaron about the rough treatment he had received, but he considered that a test of his courage anyway and was proud of the way he had stood up to it. But in any event, he agreed with his lawyer. He was through talking to any jail guard or lawman about anything related in the remotest way to this case.

"That's good, Earl, because talking is dangerous. Saying anything in words is always a risk that you might slip up somehow when you don't intend. Besides, talking at all reveals by your body movements to an experienced interrogator more than you realize. Marshall Boyle is an arrogant bastard and not worth near as much as he thinks he is, but some of his men do know how to question a prisoner. Who'd you have, Richardson or Smokes?" Aaron asked being familiar with both officers.

"I think it was the Smokes feller, or his name sounded something like that, but a younger one was here too, don't remember his name," Earl said. Aaron smiled slightly as he imagined the good cop bad cop routine interrogators religiously employed, being used on Earl Bryant, one tough customer he thought.

"No matter now, so long as you are sure you didn't confess to anything important. So tell me what happened out there on Friday," Aaron asked, leaning forward with his left elbow on the table, resting his chin on that thumb, with his left index finger curled slightly over his clean shaved upper lip, while his other hand with pen in it poised to take any notes he thought important from Earl's story on the pad of paper, legal size, he had produced from his brief case. He waited as Earl began to explain what happened and jotted down on the pad the salient points in handwriting readable only by him.

"I came into my house for breakfast at six o'clock, or six thirty, after leavin' before light to go check on my shipment. You see, I run a whiskey operation in Liberty County, down deep in the woods back in the river country, and I was planning to ship several truckloads out that very morning. The law is changing, and if I didn't get it shipped out to the bootleggers up in Leon, Gadsden, Bay, Franklin, Jackson and Calhoun Counties, there wouldn't be no other chance before Prohibition ended, you see? Once whiskey is legal and the tax revenue starts to roll in, hell, they'll skin every moonshiner alive in the region."

"I can't hide that I run a large still operation and them Federal fellers probably knew it anyways. I guess that's why them agents was down to home in the first place. They probably have a snitch on me and I think I now know who he is. My man George Drucker was just too much in the thick of things that morning and he had no business bein' down there. I should a caught that, damn! He runs the business end up country for me, but he was there that morning right after I found out about the shot and turned back to the still."

Earl explained in a manner that made no sense to anyone in the world who had not been with him that morning, and especially Aaron Martin, who needed every detail in the order in which it happened and not this quick and dirty summary in the fashion of Earl Bryant telling his wife or some friend.

Aaron made Earl tell his story over and over again, ad nauseum, looking for details that his client knew but didn't think important enough to tell, but needed to be extracted from his memory, in order to find a defense. Everything he knew eventually came out with the multiple telling. He particularly drilled Earl about his conversations that morning with George Drucker realizing instinctively that Drucker was the key to the case.

It wasn't clear to Aaron whether his client was guilty or innocent at this point, and no matter what else he learned this morning, he was not going to ask Earl if he fired the shot. He didn't know yet, even though it was unlikely he would ever call him to testify in the case, but if Earl admitted the crime to him, he could never put him on the stand as a witness. That would be suborning perjury, and that he would never do that.

It was better to ask all the questions except that one. If Earl wanted to confess on his own, then he would work out a plea deal, but if not, and if Earl volunteered he didn't do it, so much the better. This was just the way things were done in the defense of the probably guilty. The question was not whether he committed the crime or not, but whether the federal Government could prove each element of the crime beyond and to the exclusion of a reasonable doubt. It was just too early to decide whether he thought this was the case or not. Besides, his job was not to judge Earl Bryant, but to defend him. Cosmic justice was up to God.

17. Set it up

Houston Gilchrist had called the prosecutorial team together in the US Attorney's conference room that Monday morning to map out the strategy for the case. Present were Dan Fernell, US Attorney, Houston Gilchrist, Erick Driskoll, a young assistant to Gilchrist, Marshall Boyle, Interrogator Ruben Smokes and the undercover man, Ed Smalley. Dan Fernell took charge.

"All right boys, just exactly what do we have here on this case?"

"I'll take a stab at it Dan," Houston said as he summarized the evidence so far in the case. "We have Bryant in custody at the County Jail. He has not confessed in round one of jailbird indoctrination or interrogation. Ruben Smokes, here, one of the best crime interrogators around here, has put the old two step squeeze play on him, but the fellow is tough and he didn't crack. So much for the easy way."

"He has a lawyer now, Aaron Martin, Roland's son and a good one too; Bryant will not be talking any more. As to evidence, we have the murder weapon, a 30-06 bolt action Enfield Surplus military rifle with Bryant's prints all over it. The local FBI lab has already confirmed that. We have the bullet that passed through Stiller and embedded itself in the doorframe of Earl's house. We're checking with the FBI lab now to see if the rifling on the bullet matches that in the rifle with Bryant's prints on it. We've got the quasi confession from the snitch, Drucker, though it's not really clean enough to nail a conviction. Martin will turn Drucker inside out on cross when the time comes, but since we have the other evidence, I think a grand jury will find it all convincing."

"But Drucker does pretty clearly identify the weapon and one shell is missing from the magazine just like he says. Drucker puts Earl in the area at the time of the shooting. So do some of the Negro hands, who confirm that Drucker and Bryant were actually talking to each other at the still that morning, when Bryant supposedly confessed. We have motive in that Stiller apparently killed Bryant's Pappy back in 1913, and Drucker has Bryant grousing about his hatred for Stiller that goes way back. That much makes sense and will be believable. We have the gun and we have him with the opportunity."

"We won't charge Bryant with moonshining, it just messes up the case, you know Dan, adds the confusion factor. But every juror knows Bryant is a notorious moonshiner and that will help us sell the case without saying so, that he needed to put these Federal men out of the way and had the balls to do it so brazenly on his own front steps. That's about it. Did I leave anything out Tom, Ruben or you Ed?"

Tom Boyle, being the egotist that he was, could not help himself, he had to say something. "Yeah, he was arrogant when I arrested him,

Houston, I want you folks to remember that," Marshall Boyle said almost irrelevantly.

"I'm sure he was Tom," Dan Fernell said, "But that doesn't make him a murderer, and you did fine in the arrest Tom. Don't worry; you'll get credit for it." Boyle accepted it contentedly and carefully suppressed a smile.

"Now, we have to bring him up before a Magistrate and Martin will make a pitch for bail. What do we have on his record, you know, evidence of the danger to the community bit?" Dan asked the group generally, but Gilchrist mainly, for he was the one who would have to defeat the bail request, if they weren't going to lose him. Every member of the team believed that if Bryant were released on bail they would never see him again. But evidence for that proposition was another matter.

"He doesn't have much of a record of convictions at least. He has been charged with making illegal whiskey four or five times, but convicted only once. Paid a fine and was released, never did a day of jail time. Practically no record as a criminal to speak of, and that's certain. But he lives deep in the woods down in Liberty County, and that's a regular highway out to the coast with escape as easy as pie," offered Erick Driskoll, Houston's young assistant trial attorney.

"I think, Dan, the evidence is the key to denying bail. This is a likely murder indictment and it will take a few weeks to impanel a grand jury. Magistrate Henry is likely to be persuaded by the seriousness of the crime with the evidence we have for conviction. It's a novel approach without real evidence of danger and flight potential," Houston said, making the best case he could think of on the spur of the moment.

"All right men, then that's what we do," Dan Fernell said. "Houston, set up a hearing before Magistrate Henry in a day or two, that'll give Houston time to perfect his arguments for denying bail, so the delay won't violate Bryant's Constitutional rights. In the meantime, put together a request for a special setting of the grand jury. Judge Parker issued the arrest warrant for probable cause, so he'll agree we need a special set. Martin will rip us apart for delay, especially if his client has to sit in jail until the next term of the regular grand jury. It will take a few weeks anyway to get the summonses out and responded to. I don't suppose Dickey Tooms has forgotten all he knows about persuasion, so we might get lucky if we can keep the man behind bars. Hell, we may just need it in this case before it's over. Bryant is the killer and that much is certain. The only question is, can we prove it. It's up to you Houston to make this work."

"Yes, Sir, we'll do our best," Gilchrist said. The meeting concluded, the team disbursed, leaving Dan Fernell to ponder what lay ahead. A conviction of a notorious whiskey operator in the region for a charge of premeditated murder would attract a lot of attention. If his office pulled it off and got a conviction, he would get all the political credit. If the trial was botched and Bryant walked, there would be political hell to pay. But that was the way it was in his job. The people had to be protected and the guilty had to pay and by God, in the case of The United States v. Earl Bryant, he would see to it that Bryant paid, maybe with his life.

18. A robed affair

The Magistrate's hearing before The Honorable Stillman Henry was arranged for two days hence by Houston's young assistant; Erick Driskoll, with notice to Aaron Martin and the Jail, so all parties could prepare for the transport of the prisoner to the Federal Court House at 10:00 AM sharp on Wednesday morning, and arrive on time for the hearing. Earl was cleaned up well before day for the ride over to the courthouse. Aaron came out to the jail early before he had to be taken to Court to give Earl the benefit of his experience, and extract the last bits of information about Earl's record and life to include in his pitch for bail. Houston and Erick arrived in Court well before the hearing and took up their positions in the stately old courtroom, staking out the territory for the Government's position, psychologically at least. Earl was manacled for the trip to the courthouse and was led into the holding cell in the basement, where he was released from his shackles just in time to be led into the Courtroom, as Magistrate Henry assumed the bench.

"This Court will be in order. Mr. Gilchrist, I understand you have a Federal prisoner picked up on Judge Parker's arrest warrant for investigation on the charge pending for first degree murder of a Federal Agent? What say you Sir?" Magistrate Henry said, with his usual business like and no nonsense decorum in His Courtroom.

"Yes, your Honor, US Marshall, Tom Boyle, has served the said warrant on one, Earl Bryant of Liberty County, and within the jurisdiction of this Court, who is in custody and now here before this Honorable Court. Mr. Aaron Martin, Attorney at law, represents Mr. Bryant, the prisoner here, who was arrested at his home in Liberty County after one of the Federal Revenue Agents, one Mr. Frank Stiller, was shot dead on the front door steps of Mr. Bryant's home, the suspect's house. We have the gun your Honor, the bullet that killed the deceased, and the fingerprints on the stock belonging to the suspect. We can produce a witness who will place Mr. Bryant at the scene of the shooting, at the time of the murder and offer…"

"Objection, your Honor," Aaron Martin said, interrupting the flow of Houston Gilchrist's presentation, "This is a hearing to determine bail not a trial of my client's guilt or innocence. I object to the relevance of putting on the evidence for trial at a bail hearing, however summarily. The only issue at this hearing, as my learned opponent undoubtedly knows, is whether the suspect, who I have the honor to represent, will put the community in any danger if he is released on bail, not the quality or quantity of the possible evidence against him."

Earl listened quietly, and of course agreed with everything his lawyer was saying to the Magistrate. *Hells bells*, Earl thought, *if the bastards would stay away from my house and land, there ain't no danger to nobody!*

"Good point Mr. Martin, Counsel, what evidence do you have to suggest that this gentleman will, if released from custody pose a danger to the community or is at risk of fleeing this jurisdiction?" Magistrate Henry said.

"Your honor, we are prepared to show that the suspect is not just an ordinary citizen being investigated for murder but a notorious whiskey still operator from Liberty County. As your Honor well knows, and can take judicial notice of, a whiskey still operator in the deep woods of Liberty County. This suspect your Honor lives so deep back in the woods down on the Ochlocknee River that releasing him will keep the whiskey flowing in this part of Florida, and that is a danger to the community of this State," Gilchrist said.

Earl pushed back in his chair at that as he thought, *They must a busted up my stills by now; How can I make anything from that mess?* He pulled on Aaron's arm and whispered as much in his ear out of the hearing of the Judge.

"Now Mr. Gilchrist, I thought you said Mr. Bryant was arrested on a warrant of Judge Parker's for investigation for murder not moon shining, or did I misunderstand you, Sir?" Magistrate Henry said.

That's telling him Judge! Earl thought.

"Your honor, we are not sure what indictments the grand jury may hand down in this case, which may very well include a true bill for murder and illegal whiskey making so that evidence is relevant to the bail issue, your Honor," Houston argued. And he had a point there and Aaron knew it. Henry had been Federal Magistrate for a number of years, but had tried his share of cases defending illegal whiskey operators in the district, and did not have to be told about that danger to the community in the continued making and selling of illegal whiskey, or the risk of flight into the interior of western Florida. There had to be more to deny a suspect his Constitutional right to bail unless the Government could show a real risk of flight or danger to the community, and Gilchrist had done neither so far. This was a novel approach to try to use the overwhelming likelihood of conviction as a reason to deny bail but Magistrate Henry wanted to hear more.

"Go on Mr. Gilchrist, tell me what you have," Henry ruled.

"But your Honor, I object!," Aaron stated forcefully.

"Overruled" the Magistrate said.

"Exception," Aaron said preserving the record for possible appeal.

"Noted," Henry said, "Go on Mr. Gilchrist, and tell me why I should not release Mr. Bryant here on his personal recognizance, or on minimal bail, since this is at best only an investigation."

"Yes, Sir, your Honor, we have a reliable witness who heard the suspect make a confession that will establish a compelling motive for the murder in that the dead federal agent. Years ago Mr. Stiller shot the father of the suspect in a raid on a moonshine still and the suspect told the witness that he would get the man someday and see him, the snitch that is, in Mexico. We believe he did just that just last week and will run if released, your Honor," Gilchrist said.

He was convinced he had Magistrate Henry leaning his way on the bail issue, especially with that little addition about Mexico, that couldn't be proved or disproved, and wouldn't turn up at trial anyway, but darn well might keep Earl Bryant in the Jail for now. Judge Parker may be another matter at the arraignment hearing, but that was then and this was now. *One hearing at a time*, he thought.

"We can and will prove, if a Grand jury indicts on the charges of murder and moon shining, motive, weapon, and opportunity to commit murder," Gilchrist said cleverly wrapping in the moon shining and murder charges to confuse the issue.

Earl took in the stuff about the snitch and nodded to himself in an inner conviction now as to who the dirty rat was, *It's that damn Drucker, can't be nobody else. Damn his soul, if I get out of this mess, that feller better be headed to Mexico hisself!*

It was Aaron's turn to put on his case and however weak it was he must at least try. "Your Honor, there has been no evidence introduced in this hearing that my client is a danger to the community or presents a risk of flight. No criminal record involving jail time, not even a day has been introduced because there is none. Earl Bryant has been a stalwart citizen of Liberty County all his life. Just because he lives in the country makes no case of a risk of flight as my learned opponent implies. He has been arrested, shackled and dragged out of his home to a strange jail and placed in solitary confinement. That is cruel and unusual punishment and no conviction of any crime has been offered to the Court. Mr. Bryant should be released on his personal recognizance, pending a lawful calling of the Federal Grand Jury on this matter. At worst a $50.00 bond should be required, and at worst, if confined against his Constitutional rights, he should be permitted the same access to jail facilities as any other prisoner, with free, unsupervised, visitation by his family. If this Court must continue to ignore my pleas and deny my client the rights so precious to all of us, granted in the United States Constitution, then the process should be made as painless as humanly possible. I caution the Government to carefully supervise the jail personnel to be sure no harm comes to my client while there, unless you release him your Honor! The bail applicant rests his case on that, Your Honor." Aaron said in conclusion, not particularly hopeful that he had accomplished very much. Earl was impressed because it sounded reasonable to him, as he leaned forward expectantly as the Court Magistrate began to speak.

Magistrate Henry thought it was a weak case of evidence offered to be proved for flight or danger, but he would not be the judicial official to release this man pending trial for capital murder and have him skip bail into the wilds of West Florida, where even the most notorious bounty hunters would fear to tread. He would let Judge Parker exercise that discretion, if the Grand jury decided to return a true bill of indictment. *Always wanted that Federal Judgeship appointment, but damn, it sure takes courage sometimes! Maybe I'm better off right here after all.*

"Bail denied!" he announced forcefully, as if there was no doubt in his mind in the matter. "The suspect Earl Bryant is bound over for the meeting of the Federal Grand Jury, provided that proceeding is conducted in the next three weeks, or I will entertain a new motion for bail, and Mr. Martin, I will order that no isolation in the Leon County Jail or harm to your Client will be tolerated. Is that understood Mr. Gilchrist?"

"Yes, Your Honor," Houston Gilchrist said.

"This Court will be in recess!" The Magistrate pronounced it and left the bench as the lawyers hurriedly rose to show their proper respect.

Magistrate Henry had denied bail over the final strenuous objections of Aaron Martin, but Aaron liked the victory he had gotten, however limited, that the grand jury must be assembled with haste, or he would have another bite at the apple of freedom for Earl and the additional twist on the ruling. That he was able to persuade Magistrate Henry to grant that Bryant could no longer be retained in isolation, and the

Government had been warned against any persecution of him while imprisoned, and that was at least, a worthy accomplishment.

Earl wasn't quite as well impressed because he had to go back to that hellhole, as he called it, but he stoically accepted that he had no further choice in the matter and prepared himself mentally for what may lay ahead. As the hearing concluded, he conferred briefly with Mr. Martin about the next steps he might expect, was re-shackled by the jailer, and led out of the Courtroom. Earl held his head high with his gaze fixed to the unknown ahead, determined that even if the government had the upper hand for now, they would never beat him. With the prisoner returned to custody, the lawyers left the Courtroom.

19. No is no

Aaron returned from the Courthouse to bring the bad news to his father and Ellie Bryant. By the time he got back to the office, Ellie had returned and was waiting in the reception room. On the way over, Aaron was mulling over in his mind how to break the news to her. With Earl locked away in the County Jail, she would be alone down there in the deep forests of Liberty County. Aaron had left the office hurriedly on his Father's instruction and had not had time to get background information about his client and his family. For a criminal defendant in custody it was a lonely and sometimes frightening experience, but for the family who loved him or her, it was even worse. That feeling of helplessness was worse than loneliness in many ways. These were country people and they expected lawyers to do the miraculous, especially when they were paid with hard earned money.

"Mrs. Bryant, why don't you come with me back to my office so we can talk? As you can see, I didn't bring him with me and the Magistrate did turn down our bail request. But there are some good things that happened in his case and I need to explain them for you," Aaron said sympathetically and motioned to Ellie to follow him down the hall to his office. She reacted to the news internally only and followed him down the corridor, and as far as Aaron could see, the news hadn't affected her at all. He noted this reaction, shrugged in puzzlement and continued ahead of her to his office.

She was seated comfortably in the leather chair nestled next to a lamp stand, that when lit, gave off a warm glow that always made clients feel at ease. Aaron sat opposite her in the room behind his desk and leaning back in his office chair on its hinges and prepared himself for what was coming that might be painful for her.

At forty three years of age, Aaron was a seasoned trial lawyer who was not afraid to mix it up with his opponent in Court. In his youth, he had been an aggressive challenger to the established order. His friends, in those long ago years, had affectionately called him their "Wild Thing", because he questioned everything and plunged into each controversy with a reckless abandon, with no concern for what anybody thought about what he did or said. He would just as soon tell his Father in those days that he intended to do something or other even if he thought he might be punished for it. If he wanted to do it badly enough, he just disregarded the consequences and didn't mince words or hide his actions.

His good friend, Anthony "Tony" Callaway, reporter for the local newspaper, The Tallahassee Recorder, used to tell the story about when Aaron decided he wanted to buy some beer and drink it, even though his family was opposed to this practice for one so young (he was sixteen at the time), he simply saved up his money, bought the bottles from the local bootlegger, and brought them home and put them in his family's icebox. Rather than sneak around, drink it and cover up the smell of his breath with some chewing gum, as most young men did, in typical fashion for Aaron, he brought the stuff home, whether his family liked it or not, and left it in plain view. "You know what?" as Tony used to tell it, "Mr. Martin took one look at those bottles of beer, smiled and asked Aaron to share one with him." Then he lectured Aaron about the dangers of alcohol for one so young, Aaron listened and agreed he would keep the beer at home where his father could be sure he wouldn't abuse the practice. In other words, as Tony put it, "They negotiated a solution to their mutual benefit."

But that was then and this was now, for the passage of time had mellowed the rebellious streak in Aaron; however he had not lost his tenacity and forthright willingness to confront or take on any challenge. A mature Aaron Martin had become a formidable opponent for any lawyer unlucky enough to draw him as opposing counsel. He was not only combative; he had his Father's brains and experience to guide him until he got his own feet wet, so to speak, in legal practice. Every young lawyer who goes to Court to try cases, criminal or civil, has to go through the many twists and turns of experience where fear, mistakes and stupidity are left behind if he wants to become a good trial lawyer and give his clients a fighting chance to win. Aaron had weathered this process with flying colors and stood ready to take on the defense of Earl Bryant and win. And "winning is the name of the game for a trial lawyer and don't let anybody ever tell you any different," Roland Martin was fond of saying.

"Now, Mrs. Bryant, may I call you Ellie," Aaron began.

"You can call me anything you want Mr. Martin, if you explain his situation truthful and straight. I ain't got no use for smooth talk this day, its bad enough with Earl in the pokey, without my lawyer mincing words with me. Fair enough?" Ellie said forthrightly. Aaron smiled, and mulled over what he was hearing, *I think I'm going to like this lady*, and said,

"Here it is straight, Ellie. We lost a bid for bail today because Stillman Henry is a gutless Federal Magistrate, worried more about his future judicial career than following the law. I can't help that situation and Judge Parker, at the arraignment, may be no different. We'll ask again regardless, but the result is not likely to change. LoOkay, Earl is going to be indicted for first-degree murder of a Federal Revenue Agent when that Grand Jury is called in less than three weeks. I have no doubts about that. A Grand Jury is a one-sided presentation, Ellie. We don't even get to put on evidence or make argument. I won't let Earl testify, it's too risky. This will be a capital case under Federal Law and he could get the death penalty. That means death by hanging under federal law. Not a pretty picture Ellie, and I'm sorry to have to put it that bluntly, but you said you insisted I make this straight and that is about as straight as I can make it," Aaron said, giving her his un-sugar coated opinion. She came across as one tough lady; and he figured she showed just exactly what she was made of and bluntness was needed in this circumstance.

Ellie absorbed the news, which came at her like hammer blows, wiping away what little optimism, or hope she had left. She bore the news stoically in her own inimitable fashion, not letting it show on her face and features. But this was a blow more severe than she had ever absorbed before. The realization that she may lose her husband, who meant more to her than life itself, was so shocking that the iron will and fixed expression that she always hid behind began to melt from the inside out.

It wasn't noticeable at first to Aaron, though he was expert at reading a witness's emotion, and had himself been responsible for cracking even tougher exteriors than Ellie Bryant's in his years of practice. It was almost like an earthquake rumbling from deep within the earth's core. You felt it first just as a slight almost unnoticeable tremor before you could begin to see its effects.

First her shoulders began to sag as she leaned forward slightly and her cheeks began to quiver, ever so slightly at first, but increasing more and more as each second passed, until she began to sniff a little, as if a cold were just coming on. Then an audible sigh, almost like a confession at the end of a long argument, it became apparent to Aaron, just before it was replaced by a sobbing so deep within her being that it didn't sound like crying at first. But then the unmistakable loss of control flooded out of her in torrents of tears and wailing that came in waves, as it were, one after the other in an ever increasing deluge, which no handkerchief or towel for that matter could ever staunch.

Shocked at first to see this phenomenon coming from such a hard bitten exterior, Aaron finally rose from his seat and approached Ellie Bryant, pulling her from her seat, knowing instinctively that she needed to be hugged at this moment, no matter how unexpected it seemed from his observations to that point. Just like the young girl from the scene at the river those many, almost forgotten years ago, Ellie Bryant did not resist and welcomed the unexpected comfort from this stranger, this lawyer that she had insisted he give her the truth and make it straight, and was now appealing to her feminine side that so rarely was shown any more and accepting it.

"There now, Ellie," Aaron said soothingly," that's the worst of it. I pledge to you right now, Earl will have the best defense in this district, bar none. We did get a couple of concessions out of Magistrate Henry; the Grand Jury has to be called within three weeks and the jail people are ordered to stop the cell isolation of Earl and are ordered not to touch or rough him up. That's important, because if they do, our arguments will have some resonance with the Court. Now, the important thing is you have to tell me Earl's story. You know him better than anybody in the whole world and I have to know everything."

Ellie's emotional collapse was under control and the change in her was remarkable. It was almost like she had kept all that emotion inside her for so long that a new person or maybe the real person was finally coming out. She told everything she knew about Earl Bryant, leaving nothing out intentionally, and before Aaron finished his usual superb investigative interview, she had revealed things about herself and Earl that she didn't even know she knew. That's the way it is with facts, you only call to conscious memory a fraction of what memory and experience can reveal to the skilled examiner, who finally wins the witness's confidence as Aaron had, accidentally probably, with his almost brutal response to her demand that he be frank.

When they finished, both were exhausted, and Aaron then turned to the personal side of the witness problem, such as where she was going to stay and how was she to get some personal support after she left his office.

"Nothing will happen for three weeks, Ellie, until the Grand Jury is called. Where will you stay through this and who do you have, family possibly? You don't need to be alone through this, now", Aaron asked.

"Ain't got nobody, Mr. Martin, family's all grown up and gone from home. Suppose I better head on back to the Place, back home that is," Ellie said without real conviction.

"You live alone don't you, Ellie?" Aaron asked, remembering that part of her personal narrative. "Your kids are all grown up and gone, I believe you said, but doesn't one of them live in Bainbridge, that was Emily, wasn't it?" Aaron had a good memory and had remembered that part too from her story.

"Yes, Sir, but it ain't no need of seeing Emily, you see Sir, she married that Dr. Wilson up there and he won't let her see me nor Earl over this whiskey business, and she feels about the same too," Ellie said without much enthusiasm, as though comfort from there was a lost cause indeed.

"But she's family, Ellie, and families stay together in a tight spot. I suggest you go on up there and see her. Dr. Hugh Wilson, I think I've heard of him. A, good Doc, as I hear it. Surely they will welcome you at a time like this?" Aaron said unconvincingly.

The Bryant kids had apparently run away from their father's reputation, emotionally and physically, and who could blame them, really. "But what I must stress Ellie, you shouldn't be alone at a time like this, and its closer and more accessible from Bainbridge up in Decatur County than from deep in the heart of Liberty County. I need you close by, and Earl needs you too. I suggest you get a room here in Tallahassee for the trial but go on up there and make peace with Emily and the Doctor. It'll be all right, Ellie, trust me," Aaron said.

Ellie nodded her head in agreement to parts of it anyway, rose from the chair where she had been re-seated after the consoling embrace, and left the office. Outside in the truck, she started it up and headed north on Monroe Street, fully intending to turn left on Tennessee Street to head for home, dismissing the strange and unacceptable idea of going to see Emily. She could not face that, no matter how much sense it may have made to her lawyer. Ellie thought, *I ain't going to Bainbridge. Truck; turn left at that damn light! Truck, why are you headed north toward 27? You ain't going to Georgia! Truck?*

Ellie realized that some part of her mind was making decisions the rest of it would find ridiculous, but she was doing it anyway. What was going on here, she wondered helplessly? Ready or not, she was driving Earl Bryant's pickup truck straight toward a reunion, of sorts, that was highly unanticipated for Emily and the good Doctor; and for the rest of her that day, this undertaking was dreaded beyond even the fear for her husband's life. And that was saying something, indeed!

20. Friends are where you find them

The return ride to the jail for Earl was a slide down a slippery slope of despair. The more he thought about his hopeless situation, the worse his mood darkened. The jail guards had the responsibility to get him there safely. Safety to them meant essentially no accidents or escape. They were personally indifferent to this prisoner, or at a minimum of interest, only slightly curious. One prisoner was just like another to them, from short-term residents in the drunk tank, to white-collar criminal defendants awaiting trial in Federal Court.

Eddie Johnson had been a guard at the Leon County Jail for several years. He liked the pay and the fact that he didn't have to work very hard. He was comfortable in his knowledge and experience, though both were limited. His co-worker today, Eugene Barfield, was the junior man of the team and followed the lead of Eddie, though not really subordinate to him, just ignorant of what to do and how to act.

"Looks like you are goin' to be with us for a while," Eddie said to the prisoner rhetorically, just to make conversation and relieve the tension caused by his uncertainty. Earl sat silent, brooding over his situation, giving the statement about all the credit he felt it deserved. "Humph," Eddie grunted, Surprised at the non-response. He was generally a genial person and thought life ought to be passed as painlessly as possible, even considering that his charges were suffering in one form or another by their confinement, that he happened to be providing at the moment, and did not find it easy to make light of their plight, just to ease the day for the jail guards, however pleasant they might act.

Earl was no exception to this pattern, particularly considering the gravity of the charge he was facing. As far as Earl was concerned, these men were just other parts of the enemy he was facing, the government in all its aspects conspiring to deny him his freedom. Eugene kept his mouth shut, just marking time for the trip, although there was really nothing he had to say in the first place.

But Eddie Johnson was raised by a caring family and it was his way to pass the time pleasantly, if possible. The fact that this man was accused of, or was being investigated for murder, really didn't change the way he looked at this situation. He was the jail man in charge in a manner of speaking, and he was determined to make the best of a bad situation, no matter how non-responsive this particular prisoner was. So, he tried again.

"Say there, Mr. Bryant, you might be interested to know that the jail yard is open to all prisoners for exercise and such a couple of hours a day. I hear tell you have been released from isolation, which entitles you to that privilege, what do you think of that?" Eddie said. Earl Bryant heard the comment all right and did sense that this man, even though he was a jail man was trying to be friendly at least. He couldn't fault the man for that.

"Let me tell you this once, Mr. Jail Man, and then I'll keep my peace. You and this feller back here (indicating to Eugene, the silent one, with a slight nod of his head) have to get me back to that hell hole of a jail. My lawyer says there ain't nothin' I can do about it. I don't like it, jest like I don't like bein' here in the first place. You seem like a decent feller and I don't hold it against you for doin' your job. But, I don't need no chit chat and don't plan to give any. That clear, Mr. Jail Man?" Earl stated, also rhetorically just to put an end to this pretense at pleasantness. He was in hell, in his mind at least, and no jail man, green behind the ears like this one appeared to be, or otherwise was going to intrude on his brooding right now. Eddie got the point and kept his mouth shut for the balance of the trip. Eugene didn't need any encouragement and followed suit.

The new cell Earl was checked into was not much different than the other one, though it was not in the isolation wing of the jail as Magistrate Henry had ordered. Small differences, a cell like this does not make. The iron-bar door was the same, as was the cot like bed, with a mattress so thin it forgot to remind you of home. But this time he had a cellmate. The old man on the cot on the left side of the narrow cell was asleep when Earl was reintroduced to confinement, and the slam of the door and the noisy turn of the key did not appear to disturb his slumber.

Earl took one look at the form on the other cot and sat down on the side of the open one with his hands against the mattress on either side of his body, staring at the opposite wall without seeing anything, lost in his own thoughts. *Murder charge, they say, and stuck in this place to boot. Ain't that a fine kettle o' fish. And now I have to put up with some deadbeat, drunk or worse, who'll want to flap his gums at me about who knows what. Damn. I shore hate this place!*

Earl looked at the sleeping figure ,who by now was snoring unmercifully, pulled off his jail shoes, wrapped himself in the blanket folded neatly on the end of the cot, and rolled over on his side away from the racket emanating from the sleeping cellmate. In a few minutes, he was asleep himself and probably adding to the din of nocturnal noises, which reverberated unpleasantly to any who might still be awake throughout this wing of the jail. However, he heard none of it.

At six o'clock the next morning, the single bulb screwed into the light fixture in the center of the ceiling overhead in the cell came on suddenly and brightly. Within seconds, the jailer for the day, Eugene Barfield, came striding down the corridor shouting out the daily orders as he passed by, on which jail schedule depended. "Rise and shine you people, you got thirty minutes to clean up, use the toilet in your cell, and freshen up if you have to before a breakfast tray will be slid under your cell door. Then you got twenty minutes to eat and shove the tray

142

back under the door. This wing gets first dibs on the exercise yard on Tuesdays, so that means everybody in the wing gets one hour outside. You people on the chain gang, you know who you are, will turn to for shipping out immediately after breakfast. No exercise for you, you get that on the road, heh, heh, heh," Eugene chuckled, amusing himself with the thought of the hard work the chain gang men had to endure.

The chain gang was the primary application of the principle of deterrence in the southern criminal justice system. First of all, you had to be sentenced to the gang and the punishment meted out on it was done by a Judge's order, so you were reminded every day you went out to work on it that your own conduct caused this punishment. Second of all, the work was done in full view of the public and some of the people who knew you, as if that would scare these men into obeying the law.

Most didn't care what other people thought about them or their conduct, so that aspect of the system was a failure in the deterrence department. The by-product of the system was the employment of cheap labor for public projects of necessity, that no one else liked to do for wages. They dug ditches, cleared brush, cleaned out junk accumulations and other undesirable physical labor, all seasons of the year, and in Florida from the end of April to November was a hot, humid, and an uncomfortable place to do this kind of work. Not too many men were deterred from criminal conduct because of exposure to work on the chain gang, but the work system continued under the influence of that powerful force of inertia that says don't change something that you think is working.

Since Earl had not even been charged with anything, he was not a candidate for the chain gang, but as a private citizen, was well aware of its undesirable attributes. But with his own troubles much worse than that, he had no sympathy, time or willingness, to devote even a passing thought to the matter. Dealing with the man in the cell, however, was another matter. His privacy was very personal matter and that aspect of his life had been changed for the worse. He came awake instantly with the light and chatter and sat up on the cot to get his bearings. This cot was insufferable for comfortable sleep. His back hurt and his body ached all over from the normal ailments that inflict men his age. The cellmate moved a little but was hardly bounding up to face the day.

Earl took advantage of the lull to relieve himself in the open toilet bowl, flushed the waste down with the recycled, foul smelling water provided. Then he moved to the single lavatory to splash cleaner water on his now bearded face and look at himself in the stainless steel mirror that was hung behind it. He saw the two-day growth of beard, his reflected the stress and fatigue he had experienced since he had been arrested. It wasn't a pretty sight. As he dried his face and hands on the towel hanging on a ring on the wall, he heard the unmistakable sounds of his cellmate coming to life.

"Well, now, what have we here, company for Jack Sanford? This head belongs to somebody else, I don't need it no more. Damn that was some whiskey I run into last night er was it night befo' last, damn, lost track already!" Jack said to his cellmate or nobody in particular.

His bleary eyes came into sharper focus and he saw the man opposite him clearly for the first time. "What done it for you? Mine was whiskey, like always, Jack asked, or told Earl, the stranger, what he was there for, whether he cared or not. Earl sat silent regarding the man who was obviously recovering from a mule sized hangover.

Earl thought about what he had heard for a minute, *Well now, a talker this feller is, and drunk, or was recently, to boot. Suppose I'm stuck with the feller for a few days at least, might as well pass the time.*

"Befo' we get real chummy," Earl said, "You cain't be here for long, just a drunk pick up is it?"

"Well that too, but they got me for stealin' off'n the railroad commissary, so I got to be here for a right long spell, and the gang later, maybe, how bout you?" Jack said, playing the tit for tat game fairly well. Earl had implied that he might become friendlier if the man was more than a drunk, sleeping off a night of boozing or vagrancy charge. Earl was more or less trapped and figured he might as well talk to the fellow, since he was to be his cell mate for at least three weeks, maybe longer, and the silent treatment could only be carried so far. Earl thought a minute and then said,

"They is goin' to charge me for murder, Jack, sayin' I shot a Federal Revenue Agent on my own front door step. My lawyer says they is got to call a Grand Jury, or something befo' goin further, whatever that means," Earl explained ambivalently.

Jack thought a minute, not being particularly bothered by the murder charge since he had been in and out of the Leon County Jail so many times, he had had his turn and fill of cellmates of every stripe at one time or another. But the "Federal Revenue Agent" comment was interesting to him. He had been a major customer of practically every bootlegger in the region and moonshine, or white lightning, was his drink of choice. It was all he could afford when he could do even that. He was not welcome in the polite "Speak Easy" or "Bottle Club" facilities that people of means used to get their alcohol during Prohibition. He just didn't fit in with that crowd.

He had to find his drinks from the jug or hip pint handed out surreptitiously in the very face of the federal agents, who were after the sellers at times. He had barely missed being shot a time or two by federal agents chasing after the bootlegger target of the week which for him happened to coincide with his need for a drink, which was often.

Jack was a drunk, but not stupid, and he picked up right away that Earl had to have been involved in the illegal whiskey trade, or no self-respecting federal agent would be poking around the man's front door step to get shot.

"Excuse me, Sir, but I must have forgot the manners my momma taught me, "I'm Jack Sanford, at your service, and might I ask, who are you, Sir?" Jack said, following the ritual of men remembering the formality of introduction, when they had assumed no interest that was suddenly revived.

"I'm Earl Bryant, of Liberty County, pleased to meet you Jack," Earl said, reaching out his hand to shake and sounding pleasant enough under the circumstances, completing the social ritual. Jack returned the gesture and step one toward a jailhouse friendship had been initiated.

Aaron Martin had warned him that conversations in Jail were dangerous, especially concerning his case or him, which didn't leave much to talk about and there was no telling who might be a plant by the federal officers. But like all clients who get sound advice from their lawyers, which makes perfect sense at the time, the advice is generally forgotten once the familiar patterns of social intercourse begins. It is basic to human nature for prisoners or people generally, to care about themselves most of all, and to not talk about that favorite subject when given the chance is a restraint that is seldom exercised.

"Federal Revenuer killed, huh! Don't suppose you is in the whiskey business, Earl, because I been swimin' in white litnin' deeper than a river snake long as I kin remember and its done me no good, and that's certain, ere you?" Jack Sanford said and asked because he would really like to know and wasn't just passing cell talk, as it was called around the jail.

"Yeah, I'm in it all right," Earl said without giving away anything and half way remembering what his lawyer had said about idle talk around the jail. Jack somehow sensed that Earl was reluctant to talk about it so he decided to take the initiative to tell his own story, but the progress toward friendship was interrupted by the breakfast trays slid noisily under the cell door. Jack took one look at the trays and said,

"This is typical Earl, creamed beef on a biscuit or toast, sit on a shingle, the prisoners call it, but you'll get used to it, at least it keeps you regular."

"I kin see that," Earl said, as the two men took their trays and sat on their respective cots and began shoveling into their mouths the gooey mixture now chopped up into a kind of stew.

"Not bad, huh?" Jack said as he finished his plate and drank the cup of water in a tin cup passed along with the food, sitting in the tray. "I been in this here jail so many times, Earl, it's like a second home to me. Mostly from being drunk though, this stealing thing is a new one for me," Jack explained.

"Why so often, Jack?" Earl asked, curious about how the product he produced affected his customers and not really seen by him before now

"Hell, I don't know, Earl, it's in my blood I guess. My Pap, he were a drinkin' man and the only thing I ever told myself coming up, was, self, being like Pap is one thing you that you ain't goin' to be, no matter what happens. You see, Earl, Pap couldn't help himself when he got to that whiskey; and it wound him up as tight as dick's hat band, and all hell would break loose when he got drunk. He beat my Momma so much it were shameful. Damn, I hated that man and look here at me, I guess I couldn't help myself neither. Did the same damn thing as Pap, ain't that a holler!" Jack explained in his folksy, down to earth, way of talking. He had slipped so low in the world of behavior and responsibility there was nothing really to hide. He was just the way he was and might as well admit it.

Earl Bryant had helped his father, Terrell Bryant, make and sell moonshine whiskey all his life, until Terrell had been shot by Frank Stiller, and thereafter on his own. The effects on his customers had been something he had never even considered. In fact, he wasn't really considering it now, for his preoccupation was with his own Survival and not the social consequences of his profession. But it did pass his awareness that this man was in dire straits from his whiskey, and it was pretty sure, in his own way of thinking, this customer had tasted the Bryant Country Whiskey at one time or another, though Earl had never seen the man before. By this time the bell had sounded for Wing Four of the jail to turn out to the exercise yard and for Earl, at least, this was to be a new experience.

21. Lost but not forgotten

Ellie drove the truck up Highway 27 north until she got to the Georgia line, where the paved road ended and the sign for that highway indicated Bainbridge 20 miles away. She was still fighting with that part of herself that seemed to be driving this truck, because all of her feelings wanted to go in the opposite direction. The denunciation and rejection by Emily Bryant, now Emily Wilson, the wife of a respected Bainbridge physician, had been so painful to her motherhood instincts she had almost abandoned them. The thought of confronting Emily again and what made it worse to ask for her help was too painful to contemplate.

And yet, here she was bumping along a Georgia red clay highway, if highway was a good name for this challenge to the health and safety of the driver's and passenger's spinal columns, and somehow losing the argument with the feeling side of her nature. Since, as there was nobody in the truck but her, thinking and talking were synonymous, she voiced her concerns from the feeling side, to the audience of the rational side, in a steady stream of emotional and rational dialogue with herself, as it were.

Emily will ask me and rightly so, Why in the hell did you drive all the way up here to, one, tell me Daddy has gone and gotten himself arrested for murder and then , two, expect me and my husband have made it crystal clear, time and time again, that we want nothing to do with you or Daddy, to stop everything and say welcome Momma. Come on in here and stay with us so that all our neighbors and my husband's professional colleagues, not to mention his patients, can learn firsthand that your daddy is a murderer and a moonshiner, would you answer me that please?

I can hear her now! her feeling side said convincingly, driving home the point. "Your lawyer says, rightly so, I might add, that you need some-one right now to be with. She's flesh and blood and when the chips are down, blood is thicker than water, she'll melt, trust me," Her rational side said in a counterpoint reply. The emotional side of Ellie had the stronger case, it seemed but for reasons she could not fathom, she kept driving the truck north toward Bainbridge.

She pulled into town and stopped for gas at a Mobil Station, just inside the city limits, and asked the young black man pumping the gas, "Do you know or have you heard of Dr. Hugh Wilson and could you give me directions to where he lives at, please?"

"Yessum, he live on Franklin Street or the other side of that hospi-tal down by the river. Turn right at the light past the hospital, that's Franklin, and it's the white house on de right about half the way down there. Have a big porch wrapped round the house. You cain't miss it, ma'am. I been there lots times to deliver kindlin' and such. Dr. Wilson is a fine man, Doctor, too, I hear," the black attendant said as he finished filling the truck's gas tank. Ellie paid the requested sum and drove into town looking for the hospital with much trepidation. She found Riverside Hospital easy enough and the light beyond as the young black man had said, turned right on Franklin Street and noticed the quiet well-kept neighborhood of residences that reflected the best the City of Bainbridge had to offer.

She was proud of her daughter, Emily, for making her way out of their home and marrying an upright member of the community, no matter how painful the fear of the upcoming encounter was welling up in her heart and gut, like a balloon ready to burst.

The white house, about half way down Franklin Street, did in fact have a screened porch, as the young man had described, and right in front of the house was a sign that, unmistakably, identified the place as the Wilson residence. There was ample evidence that someone was home as she heard music playing on a wireless set, something she had heard about but never experienced herself, and a truck with hand painted letters that said, Kingston Laundry" on the side was parked in front.

She wasn't relieved, however, because she had secretly hoped that nobody was home and even better, her emotional side hoped that the Wilsons had gone to Atlanta or someplace away from here, and that she would have no choice, emotional or rational, but to turn the truck around and head back to Liberty County. No such luck was in store this day because the laundry truck was just leaving, and the Wilsons' Negro maid was paying the bill and saying goodbye to the driver, obviously a friend.

"Ya'll come see us," the maid said, and stopped as she noticed Ellie's truck drive up and stop. Ellie sat still for a moment staring at the maid, and the maid stared back, each taking the measure of the other. One of the jobs of Elvira Henderson was to announce the arrival of guests and to screen out "riff raff", such as unwanted solicitors that often tried to sell something or the other to the Wilsons and other local residences. The economy had been so poor with the onset of the depression, that people were selling anything and everything that they owned or sometimes things they didn't own. It was strange she thought, to see a white woman driving an old truck in a residential street in Bainbridge. Something wasn't right with this picture.

Ellie's rational side, and the courageous spirit that dwelled within her, finally won out in the contest and climbed out of the truck and slowly approached the front door, although not without a good dose of fear and uncertainty.

Elvira waited patiently, assuming the posture of politeness and skepticism, all in the same demeanor. Maids like Elvira Henderson had practiced this posture to perfection, and could turn on the charm in a moment's notice, or throw the bastard or bitch out if the need arose.

"Can we help you Ma'am?" Elvira said, giving Ellie the benefit of the doubt as the first line of defense requiring the stranger to state her business, which would govern the next response depending on its nature.

"Yes, please, is Mrs. Wilson home? I would like to speak with her, if she's home, and if she don't mind," Ellie said, not tipping off the reason for her visit. It was always possible that Emily was not home, though she doubted it very much.

"Who may I say is calling, Ma'am? Mrs. Wilson home, but she will want to know so she can properly greet her guests," Elvira said, maintaining the southern social ritual.

"You can tell her its Mrs. Earl Bryant, from Florida, her mother, to see her," Ellie said watching carefully the face of the maid to see if her daughter's estranged family relationship had been explained to her help, as a tip alerting her as to what lay ahead. There was nothing on the Negro woman's face that registered a warning sign, which didn't help Ellie to prepare herself.

"Yes ma'am, I'm Elvira the Wilson's maid and why don't you come in Mrs. Bryant, Mrs. Wilson didn't tell me she be expecting family, is you had a hard drive?" Elvira turned on the southern charm, reading this as a safe introduction, although she thought it strange that her mistress had not expected her mother to visit, which was usually a time of expectation for southern daughters to have.

But come to think of it, she thought, *Miss Emily never say nothing about her momma, not never. Why you suppose that is? Elvira, something strange going on round here. But, Mommas is Mommas, till they tells me different, I always say.*

"Please come in, Mrs. Bryant, here in the parlor, would you like some tea?

"No, thank you Elvira, just go tell Mrs. Wilson her momma is here.

Elvira made her way to the back of the house where Emily was working in the kitchen supervising the preparation of the evening meal. Her coOkay, Annie Blakely, was peeling potatoes and Emily was chatting with her neighbor, Geraldine Nelson, who had dropped over from across the adjoining back yard for some tea and socializing, being a common occurrence for the two women neighbors who had become fast friends.

"Mrs. Wilson, you have an unannounced guest, the lady say she your Momma from Florida," Elvira, said and watched with shock at the look of horror on her mistress' face. In fact the look was so strident that Elvira feared she had missed something terribly important and fully expected to be let go that very evening. Emily absorbed the shock quickly and turned to Geraldine with a request only good friends will honor.

"Gerrie, I have a terrible favor to ask, could you excuse me? My mother has dropped in unannounced, so there must be some kind of an emergency. Normally, I would love for you to meet her and visit for a while, but this is different, you see, don't you?" Emily pleaded with her friend, reaching out to her and holding her hands and being the true friend that she had become.

Gerrie nodded her understanding and without a word, excused

herself and left quietly out the back door, smiling a signal to Emily that she completely understood, although that was far from the truth, because she understood nothing about this at all. But Emily was her friend and if you can't trust friends not to have to explain in an emergency, then it must be important. She would come back later and be ready to support Emily whichever way she was asked. But for now, the thing to do was leave.

Emily closed her eyes in that expression of relief common to womankind, grateful that she did not have to face her Momma in front of anybody, for what she had to say would be rude and unpleasant to anyone, and especially embarrassing to her friend. Emily was well fixed in her position on motherhood, Bryant style, and whatever the emergency was, and she had no idea of what this could be about, the response would be the same. Leave now and stay away, period!

Emily left the kitchen furious at her mother for intruding unannounced like this and strode into the parlor ready for confrontation. It was like every other such meeting had been ever since she had left home as a teenager, disgusted with the lifestyle of her parents, especially the illegal whiskey still business, in which her Father was engaged. The sight that met her was far different than she expected. Ellie Bryant sat disheveled in a chair near the window gazing out into the street as if she wished she were there and not here facing her daughter.

Emily knew her Mother well from those childhood years as an uneducated, tough-minded, unsympathetic custodian of a troubled household. Defiance was a word that crossed her mind, as she had thought about her mother, from time to time, over the years since that fateful day many years ago when she had finally had her fill of the berating and belittlement of her person.

Any sixteen year old has a tough time reconciling the need for independence and the rebellion against authority, and she had failed.

Ellie had let her go, even though she, Ellie, was at that time, physically strong enough to overpower her in departure.

"Good riddance!," had been her parting shot that morning as Emily had bolted out of the house and headed up the dirt road to freedom on foot never to return. In this case, home was where the heart wasn't, in her way of looking at things in Bryant Country.

Ellie turned from gazing out the front window and fixed her focus on the determined and angry face of Emily Wilson.

"Well, Momma, what part of stay the hell out of my life did you not understand?" Emily fired away rhetorically, for there was really no way to answer that loaded question.

"Good to see you, too, Daughter!" Ellie said meekly, in a softer and far less belligerent tone than she would have used those many years before on Emily's escape from family control. In fact, it was almost humorous to Ellie from the rational side of her being, but full of pathos from the emotional side. The look on her face was a pathetic mixture of the two that left Emily confused or puzzled.

What on earth could bring her to my house unannounced, but docile, isn't she, for a change? Interesting, no, curious is the word I'm searching for to explain this. Something terrible must have happened or she'd never be here!

"Let me guess Momma, there's trouble at home? Daddy beat you up? Don't see any marks though. Oh, I get it its Prohibition ending isn't it? The illegal liquor business has competition now! Daddy has it a financial snag and you need our help? Well, you can forget that! Hugh won't speak to you or Daddy, much less help out even if you're desperate for money," Emily said in a question and statement way that defied a logical point by point rebuttal or answer, which is what she intended.

"There's trouble all right, Daughter, far more trouble than even you kin imagine we're in. Yore Daddy's been arrested and he's sitin' down there in that jail house in Tallahassee, locked up tighter than a snuff can lid," Ellie said but offered nothing by way of explanation, and just sat there staring mournfully at her daughter's shocked and frantic expression.

Jail! Did I hear right? Still raid, most likely, but that's not enough for this. She's devastated, that's clear! But Daddy? Been there done that he'd say and do his time, tough as flint with no wear and tear to speak of and kettles and such can be replaced. Worse? How worse?

"There must be more, Momma?" Emily said softer now in spite of her attacks from before, which had been dripping from old wounds, like oozing puss, foul and just as deadly to what little relationship was left between them. There was a human side to her after all and she was melting into caring to some degree, in spite of her determined will and exploding resentment that had faded somewhat.

"Your Daddy is in the dock for murder, Emily; they say he shot a federal man down at the house. That part, the where it was done, I mean, is not disputed, cause I was there that morning. Shot dead by somebody all right on my front door step. Course, them federal men think they know who done it and that's my Earl, your Daddy," Ellie said.

"Shot? Murder? Daddy? That can't be. He's tough as green shoe leather but murder? No way Momma, not him," Emily said safely from her memory and conviction. This did it, it seems, for the love of mother instinct instilled so deeply in the genes, or the repressed emotions of a child, and the love of offspring a mother reciprocates for child, no matter how estranged they had become, was returning in a wave of feeling for both of them, which neither could explain or control.

Before either knew what they were doing, Emily fell into her mother's arms just as Ellie rose up in a desperate mutual longing for that lost affection, and they wrapped themselves in an embrace that clung together in a vice grip of longing and regret.

"I'm so sorry, Momma" she said.

"It hurts so much," the other said and the tears were mixed together on their faces as they kissed, caressed, and embraced beyond longing or meaningful words. They simply rocked together to the music of grief suddenly and unexplainably released.

After a few moments, the tears subsided and they were able to separate to say and ask the necessary things to and of each other, as only a reunited mother and daughter can do.

"Did he?"

"Don't know and I'm a feared to ask"

"Maybe better that you didn't"

"Yes, better maybe, don't know anymore"

"Does Daddy have legal help?" Emily asked returning to the practical.

"Yes, we got a Tallahassee lawyer, good one too by all accounts. Actually, if it weren't for Mr. Martin, Aaron Martin is his name, I wouldn't be here. Damn, Emily, this was the last place I wanted to be at, with all that's gone before, but he kept insistin' I needed somebody for support. Little chance that, I told him. But the funny thing was, I left his office headed home and that truck would not make that turn to home, drove straight up here with me cussin' it all the way. Demon possessed, I was thinking. But he, the lawyer, I mean, knew best it seems, and hear I is," Ellie concluded helplessly unable to understand her feelings, much less her actions of the morning. But what about Dr. Hugh, he ain't softened up like you is, Emily?" Ellie asked, sincerely concerned about where she stood with the man of the house, who should be returning any minute for supper.

It was a legitimate concern, too, for even though Emily was a hard case to crack as far as her mother was concerned, Hugh Wilson was impossible. As an older man, an old bachelor it seems, he had fallen for the much younger Emily Bryant, and had agreed to marry her in spite of her family, but he did not have to like them or tolerate the presence of any of them in his house or their lives. He was a kind and caring country medical doctor, but he had seen the ravages that moonshine whiskey had caused in the lives of too many patients, and could not tolerate any contact with a man who had spent his adult life contributing to the destruction of the male population of South Georgia and north Florida where he practiced medicine.

He loved Emily and admired the way she had risen from the mire of the depraved upbringing under the tutelage of her parents, but for him, socializing with moonshiners, even if her father, was a line he would not cross. That line was about to be tested because the sound of Doc Wilson's Chevrolet could be heard pulling into the car port on the side of the Wilson residence. It was suppertime and Dr. Hugh Wilson was never late. Emily didn't know what she would say to her husband, the good Doctor but she would have to think of something.

22. Stretch your legs

The exercise yard at the Leon County Jail had a barren dusty clay floor surrounded by a chain link fence, topped by an inward slanted panel of barbed wire, all positioned under a relentless scorching sun most of the year, and the ground a reddish colored mud pie when it rained. Time in the yard was a precious diversion to the men that populated the jail, from the gloomy darkness of the individual or two man cells eagerly anticipated each day, rain or shine.

Some of the men walked about in an impromptu exercise regimen. A few went through individual calisthenics, but most congregated in cliques made or resumed in the pattern of regular inmates passing through again and again the criminal justice system, which was provided in a jail setting like this. As in all populations, but especially in jail or prison ones, there was a pecking order of toughness, with enforcers for the prevailing power structure readily forming to keep all those in line who failed to toe the line of their proper place in the pecking order.

That line drawn was simply that the rule of force among desperate men was the only recognized determiner of right and wrong. It was a rule of a different kind of law; it was literally, their way or take your chances. It mattered not whether there were jail guards in easy reach, punishment for the disobedient or rebellious was swift and sure. Jails unlike prisons, however, where the terms were longer, the turnover in the county jail gave inadequate time for a structure to develop with captains, lieutenants, sergeants and privates or their like but that didn't change the dynamics common to human nature. In a case of combinations of lawbreakers, where morality for most had been abandoned, somebody is bound to hurt someone before the day is through.

Jack Sanford rose from his cot and signaled Earl to follow in a sort of show you the ropes gesture, as the cell door was opened; and following him, the two men walked down the corridor toward the exit into the yard. Groups of no more than four prisoners at a time were escorted by guards armed with nightsticks. Guns on the belt were too dangerous, or at least, tempting to these freedom starved inmates. Although in December, the sun was out; the air cold and the yard dry that day for Earl's first introduction to communal living, jailhouse style.

Jack shielded his eyes as the blazing sun in the cold morning air assaulted his vision as if to say, you think that hung over head hurts now, try this! Jack made his way to the far corner of the yard where a group of prisoners had congregated in the dominant grouping of the Wing Four jail population.

"This here is Earl Bryant, boys," Jack said in a casual introduction to the group. "You'll like Earl, especially when you learn he's the man in

Liberty County that runs the business, you know. But don't mess with him, you see, he's likely to git out'n here and will cut yore supply off," Jack good naturedly and enigmatically said, though putting a personal point on it, that none of the gang of drunks could miss.

The most common reason these men were arrested and in jail were due to moonshine. They either drunk too much of it or stole something when the money ran out because of it.

"Howdy Earl, I'm Frank," one of the newer and less experienced inmates said, reaching out a hand. The others followed suit and before long Tom, Dick and Harry or whatever their given names were that had floated over Earl's head beyond recall, consciousness, or at least memory, had after a fashion, introduced themselves.

Jack's clever way of introducing the most notorious moonshiner in north Florida to this gang of drunks was understood loud and clear. He had done it without spilling to any unknown jailhouse snitch, evidence that would betray him to the authorities. Only paid snitches, desperate for the relief, promised by the authorities on pain of detection and a punishment by the gang that would be long remembered in the annals of Leon County Jail lore, would dare to disclose secrets learned from fellow inmates. Among these north Florida men, you just did not turn in one of your cell or yard mates, no matter what might be promised.

Earl looked each man in the little group in the eye trying to see inside of each soul but it was a fruitless effort. These men were so beaten down by life there was little left to share outside either their depression or despair. This was fine by Earl for under his circumstances, which he was not about to explain to this bunch of losers, as he saw them, the less said in conversation the better. So no one having much to gain in idle chatter, the group just milled around mumbling, swinging their arms in a kind of defacto attempt to warm up their bodies in the rapidly growing cold, winter air.

There was nowhere to sit either, so before long there was a kind of pairing up in twos and threes, as social interchange is given to do, even among prisoners. One shared a little bit about family, another recalled the last time he had a job, and still another bragged on the best jug he had ever bought or the worst hangover he ever had. From what Earl could determine the common denominator of the problem he saw with each man he talked with was the drinking.

It was a side of his business he had never seen before, so like most people engaged in a socially destructive occupation, he ignored it for the moment and just put each one of these guys in the category of loser, which to Earl made it their problem, not his. If he had to spend three weeks in here that was bad enough, but to mingle with a bunch of drunks, that was a horse of a different color. He decided to keep his mouth shut and his eyes open.

Old Jack Sanford seemed all right so opening up to him a little bit was fine, but beyond that he wasn't seeing much human value around here, to invest much of himself.

23. Call them up

The US Postal Service trucks made their deliveries all across Tallahassee and by transport to nearby communities, where a legion of footsore postmen began their daily ritual of connecting the arteries of America. Unnoticed to most of them, in their bundle of personal mail to be delivered, was a special envelope postmarked the day before in Tallahassee from the United States District Court Administrator announcing a Summons for a special Grand Jury called on the Order of The Honorable Benjamin Parker, Jr., United States District Court Judge for the Northern District of Florida.

Magistrate Stillman Henry's Order or a suggestion really, because he had no authority over Judge Parker, that the Grand Jury be convened to consider Earl Bryant's case within three weeks, had caused a flurry of administrative activity. The work of screening the voter registration lists and weeding out the deceased, relocated and otherwise unqualified potential jurors, had been laborious and time consuming but the hard working court staff had somehow managed to get them out in time for mailing the day before. The Magistrate had set that deadline and they had made it, barely.

The mail box at the auto body shop on Calhoun Street was positioned out on the street where the postman could conveniently stuff the day's deliveries into it as he drove his van by street side. Bill Haskins walked out to the box as soon as he saw the mail man stuff the box and leave he sorted through the days' offering.

"Wilson's Store bill, Ruby's stuff huh, movie flyer, advertisement ugh gas bill, double ugh, what's this?" He cocked his head and examined the envelope addressed to him at the auto body shop, where he maintained a residence behind the shop down a long lane deep into the acre lot he owned. "United States District Court Administrator," he read from the return address on the envelope. "Grand Jury Summons, damn!" said Bill, as the significance of the bad news sunk into his consciousness; which meant that he would have to find someone to run his business in his absence, and that would be difficult at best, to do.

However, the Court's warning that the Summons must be obeyed on pain of fine or imprisonment was not something Bill Haskins would take lightly. Like it he wouldn't but obey it he would, or at least take a shot at trying to talk his way out of the service call when he answered the summons.

Surely they must allow people off this *thing for running a business? Let me see, which one of the boys could best take charge in my absence if I have to do this thing? Steve? Elliot? No, I think Billy Jackson will be the one,"* he thought and tossed the envelope and Summons over on his mail desk and walked out of his cottage up to the shop to do the tedious paperwork for the day that he hated.

Whichever sombitch has gone and brought this here job on me had better have a good story, is all I say! Bill Haskins thought.

Phyllis Smithson, Perry grade school teacher, opened her summons envelope and had a similar reaction. *Who will look after my class? Three weeks possible they say! Whew! That's just not fair. All the way to Tallahassee? Where will I stay? I can't commute! Who can I call to get out of this,* she thought as she sat in the classroom where she had brought the daily mail in to read after a quick trip back home for a hastily prepared lunch.

Her principal at the school the next day agreed that she had no choice but to go. He would find a substitute for her class for the three weeks if necessary. The kids were resilient and they would probably enjoy the change of pace. She didn't like this one bit but was resigned to the inevitable task ahead, whatever it turned out to be.

Phyllis, like all people called by aptitude and interest to teaching, turned her curiosity about the grand jury assignment into some research from her limited resource materials available at home that evening, her old encyclopedia set. There was an article she read on the history of the development of the grand jury in English Common Law, and why the device was relied upon to gain the truth about the facts presented before it. She was fascinated to learn that the jurors themselves had the power to take control of the investigation process, call witnesses and get to the bottom of a case presented before them. She wondered whether that report was about practical reality or some writer's ideal of how the process should work. *This may be interesting after all,* she thought as she put the volume back on its shelf set and made ready for bed.

The mailbox at the Ballister Farm was stuffed with its own Court Summons but wasn't delivered until late in the day, due to the longer mail route into the further parts of the District, but delivery was made. Ernie Ballister had returned from a hard day of fence repair to his single story farmhouse, where he and Rachel housed and raised their six children on his three hundred fifty acre general purpose farm.

Ernie, who could barely read himself, brought the day's mail into the kitchen where Rachel, his lovely wife, who read far better than he, could interpret the confusing document that met his eyes upon opening the Court issued Summons. His reaction was the same as the others in terms of preference. He had rather not go in and would instead prefer to tend to his chores on the farm; but if called, he might as well report as ordered. It was a relatively slow time of year on the farm in December and going to town every day could be endured without too many painful consequences.

He just didn't know how to ignore a call that was made by the Honorable Benjamin Parker, Jr., the Federal Judge, known for his tough administration of justice in the District. He cared about law and order in the community, but didn't particularly feel that it was his responsibility to dispense justice. Besides, he never heard of a Grand Jury before and wondered what that was all about in the first place. Ernie put the matter out of his mind and turned up the old radio the family owned and settled in for an evening of The Green Hornet and other serial favorites that he and Rachel enjoyed.

Willis Cole finished the dusting of the merchandise in the his dry goods store down town before closing up the store, picking up his lunch pail and locking the front door on his way out and toward home. It had been a slow day for business and Willis was ready to get on home to his wife and family where the evening meal would be prepared and waiting by now or soon.

Willis had been out of school for fifteen years now and his high school sweetheart, Gail Hinson, now Gail Cole, was the light of his life, second only to their three boys, Scott, Bryan and Alex, who as budding young athletes in the early stages of puberty had taken their natural athletic talents to new heights. They played football in the fall, basketball in the winter, followed by their true love, baseball, in the spring and summer. They played them all well.

Willis had some ambition to build a future for his family but the depression economy had limited his ability to achieve to a snail's pace, tied to the absence of any growth in his retail business in town. He had inherited the store from his father, Ellis Cole, who had died early from a heart attack, leaving everything to his only child, Willis.

Every dollar, if not penny, was precious, but the Cole family was adept at getting by with very few possessions or luxuries, like most people in the community. But they had each other and happiness was something you did not have to buy with money, if you loved each other and believed that everything would work out well in the end.

Willis, Gail, and the three boys had a solid faith in their God, and he served as a Deacon in the First Baptist Church. Life was hard for those depression years, but they made ends meet and were even able to save a little each month. The evening mail, however, contained the Court Summons that was to change Willis's life.

He had a strong sense of civic duty, but reading the Summons brought a chill of fear to his constitution and rattled him to the bone. He whistled as he took in the command to appear at the Federal Courthouse at the end of the week for a potential three-week tour as a grand juror.

Dear God, he prayed silently, *I accept that all things come from you, but this is a hardship I am not sure I can bear. Can't afford to hire somebody and can't close the store. Duty to You, I understand and accept, even if it means the loss of my business. You know all things and I can accept that. But this, Oh God, is the work of men, and bad men at that, if the job means what I think it means, to judge men for their sins. You have said in the good boOkay, "Judgment is Mine," but this calls that terrible burden on me. I do not feel equipped for that Oh God! Didn't our Lord pray, let this cup pass? I ask You the same?*

Willis paused for a few minutes as if the answer would come and then a realization like acceptance, or at least resignation, settled on his inner being and gave him a kind of peace about it. *If it be Thy will, Oh God.* Then he said out loud, to no one in particular, since the front room of their small house was empty, "Come to think of it, He said that too, didn't he?"

Gail came into the front room about then to announce that dinner was ready and asked, "Who are you talking to in here Willis, I don't see anyone?"

"Just praying, Gail, I've been summonsed for Grand Jury, the Federal Grand Jury for a special session the end of the week, and I sense God telling me I have to go," Willis said handing her the opened Summons.

She quickly read it and said, "Have to go? Course you have to go Willis, it's the law isn't it?"

"Well of course it is, Gail, but I didn't mean to imply I would ignore it. I meant that I was accepting the consequences without worry, if my faith is true and I feel that it is about this. Your brother is not working right now, do you suppose you could go see him tomorrow and see if he would run the store for a few weeks?" her husband said.

"Yeah, I'll ask Darrell, he'll probably help us out, but dinner is getting cold and the boys are hungry, come on in Willis," Gail said and they walked into the dining room to have their evening meal.

It was an evening class in literature at the Florida State College for Women in Tallahassee, Professor Erik Jorgenson at the lectern. His subject for the night was a survey of the early American Literature with a lecture tonight on Melville's, Moby Dick. Erik had been a graduate of Emory University in Atlanta, holding a PhD in American Literature, and his love for the written word and its power to persuade or inform people about the meaning of life had inexorably drawn him into teaching the subject. He had a personal ambition to achieve fame, or at least recognition, as a writer of fiction literature with a special attraction to the period following the Civil War and its effects on the minds of Southern people. However he had made little progress toward that goal because of his absorption with learning all that might be taught to impressionable young female minds submitted to his charge. The class had been running about an hour and was approaching the mid class break point when a message from the office of the Dean was delivered by a young volunteer assistant. Richard reached out to take the folded over note and said, "A moment if you please class", and read the note. "Erik, your wife has come by with news that you have been summoned to the Federal Grand Jury for three weeks. Come to the office as soon as you can take a break and lets discuss this." The note was signed, Dean Roberts. Richard looked up after reading the note, saw from the clock on the wall that the break time was near and told the class, "Class, we will take our evening break now, please be back in your seats in twenty minutes, class will be in recess", and with that he gathered his papers and hurriedly left by the rear door to see what this news was all about.

Dean Roberts was sitting in his rocked back leather chair when Erik came into the office "Oh, that you Erik?" Dean Roberts said, putting down a summary budget sheet he had been reviewing, and gestured for Erik to take a seat. "Have to get you out of this Erik, that's all there is to it, I'll call the US Attorney's office tomorrow and arrange it, or Judge Ben for that matter, if necessary, but thought you would want to know right away," Dean Roberts said as a matter of fact.

"Not so fast, Dean. Did Amy leave any papers or notice for me?" Erik said, staking out his independence in the matter. He was a careful intellectual thinker by habit and not prone to jump at every suggestion even the Dean's.

"Oh, yes, it's here someplace," Dean Roberts said, shuffling through the papers on his very busy desk, before finding the Summons and envelope from the Federal District Court and handing it to Erik.

Erik read the document, noticed that it required his attendance for three weeks and saw that he must report by the end of the week. He scratched his head a bit nervously, pulled his pipe from the pocket in his vest, twiddled it a bit as he thought and then said, "Dean, I don't like this anymore than you, but there is my civic duty in this, isn't there? What does it say to our common man if College Professors, the upholders of truth, scholarship and justice for the world, duck their duty to serve the public just because it's inconvenient?" Richard said.

The Dean thought about that for a minute and said, "You have a point Erik, even though no one who matters, would ever know I pulled strings to get you off jury duty, we would know, wouldn't we?"

"Yes, Sir, and that's the important thing, you know. Can you get one of the student assistants to fill in? I'll pull my lecture notes together for them", Erik said. The Dean nodded; Erik excused himself and left the office to return to his class and Moby Dick.

These were just typical reactions and a sampling of the deliveries to the thirty six such summonses for Grand jury duty that were sprinkled across the District like so much confetti in a Memorial Day ticker tape parade on New York City's Wall Street. There wasn't much confetti or anything else happening of note on Wall Street that year as the shock effects of reaction to Black Tuesday in 1929 had hardly worn off. But summons the people, the jury notices did in an effective call to service which was hardly ever ignored, unlike modern times where a vast number of jury summonses must be issued each term to have a chance at filling the twenty-four qualified grand jury positions. The sad practice for some in a total disregard of civic duty is to just ignore the call, something unheard of in 1933.

On the appointed day and hour the thirty-six citizens, registered voters all, drifted into the assembly area of the Federal Courthouse as directed in the Jury Summons. Some of them knew each other, but most were strangers, coming from far and wide across the District. The assembly area was a large meeting room in the basement of the Federal Courthouse that had at one time been a file storage area until the annex building had been built ten years before, and the files had been moved there by freeing up the room. The jurors milled around the room waiting for someone to tell them what to do. They didn't have long to wait. A Clerk of the Court came into the room with the jury list and yelled out for everyone to take a seat. The group fell into silence with an attitude of curiosity and respect for the office of the Court, represented by the Clerk and waited to hear what exactly was ahead of them in this Grand Jury assignment. Every one of them regretted that their lives were to be put on hold for the three-week upcoming term but, since already committed and present in the building, the attitude was fairly positive, all things considered.

"Listen up, people, I'm Frank Hopkins, Deputy Clerk of Court. You have each been summonsed here by the Order of the Honorable Benjamin Parker, Jr., United States District Court Judge for a special call of the District Grand Jury. The term of the jury will be three weeks and you will appear every day at 8:30AM, sharp' for work. You will be paid the standard jury fee and transportation fee; and all those jurors empaneled from outside of Tallahassee will be put up in the Duvall Hotel at the Government's expense. Lunch will be brought in every workday, Monday through Friday, and the rest of the week you are on your own. The United States Attorney, or his deputies, will present the cases to you. You will hear the evidence or summaries of it from reports of witnesses and investigative efforts made by the Government in the cases and decide whether an indictment will be handed down or not. The decision is entirely up to you. Judge Parker will address you at the first session and explain the law to you and hear all requests for being excused from duty. Severe hardship will be considered, as will physical impairment. I must tell you, however, not many requests for being excused are granted. How many of you intend to make a request for excuse from service?" Frank asked, not really expecting much in opposition to service, for this was after all his grand jury and what could be more important than that.

A few hands began to go up and the others, seeing what they had hoped for but not expected, slowly began to add their hands to the response until the entire panel, except for Erick Jensen, one of the older jurors summonsed to appear, who had already fallen asleep in the back of the room.

Frank was taken aback by this, but not for long, as he turned on the authoritarian manner he had practiced and developed to a science over the years and spoke to the rebellious group.

"Now listen people, maybe I didn't make myself clear when I said that only extreme hardship will be considered. My guess is Judge Parker will let only a dozen off because we need to empanel twenty-three of you, which should allow ample allowance to excuse the truly needy situations. However sixteen of you must be present at all time or the proceedings will cease. Now enough of this, follow me and we'll go upstairs and talk to the Judge," Frank said, and gestured toward the double doors leading up to the staircase where the group could climb up to access the main courtroom on the first floor.

The jurors pulled down their hands and meekly, but not without grumbling, followed the Clerk out of the basement room and toward the stairs. It was anybody's guess who or how many would find the courage to ask Judge Parker to let them off. Each one secretly thought, he'll have to consider my excuse as exceptional.

The first floor courtroom was only partially filled to capacity with the thirty-six potential jurors seated in the first five rows of the ancient courtroom, spaced for comfort, with the few who were acquainted seated by each other. The others kept their glances and thoughts to themselves. The Judge's Bailiff stepped to the front of the courtroom and boomed out the announcement of the beginning of the session. "Hear Ye, hear ye, the specially called Grand Jury for the United States District Court, Northern District of Florida, is now in session, The Honorable Benjamin Parker, Jr., presiding. All rise!"

The potential grand jurors rose quickly to their feet as Judge Parker came in from Chambers at the rear of the courtroom in a flowing black robe and took his seat behind the bench and bar. Judge Parker, wasting no time with formalities, boomed out, "Be seated, ladies and Gentlemen, let us begin. You have, each of you, been called to serve on a special term of the Federal Grand Jury called into session under an emergency of sorts to consider the charge of murder of a Federal Revenue Officer. The Grand Jury is a compilation of citizens given the awesome responsibility under the Constitution to decide in Capital cases whether the charge of murder can be brought before the Court for adjudication. This case has the potential for the imposition of the death penalty, so it is a serious matter." Judge Parker was a graying man in his early 70's, still having an active mind and a keen eye for justice. There was no doubt who was in control in his courtroom, The Federal Grand Jury proceeding involving Earl Bryant's charge being no exception.

"The evidence will be presented by the US Attorney, or his deputies and witnesses will be called to present evidence before you on the facts of the case. If twelve or more of you find that there is sufficient evidence to bring the charge based on the standard of what we in the law call probable cause, you may return what we call a True Bill of Indictment. Probable Cause is a term of art that simply means that the evidence presented is more probable than not to indicate guilt. It is not your job to determine guilt and you will not hear a defense presented, only the evidence of the Prosecutor. The determination of guilt or innocence on the higher standard of proof beyond a reasonable doubt will be the job of the Petit Jury in my Court, if you authorize a charge to be made. So don't concern yourself with that heavy responsibility. You can rest assured you will not be allowed to serve on the Petit Jury for this case if there is an indictment. This effort is your only contribution in this case. You should know that the accused is in custody on an arrest warrant for investigation, so the sooner you conclude your business, the better for all concerned."

"Now, this is important, very important indeed, so listen carefully to my instructions. The US Attorney, Mr. Daniel Fernell, or more likely his Chief Deputy, Mr. Houston Gilchrist, will be in charge of the case; but he is not in charge, nor does he have the authority or the power to decide this matter for you. In the end, you alone by majority vote will decide whether to return a True Bill of Indictment. That rests exclusively with you. If you decide you want to hear more witnesses, or look at more documents or other evidence before deciding, you tell my Bailiff, Mr. Ervin Floyd, who will always be accessible in these proceedings, and he will arrange to have the witnesses, or documents brought before you. Now, if there are any disagreements between you or Mr. Fernell's office over anything, or you have legal questions or procedural questions, anything, you contact Mr. Floyd here (gesturing to the bailiff seated over to his left in the Courtroom) and he will bring the matter to my attention for decision. Any questions before we begin on requests for excuse from jury duty?" the Judge concluded. There were none. The Clerk will now call the role of those summonsed to appear in this Court," Judge Parker said and Frank Hopkins, Deputy Clerk on duty, called the jury list. They all answered present.

"Is there anyone here suffering from an illness or disability that would, in your opinion, interfere with your duty to serve?" Judge Parker asked.

"What'd he say?" Ed Falls cupped his hand behind his ear and asked the person next to him, a stranger. "Can't hear back here Judge," Ed Falls yelled out in that excessively loud manner customary for the deaf or hard of hearing.

"Juror Number 7, Mr. Ed falls, are you hard of hearing, Sir?" Judge Parker asked after checking his juror list.

"What's that Judge?" Ed said, clearly unable to hear the rather penetrating voice of Judge Ben Parker.

"Mr. Falls, we will excuse you, sir, on grounds of hearing difficulty, you may leave now Sir." Judge Parker said.

The man seated next to Mr. falls shouted in the old man's hear from close range so he could actually hear it that the Judge said he could leave. Ed falls gladly left.

"Anyone else?" Judge Parker asked.

"Judge, I'm Mary Ellis and I think I am too sick to serve, Sir, I'm suffering from emphysema and breathing is difficult for me, Sir, making it hard to pay attention.

"Very well Ms. Ellis, you are excused. "Anyone else?" Judge Parker said. No more raised their hands on this question. "Now, work related hardships, where are we on that for the rest of you people?" the Judge asked and the hands shot up all over the courtroom. Judge Parker patiently heard every excuse known to modern man before excusing eight of the jurors out of the petitioning fifteen. This was cutting it close with two extras left as an allowance.

"Are there any of you who, for reasons of opinion or philosophy on the death penalty or other moral reasons, believe that you cannot fairly sit in judgment on this case?" the Judge asked and eliminated two more jurors who convinced him that they were so opinionated or insensitive to the truth determining process that they were not suited to occupy the important office of grand juror in his Court.

That was it for the weeding out process for now, the jury in the statutory requisite manner had, been empaneled and was ready to be sworn in and get to work. He explained that their first duty was to elect a foreman to speak for the panel and to get ready to hear Mr. Gilchrist's evidence. By now, the morning was gone and the difficult selection process was through in rather short order.

This process was dramatically different from a petit jury selection where the lawyers for both sides searched with penetrating questions for any reason under a limited number of challenges called "pre-emptory." Each side wanted favorable jurors to their side of the case and often by a process of elimination, got them.

"All right, now, the Clerk, Mr. Floyd, will swear in the jurors by oath and then you can leave for lunch over at the Garden Grill next door to the Court House and report back to the Clerk at 1:30 PM. Mr. Floyd, do your duty, Sir," Judge Parker said.

The Clerk of Court proceeded, "Raise your right hand (they all did) and answer each one of you the following question, Do you so solemnly swear to do your duty as a Grand Juror of this Court and faithfully carry out whatever tasks are required by law, So help you God?" Each Grand Juror answered more or less in unison, "I do!"

They rose on the command of the Bailiff as Judge Parker hastily left the bench and then left for lunch.

24. News of the day

Anthony (Tony) Callaway, news reporter at the Tallahassee Recorder, sat in the newsroom the day the Special Grand Jury was scheduled to hear evidence in Earl Bryant's charge for murder when the phone rang.

"Hello, this is Tony, how may I help you?" and the voice on the phone whispered something very difficult for Tony to understand. "Speak louder, can you please?" Tony asked the caller not recognizing the voice.

Tony Callaway at age 43 was the senior writer on duty in the newsroom that day. Tony was a local man, having been born and raised in nearby Gadsden County and a graduate of the University of Florida in Gainesville, who had desired to make writing his career. Writing news copy and later stories for by line on the paper had been the only thing available to him that satisfied his need for creativity and expression. Besides it was the only job he could land at the time. He had thought during college that he might want to teach literature and satisfy his creative urges from that platform, but although a graduate degree at that time was not beyond his financial reach, the desire to get on with his life just seemed to postpone that choice until he was, by the inevitable forces of inertia, committed to a career in journalism.

Tony was an intellectual by aptitude and curious as a matter of interest, and he was one of the smarter young reporters on the staff when he first joined the paper after college in 1911. His job with the paper as a beat writer had evolved by 1916 to senior news writer, a remarkable accomplishment for any but the precocious; however those connections and accomplishments had saved him from the draft during the European conflict in France and Belgium. He had managed to escape the slaughter fields in France, but wrote long pieces on the effects of the war on local families, including people close to his own.

"I have to whisper Tony, or the Judge will hear me, we're in court,"

Ervin Floyd, Bailiff to Judge Parker said. Tony understood immediately the phenomenon of listening and speaking on his end full volume while remembering that the whispering caller in secret can hear you just fine. The tendency is to raise your own voice when you can't hear just like what everyone does with a deaf person or a foreigner. Tony grabbed his metal ringed steno pad and trusty yellow pencil and furiously began to take notes from his conversation with one of his important contacts and friend, Ervin Floyd, Bailiff to The Honorable Benjamin Parker, Jr.

"The Grand Jury has just been convened, Tony, and they start hearing testimony this afternoon in United States vs. Earl Bryant, for shooting that Revenue Officer down in Liberty County," Ervin said by whispering. Tony was on his wavelength now being generally familiar with the arrest and jailing of the notorious Liberty County moonshiner.

"I understand Ervin," Tony said and continued to listen and make notes as fast as he could.

"Twenty-four, general mix of voters, Professor Jorgensen at College, Marshall Boyle to testify today, Bryant denied bail, Leon County Jail" were the notes Tony was able to make as Ervin Floyd blurted out what he had to say in a terrific hurry. Tony, realizing his friend was taking a big risk calling him at all, but friends are friends and risk taking is something you just do for them. He would never betray that confidence even on pain of jail or death.

Tony hung up the phone and grabbed his coat, because in December in Tallahassee is still chilly, no matter how warm Florida is considered to be or is the rest of the year, and headed out to the parking lot to drive his Ford sedan over to the Courthouse. If he was lucky, he could catch some of the jurors on the way back from lunch at the Garden Grill where they always were taken the first week of the session and add some personal information to his story. He would clear it with his boss later that day and save some space in the City Page for this breaking story, which he intended to personally cover from start to finish.

Tony knew he could not get the jury list, but the tip he had from Ervin that Professor Jorgensen from the College was in the panel was a tremendous start. He knew Dr. Jorgensen, a professor in American literature, who was a wanna be fiction writer like himself. He had met Dr. Jorgensen on several social occasions and that would be enough of an introduction if he could be lucky enough to find him before the Grand Jury session started. Tony only wanted to make contact with Dr. Jorgensen from a human-interest angle for his story and not to influence or embarrass him in any way.

Tony parked his Ford strategically along the street between the Garden Grill and the Courthouse, the only path the jury would take on their return trip. This would be dicey to pull off because Ervin would be escorting the jury members back and would be instructed by Judge Parker to run interference for any reporters or others interested in having an input with the jurors. Friendship could only go so far so he would have to be careful.

As he sat on a park bench along the expected path for the jury, Tony noticed the group headed his way in mass. But as walking groups are prone to do, they quickly spread out with Ervin Floyd at the head, like a football coach running onto the field ahead of his team at the start of a game. Tony let most of the group pass by and fell in alongside Professor Jorgensen as if he was part of the group. In reality, Richard hadn't been in the panel long enough to meet everyone yet, so this was not a tip-off that Tony Callaway, *Recorder* Reporter, had infiltrated the column.

No one in the jury group understood yet the protocols of secrecy which would be drilled into them once they started. Judge Parker had that important function yet to do before they actually convened deliberations. Consequently, talking to strangers would not seem unusual to Dr. Jorgensen at this point.

As any clever news reporter knows, you don't look a gift horse in the mouth until somebody official slams the door to the barn and tells you to stay the hell out with the gift horse safely inside.

"Dr. Jorgensen, I'm Tony Callaway from the *Recorder.* We met a time or two on social occasions as I recall, how do you feel about serving on the Grand Jury in this case, does a murder, death penalty case cause you any personal concern?" Tony threw out several questions at once realizing he might not get more than one round answered and he was trying to be cautious so as not to compromise his friend and source. Anything he got at this point would be pure bonus. *Maybe a book someday* was a thought that ran through his creative and ambitious mind.

Dr. Jorgensen seemed startled by the questions and being an intelligent man himself was not totally ignorant of the need for secrecy in grand jury proceedings, but this was before they actually started and no one had told him not to talk to the press. He believed in the First Amendment freedoms in the Constitution and was not unsympathetic with the need for the press to dig out and publish the news.

"Oh yeah, I do seem to recall we met once, that fund raiser at the College last year, wasn't it? Hmm, don't think I should be discussing this case, but can tell you this much, I consider it a duty to serve and I will fulfill that duty, murder, death penalty or not," Erik said.

Tony quickly followed up, respecting the position of his renewed acquaintance and news source. "Is it a burden on you or the College for you to be over here possibly for a few weeks? How will the College cope, or is it the same for everybody on the panel?" Tony asked.

"We'll manage with teaching assistants, but you're right, it is a burden, but it's a price we all pay. Everyone in this group has to give up his or her job, and in some cases family. I met one lady from Perry who's serving," Erik explained.

"I can tell you this much," one of the other jury members said, listening and joining in the conversation between Tony and Dr. Jorgensen, it's a damn imposition on me. I run a small auto body shop and I had to risk my business by trusting things to one of my men, ready for the responsibility or not. The judge wouldn't agree that as a good enough excuse."

"Your name Sir?" Tony asked and wrote down quickly the details of the comments of Bill Haskins, shop owner and upset citizen to boot. "How do the others feel," Tony asked generally as the circle of walkers had widened with Tony in the center of the arena, so to speak.

Tony realized he was near the end of the risk he was willing to take for the sake of his friend and source Ervin Floyd, so he took down a few comments of disgruntled Grand Jury members striving to get names, descriptions, and where possible, quoted remarks.. He excused himself just before Ervin, glancing back at the straggling group, came back to investigate.

Just in time, Tony slipped out of the walking crowd and made it safely to his Ford and perfected his escape without danger to his friend. He had some research to do about moonshiners, Earl Bryant, the murder story, and the socio economic ramifications of an illegal whiskey business in the context of the repeal of Prohibition. That was his next task.

That connection between the repeal and the apparent increased enforcement activity just seemed to leap off the page of the relationships he now perceived. Tony could just smell a story coming on and he was eager to meet the challenge of putting it all together. He would return to the office, clear the story with his Editor, and type out a lead story for tomorrow's early edition alerting his readers that this jury was deciding an important case and a personal sacrifice was being made by all those answering their government's call.

25. Change of heart

Dr. Hugh Wilson had seen his last patient on end of day rounds at Riverside Hospital in Bainbridge, and left the hospital in time to make it home for supper. Hugh enjoyed his medical practice, and especially he liked being able to help his patients through the crises of their illnesses. He had just finished medical school when the World War I in Europe had broken out and had been called to serve as a field surgeon at many of the bloodiest engagements of that terrible war.

It was an internship he would rather have avoided, but he came out of the experience dedicated to helping people in medical distress. His treatment of hundreds of soldiers suffering from the worldwide influenza epidemic, following the war with many dying in spite of all the heroic efforts employed, had left him capable of facing any tragedy with cool professionalism.

After the war was over, he had returned home and opened his practice. He had a reputation in Bainbridge as a competent, caring professional and was loved by the community. He was content also in his private life, happily married to his younger wife, Emily, and accepting of much of the diversity of life he encountered. However, he had drawn the line as to compassion when it came to Emily's family.

He had known Emily's father was an illegal whiskey man in a rural part of north Florida, but had fallen in love with her when she worked in Riverside Hospital as a nurse's aide and studying at night, by correspondence, to become a registered nurse. She was young, beautiful, and had an inquiring mind that appealed to Dr. Hugh in all her qualities.

When he had proposed, he had broached the subject of her family, and made the offer of marriage contingent on her agreement that the Bryant clan would forever be persona non-gratis in the Wilson family home and associations. This didn't matter to Emily, because when she had left home at age sixteen. It was good riddance, sayonara to home and family permanently as far she was concerned. The return home by Hugh today, however, would test that hypothesis more than either had expected back when the commitment had been made.

Hugh came in the front door, hung his coat in the hall closet as usual, and surveyed his face in the mirror on the wall of the entry way, surrounded by pegs for hats, umbrellas, and coats to see if the long day had accelerated the aging process, he believed he could detect in his reflection. He confirmed the likely imperceptible change from the morning and turned to greet Emily in the parlor as was his custom. He expected she would be there with a cup of hot tea, ready to sit with him and hear the stories of the day's patients and challenges. As it turned out, he faced something far bigger by way of challenge and having to make a decision he thought he would never have had to make, including the presence of who he thought was a stranger to him standing by Emily in the parlor.

"Hugh, you've never met my mother, Ellie Bryant of Liberty County, Florida, Mother, this is my husband, Dr. Hugh Wilson," Ellie said in an unusual formal introduction, as if she were introducing her husband to an unexpected guest from the local Garden Club.

Hugh took one look at Ellie Bryant seated quietly in his very own reading chair in the parlor, much less anywhere else in his house, which had been off limits to Emily's family by settled agreement and years of practice. However, for once in his life, he could think of nothing to say.

Southerners have a strong tradition of courtesy to guests, but he and Emily had an agreement about this, and Emily apparently had broken it. It was a dilemma that he was not sure how to resolve. It did not take him long to get past the dilemma.

"Mrs. Bryant, I must say I cannot tell you that I am pleased to meet you, or that you are welcome in my house. Emily and I have had an agreement since we were married, that her family could not be permitted in our house or our lives. You see, Mrs. Bryant, I abhor the damage your husband has been doing to the health of the poor ignorant people of south Georgia and north Florida, many of whom by type, if not actual customers of your husband's illegal moonshine whiskey operation, I have to treat in hospital or the local county jail on occasion. I must ask you to leave and not return, Mrs. Bryant!" Dr. Wilson said gravely and with firm unshakeable conviction.

Emily spoke before the shocked and subdued Ellie Bryant could think of what to say. "Hugh, we have a family emergency in that Daddy has been accused of murder and is in jail in Tallahassee awaiting trial if the Grand Jury indicts and from what Momma says, is likely. Momma has nobody to be with during this time and she came to me as the only family within hundreds of miles. I know we agreed about this Hugh, but this is different. Momma is not on trial and she needs me. I want her to stay for a few days until she sees her way clear to go home or move to a hotel in Tallahassee for the trial. I had the same reaction as you did when she first arrived, only worse. But we're over that now and she's still my Momma. I ask you to make an exception to our agreement," Emily said, laying out her case.

What happened next Surprised even her. Hugh took another look at Ellie Bryant and saw a desperate, wounded soul, utterly dependent on them, the only haven she could possibly have run to for some support. He could only imagine how hard it must have been on her pride to come all the way up here and confront her daughter, knowing the history between them. The logic of his position was impeccable, but the suffering he could see in Ellie's face was no different than the soldiers with yellow fever or the Negro men coming into his emergency room with knife cuts or gunshot wounds. They were all suffering human beings and the cause was not that important then, or heaven help him, he thought, even now.

"Mrs. Bryant, after what I said when I first saw you in my house, you must accept my apology. You can stay with us as long as it takes to get through this time of trial in yours' and your husband's lives. We'll put our family agreement aside for this once and pretend for now, anyway, that you are our guest. Will you forgive my words and actions, Ma'am?" Dr. Wilson graciously said.

Ellie was too much in shock over this and everything that had happened to her in the last few days, to single this event out from the moil of reactions she was having about now, but said, "Dr. Wilson. Yes, I forgive you and thank you for yore kindness. I did not expects this," Ellie said, and rose to offer her hand to shake that of Dr. Wilson which probably was not the appropriate gesture, but by God, she had to do something other than just sit there.

Emily saw the awkward moment and jumped up to say, "Elvira will have supper ready by now so why don't we go on back to the dining room and have some supper. Did you have a hard day, darling?" Emily asked her husband as if nothing new was in their lives. He appreciated her spreading this social balm over an awkward moment. They would talk more at dinner and he would find out about this murder case Mr. Bryant was headed for and try to understand his guests suffering even better. It wasn't a wound or infection in the traditional sense, but emotions can get you sick too and Dr. Wilson was above all else, a healer in the proud medical tradition of the Southern general medical practitioner.

26. Let the probe begin

The jury returned from the Garden Grill, anxious to get on with this annoyance and interruption to their routines. They filed into the basement of the Federal Courthouse where Grand Jury proceedings were conducted at the appointed hour of 1:30 PM. Ervin Floyd directed them to the twenty-four seats provided across the raised platform, separated by a bar of sorts in the form of a railing. There were no spectator seats provided because Grand Jury proceedings are closed to the public, even the press. Judge Parker came in shortly after they were situated and addressed the panel. "You have been told your duty and you will entertain all evidence presented by the US Attorney starting in a few minutes. Please remember, ladies and gentlemen, these proceedings are secret and nothing discussed or presented here can be discussed by you outside of your deliberations. You will entertain no questions from the press or curious friends and family. Any violation of this restriction should be reported to Mr. Floyd here for me to deal with. Are there any questions?" Judge Parker said.

Immediately, Erik Jorgenson and one or two others wondered whether they should report the incident with the news reporter before they had been cautioned against that very thing. *Wow, that little talk with, what was his name? That would violate the rules but I didn't know it at that time. It would only mess things up for him and nothing important was revealed, I guess,* Erik thought. The others, who even remembered the brief encounter, really didn't think about it, so luckily for Tony Callaway nothing came of it.

"Your first job will be to elect a foreman and report that decision to my Bailiff, Mr. Floyd, and tell him that you are ready to proceed. Mr. Hopkins, the Deputy Clerk of Court, will maintain a record of these proceedings, swear in all witnesses and generally preside.

With that, Judge Parker left the room with Ervin Floyd and the jurors were alone in court for the first time. The jurors sat there, looking at each other, not really sure how to go about this foreman selection process. The lack of direction and indecision permeating the group reached the point of pressure where somebody had to say something. At that point, Willis Cole spoke up,

"Well, I'm Willis Cole and I have no idea how to do this, but does anybody want to be foreman?"

Phyllis Smithson, the school teacher from Perry, joined in, "I am not interested in that job but it seems to me it ought to be someone with some kind of leadership experience. Has anyone been elected to something in school or whatever?"

"I haven't been elected to anything," Erik Jorgenson said, "but I teach at the College and I serve on the faculty student disciplinary committee as chairman, if that is experience of interest to you and I would be willing to take this on, if nobody else wants it." The silence was deafening as it became apparent that nobody else really wanted to be here, much less take on the job of foreman.

Finally, Bill Haskins, the disgruntled auto body mechanic, suggested that the Professor take the job, since nobody else seemed to want it and the others nodded their agreement.

Erik took that as his selection and said, "All right, it seems I'm it. I'll go tell the Bailiff that we have selected a foreman and that we are ready for the US Attorney to begin.

Houston Gilchrist and Erick Driscoll had been meeting with Marshall Tom Boyle, since early morning to prepare their case for presentation to the Grand Jury. Judge Parker's office had called late in the morning to notify the Prosecutor of when they should be ready to proceed. At the same time, a Subpoena had been perfunctorily served on Earl Bryant at the jail to appear the next day, with a copy to Aaron Martin's office.

Even if a client testified before the jury, his attorney could not appear with him and had to stay outside the room where deliberations took place, only to answer questions and confer with his client when the client decided he needed help. If the client needed to be briefed, if at all, by his counsel before the secret proceedings started.

No evidence for the defense is presented and most grand juries had no difficulty handing down an indictment as requested. Of course, no one expected Earl's attorney to permit Earl to testify, relying as always on the Fifth Amendment prohibition against self-incrimination. The Subpoena was served anyway and Earl would be dutifully transported from the Leon County Jail to the Grand Jury room, where he just as routinely, on the advice of his lawyer, would refuse to testify as expected. The ritual went on regardless of what every knowledgeable person in the world fully expected in these matters and just as predictably got.

Gilchrist, Driscoll, and Marshall walked into the Grand Jury room and took their seats out in front of the large jury box as soon as they were notified by Judge Parker's Bailiff that the jury had finished the selection of a foreman and were ready to take evidence. Most grand jury proceedings were not presented direct evidence anyway as everyone more or less accepted the short cut of summaries of evidence presented by the law officer involved in the supervision of the investigation of the case. No one told this Jury that, but the assumption by Houston Gilchrist was that everyone wanted to get this over with as soon as possible, so the short cut method was selected and utilized.

Not waiting for formal direction to begin and experienced in this from many cases presented, Houston Gilchrist arose and addressed "his" grand jury. "Ladies and Gentlemen of the Grand Jury, my name is Houston Gilchrist, Deputy United States Attorney for the Northern District of Florida, and this gentleman (indicating Erik) is my assistant. We call to testify before you the Honorable Tom Boyle, United States

Marshall for this judicial district. Mr. Hopkins will you swear in the witness, Mr. Boyle.

"Do you solemnly swear that the testimony you will present is the truth, the whole truth and nothing but the truth, so help you God?" Frank Hopkins said.

"I do!" answered "The Great One" forcefully, as if no one should question him about truth, especially lowly members of a public grand jury or some clerk for that matter, as he saw things.

"Take the witness chair Mr. Boyle," said Houston Gilchrist and the story of the case was about to be told. "State your name and Office, please, Sir," Houston said and Tom Boyle revealed with some relish that he was The United States Marshall as if there was only one and the jury had sure better take notice of that, was the implication from his tone. "Please tell the Jury, Mr. Boyle, what evidence you and your office have accumulated in the case before this Grand Jury," Houston said and sat back expecting "The Great One" to take center stage and tell the whole story to his own glory and hopefully making his case for probable cause for the indictment.

"Well Sir, my office was notified that on December 5th this year, two of the federal revenue officers for this District were sent to the residence of the suspect, one Earl Bryant, a well-known moonshiner in Liberty County Florida, in this District, on a tip that an unusually large shipment of illegal moonshine whiskey was being shipped that day out into the Surrounding counties. This search of theirs was in the hope they could intercept that shipment.

"The two officers were Officer Frank Stiller, the most senior man in the service in the District, and Clyde Browning, his junior assistant. They arrived at the residence of the suspect before the expected break-fast hour at the Bryant household, based on another tip from the same undercover sources, and stood on the front steps knocking to gain the attention of the occupants of the residence, when a rifle shot fired and Mr. Stiller fell dead across the front step where he was standing. Mr. Browning, fully expecting he was the next target, sensibly left the scene as rapidly as possible."

"When Mr. Browning returned to Tallahassee and reported this dastardly crime to his superiors, a search and recovery team was hastily sent back to Liberty County to recover the body and as much evidence as possible without waiting for warrants. After all, Mr. Stiller could have been still alive and speed was everything. The search and recovery team found Frank Stiller dead and the Coroner has concluded that he was dead by gunshot wound and the time of death was instantaneous with the entry wound. In other words, he was dead on the spot when shot."

Boyle smiled just a little at the rhyme of his words, but quickly throttled his self-appreciatory humor, as he noticed no appreciative reaction from the jury.

Boyle continued, "The crime scene investigators found that the bullet that killed Stiller entered the door frame right behind his body and that the path of the bullet came from away from the house on a low trajectory from someone either crouched while shooting or very short in height. Mr. Bryant is slightly over five feet tall. The team also found a possible knee print and the spent cartridge casing approximately one hundred fifty yards from the house in a position consistent with the path of and the angle of the bullet."

Mr. Boyle continued his remarkably smooth account of the case with no interruptions. "The Federal Revenue Service operating the so called "Still Buster Team" empaneled to clean up and stop the illegal whiskey business in this District, had engaged the services of an undercover agent, one George Drucker, who is employed by Mr. Bryant as an operations manager. This Mr. Drucker was the witness who provided the information about the unusually large shipment of illegal whiskey due to be trucked out on the day of the shooting. Mr. Drucker was in the area the day of the shooting as previously arranged by his employer and obtained additional evidence, which I will summarize for you, Ladies and Gentlemen.

Mr. Drucker can testify that Mr. Bryant was in the immediate area at the time of the shooting and that Mr. Bryant's rifle was in the whiskey still structure when he joined him after the shooting. He had the opportunity that morning to examine the rifle and found one shell missing from the magazine and will testify that Mr. Bryant always carried his rifle magazine full of shells. Mr. Drucker will also testify at trial that Mr. Bryant practically confessed to the shooting." At this point in the dialogue, the members of the jury panel leaned forward eagerly in their seats, as this part of the story seemed very important.

One of the jurors from the back row raised his hand to speak, but quickly saw this was not like a classroom with a teacher to recognize him, so spoke out his question nonetheless, "You say, Mr. Boyle, he practically confessed? What did he say exactly?"

"The Great One" was ready for this and pulled out of his pocket several three by five cards and found the right one and read to the jury. "He said, words to the effect that this man Stiller had been a burr under his saddle for many years and that no body but him would have the brass ones to shoot him on his front door step." The juror absorbed the rather remarkable quotation and said nothing further.

Marshall Boyle continued, "We recovered Bryant's gun from his own house at the time of the arrest and our forensic experts have determined from the rifling marks on the bullet that the rifling grooves in the barrel match. It's the same gun, ladies and gentlemen. Bryant's fingerprints are naturally all over the gun. The final bit of compelling evidence is that George Drucker would testify that he was close to the heart of the Bryant whiskey operations, and that Bryant, himself, has supplied a motive more specific for the killing. We have discovered from historical records of the Department that Frank Stiller in 1913 shot Terrell Bryant, Earl Bryant's father, in a whiskey still raid and Drucker would testify that Earl Bryant witnessed it. We contend that the evidence will show that Bryant killed Agent Stiller for revenge and to eliminate the interference with his illegal whiskey still operations in this District."

Satisfied that he had laid out a case sufficient for indictment since he believed beyond a shadow of doubt that Bryant was guilty, he stopped and waited for what the US Attorney or the Grand Jury would do next.

"Does the jury have any questions for this witness?" Houston asked, really expecting none.

A juror spoke up, "What did the suspect do when arrested, did he put up a scrap or come peacefully?"

Tom Boyle was ready for this one also and said, "That did surprise me a little. He was sarcastic and resentful but he came out of the house peacefully, offering no resistance. Quite frankly, we had expected him to run and hide in the woods, but he was at home as if nothing had happened. That was surprising," Boyle said.

"Any further questions?" Professor Jorgensen asked, taking over his role as foreman of the Grand Jury. There was silence that greeted his question. "There being none, we will confer on this summary of evidence and decide what to do next. Do you have anything further you wish to say Mr. Gilchrist?"

"No, Sir, if the jury desires further evidence, contact me through the Deputy Clerk, Mr. Hopkins. With that, the lawyers and the Marshall left the Grand Jury room so the jury could deliberate.

After they left, the jurors relaxed a little more and began to discuss the case among them. Of course, none of them knew what they were supposed to do, so they waited around engaging in small talk and waited to see what would happen next. Phyllis Smithson, the schoolteacher from Perry finally said,

"That's pretty damning evidence, it seems to me. He was there at the time, he had a motive, and that gun evidence seems persuasive to me."

"Yeah," Bill Haskins said, anxious to get this over with so he could get back to his shop, "What are we waiting for, let's indict and go home, what da' ya' say?"

"I think we need to consider this carefully, a man's life is at stake here," another juror said.

"I agree," Willis Cole said. "We have the authority to demand that actual witnesses come and testify or call witnesses of our own, don't we?" a third juror said.

"An awful lot of the Government's case rides on that fellow Drucker, he was the whistle blower on the whiskey operation, put Bryant at the scene, supplied evidence of a motive, and told that almost confession from Bryant," Erik Jorgenson said.

"I think we ought to hear from him directly and not get it all through the words of the Marshall," Willis Cole said, being careful to do his duty thoroughly, after he figured out that God wanted him to serve in that capacity faithfully.

"That would just take extra time, why would Marshall Boyle get it wrong? I want to go home now," another juror said.

"What troubles me," Professor Jorgensen said, "Drucker was a key man in Bryant's whiskey operation, and he may just be setting Bryant up to take over his empire, so to speak. I want to hear the man say the words in front of us, not just repeated by the Officer."

Several others nodded their heads. Erik put the matter to a vote, having been told that a majority was their voting standard. The vote was thirteen to eleven in favor of hearing from Drucker, a bare majority. Erik left the room to find the Deputy Clerk, or the Judge's Bailiff, to have the Court issue the appropriate Subpoenas. By then, the afternoon was gone and the jurors were released for the night with the witness, Drucker, to be called the next morning having been assured by the Assistant United States Attorney that witnesses would be available on short notice.

When Houston Gilchrist got the news that the Grand Jurors actually had voted to call direct witnesses, he recovered from his shock rather quickly, although Tom Boyle, "The Great One", saw it altogether differently. He could not understand how anyone could question his summary of the evidence, not in a grand jury proceeding anyway.

When Houston got back to the Office of the US Attorney and reported the disastrous turn of events to Dan Fernell, Tom Boyle was directed, no ordered, to send word to Elliot Erikson, his assistant, to contact George Drucker at the Duvall Hotel. He had been brought to Tallahassee just for such an emergency, and together they planned to spend several hours that evening preparing the witness to testify the next morning.

He was guarded in the far end of the Duvall Hotel under the then version of the witness protection program, so that he had no chance of running into the out of town jurors also housed there. George Drucker, on being told of this disastrous turn of events, suddenly for the first time began to realize that this was serious business he was engaged in and it was time to do some serious thinking about what he would actually say in court.

He didn't have long to deliberate, for Gilchrist and Fernell would take no chances on tomorrow with this out of control Grand Jury, as they saw it; and they would grill him mercilessly, all night if necessary, until he got his testimony right. The US Attorney was not about to lose this case without an indictment. If word of that ever got out, Dan Fernell's political career would be over before it really got started. He would have none of that.

27. The story's the thing

Tony Callaway had made his way back to the *Recorder* that afternoon to write his first installment of the Earl Bryant story, making sure he finished it in time for the Editor's review at six o'clock. He didn't have much by way of detail as yet, but this first story would set the stage for the written coverage of the eventual trial, which might even attract national attention.

His contacts in the US Attorney's office, speaking of deep background, had revealed that the Federal agent had been shot on Bryant's front door steps in a push to stop the major illegal moonshine whiskey operators and Bryant's was one of the main ones. He was the lynch pin, or so it seemed to the Feds, in the network of mostly small producers of corn liquor that had to be stopped if legal whiskey was coming to town. The Federal Revenue Service couldn't have both, especially since the legal stuff now generated substantial federal revenue and the moon shiners' sales, generated none.

The source inside the US Attorney's office didn't say so, but Tony figured this was a bureaucratic response to the practical problem facing law enforcement, with this paradigm shift in the regional if not the national culture. A small town news reporter always dreamed of such a chance to be in the catbird seat, so to speak, of such a breaking story of such sociological and historical significance. Fate had placed him in the right place at the right time and he was ready to take advantage of it.

In college, during his idealistic days, he had dreamed as all young men dreamed, of being rich and famous someday; and if a choice had to be made between the two, famous was really more appealing than rich and the more likely opportunity for a small town news reporter and aspiring writer anyway. As he sat at his desk in the newsroom that afternoon, he collected his thoughts and reviewed his hastily scribbled notes from the adventuresome, though risky, walking interview with the Grand Jury, before turning to his typewriter to compose his first draft. *Let me see,* he thought, *Prohibition is ending early next year and the pressure on men like Earl Bryant by the Feds surely led to this confrontation and the unexpected and tragic shooting. Grand Jury proceedings will be secret, but they will likely indict and trials are public property. A notorious moon shiner kills a highly respected Revenuer? What more drama could you ask for? This is great! Headline?* Tony began to type and the draft of the story emerged from the beat up old typewriter, like an artist's sketch that presents the subject and theme of the picture to be filled in later with color and textural strokes as inspiration and the facts and circumstances permit.

GRAND JURY CALLED FOR FEDERAL MURDER PROBE
By Tony Callaway, *Recorder* Reporter

"Twenty-four residents were called to serve in the Federal Grand Jury investigating the murder of Frank Stiller, career Federal Revenue Enforcement Officer, on December 5th. The prime suspect's identity has not been officially revealed because Grand Jury proceedings are secret; but local sources, on requests for anonymity, reveal that Earl Bryant, age 54, Liberty County man is being investigated for the crime. The Federal Grand Jury commenced deliberations today with a cross section of north Florida citizens tabbed for the duty.

This reporter learned today that the Grand jury is comprised of, among others, a College Professor, an area Elementary schoolteacher, mechanic, farmer, and day laborer thrown together with nineteen of their fellow citizens to decide the fate of Bryant. The sentiment of some is that this call to duty is a terrible intrusion into their private lives and resent the sacrifice. Others see the call as a necessary evil to make the judicial system work for the protection of us all. Student Assistants at the College, junior men in the businesses, relatives, or temporary hires filling in for the absent jurors were typical adjustments to be made as related to this reporter.

Judge Benjamin T. Parker, Jr., Federal Judge in charge, was hard to convince on excusing people, the jurors reported. US Marshall, Thomas Boyle, who headed the criminal investigation and made Bryant's arrest, was expected to be the first witness called at the session this afternoon.

Bryant was denied bail in the Magistrates hearing on Monday and waits in Leon County jail cell as the Grand Jury has his fate in their collective hands. Earl Bryant is reputed to be a moonshine still operator from the backcountry of Liberty County, so well-known in federal law enforcement circles, that his domains are respectfully called "Bryant Country."

Up till now, federal officers have avoided plunging into Bryant's risky territory, but the repeal of Prohibition by Congress in February and the immanent ratification of the repealing amendment by the states early next year, apparently have changed the emphasis in the enforcement of federal law against illegal moonshine whiskey, now that legal whiskey will soon be available in most states. Anguish and worry will undoubtedly fill the hours between now and the session tomorrow for Earl Bryant as he waits after lights out in his lonely, Leon County Jail cell.

The Citizens of Tallahassee will learn more of this sorry tale as the proceedings unfold."

Tony finished the story adding optimistically his name as a byline and hurried from his desk to meet with Dick Powers, News Editor. Unlike Tony, whose writing was confined to a desk in the newsroom proper, Dick had a private office commensurate with his hard earned rank. He had written for the military service paper, *Stars and Stripes*, during the recent conflict.

The Publisher, Stinson Bullet, heir to the Bullet turpentine fortune, was a patriotic soul who although he had assiduously avoided military service himself, never tired of talking about the great conflict as "the war to end all wars" was called and was so impressed with Dick's pseudo service for *Stars and Stripes*, that he had hired him as News Editor for the paper.

His job every day was to review the work product of the staff writers under him but more importantly, to decide what news each day made the cover page of the *Recorder*. Dick had a talent for creating news copy all right, but his judge of other's work left a bit to be desired. Fortunately in this case, he trusted Tony implicitly, who had never failed him. Dick's approach was to weed out junior men every time a mistake was made to provide a scapegoat to save his reputation, even if his poor judgment and lack of leadership was really to blame.

Stinson was so feckless and lacking in talent himself that he was continually being fooled by Powers' "mistakes." Somehow the paper had survived in spite of Dick Powers misjudgments. Tony's writing skills and good nose for deciding what was really news, had saved Dick more than once. The paper, in spite of this built in weakness, had somehow managed to avoid being sued for liable, although the Bullet family money had been required to settle a few matters quietly and discreetly.

"What you got Tony?" Dick asked, barely glancing up, as Tony came into Powers' office and tossed the typewritten by line on to Dick's desk.

"Probably the next Pulitzer, Dick," Tony laconically replied, taking his seat across from Dick and leaning back in the tired old spring recliner Dick kept in his office. The weak hinged chair served alternative dual purposes for Powers, either to force the young or at least junior to him reporters to either sit on the front of the seat appearing too eager or surrender to the shape of the thing and appear indifferent.

Both choices were wrong since the reporter never knew how to anticipate Powers' mood of the moment, which was precisely what Dick Powers wanted, keeping them off balance, never knowing what to expect from him.

The not so subtle hint of Tony's bold belief in the quality of his offering immediately caught Dick's interest, although not to the level of excitement yet, as he raised his eyes from the copy he had been editing and looked across the desk at Tony curiously.

"Pulitzer, you say?" Dick asked equally laconically and waited for Tony to take the initiative, which wasn't long in coming.

"Earl Bryant is so well regarded, I really mean feared, as a moonshiner in the bowels of Liberty County that until now, Federal agents have been afraid to go in and arrest him. That is, if they even cared, since no tax was being collected on any whiskey, legal or illegal, until now. The new income tax hasn't generated enough revenue it seems with the depression going full speed and all, so the Feds are looking back at the excises such as the liquor tax for help."

"In conjunction with that, the repeal of Prohibition apparently has put enough pressure from Washington on the Federal Revenue Service that they threw caution to the winds and sent two men deep into what the locals down there call "Bryant Country." The purpose was to interdict a planned large shipment of illegal whiskey just ahead of repeal as revealed by a snitch in Bryant's organization."

"Well, one of the men got shot. He was a highly regarded agent by the name of Frank Stiller and the snitch who had told about the shipment that day has ratted on Bryant, leading to an arrest warrant. He's held in our local jail awaiting charging, which under the Constitution requires a Grand Jury indictment for capital murder. Grand Jury proceedings are secret and usually a rubber stamp of the US Attorney's wishes, but my sources in the Court and US Attorney's Office say that the jury has gotten independent and demanded to hear actual evidence, rather than a railroad story by the Marshall's Office in "The Great One", Tom Boyle, himself. You know him don't you, the one who was in France about the same time as you in 1916?"

Tony paused just long enough to let the slower Dick Powers absorb all the historical and sociological content he had thrown at him. Picking up the end of the line first, Dick said, "Boyle, isn't he the guy that wants everybody to think he won the west single handed and it all happened in Leon County?"

"Yeah, he's the one all right. Everybody calls him "The Great One", but never to his face, because he might pull out that pistol he always carries and shoot you on the spot, heh, heh, heh," Tony chuckled. "He served with Black Jack Pershing in France and parlayed that to the harmless office of US Marshall for the Northern District of Florida. But what's more important Dick is we, and by that I mean our local Grand Jury, is likely to indict. And after that, a local petit jury will have to try a death penalty case on the cutting edge of societal evolution, so to speak. We will have the story of the new century handed to us like a gift, don't you see Dick? Right here in little old Tallahassee and with the *Recorder* at the forefront like it or not" Tony pleaded, to head off any reluctance of the dull witted News Editor to object on some silly grounds such as the possible violation of the Grand Jury secrecy rules and having to defend the First Amendment for God's sake!

Dick read the story with interest now that he had the significance of the overall story so eloquently pointed out for him.

"I get it. You start out with the public interest aspect of the burden of serving bit to whet the appetite of the readers who missed it, by God! "I would gladly serve" and all that other bullshit our readers will think or even say to each other in the market or in church even though it costs them nothing when they aren't the ones called to this duty.

A murder story will sell papers and paper sales will sell advertising.

Tony, my boy, I think you are on to something here. I'll tweak it here and there and we put it on page one tomorrow as the lead story. Get to it, Son!" Dick Powers patronizingly said as Tony grabbed the copy knowing all that tweaking talk was wasted words and quickly forgotten anyway. He would have to hurry to meet the six o'clock print deadline that was rapidly approaching. Powers didn't even notice that his subordinate had just bypassed his editing of the story as he dreamed of the fame that Tony Callaway would bring to *The Tallahassee Recorder* and indirectly, him. *After all,* he thought, *I'm the one in charge and it happened on my watch!*

28. Prep him

Elliot Richardson, the Assistant US Marshall, got his marching orders by phone, and before the hour was out, George Drucker was packed up, bag and baggage and hauled over to the US Attorney's Office for the prep session that evening. Dan Fernell's secretary ordered in some food for dinner and the prosecutorial team assembled in the large conference room with the physical evidence arrayed, such as it was, for easy access.

"Houston, why don't you have Erik contact the local FBI Crime Lab and see if they have someone over there that can dredge up the home phone number of Bill Stevenson, that firearms ballistics expert, and have him ready to testify before the jury tomorrow after we conclude with George. If it looks like they are still wavering, we'll run him in to testify. He can bring the fingerprint studies lifted from the gunstock and testify as an expert on prints and forensic logistics. That ought to satisfy this damn jury that wants direct evidence. I'm not taking any more chances with this crowd." the US Attorney said.

"Dan," Tom Boyle said, being the only one in the room with enough courage this night to call Dan Fernell by his first name, "I still don't get it! I told these people exactly what happened and damn well too, if I must say so myself, the nerve of these red neck farmers, soul searching Christians, and that pin headed intellectual Professor to question me on evidence, The United States Marshall for the Northern District of Florida!"

"Now, Tom, settle down. We're all on the same team here, so get your head out from your ass, if I must speak plainly, and let us get on with the preparation for tomorrow. Phyllis will be pissed off when I come home late tonight as it is, so don't prolong this any longer than we have to, you get it?" "The Great One", suitably put in his place, turning three shades of red in utter embarrassment, shut up and sat down in an harrumph.

"Houston, I'm not trying to tell you how to put on your case, but, why don't you take Drucker here through his paces with a lead up to the almost admission, followed by the motive testimony as the wind up?" Dan said.

Houston Gilchrist, not being the egotist or blowhard that "The Great One" was, took the suggestion without offense, and then went on to explain to George Drucker how they would proceed.

"I ask the question George, like this, exactly what did he say that morning when you got to the still?" Houston explained, and George got the drift of the direction he was heading.

"You mean, Sir, I answer with the part about how there was no one else with the brass balls to shoot Stiller and stuff like that?" George asked.

"Well sort of George," Houston said, "but there are good Christian citizens on that jury and they may take offense if you talk about brass balls. Tom here has used the term "brass ones" which softens it a little bit, you understand, and we don't want you contradicting Tom in his summary. We have the transcript here tonight and Erik Driskoll will go over Tom's testimony with you so you don't screw it up."

They continued this way for a while until George began to get the hang of the part he was going to play. "The main thing George, you need to relax and just tell the truth. The other main thing is the jurors have the right to ask questions and they are not lawyers, hell they may be even doing their jobs and are looking for the truth, so watch out for that," Houston said as George nodded his head in agreement.

"Now George, you haven't said yet, as I remember, as to how you learned that Earl witnessed the shooting by Frank Stiller of Earl's father, Terrell Bryant, giving him a motive to kill Stiller, which a juror just might be curious about, how would you answer that?" Houston said.

"Well, I'd say it like this, any fool down here knows that Stiller killed Terrell Bryant. That is common knowledge among whiskey men. Besides, Earl talked about his old man like he weren't no damn good, but that Frank Stiller ought not to have shot him with that Colt 44 of his. I asked him one time how he knew it was a 44 and he said he seen it. That's how I know he knows," George said, as if perturbed that anybody would question what he thought everybody in north Florida knew anyway.

"Ok George, that's good enough for a grand jury hearing but do you know when and where, that kind of stuff?" Houston asked hopefully.

"If I knew that much detail about it, now who would believe George Drucker?" George said convincingly.

Houston and Fernell took turns grilling Drucker on the details of his testimony until they were sure he had it down pat. Dan Fernell was going to take no chances with a criminal for a witness and this review session was the proof. By midnight that night, all the Prosecutors were finally satisfied that they were ready for tomorrow's test for George

Drucker before this independent grand jury and the meeting ended with everyone dead tired but satisfied and headed for home or hotel.

29. New friends

Earl Bryant sat forlorn in his cell totally unaware of developments in his case. The morning paper was not delivered to the Leon County Jail and especially not made available to its inmates. His lawyers were likewise in the dark, for unlike the litigation of a criminal case once charges were filed or in the case of a grand jury, once an indictment has been handed down, which is thereafter open to the public and lawyers alike, the grand jury operates behind a veil of secrecy. However, *The Tallahassee Recorder* story that was blazed across page one the next morning and was the subject of the talk of customers of coffee shop and breakfast restaurants all over town, as well as the inner offices of Martin & Martin, had peeled away some of the secrecy normally expected in such proceedings.

Aaron sat in his father's office across from the Senior Partner of the firm and each had their noses buried in Tony Callaway's by-line story.

"Damn!" said Aaron, "How do you suppose Tony got to that jury? I know that guy is smart, I grew up with him, a close friend at that, but talking to grand jurors and reporting an inside scoop from the Prosecutor's Office? I am impressed!"

Roland Martin said nothing, poring over the details of the story looking for facts that might help their case.

Aaron continued, "That guy used to come out with some of the most insightful comments when we were just kids. He had read Homer's stuff, you know the *Iliad and Odyssey,* by the time we were twelve, but this grand jury penetration took cunning and guts, I'll bet."

"Yeah, but there's neither surprise nor help for us here either. You know that young guy over in Dan Fernell's office, Driskoll, isn't that his name, don't you? Why don't you give him a call and, you know, just feel him out about how long the Grand Jury will take, and naturally he won't say if he knows, but maybe you can read something useful between the lines from what he does say. Then get out to the jail and let our client know we are doing something. He's probably hopelessly depressed by now, not hearing anything. It's not anything important to our case but it is important to keep his spirits up," Roland said and Aaron nodded his agreement, folded his copy of the *Recorder* under his arm and left his father's office.

He planned to drop by the Garden Grill after calling Erick. They had been at law school together, and there might be an angle there. The Grill was the most popular eating-place for the people hanging around or working near the courthouse. This would be an unnecessary breakfast since he had already had breakfast at home. He would go there anyway, just on the outside chance he could catch up with someone involved in the case, or at least to make his face known around town. Publicity is important for a lawyer even in the middle of a case, he thought.

Earl's cellmate was still sleeping, so he sat there on his bunk with his elbows on his knees and hands cradling his chin like a cup, thinking about the mess he was in thus far. Jack Sanford rolled over on his cot and made the unmistakable sounds of a sleeping man coming awake. Earl leaned back to a sitting position and waited. Jack raised his head, blinked and turned toward Earl and said, "Morning there, what's happening mate?" Earl stared at Jack and shrugged, not really ready to engage the man in morning chitchat, but not wanting to avoid some social contact either. He was lonely, wanting company but content to be alone, desiring solitude all mixed up together. The contradiction was not apparent to him with these mixed feelings. But like it or not, companionship was forced on him in this small two man cell and neither man was content to avoid it altogether.

"You got anything scheduled in your case today as far as you know, Earl?" Jack inquired; hoping to find some subject his cellmate was comfortable discussing.

"Nothing I know of," Earl cryptically said, hoping to end the conversation, as the solitude side of his longing seemed to have the upper hand. Jack was feeling terrible himself with the full effects of a king sized hangover that every alcoholic has, no matter when he had his last drink and can't get more immediately. He had been here, done that so many times, that making the best of jail time was a skill he had acquired many years before, and a solitude seeking cellmate was just not going to be tolerated.

He needed a diversion from the throbbing head and the beginnings of delirium tremens that were rising up in his bones like the premature rumblings of an ancient volcano. The explosion would come soon enough, but he had learned the hard way that the more engaged he could become in human contact, the longer the explosion was postponed. The benefit of that delay was the best he could expect, and was well worth the effort required to penetrate the stubborn desire of a cellmate for solitude.

"This is your first serious charge ain't it Earl? I can see that in your airs," Jack said enigmatically. This caught Earl by surprise, since he had not said anything about whether he had been in jail before and had not the slightest idea what his cellmate meant by his "airs." But Earl was well acquainted with how not to directly answer an embarrassing question, changed his tack and said,

"You look like shit, Jack, do you feel near as bad as you look this morning?"

"I had to wait the thing out once Earl," Jack said, also avoiding answering an embarrassing question, because the last thing he would do is engage in a discussion about how he felt this or any other morning. He continued, "They had me on a theft once, charged me with it that is, and I had to sit in this hell hole longer than what's right until that damn prosecutor made up his mind that he had no case and let me go. Waiting that out was worse than the chain gang and I done them, too, more than once. If the black dog gets you, there's no telling where the hell he'll let you get to," Jack said, having drawn Earl into a cell conversation in spite of himself, except that Earl and Jack in their desire to avoid certain subjects, kept passing each other like two cars in a tunnel with the lights out.

Earl liked this old drunk better than he had expected and Jack felt there was some mutuality to it too. "You probably had some of my whiskey and never knowed it," Earl said.

"Yours and everybody else's, if common sense applies to this situation, I'm thinking. I been drinking moonshine whiskey since my Pap introduced me to it as a boy and it damn near has kilt me, Earl," Jack said. "That stuff is the death of the people what drinks it, if my thought on it is true and proper," Jack offered prophetically. "You cain't leave it alone and it won't let you alone neither," Jack continued.

"What do you mean, it won't let you alone, Jack?" Earl asked, really curious by his comment, never having given much thought to the problem his customers might have experienced and not understanding at all what Jack meant by the stuff leaving the customer alone, as if the whiskey was not just the problem but the one behind it.

"That whiskey you make Earl, its evil, is all I kin say about it, and when it gets a hold of you like it's done me, part of it gets in you and stays there and answers every time you get close to one of them bootleggers. I swear it's like this siren calling out as you run past it. You know its callin' and that part inside you answers back like they was singing one of them duets at church, except there ain't no God in this business at all. You hears them singing, that one inside and that other one outside and the music is so pretty you can't bear to break them up. One strain without the other won't sound just right but together, that's music. And you can sing for a while at least! You see what I mean, Earl?" Jack tried to explain but not making much sense.

"No not really, Jack," Earl said plainly, really puzzled as to what his new friend meant, and Jack Sanford was becoming that to Earl, little by little, even if he could not have articulated that sense of their beginning relationship.

Friends are usually two or more people who don't stand face to face, but side by side, having a common interest finding that special kind of love reserved for that rare combination of emotion expressed only in this way. There is no jealousy in it, no conflict over who gets the object first, and no limit to the number who can share in it. Most people, men particularly, go through a lifetime and rarely make more than a couple of them; but when they do, the priceless nature of it is apparent to all of them engaged in the process. Something strange was happening in this otherwise lonely place of hopelessness, and despair and neither man really understood yet the thing of beauty that had been hatched. They were too busy figuring out how to get through the trouble that each day was bringing them. And for Earl, that trouble was brewing in a mixture he could not even yet imagine in his worst moments.

30. Finally started

Professor Mathewson was the first to arrive in the jury assembly room at 8:30AM, as ordered by Judge Parker at the preliminary meeting when the procedural instructions had been handed out.

He was a punctual man by long habit and could not alter it if he tried without great discomfort or unease. He just felt better if he was on time. It was not so much the avoidance of the imposition on others, which was a factor to be considered, but in his case, it was simply the way he had been trained since childhood by a mother who had the same trait, indelibly ingrained in her as well. She had simply imprinted this rather desirable trait on her son. Most people are not that punctual caring more for their own conveniences than the imposition on others, but it was a big matter especially today for the they all had to decide the fate of a fellow human being no matter how heinous an act he was accused of committing. This was serious enough to bring them all into the assembly room within five minutes of the appointed hour.

When all the jurors had arrived, checked in, helped themselves to the free coffee the Federal Court had provided as a courtesy, and been called to order by the Deputy Clerk of Court, that day's session of the Earl Bryant Grand Jury was about to begin.

"Ladies and gentlemen, at your request and pursuant to a subpoena of this Honorable Court, the Government calls George Drucker as its first live witness before you. The Clerk may swear the witness to tell the truth," Houston Gilchrist said with stentorian effect. He was so sworn. "Your name and address, Sir? And spell the last name please for the Court shorthand writer"

"George Drucker, D-r-u-c-k-e-r . I stay at the Duvall Hotel for now and after this, Lord knows where I'm staying at," George said sincerely.

"Please tell the jury your occupation, Sir."

"You sure I ought to tell them that Sir (looking nervously toward Houston, who nodded yes and he continued, "I ain't got one of them occupations, far as I know, but up till yesterday, I ran the business end of the Earl Bryant whiskey stills down in Bryant Country," George said proudly once he figured out he was in the clear for illegal moon-shine work being that he was here in court at the beck and call of the Federal men.

"Just exactly what is Bryant Country, George?," Houston said trying to sound personal like George and he were just having a good old time talking about things, nothing important yet, just background stuff.

"Well it's like this Sir," George said, Earl Bryant is the kingpin in the illegal whiskey business in Liberty County and near the whole County, too, so folks call it all Bryant Country, but the main place of it is deep in the river country at the Lagoons where the main still is located."

"How big is the operation down there George, how many kettles, that is?" Houston asked hoping George would elaborate on the size and complexity of the operation in the deep river country behind Earl's house, where the shooting took place.

"He has six coppers with an assortment of mash barrels and cooling barrels with worms in them at that location at the Lagoon, all covered up with a tin roof showin' only grass and small trees from the air," George said confidently, as if every man and woman on the jury knew exactly what he was talking about, but they of course knew none of it, just sitting there with a puzzled look on their faces which Houston, the experienced trial lawyer, noticed immediately.

"You might explain about the worms, George, most folks would think you were talking about fish bait or something," Houston said, smiling knowingly to himself.

"Well, the worms, Sir, they is the coils in the coolin' barrels that bring the liquor out after it evaporates from the coppers heated by a hickory fire underneath, made in a spiral like," George said, twirling his fingers opposing each other to signify the coil effect which now registered with most of the jurors.

"Where were you on the 5th of December last, George?" Houston asked ready now to bring George to the critical part of his testimony and lay the foundation for the inference of guilt.

"I had been called by Earl Bryant to come to the Lagoon to help with the shipment out into neighboring Counties, but I was a little bit late that morning walking the way of the River Road east of Earl's house and I got there right after Earl did. Soon as I come into the factory, the men called it the "factory" like we was manufacturing plow stocks or something, but what we was making was something for plow hands stead of stocks, you might say," George said, making a kind of a joke, but nobody was laughing yet it seemed.

"Did you notice whether Earl had been carrying a gun, George, when you came in, I mean?" Houston asked, tipping George off with his cue that he was to testify about the gun magazine and that Earl always carried a full clip and that morning one shot less than full was readily apparent. George explained this to the satisfaction of the jury as far as Houston could judge by his reading their body language and moved on to the confessions, which was the key testimony as far as he was concerned. "Now, George, what did Earl Bryant say about the shooting?" Houston asked with the cue card question again.

"He asked me if I heard that shot and I said I didn't and then told me that there Stiller feller, a Federal Revenuer, had been shot on his own front doorsteps. He said he had a good look at him and told me he was the one what had been giving him a burr under his saddle for years and who else but he would have the brass ones to do it," George said.

"George, this is important now, are you sure he said exactly that?" Houston asked, as if questioning what he wanted the jury to have drummed unto their memories by repetition.

"As sure as I'm sitting here, Mr. Gilchrist, I swear he said it!" George said, putting an explanation point on his sentence, making Sir he convinced this jury because that was his ticket to safety, or at least a pass to stay in north Florida rather than to run to Kentucky or someplace up north, if Earl got out of the frame George was trying to put him in. The stakes were high all right and George Drucker would pay any price for it, it seemed.

Houston had one final question for George before turning him over to the independent Grand Jury and that was the motive question. "George, besides that, can you tell this Grand Jury anything that might suggest why Earl Bryant would shoot Frank Stiller, anything at all that comes to your mind?" Houston asked as if the two men had just met and had not spent four hours the night before drilling this very question and the answer that was coming into the memory and consciousness of George Drucker.

George seemed to think for a few seconds as if he had never thought about this before and then he began as if he was a thespian on center stage and trying his hardest not to sound rehearsed. His acting was a bit over the top but it had a plausible ring to it if not truly, credibly authentic as he said,

"There was a reason he would do it, Mr. Gilchrist, because he witnessed the killing of his Pappy, Terrell Bryant, in 1913, I think it was, by the same federal man."

"Are you saying, George, that Earl Bryant had a motive for killing Stiller?" Houston asked incredulously.

"Yes, Sir, he did and he revenged it, I'm thinking!" George said.

"Now how do you know that he witnessed that shooting, 1913 was it?" Houston asked.

"He told me, Sir, numerous times he did, we was close like that, me and Earl," George said.

"Sit right there, George, the jury might have some questions for you," Houston said, and turned to the jury that had been captivated by the testimony of the snitch. Professor Jorgensen stood up first and directed the first question to George,

"Mr. Drucker, why did you come down the River Road that morning and not by Mr. Bryant's house, were you expecting trouble?" he asked. He had George there in a sense because if he, George, was in charge of the business operations, supplies, inventory and that kind of thing, one would think he would have been close enough personally to Earl to come by the house, maybe for coffee at least, since it was breakfast time when he headed for the "factory" site.

The Professor didn't have an axe to grind the point on one way or the other and was just cleverly looking for holes in the story of the man who the Government was relying on for its case just to be Sir the evidence was solid enough to indict him with.

"I weren't expecting no trouble, No, Sir, I was just late, that's all, slept in that morning and the Back River Road was quicker," George answered.

"I see," Professor Jorgensen said, being satisfied for now with the answer.

Lucas Jones was one of the quieter, more withdrawn members on the Grand Jury but being a farm hand on one of the Gadsden County tobacco plantations, from Greensboro, had been raised in the woods himself, down near the big swamp country near the coast before his family had drifted up north to take day labor jobs in the tobacco fields, after the turpentine harvest had played out and was interested in the fact that Earl had been carrying a rifle that morning. He was just curious and not at all suspicious of George's testimony so he screwed up his courage to ask the question, "Did you consider it odd that Mr. Bryant had his deer rifle with him that morning on a regular work day?" George thought a minute, longer really than you might expect for so simple a question, and answered,

"Well, yes and no, I guess," he answered enigmatically. Houston saw the opening and sought to close it by saying,

"You had seen him with the gun many times before then?"

"That's right, Sir, he carried it everywhere he went," George said, cooperating with the leading question with no defense lawyer available to say, "I object, leading" and no Judge to say "sustained, you know you can't lead the witness, Mr. Gilchrist." But old Lucas might have been a field hand to them, but he had not just rolled off the labor truck that morning either and pressed on by saying,

"Then how was it odd, if he normally carried it with him, Mr. Drucker?" as George pondered how he was going to get out of this jam, Houston simmered with anger at the stupidity of his witness. *You can train um till the cows come home, but by God that stuff comes out anyway*, he thought.

"Well, odd in the sense he weren't hunting that morning and there ain't no bears at that still," George said, recovering nicely as the rest of the panel chuckled at the reply.

Phyllis Smithson, the schoolteacher from Perry then asked, "Did you carry a gun too, Mr. Drucker?"

George really had to think about this one, because of course he had carried a rifle that morning himself, and for the life of him, he could not remember whether he had told the Prosecutors that he had or, more important, whether any of the Negroes at the still had seen him. He had seen none of them or anybody else from down there since that fateful morning and the details from his memory were getting fuzzy. He decided to add nothing new so he simply denied it. The jury seemed to accept that because no question was raised by any of them.

"Speaking of guns," Bill Haskins, the disgruntled auto body shop operator said, who had finally gotten over his frustration of having to virtually donate his services to the process, "I for one would like to hear some of that ballistic and fingerprint evidence your Marshall Boyle claimed you got. It seems to me that if Earl Bryant's gun done the shooting, we ought to hear the proof of it or not and we can get this over with and go home!"

Houston had seen that coming, so he rose from his seat at the counsel's table in the Grand Jury hearing room and walked to the double doors, opened them and called out to FBI ballistics expert, Bill Stevenson, who had been cooling his heels all morning in the court house corridor, just waiting for the expected call to testify.

Bill Stevenson was one of those small, wiry, bespectacled men that made you think he was more at home behind a desk with the proverbial green eye shade and hanging light fixture that moved back and forth in the summer as the breeze blew into the accounting office. That all changed as soon as he opened his mouth in response to Houston Gilchrist's first question about the murder weapon. After Bill was sworn to testify, Houston asked him to identify the weapon used in the crime.

He began by saying, "The weapon used in the crime was a US Army Surplus, 30.06 Enfield, bolt action shoulder weapon, standard issue to our troops in the late conflict. We matched the projectile to the rifling in the barrel of that particular rifle and the bullet that killed Frank Stiller and which bullet our people dug out of the doorpost at Earl Bryant's front step was one and the same."

"You are sure about that, Mr. Stevenson?" Houston asked, watching the jury's captivation with this intelligent and experienced little man.

"It was the same gun, Sir, I stake my professional reputation on that," Stevenson said.

"How do you know who fired the gun, Sir?" Houston asked.

"We lifted fingerprints off the stock and barrel, Sir, that's how," Stevenson said convincingly.

"And from those prints, could you determine who put them there?" Houston asked setting up the question for the winning point.

"Yes, Sir, they belonged to the suspect, Earl Bryant, based on prints on file with the FBI Office, from when the suspect applied for a farming exemption from military service with the Liberty County Draft Board before the last war and transferred to the national fingerprint bank in Washington, DC, Sir. It was him all right and you can be Sir about that," Stevenson said. With that, Houston turned back to the Grand Jury to see if the independent bunch had any questions left.

Willis Cole had been sitting quietly in the back row of the jury area not saying much one way or the other, possibly praying a lot. Just when it seemed that the jury had no questions and even Professor Jorgensen was about ready to confer for a decision, he spoke out.

"Excuse me, Mr. Stevenson, Sir, could you tell us how the gun was found?" Ernie Ballister, the illiterate farm hand who had also had nothing to say so far, spoke up before Houston could explain the point, "Marshall Boyle testified, didn't he, that there gun were at Earl's house the same morning of the arrest?"

"That's my point," Willis said, but of course nobody yet got his point and as he noticed this, he went on. "If Mr. Bryant, the suspect here, shot the man on his own front door step with the bullet buried deep in the wood of his own door frame, why in blazes would he bring the gun with his fingerprints all over it and leave it in his own house where the Marshall's people were bound to come get it? It don't make sense to me, is my point."

"He doesn't have to be smart to be guilty does he? Dumb criminals get caught all the time," Mary Easter, the seamstress from Chairs said.

"She has a point, people," Professor Jorgensen said, "We have to look at the evidence we have, not the evidence we don't have."

"You should remember folks, that Mr. Bryant does not have to testify here and has decided not to testify and you must not give any credence to that one way or the other," Houston said, cleverly reminding the jury of exactly the opposite point in that speech, all in his civic duty you understand, as an Officer of the Court.

The jury apparently got it, for when Houston asked if the jury wanted to hear any more evidence, his question was greeted with a silence that to Houston at this point was golden.

"Hearing no further calls for evidence or witnesses let me sum up things presented before you. Marshall Boyle testified that Earl Bryant was arrested at his house with a weapon that Mr. Stevenson, the ballistics expert from the FBI, confirmed as the murder weapon. You heard from George Drucker, an inside man in the Bryant whiskey operation, testify that Bryant had opportunity and motive for the killing. We contend Ladies and Gentlemen, that Earl Bryant saw an opportunity to even an old score for the killing of his father, Terrell Bryant, back in 1913. Mr. Stiller was a burr under Bryant's saddle and he as good as admitted the crime to George the morning that it happened. Of course he did not say, I did it, but he did the next best thing when he said, "Who else but me would have the brass ones to do it," pardon me ladies for that, but that was the testimony of the witness.

The government contends that on December 5th, 1933 in Liberty County, Florida, Earl Bryant with malice aforethought, deliberately shot and killed his old nemesis of the whiskey wars and satisfied an old grudge by revenge in the process. We leave this matter to the jury for a vote as to whether to return a true bill of indictment for first-degree murder", and with that, he, Earl Driskoll, Bill Stevenson and a subdued for once, Marshall Tom Boyle, "The Great One", left the courtroom. The jury turned to deliberate and decide Earl Bryant's fate.

31. Still remains

There had been no reason for Hub and the other Negro workers to return to The Lagoon after the Still Buster Team had done its dirty, but thorough, work of destroying the cooking kettles, mash fermenting barrels and cooling barrels that chilly December morning. The worms inside the cooling barrels were smashed flat and useless, which was the main object of the raid. The worms were the hardest to replace for there was a special skill in their making not many men knew how to do. But after a few days, curiosity or was it despair, got the better of Hub Douglas.

Herbert or Hub, as he was usually called by blacks and whites alike, was the youngest son of Mack Douglas, lot and handyman for Roland Martin, farmer-lawyer from the area. Hub had abandoned the comforts, such as they were, and the security of home, as many young Negro men did in that age and time, for adventure, rebellion or just a change of pace in a different place.

Mack Douglas and his wife Mary had raised the five boys and three girls with tenderness and discipline. The children all worked in the Martin tobacco fields and learned what it meant to be on time to work, carry your share of the work load, and do whatever you said you would do. Hub received that imprint on his character fairly well.

Hub, on the other hand, was always bucking against the stream of what was expected of him; and on more than one occasion, had gotten into trouble in the fields by talking back to the field boss or worse yet, even once did so to Roland Martin, the owner himself.

Mr. Martin was a lawyer by profession well connected in District politics, the senior partner of The Martin Law Firm that represented his boss, Earl Bryant. But from where he stood today, Hub knew nothing of this. That was White Folks' business and all he knew and understood very well was that with Earl gone from the still, everything in the business and the money for wages, pitiful as they were, came to a screeching halt. The thought of that finally overcame the fear he had experienced that fateful morning when he and the others had hightailed it out into the river swamp to where they lived.

Hub lived in a makeshift cabin or dwelling, one of several scattered across a ridge, separated by small garden plots and some stock enclosures, deep in the forest of Bryant Country in a small community of other Negro workers. The men of this community were all engaged in the business of tending the Bryant moonshine operations, the service of which earned them just enough to meet basic needs, but not much else. The limited farming in and around the little settlement known to the hands as "The Quarters" was permitted by Earl Bryant and encouraged as a supplement to the cash money they were paid from the still operation.

It was to this dwelling of his that he had retreated to that fateful morning after the still at the Lagoon had been smashed. Like most young Negro men in the community, he had taken up with a woman for their mutual satisfactions. They were not family yet in the sense that his father and mother had been, and as he had known it back at the Martin Farm, but life was regular and their basic needs were met.

Hub's woman, or girl really, Lizzy Spooner, was younger than him and the main attraction, for both of them at this point in the relationship, was sex. As normal young people, with sex hormones raging through their blood, there was thought of little else but sex each evening when he returned after a long hard day for Hub of cutting and stacking firewood or stacking and moving around the raw materials for whiskey making around.

They had a true passion for each other and given enough time, the physical attraction that bound them temporarily together would mature into some more permanent kind of a relationship, if not actual marriage. Since making illegal whiskey was the prime purpose of the community, a sense of law and other institutions that established morality that usually comes from the tradition of its observation, was missing. Fortunately for both of them, no children had been produced from the passion of the physical attraction between them and responsibility for the lives of others was beyond either of their desires or capabilities.

"What you doing home Hub before night, Boss Man know you down here?" Lizzy said, with a seductive smile in her voice and not particularly critical at that, as he came inside the door. An occasional morning or afternoon escape from work for a "nooner", was not that unusual.

She was typically obliging and the thought about sex this morning had crossed her mind more than once, as she remained busy with home duties. But today was different as she could see immediately the fear and panic in Hub's face and could hear the clamor of activity in the nearby cabins, which told her instinctively that something was terribly wrong. One man slipping away from the Lagoon for a secret indulgence was an ordinary occurrence but for more than one at the same time, that was strange, if not alarming.

"Where my jug, Lizzy?" Hub asked, stomping into the cabin, looking frantically for his jug of corn whiskey that each of the men kept in their cabins. Earl was aware the men drank some of the products of the still, but so long as they managed to come to work reasonably sober, it didn't bother him all that much.

"You know where it at, Hub Douglass! What's wrong with you, something happened ain't it?" Hub thrashed around the cabin saying nothing until he found the missing jug and drained what was left in it as fast as he could, seeking the comfort of the liquor to quell the fear that gripped him this morning.

He dropped into a homemade chair situated in the corner of the room next to the fireplace that Lizzy kept a fire going during the winter months and this December morning was no exception. She wisely left him alone with his thoughts and sat next to her man on the floor of the cabin and waited until the alcohol in the potent corn liquor did its work, calming the immediate fear or blanking out his reaction to what had happened. As the intoxicant sedated him, he finally realized that he needed to explain to Lizzy what had happened, as he tried to figure out what he should do next.

"Gov'ment men done busted up the stills this mornin' and before that, me and Nooby done heard them white folks talking bout a shootin' that took place up at Mr. Bryant's house this mornin' when one of them Gov'ment men was shot dead!" Hub said, in a confusing explanation of events that had all run together covering the entire day before his hasty departure when the Still Busting Team had flattened the still at The Lagoon.

He, Nooby and the others had no idea who had been shot or who did it but the strange conversation between Earl Bryant and George Drucker taking place in their hearing had not gone unnoticed. Neither had the comings and goings of everyone involved in The Lagoon operation. Little was missed by the men working there. "It Sir weren't no surprise when them Govment men come bustin' it up after that and we naturally heard the warnin' of it from the front men before they come on us and we got the hell out of there and I run home" Hub said.

"What we going to do, Hub? Boss Man won't get set up again before next month and that man ain't goin' to pay nothing if you ain't workin' and you ain't workin' if the still shut down?" Lizzy asked and explained all in the same thought.

"We ain't going to get set up next month nor next year neither, cause Nooby done heard the law done come for Boss Man and he in the Leon

Jail, maybe for good!" Hub said, looking around for his back up jug of corn liquor, since the dampening effect from the first drinks from the now empty jug had begun to wear off. Meanwhile the old fear, plus a panic about his own future, had begun to sink in to his consciousness.

The corn liquor had done its work well by now and Hub's courage had returned somewhat, so he decided to make a return visit to the factory to see just how bad everything was and what items of value just might be left lying around that he could sell somewhere. If Mr. Bryant was shut down and Mr. Drucker was gone too, there wasn't any point in leaving anything valuable around for the rats to eat up or somebody else to steal. He told Lizzy to stay put and left the cabin to head back over to the river country to see what he could see. There just may be an opportunity in this disaster. Lizzy on the other hand had other plans.

Hub approached The Lagoon cautiously, sitting for over an hour well out of gun and ear shot, with a good line of sight of the now decimated "factory" just to be damned Sir that no Federal Agents were laying in the weeds just waiting for Hub Douglas to show up and admit to being in the employ of the owner of the Bryant Country factory operation. When he thought the coast was clear, he cautiously slipped into the back entrance to the old still site.

It was a mess. The six copper kettles were smashed almost beyond recognition and definitely beyond further use. The mash barrels were more like bent sticks bundled by wire hoops than the proportionately curved oak pieces bound by stays. The cooling coils looked more like leaf springs than coils. The whiskey jugs containing the finished whiskey inventory were smashed and drained into the dirt floor of the factory. None of the sugar or corn inventory was left and the flash fire set after the destruction had been complete had burned the roof and supports.

As an experienced hand for those monotonous years after he left the Martin Place and worked down here at the river in the whiskey business, Hub Douglas could see in a minute that the destruction had been complete. He surveyed the walls of the room noticing the gun rack still pegged into the dirt wall on that side of the structure and remembered that Earl and Drucker had each brought guns into the factory that morning and hung them side by side next to where they had that conversation about the shooting.

The scene was a disaster and the hope he had had about finding something of value he could sell, evaporated as quickly as the liquor business of Earl Bryant that morning. He took one more long look around the place that had occupied his working hours for so many years, fighting off the nostalgia of the familiar if not the pleasant memories; and slowly made his way out the same way he had come and returned to the settlement to further drown his sorrows in the last whiskey jug he had left in his cabin.

When he entered the cabin, he saw immediately that Lizzy was gone and a quick look around told him, judging by the things of hers that were missing, her departure was permanent. No goodbyes, no farewells, no "enjoyed it while it lasted", and worst of all, no one more time in the sack to satisfy his desperate need for something pleasurable this morning and to remember her by. The long and short of it was she was gone forever. He had no job left, no money and soon would have no whiskey left. He must decide what to do about the future. He considered his options, found them limited or hopeless, and sat down on his cot to drown himself in the memories of when things had been better. After that, he would decide.

A day or so later, he came into the conscious state of one who was gripped like a vise with the worst hangover known to mankind, the moonshine hangover. It was terrible and worse yet, the only known remedy, to drink more of the poison, was not available to him. He had finished all the liquor he had left. He laid on his cot groaning and wallowing in self-pity and seeking one person or the other in a desperate need to blame someone, anyone other than himself and the choices he had made.

It had seemed so reasonable, so much fun to run away from home, being finally free of the moral constraints there and hide down in the river country of Liberty County, accountable to no one but himself. When he had left home those years before, the chaffing at the authority of accountability and discipline imposed by his father were the straws that had broken the back of his acceptance of home and relative safety in search of excitement and opportunity.

Home looked rather appealing to him now in spite of the faded memory of his objection to what had been good for everyone else in the family except him. He wondered to himself, could he go back? "It weren't so bad back then, had food, had work, and had family who cared about me. Mr. Martin never done nothin' bad to me, and Daddy did care about me didn't he? Cain't be worse than this. Besides, ain't got no choice has I, this business as such is over." He said this to no one except himself since he had been alone in the cabin for over two days.

His rationalizations were suddenly interrupted by the sound of approaching footsteps and Nooby Oakley, the closest thing to a friend he had, popped his head into the cabin.

"Hub, what's up?" Nooby said.

"Nothing up Nooby, it's all down, Lizzy done gone. Nothing down here for her or me so I'm next, I figure," Hub said.

"Why you leaving Hub, ain't nowhere to go to, is there?" Nooby said.

"Uh huh, I hear you, but going anyhow," Hub said.

"You ain't scared of them Federal men comin' back is you?" Nooby asked, fishing for a motive.

"Uh huh, maybe they is," Hub said.

What you up to Hub Douglas, you ain't in this mess is you? Nooby thought.

"You think them police going to leave these woods to let the next one take over the Lagoon? Ain't happening," Hub said enigmatically.

Nooby was truly puzzled now. He had seen Hub leave the still a few minutes before George Drucker came in, and tried to set up Earl Bryant and come back just in time to hear their conversation in detail, especially the part about Bryant having a motive to kill the Federal Officer, when nobody else heard or remembered it. It was almost like he might have been in on it with Drucker, Nooby was thinking. *He claim he be down but where he going go to anyways, where any of us has a place to go to? That boy is in this mess, for Sir! He cain't tell me and be safe, so he keep it to himself. Makes no nevermine to me. Huh! Better let this go or I be up in this mess, too. We is all still men and them Federal Men won't forget that. If he got something to hide, so be it!* Nooby reasoned to himself.

"Okay, Hub, if you be going, then be gone, I'm staying with them other boys. We goin' to live off the woods, the river and such until something turn up. If not, then we be gone too. You been my friend Hub and I ain't goin' to forget it", Nooby said. Hub did an unpredictable thing for a young Negro man; he reached out to his friend and tried to hug him. Nooby hesitated at first and then returned the favor, genuinely impressed by the emotion and gesture of the moment. He said his goodbyes and left.

Then with one look around the now empty cabin, Hub grabbed his few clothes and some food that was left, tied them up in a bundle, slung the sack over his shoulder for the long walk back to Gadsden County; and without another thought or regret, unlike Lot's wife, he left his "Gomorra" behind without so much as a glance back at what had been his home for years. It was a long hike out of the river swamp country back home, but he resolutely headed up the road north towards home, not sure what lay ahead but confident of one thing and one thing only, he wasn't coming back to this place. He had not told his friend where he was headed partly because he was ashamed of not staying like the rest, hanging onto the camaraderie, which was the only positive thing in his life right now. But mainly it was because he was not Sir he would have the courage to make it that far.

32. Decision time

"All right people, listen up," Professor Jorgenson said, "We have now heard all the evidence we are going to hear, so now it's up to us."

"It seems open and shut to me," Bill Haskins said, "any doubt about our responsibility to indict left hanging by that blow-hard US Marshall was filled in by that Drucker fellow's testimony. Bryant obviously had it in for Mr. Stiller and killed him for revenge. It's pure and simple it seems to me"

"And don't forget, that FBI man's testimony on the gun," Mary Easter said, "It sounded convincing to me, how else could the gun that killed him get Mr. Bryant's fingerprints?"

"That Drucker fellow bothered me," Willis Cole said, "He is a snitch and I don't like snitches. What other motives did he have to expose whether he was telling the truth?"

"Yeah, I didn't like Drucker," Lucas Jones said, he was slimy to my way of thinking." "We have to stick to the evidence we have, not our feelings about somebody," Professor

Jorgensen, the foreman said. "Let's take a vote people, just to see where we all stand and to save time if the majority has already decided, OK?"

The group nodded approval and a secret vote was taken by passing around slips that Frank Hopkins, Deputy Clerk had provided for that purpose. Professor Jorgenson counted the slips on the initial vote and the count was evenly split with one abstention, one vote short of an indictment. Since the voting was secret, nobody knew who abstained and who voted for what.

Bill Haskins had been the most reluctant juror to serve on the case because of the serious imposition, as he saw it, to his business. He had tried to be excused and failed due to economic hardship, had balked by feigned inattention in the beginning, but finally after he was resigned to sitting there anyway, had finally become interested in the case. He thought Earl Bryant was guilty and didn't care whether Marshall Boyle was a blow-hard or George Drucker a snitch. The gun evidence was the most important evidence to him, which left no room for doubt. This combined with his desire to quickly end the matter and go home warmed him to the task of persuading the hold out or some of the doubters.

"LoOkay," he said, "No matter what you think of George Drucker or the Marshall as people, you can't deny the importance of the gun. The gun was found at Bryant's house, and it matched the murder weapon description and the bullet from it to a tee. There's simply no getting around that. He did it and the evidence proves it."

"But why on God's green earth would Earl Bryant leave the murder weapon with his finger prints all over it in his own house, if he was the guilty man?" Willis Cole asked.

"Yeah," another said, "nobody in their right mind would do that."

"We've been over that," Professor Jorgensen said, "remember, we have to look at the evidence in the case, not the evidence left out that doesn't exist. Mr. Bryant will have his opportunity at trial, or at least his lawyer will, to make that point, and it's a good one, but we don't decide the guilt or innocence, only whether there is sufficient evidence to go to trial. The suspect is in jail and will stay there because this is a capital case with a death penalty the likely result, and we can't turn him loose on the amount of evidence we have presented to us, don't you see?"

"Would those not yet convinced, please speak up so we can decide how to proceed," Professor Jorgenson argued, hoping to convince at least one undecided juror to change his mind.

"I'll speak up," Willis Cole said, "I am one of the nay sayers because the life of a man is too important when I have some doubts in the evidence. I believe men do what makes sense to them and I can't see a guilty man that careless with the murder weapon. It looks like a frame up to me. That Drucker fellow was a little too slippery to suit me and his word alone is what we have to go on."

"Stupid is not a defense to murder!" Mary Easter argued, looking right at Willis. "I care about life too and Frank Stiller did not deserve to die either. It's not up to us to decide that but there is enough evidence to indict. Let the regular jury decide guilt or innocence. I was one of the doubters too but I am now convinced, so let's vote again."

"All right, folks, it sounds like it's time for another ballot," the foreman said and handed out twenty-five blank pieces of paper for the second vote.

The final tally was fifteen to ten with a clear majority in favor of indictment. Erik took the ballots and handed them to the Deputy Clerk, who left the courtroom to see the judge. Judge Parker was still in his chambers reviewing a brief for an argument later in the day to come before him in another case.

The Judge took the ballots, recounted them, and sealed them in an envelope as a part of the formal record should there be an appeal. Then he rose from his seat and walked out of his chambers into court where the Grand Jury was assembled, hastily called back to their seats by the Deputy Clerk.

"All rise," said the Clerk as Judge Ben Parker, Jr., came solemnly into the courtroom and took his seat majestically behind the massive bench on the raised dais overlooking the Grand Jury room. The jury stood quietly waiting for what would happen next.

"Be seated, please," Judge Parker said. "I understand you have reached a majority decision on the matter of the killing of Frank Stiller. Mr. Foreman, would you inform the Court of that decision", the Judge said. Professor Jorgensen rose and took his place in front of the lectern, a place he was, in a manner of speaking, not unfamiliar with as he regularly spoke to his students from a similar posture at the Florida State College for Women.

"Thank you, Your Honor, we have heard the evidence presented by the United States Attorney's Office and voted in favor of sending down an indictment by a majority vote, as I tabulated the ballots as you instructed. We, that is, fifteen of us at least, feel there is enough evidence that could lead to a conviction of Earl Bryant for the First Degree Murder of Frank Stiller.

"Very well, the Clerk will issue the indictment as a True Bill for which a warrant for the arrest of Earl Bryant for First Degree Murder shall issue and be served by the Government on the prisoner out in the Leon County Jail, where he is held for investigation without bail. That is the Order of this Court," Judge Benjamin Parker, Jr., pronounced and hammered his gavel down on the pad on his bench, as if to add a forceful conclusion to the mater already decided as he signed the order.

"The jurors are excused from further duty in this matter and shall return to work on the next case in this term. This Court shall be in recess and the jury dismissed for the remainder of the day. You will report first thing tomorrow morning for the next case," Judge Parker said and rose with the command of the Clerk, with all twenty-five of the jurors and returned to his Chambers.

Another day another indictment, the Clerk thought, but the Grand Jury members saw this as just another day of inconvenience that must be endured for the remainder of their term of three weeks. Some of them wondered whether justice had been served but there were always doubters in every group this size. On the whole it had been a different kind of experience for them, and the majority at least thought it had been the right thing to do. The trial on the other hand, might be an entirely different matter.

33. Ear to the ground

Aaron Martin was having his late morning coffee break at the café just down the street from the courthouse, when he saw out the window that the jurors were streaming out of the Federal Courthouse.

"Well, well, well," he said to Bill Nelson seated across the booth from him in Annie's Café, "Looks like the Bryant jury is out early Bill, that's a sign I reckon, but trouble is, I could take it either way."

"Yeah, you can't tell with early grand juries like you can with petit juries where a quick verdict usually means guilty," Bill said.

"Don't know about that, Bill, I remember that Smith case, you remember the guy who couldn't keep his pants zipped, a flasher kind of guy. That jury was out less than two hours, and with two eye witnesses too, and be dammed if they didn't acquit," Aaron said.

"That's because you are the master trial lawyer, Aaron Martin, with anybody else that guy was headed for Raiford," Bill joked in cutting at his friend with false praise.

"That's "BS," Bill and you know it. We lawyers don't control these cases, the facts do. We just point them in the right direction and sometimes they bring it on home, and you always forget to tell about the time the guy went down the river when a nervous law student should have been able to get an acquittal. The wins are the only ones that make the stories, right? I better get on over there and see what the hell they actually did with my client, see you around, fella," Aaron said to his longtime friend, dropped some change on the table to pay for his share of the coffee and headed out of the coffee shop.

Bill returned to reading the morning edition of the *Recorder*, and concentrated on the lead editorial that blasted the Republican Governor's Administration for the joblessness in the county, something he had absolutely no control over in the middle of a worldwide depression, but was taking the lion's share of the blame because it happened on his watch.

Aaron strolled over to the Courthouse as if nothing in particular was happening when his client's legal fate was hanging in the balance, and the anticipation was welling up within him like water bubbles in a compression chamber. He climbed the steps to the Courthouse and made his way down to the Clerk's Office at the end of the hall where the Court lodges all orders.

"Hello Mary, Frank back yet?" Aaron asked the Deputy Clerk on duty at the filing window.

"No, Mr. Martin, he's back with Judge Parker now that the Grand Jury's through," Mary Jergens said. She leaned forward conspiratorially and whispered into Aaron's ear, "they handed down an indictment for first degree, the warrant is to be served in an hour, thought you would like to know."

"Thanks Mary, I owe you one," Aaron said as he smiled and turned graciously away and headed out of the Courthouse on his way to see Earl at the jail. Earl couldn't evade the arrest if he wanted to, since he was held without bail, but he thought he ought to warn his client that it was coming.

Aaron had made it a point to stay on good terms with Courthouse personnel, especially the junior level clerks who had less of the affliction of egotism that most Chief Deputies or the high and mighty Chief Clerk himself had. Those guys were untouchable and the thought of being friendly to defense lawyers or lawyers generally was anathema to them. His friendliness with Mary Jergens, this time had paid off. He made a mental note to say a few more kind things about Mary to one of her friends who attended the Centenary Methodist Church where he did and they saw each other there from time to time. He had to be careful. Gifts and that sort of personal commentary, even if never financial in nature, would be frowned on by Judge Parker, if he ever got wind of it.

Earl had been delivered to the interview room at Aaron's request and left alone with his lawyer as the protocol demanded.

"Well Sir, is it up or down?" Earl asked his lawyer, sensing from Aaron's demeanor that something had been decided concerning him.

"Bad news, Earl, there's going to be a trial" Aaron said solemnly.

"Damn!" Earl said, "Guess that were inevitable, weren't it."

"You remember, I predicted this, but don't be concerned just yet. They still have to prove you did it," Aaron said, without much conviction. "How's Ellie, she been to see you yet?"

"No. Scared, I reckon, better that she stay away," Earl said.

"Now, I disagree about that, but where's she staying anyway?"

"She's up in Bainbridge, most likely with the daughter, if she can make it past that holier than thou, Doctor husband she has," Earl said.

"I'll get word to her. She ought to know what's coming and come see you too, what's that Doctor's name, the saintly one?" Aaron said somewhat with a slight hint of sarcasm in his voice following his client's lead.

"Wilson, Hugh Wilson, M.D., and don't you forget it, he'd say, up there at Bainbridge in South Georgia," Earl said.

"I know where Bainbridge is Earl, besides; we need to go over that evidence again now. What concerns me is George Drucker. Their whole case depends on that snitch, what else can you tell me about him?" Aaron asked, with some memory of the name rattling around in his brain.

While waiting for Earl's answer, thoughts whirled through Aaron's mind. *Drucker, George Drucker, where do I know that name? Not Pete Drucker's family, by God! Could he be the worthless older brother of my old friend Pete up in Havana?*

"He came from up in Gadsden County.," Earl said.

I thought so, Aaron thought.

"His old man was a moonshine man, small time operator. Never amounted to much, I hear tell. George was up to no good as a young man, you know small time crime, thieving and that sort of stuff. Did some time on the chain gang and was headed for Raiford till he took up with me in 1925, I think it was. He drifted down to Liberty County, running from the law were more like it, till I took the fella in and put him to work on a still. He took right to it and I seen he had potential. He had a knack for organizing, keeping up with supplies, corn, sugar, and that stuff. He could sweet talk them suppliers into hiding a sugar shipment and make it look on the books like a load of tobacco fertilizer, or corn meal, if the damn tax auditors come a calling."

"I put him in charge of that sort of thing and he run it out of that little store I run up in Telogia. We called it the office," Earl said.

"Where's that Earl, I thought I knew Liberty County pretty well, but never heard of Telogia?" Aaron asked, trying to get the geographical placement of the key events leading up to the alleged murder by his client.

"It's just south of Highway 20 at Hosford, where 65 join it, west of the river about six miles, the road what connects all of West Florida to Tallahassee. I trusted that damn feller like a little brother and to have the bastard turn on me, well it hurts Mr. Martin." Earl said with almost a groan of disappointment.

"Had he come directly from Telogia that morning, Earl?" Aaron asked, wondering why George would claim to come by the Back River Road to get to the Lagoon and miss being in the neighborhood at the time of the shooting. He had remembered Earl's story from the repeated telling he had forced him to give of the events that day, and recalled it with a trial lawyer's gift for the remembrance of details in the evidence. "I mean, if he had come straight on down 65 to Taylor's and then southeast down the main road to your house, he couldn't have missed the excitement, judging by the time he arrived at the Lagoon, could he have?" Aaron asked further, probing for any weakness in the government's case.

"It seems so, but there is a short cut road from Telogia to Sopchoppy and the coast, with a cut off into the river swamp where the Lagoon's at. We call it the Back River Road and its six to one or the other, you might say," Earl said.

Aaron made a note on his legal pad to digest later in his trial preparations. "So what he said could be true or not, you simply don't know, right Earl?" Aaron asked trying to confirm what he believed his client was telling him, that he really didn't know one way or the other.

"All I know is he showed up at the factory right after me and said he come by the Back River Road," Earl said.

"Well that's enough for today Earl, it will be several weeks before the trial and we can go over this again. The next step is the arraignment before Judge Parker and that happens tomorrow. You will enter a plea of not guilty and I will make another pitch for bail but again don't count on it being any different result. This is a murder case and the Grand Jury voted that there is enough evidence to bring you to trial. Judge Ben will not want to risk that you might run away, but we'll see. After that, I get a list of the Government's evidence and we will hire our own ballistics expert to examine the bullet and the gun barrel rifling. I will see you in Court and won't come out here before hand. They have to bring you before a Judge now and Judge Ben will take charge of the case from now on. He's a fair man; we'll leave it with him. All right?" Aaron said.

"If you say so Mr. Martin, but I don't trust no Govment men, Judges or any other kind.

"The Judges are all we have, Earl and it's the fairest system anywhere. Perfection will only come in Heaven, but don't you lose hope now, you hear me?" Aaron said forcefully as if stating it so could change the hopelessness that pervaded the whole atmosphere of the jail and in the soul of Earl Bryant.

"Yes, Sir", Earl said with a total lack of conviction. With that, Aaron rose, shook Earl's hand and hailed the guard to come and open the secure interview room. In moments, he left and Earl was returned to the gloomy environs of his jail cell to commiserate with Jack Sanford until tomorrow's Court appearance.

34. A call to family

Aaron leaned over his desk to touch the intercom button to speak to his secretary. "Anna, Doctor Hugh Wilson lives in Bainbridge. Get his number for me, office or residence, no matter, would you please?"

"Yes, Sir, Mr. Martin, coming up, be just a minute," Anna said and turned to her phone and lifted the handle.

"Number please?" the Operator said in that lilting melodious voice the typical telephone operator in the deep south had in that era, practiced to perfection.

Recognizing the familiar voice, Anna said, "Mrs. French, could you inquire of the telephone company in Bainbridge and connect us with the number for the home or office of Dr. Hugh Wilson?"

"Sir Anna, just a minute please," and Anna held the phone for the few seconds that it took and heard the telltale ring, ring, ring, click,

"Hello, Dr. Wilson's residence, who you want, please, this Elvira, the Maid speaking."

"Elvira, my name is Anna Devlin, Secretary to Mr. Aaron Martin, Attorney, in Tallahassee, Florida, is Dr. Wilson or Mrs. Wilson there?" Anna said.

"Jest a minute, please, Dr. Wilson just come home from the hospital where he work at," Elvira said, "I go get him."

In a moment, the sonorous voice of Hugh Wilson, MD, came across the phone line.

"Elvira said you're calling from a Tallahassee Lawyer's office, what's this all about, please?"

"Excuse me, Dr. Wilson, but I'm Anna Devlin, Secretary to Aaron Martin, Attorney, and he would like to speak with you, Sir, if you don't mind?" Hugh held the phone a few seconds until Aaron came on the line,

"Dr. Wilson, I'm Aaron Martin, I represent Mr. Earl Bryant down here on a case in Federal Court and I understand from Earl that his wife, Ellie, is staying with you and Mrs. Wilson, their daughter, during the trial of his case, is that correct, Sir?"

"Maybe you ought to speak directly to Ellie, she is here Mr. Martin, just a minute," the line went silent as Wilson went to fetch Ellie to the phone.

"Hello ," Ellie said, "is that you Mr. Martin?"

"Ellie, we go to Court tomorrow for Earl to enter his not guilty plea and make one final pitch for bail and I want you down here. The Grand Jury has returned an indictment for murder and it would help Earl if you could be here, you know, to show the Judge that his family is behind him. Could you manage that, Ellie?" Aaron asked.

"Yes, Sir, what time and where?"

"Ten O'clock tomorrow morning in the main Courtroom at the Federal Courthouse in Tallahassee. I would like you to be prepared to tell the Judge what Earl is likely to do if he turns him loose on bail, could you manage that and to spend some time with Earl, he's a little low about now?" Aaron asked, not at all Sir how Ellie, a private person from the country like she was, would take to that.

"Yes, Sir, I'll be there and see my man, Earl, too after it's over," Ellie said.

"Thanks, Ellie, he'll never say so, he's too proud to, but he does need you and will deeply appreciate that," Aaron said and concluded the call.

"What's happened Ellie," Dr. Hugh said, seeing the distress Ellie was undergoing, having gotten over the judgmental attitude he had taken with his wife's family for years, and saw her as a suffering human being no different than the patients he saw every day in their own sufferings from the ravages of disease, accident, or deliberate damage, and was quite prepared to support her now in this time of struggle.

"It's the jury. They done handed down one of them indictments and my man, Earl, he have to go to the trial, but tomorrow he speaks up that it weren't him or something like that and the lawyer want me there for support for the bail business," Ellie explained.

"Well, I can't get away but Emily will drive you down and be with you, right Em?" Dr. Hugh said, looking over at his wife who nodded her agreement. Ellie had won over the entire family by this time and the feeling was genuine. "Let's have dinner so you can get some sleep because you will need an early start tomorrow to make that ten o'clock court thing in Tallahassee. If you get your mother there a little early, Em, she will have a chance to see Earl or at least let him know that she's there. That will be important to him."

They turned together and made their way into the dining room where Annie, the family coOkay, had prepared and set out a wonderful and delicious dinner, which she was proud to do and at the same time meet the standards of excellence Dr. Hugh expected in his office, hospital and home. Tomorrow would be an eventful day for the Bryant relatives and having Emily's family behind her was a proud moment for Ellie Bryant. Maybe some good would come out of this after all.

35. They are gathered together

Tony got the word from his source at the Courthouse that the Grand Jury had returned an indictment for murder and knew from experience that an arraignment would come within a day or so. He had also been able to learn that the arraignment was scheduled for the next day before Judge Parker. He was tempted to call his good friend, Aaron Martin, who was defending Earl Bryant, but he understood the attorney client privilege and his friend's character well enough to not try that avenue as a source for news.

He admired Aaron from their days as boys growing up and in college together and from what he had observed of his law practice in Tallahassee, from where he sat in the news business. Tony was thinking of an angle for his story of the impact of a conviction of a well-known moonshiner on the communities where men like Earl Bryant lived. Since most of the stuff was produced in the less populated outlying counties Surrounding the State Capital; and since those folks had depended on the illegal whiskey business for their livelihood and consumers from the whole northern part of the state for their taste for whiskey as a sedative against the pressures and boredom of life during prohibition and depression, the whole change in the culture would likely be substantial.

There was no getting around it, to write such a story he would have to spend some considerable time in those areas, getting to know the people actually affected by the change. He decided to first go ahead and attend the arraignment and interview those people who showed up in support of the Defendant, Earl Bryant, and follow up on them with a later visit to their home counties. He was willing to bet that there would be some family or sympathetic folks in attendance and he planned to find a way to get close to them. But their natural distrust of city people, especially newspaper reporters, made this a difficult assignment. He thought he had the Editor's support for the effort.

The word had spread rather quickly around town that something important was happening the next day at the Federal Courthouse. A clerk's assistant mentioned it to a friend at a bridge game in the evening after work and each person there mentioned it to someone else in a telephone conversation and so on. Before breakfast was over in many of the local cafés and coffee shops the next morning, the news was broadcast as effectively as if a town crier with a bullhorn had made his way up and down every street shouting: "come one, come all, see this public spectacle about to be paraded before you."

The Federal Courtroom of the Honorable Benjamin T. Parker, Jr., was sedate in its hand crafted oak paneling, in its seats and walls that had been there so long that the original light color that white oak makes when finished and stained to a slightly yellowish hue had faded or been burnished by the atmosphere so much over the years that it gave the impression it was darkened by the smoke of countless candles or cigars, possibly.

The effect was, that in this room is a place that signifies age, respectability, wisdom and yes, even justice, for all those who enter these hallowed halls. The courtroom filled quickly as soon as the Judge's Bailiff unlocked the two massive hand carved doors that hung from iron black hinges and met together in the middle, creating the impression when opened inwardly that if you follow the vortex into the interior of the chamber, you enter into the mystery of law, truth and justice.

Those who approach the bar of justice as Defendants are indubitably awed by the prospect that their freedom or property hangs in the balance to be weighed on the scales of justice with outcome uncertain. This was especially true for criminal defendants like Earl Bryant and all those who came this morning with some kind of emotional stake in the outcome. The pure spectators like always risk nothing of themselves, but the mundane nature of their private lives weighed against the prospect of entertainment. Entertainment always wins!

The lawyers, prosecutor and defense, arrived first, followed soon after by the Defendant delivered in shackles from the Leon County Jail. After Earl was released from that cruel and humiliating bondage for now at least, he took his seat at the defense table next to his attorney Aaron Martin.

Tony had managed to slip into the courtroom about the same time and made his way up front to have a chance to say hello to his good friend, Aaron Martin, at counsel's table. Shortly after Tony, Emily Wilson and her mother Ellie Bryant came into the courtroom and made their way into the front row, just behind counsel's table in the pew-like bench seats on the Defendant's side of the courtroom.

Earl heard the familiar sound that his wife made while walking, which only those close to each other by years of living together can detect, at about the same time as Aaron touched his shoulder to signal that he should turn. He rose up to greet her with a bear like hug of one deprived of that comfort for what seemed like ages. She buried her face in the front of the hideous pastel pink colored coveralls, giving no thought to the attire, but absorbed in the moment of the reunion with her lover.

She was held in the mutual embrace for what seemed to the others as forever, but actually only seconds, to she and Earl, before they separated slightly so that Ellie could look straight up in his face and said, "They treating you fair, Earl, ain't been messing with you have they?"

"Never you mind bout that Ellie, have you been looked after?" Earl asked, with tears beginning to stream down his unshaved face in his odd way of expressing his deeply felt concern for her. He had kept all these feelings to himself ever since he had been arrested that fateful morning, and had let on to no one, not even his lawyer, that he had a personal need. But here in front of the lawyer, prosecutor team, his daughter he had not seen for ages, and the fast gathering crowd of interested spectators, he was melting down emotionally like an over-heated butter churn.

Emily ran up to where her mother was embraced by her father and joined in the expression of mutual sharing of the pathos of the moment. Earl was Surprised and heartened by the recognition of his daughter.

While the emotional healing was working its way to the surface from the long buried cloisters of the hearts of father, wife and daughter, Aaron stood by the side chatting briefly with his old college roommate on duty that morning for the *Recorder.*

In the back of the courtroom, unnoticed by any of the direct participants, stood a bearded, short, stocky old man in overalls watching the reunion up front with interest. He smiled as he recognized his old friend Earl Bryant, his wife Ellie, who he knew like the back of his hand, but the young woman also locked up in the embracing he was not Sir about, but took to be Emily, the long departed daughter of his friends the Bryants.

Johnny Caldwell, fisherman, and genuine Liberty County curmudgeon, on the special request of Bryant's lawyer, had made the long trek from the Ochlocknee at Salty's Place by catching the bus if you flag it down, that sometimes stopped on Highway 20 on its trip east to the State Capital.

Johnny didn't drive anything but a mule and his coal black yearling mule would not ever make the courthouse in time, so he had never even considered going that way.

As Johnny watched the touching scene, he thought about things. *Who is that feller talking to Earl's lawyer? Can't be a cop or Federal man, can it? Must be friendly with the Bryant side of this mess. Hmm?*

He took his seat mid-way the courtroom so that his partial deafness would not interfere with his ability to learn what was happening to his friend this morning and where he could tell when he would be called to testify, if necessary.

The rest of the courtroom was filled with local spectators, and with the exception of a few newsmen besides Tony, were more interested in the spectacle of the arraignment rather than the specifications of the indictment. In the minds of most of the public, especially those present in the courtroom other than the few family and friends of the Defendant, the mere bringing of a charge of murder was evidence enough of the Defendant's guilt. The jury would just confirm, in their view, what most everyone in Tallahassee that morning already believed, that Earl Bryant was guilty as he was about to be charged.

36. The arraignment

"All Rise," said the Bailiff as Judge Ben Parker, Jr., strode authoritatively in to the courtroom from his chambers behind the large imposing bench situated in the center of the large raised area or dais in the center of the large courtroom. His stately black robe flowed behind him like a spectral cloud and as he then took his seat in the high black leather executive chair as the Bailiff announced to the audience, "Hear Ye, hear Ye, the United States District Court for the Northern District of Florida is now in session, the Honorable Benjamin T. Parker, Jr., presiding. "Be seated please,"

Judge Ben said and looked up from his docket book in front of him, "The docket before me today is the case of the United States versus Earl Bryant, Number 4567, can we have appearances, please", and he looked out at counsel in front of him, first at the government's counsel.

"Good morning, Your Honor, I am Houston Gilchrist, Assistant United States Attorney, appearing as Counsel of Record for the Government prosecuting in this case," Houston said rising and then returning to his seat.

"Good morning Your Honor, I am Aaron Martin, private counsel for the Defendant, Earl Bryant," Aaron said, also rising to announce himself for the record and then returned to his seat.

"Very well, gentlemen, we have Mr. Bryant before me, I understand, will the Defendant and all Counsel please rise?" Judge Ben said and the lawyers for both sides and Bryant rose obediently and remained standing, waiting for what the Judge would say next.

"Mr. Bryant, you have been charged by the specially convened Federal Grand Jury with a True Bill of Indictment for Homicide of a Federal Agent, one Frank Stiller, with the charge of Murder in the first Degree, meaning the commission of the crime of murder of Frank Stiller with malice aforethought. This means, Mr. Bryant, that the Government's lawyer here, Mr. Gilchrist, must prove with evidence beyond and to the exclusion of a reasonable doubt that you killed Mr. Stiller, with malice aforethought, meaning that for one instant at least, you knew and intended to kill him.

The charge of first-degree murder under the Federal Statute you are charged with, bears a maximum punishment of death by hanging. This is a serious charge, in fact the most serious charge under Federal Law, except possibly a charge of treason against your country in time of war. Do you understand the charge that has been brought against you?

"Yes, Sir," Earl said.

"Has your lawyer, Mr. Martin, explained the risks to you and the plea options available to you in lieu of a trial?" Judge Ben asked.

"Yes, Sir, he have done that, Your Honor" Earl said.

"Then how do you plead to the charge, Mr. Bryant?" Judge Ben asked methodically, assuming he would hear the typical not guilty.

"I didn't do it, Your Honor!" Earl said with all the force at his emotional command. The Judge looked over at Aaron, requesting with a loOkay, which was all that was required, to correct the terminology for the Defendant.

Aaron took his cue and said, "Your Honor, the Defendant pleads not guilty and moves the Court for the setting of bail."

The hearing on the bail request was pretty much a mirror image of the one conducted in Magistrate Henry's Court except Houston Gilchrist did not make the same mistake of arguing against bail based on the probable guilt of Earl because the Grand Jury indictment had relieved him of that burden. The Judge was aware that the jurors had been an independent lot, calling witnesses of their own before returning the True Bill, so he was relatively confident that no mistakes had been made in the arrest and confinement.

"Mr. Martin, you can spare me your standard speech on the presumption of innocence and get right to the only issue I will consider on your request, namely the likely harm of a repeated offense of the type the Defendant has been charged with and the likelihood that he will flee the jurisdiction of this Court." Judge Parker said, trying to shorten the length of the hearing, because he had a dentist's appointment with Dr. Morgan later in the morning that had been postponed twice before, and he wasn't about to inconvenience the good Doctor anymore because of unnecessary litigation on a request he was predisposed to deny anyway.

"Thank you, Your Honor," Aaron said and commenced with this pitch for bail, "Mr. Earl Bryant has been a lifelong resident of Liberty County, Florida, and prior to this arrest, has never had any trouble with the law and more importantly, never been charged, much less convicted of any serious crime, much less the murder of any man. Just because Earl Bryant lives far into the timber country of west Florida is no indication, much less proof that he would flee this jurisdiction if released on bail. I call to testify on this issue, Mr. Johnny Caldwell, citizen of this State in Liberty County who is present this morning in this Court." Judge Parker summoned the witness forward and instructed the Clerk of the Court to swear him to tell the truth.

Johnny made his oath, lifted his hand from the old leather Bible used by Judge Parker's Clerk for that purpose, and took his seat in the witness chair. Aaron commenced with the usual background questions to qualify the witness to testify about Earl Bryant's credibility and connections to the country community of west Florida.

"Is there anything about Earl Bryant that you have noticed in the many years you have known him that suggests to you that he would leave the country if released on bail and allowed to return to his home Mr. Caldwell?" Aaron asked.

"I have knowed Earl Bryant longer than squirrels run up oak trees, and if there was anybody that stay close to home more than him, I ain't met them yet," Johnny said.

"What has he contributed to the way people live where you do, Mr. Caldwell," Aaron asked having carefully avoided asking any question that might lead to a discussion about moonshine whiskey, a point he had cautioned Johnny about before he was called to testify.

"Earl have sent food by Ellie, that is his wife sitting over yonder (pointing toward Ellie Bryant seated behind the Defense counsel table), when people have got sick. He knows practically everybody in the County, I'm figuring, by name or on sight, and I ain't never seed him snub at nobody as lesser than he is, not even the Negroes," Johnny said.

"Have you seen him in Church up in Hosford or Telogia?" Aaron asked.

"I ain't no regular attender at Church myself, Mr. Martin, though the Good Lord knows I ought to be, but I see him and Ellie all dressed up on Sunday morning goin that way quite regular and there ain't nowhere up there else to go on Sunday cause everything else is clear shut down on Sunday tighter than Dick's Hat Band. Yeah, they is Church people all right," Johnny said.

"Your witness," Aaron said and nodded to Houston Gilchrist for his cross-examination of the witnesses.

"Mr. Caldwell, you have known Earl Bryant longer than squirrels have been running up oak trees, I believe you said," Houston asked as the courtroom twitter was noticeable as he sarcastically referred to Johnny's down home expression.

"Yes, Sir, I is," Johnny said, remembering correctly Aaron Martin's admonition to answer the prosecutor's questions without elaboration.

"In fact, it would be fair to say that you and Earl are friends, good friends, correct Mr. Caldwell?"

"Yes, Sir," Johnny said.

"You fish together, visit each other's houses and are acquainted with the same people, right? In fact, you would help him out in a jamb, wouldn't you, Mr. Caldwell?" Houston said. He was violating the lawyer's conventional wisdom that you never ask a question you don't know the answer to and leading also but was gambling in this instance being fairly confident that Judge Parker would not let a Defendant indicted by one of his grand juries for first degree murder out on bail. It wouldn't matter how many of these country yokels Aaron Martin was prepared to run past Judge Ben this morning saying he was an upstanding member of the Liberty County piney woods community.

Aaron pretty much knew this too so didn't bother with an objection.

"Yes, Sir I would help, shore, if he needed it, shore I would," Johnny said, giving Houston the opening he was looking for.

"You would do anything he asked you to do, wouldn't that be fair, Mr. Caldwell?" Houston said.

"Yes, Sir, I have knowed Earl Bryant all my life. Earl is a good man and did not shoot that Stiller feller no matter how many juries you run at him, if you want my feeling on it!" Johnny said, giving Houston much more than he wanted with the answers to that question but after all this was not before a jury and the risk was acceptable even if it did backfire as far as it went.

"We rest, Your Honor," Aaron said, not bothering to make argument on this rather routine matter and very much aware that Judge Ben had already made up his mind and a few words of lawyer talk was not going to change anything.

Houston signaled the same thing with a wave of his hand.

Judge Ben announced his decision in rather stentorian and judicial sounding manner. "This is a first degree murder case against a Federal Revenue Agent. A Grand Jury regularly called, has reviewed the evidence presented by witnesses called by them and the Government and returned a True Bill of Indictment. I cannot lightly disregard the probability of a conviction in this case. Mr. Bryant has had no record of convictions or even arrests for serious offences, so I must consider all the evidence presented as to the likelihood that he would either commit another crime or flee the jurisdiction. I am convinced that Mr. Caldwell believes that his lifelong friend is a good risk for bail, but I am also aware that friendship sometimes will go the second mile for itself even when the conclusion reached is wrong. I must consider the location of the Defendant, which should not be held against him, but the temptation to drift away into the backwoods of this state and never be heard from again is one risk I am unprepared to take in the matter of a Grand Jury indictment for first-degree murder. I will deny bail, but grant an expedited trial schedule to get this matter heard sooner rather than later. If Mr. Bryant is innocent of this crime, as Mr. Caldwell so forcefully has stated, he should be given a chance to see whether the Government can prove its case to the Constitutional standard we must observe. The trial of this case will start in this Courtroom on Monday, February 15, 1934, at 10:00AM. The Defendant shall remain in the custody of the United States Marshall at the Leon County Jail until then, with a case schedule to be released by my Clerk later today for procedural matters. This Court will be in recess."

The Bailiff cried out the "all rise" and the Judge left the bench.

The scene in the courtroom was a buzz with the developments in the case, especially among Aaron, his client, and few supporters. Tony Callaway hung around the fringe of that group, hoping to gain an introduction to Johnny Caldwell, the perfect window view of the scenery of the Liberty County culture he had been hoping for. Now all he had to do was sell Johnny on the idea.

37. Escort to Liberty

Just as soon as the Judge left the bench, Ellie, no longer able to restrain herself, left her seat on the front row and rushed up and threw her arms around Earl who was absorbing in his mind what had just happened to his body in court. He could deal with the denial of bail because his lawyer had prepared him for that, but the thought of the trial with live witnesses testifying about him and what he was supposed to have done brought a new feeling to this fiercely independent and self-confident man he had never had before. Never in his life had he experienced a fear like he did at this moment.

That Judge actually said death by hanging. Ain't never been faced with that. That damn fool George Drucker would say any damn thing they want him to. My ass is done for, but I ain't quitting, by no long shot at it.

He turned around in the desperate embrace that Ellie had about him and held her fiercely as though this was the last time and he might never see her again. He saw Emily also standing by, and was amazed to even find her here, much less showing that she really cared as she obviously now did, or she wouldn't be here in Court. That encouraged him, but it didn't change the predicament he felt he was in.

His lawyer was explaining some nonsense or other about procedure, or so it seemed to him, as he contemplated what he was really facing in this thing. Nothing to do but fight it he thought, for Earl Bryant, by God, was not going to give that George Drucker the satisfaction of him pleading mercy before the Court to spend the rest of his life at Raiford and then walk out of the courtroom and Tallahassee and pick up the pieces of his whiskey business that had taken him a life time to build in Liberty County. No, Sir that would never do, not without a fight.

Elsewhere in the Courtroom, Johnny Caldwell rose and slowly headed out of the courtroom feeling, dejectedly, that he had let his friend down, since bail had been denied and he was the only witness.

Tony finished his brief discussion with Aaron and hurried out of the Courtroom to try and catch up with Johnny Caldwell. Johnny got outside of the Courthouse and stood there on the sidewalk for a few minutes trying to figure how he would find one of those buses to get him back home. The lawyer had given him a roundtrip ticket, but he had no idea how to find the bus station. Tony came along side and introduced himself.

"Mr. Caldwell, I'm Tony Callaway, Reporter for *The Tallahassee Recorder* covering the Bryant case. I would like to ask you a few questions if you don't mind; it's for my story about Earl and his case."

Johnny looked at Tony and thought, *Newspaper Reporter, he said, ain't got much use for them newspapers. Cain't read anyhow but he did seem awful friendly with Earl's lawyer before the start of things. Must be an "OK" feller for that.*

"You say Newspaper? You will put my name in one of them damn things if I talk to you?" Johnny asked, trying to feel him out as to his intentions about this interview, looking Tony square in the eye, trying to determine whether he could trust this man.

"Not really, Johnny, unless you want me to, I'm more interested in the effect the moonshine business has had on the people out there in the country and the little towns across this part of the state. We're headed into a new thing with Prohibition ending soon and I figure it's going to hit some people pretty hard. I don't know any of those people, they wouldn't talk to me anyhow, but you might make it possible for them to trust and talk to me. What do you say, I give you a ride back home and we get acquainted, sort of. I won't write anything to hurt your friend, not personally anyway, and you give me a chance to prove it. What about that?" Tony asked, measuring up this grizzled old man and seeing in him a kind of brutal honesty, the kind that wouldn't mind telling you to take a hike if you got out of line as he saw it, or level with you if you didn't.

Tony had learned the hard way to be frank with people and to not try to be too clever. No one likes to be manipulated and the little gain that you got from it was collected back against you the next time you tried to get to know a source really well. It just worked out that way, he thought, so he had just quit trying that approach long ago.

"Well, I do got to get home somehow and it might jest as well be you as some bus that I get to ride in," Johnny said.

"Fine then, Johnny, why don't we get a bite to eat first and then head on back to Bryant Country," Tony said, and the two men walked at Tony's suggestion over to the Garden Grill where Tony or the *Recorder*, more accurately, financially speaking at least, hosted lunch. If Johnny Caldwell had ever been in a restaurant like this center of political gossip before, you would have been greatly Surprised, observing the way he acted. He walked in quietly and remained that way during the lunch with Tony. The other customers that day were all a buzz about the newest case in town and there was nothing else on the minds or lips of the Grill customers.

"When we get to Hosford, where do I turn?" Tony asked Johnny, having no idea where he was headed.

"Left up ahead at that there cross roads once you get into town," Johnny said.

"How do you make a living Johnny, if you care to tell me?" Tony said, hoping to open up a connection with this old friend of Earl Bryant's and gain his confidence enough to reach the underbelly of Liberty County society with which only with a man like Johnny Caldwell he could connect.

"You ain't there yet," Johnny said as Tony's car barreled down Highway 20 approaching the Ochlocknee River Bridge at the breakneck speed of forty-five. They were in a 1933 four door black Ford Sedan, newly acquired for Dick Powers, Editor, as a *Recorder* company car for his personal use only and only loaned out to Tony, for what Dick considered a harebrained assignment.

"You never can tell Tony, what those Liberty County hicks will do once they see an automobile; hell, they'll never talk to anybody with enough cash money to buy a new automobile which automatically makes them a Republican in their eyes, and they damn Sir won't talk to a newspaper reporter with one of these," the Editor had said that morning before Tony had successfully twisted his arm with those dreams about a Pulitzer Prize coming under Dick Powers' watch.

"Well give me an old one then," Tony had said, implying Powers might miss out on his great chance for vicarious fame if he didn't let him borrow it; but there was only one and it was either this or nothing, and Powers had reluctantly agreed to the loan of his new car for the trip.

The Ford had barely made the edge of the bridge when Johnny sat up like a start in his seat and shouted, "Damn, Mr. Callaway, that river is clean out of its banks and climbing. Dam must have blown out!" Just as he said that Tony noticed that the water was flowing through the steel railing and over the driving lanes in a rapidly increasing surge like a wall of water overflowing a saucepan.

The water had covered the surface and was rapidly rising above the Ford's tires as Tony slammed on his brakes that caused the new Ford Sedan to skid uncontrollably until it became buoyant in the rising water like a crude boat.

Damn, Tony thought, with a speed too quick to formulate actual connected words he would have written in his paper describing the maelstrom he was witnessing, *flood over, where'd that come? Why? No warning! Get out before too late, hurry!* But even thinking, which can move at the speed of light in a dark cavern, was not fast enough to change the disaster they were facing. The Ford banged off the left guard rail before tipping over violently as the whole bridge was torn loose from its foundation and dumped Tony, Johnny, the Ford and for a few brief seconds, the bridge structure itself. Then, before anything that wouldn't float, sunk out of sight, into the unnatural raging current of the Ochlocknee River, like an ungainly cork striving to find its balance in a topsy turvy world they found themselves in the middle of the maelstrom.

The Ford was made well in its frame, but it was not watertight, and by the time it had floated for a few seconds, it began to take on water like a torpedoed merchant ship in front of one of the Kaiser's Wolf packs.

Tony understood little of what was happening to him and Johnny, but they had sense enough without having to debate the point, to get the hell out of the sinking ship the truck had become. He and Johnny scrambled unceremoniously out of the side windows which fortunately happened to be rolled down and hung on for dear life as the sinking hulk drifted southward away from Highway 20; and was soon out of sight of anybody who happened to be standing on the main road just short of the flooded bridge, but as bad luck would have it, there happened to be none.

Putting all this into a timeframe, by the time he and Johnny had finished lunch in Tallahassee and Tony had argued with his Editor for an hour or so to get the car, and made the trip west on Highway 20, where they had reached the bridge disaster scene on the Ochlocknee, it was already starting to get dark.

No self-respecting City slicker from Tallahassee would be caught dead in Liberty County after dark this time of year, but Tony was determined to find his story and he had Johnny Caldwell, a native son, along for insurance if not protection. But the rest of the folks had long ago pulled into home or other safe destination for the evening and no bystanders happened to be available to heed the cry for help Tony and Johnny were sending into the unforgiving, dark otherwise, soundless air. They would have to sink or swim it appeared, and swimming was the far better alternative of the two for now.

38. Cellmates

Earl was transported in cuffs and shackles all the way back to the hell pit of a jail where he was forced now to wait for his trial in February. There would be exciting and even optimistic moments as his lawyers put together his defense, but the bulk of the time would have to be endured as a trapped and cornered man facing an uncertain future. There was nothing for it now but to hunker down and endure it.

He was led back into his cell where Jack Sanford waited for anything; even another man's suffering to relieve his boredom. Jack took one look at Earl's long face and asked as soon as the guard had left,

"I take it you ain't getting out of here on no bail money, Earl?" The one protocol that was certain in any penal institution in America is the unwritten rule that you don't talk freely in front of the enemy. That risk was gone, as it seemed to Jack. Jail guard or prison wardens were all the same as far as the inmates were concerned, enemies to those longing for freedom, whether justified or not. The only risk in talking freely to a fellow inmate was that he might be a plant for the prosecution. Earl had decided he could not be too careful so he didn't respond.

"No bail, Jack. Looks like you're stuck with me till February, whether you like it or not," Earl said, and plopped down on his bunk and rolled over against the cell wall placing his back between he and Jack Sanford, signaling he really didn't want conversation right now. Jack understood this reaction but pressed forward anyway.

"Shore enough now Earl, the lawyer didn't spring you out of here?" There was a stony silence from the other side of the cell for a few long minutes before Earl answered softly.

"I aim to set my mind on it Jack and it ain't pretty," Earl said, still not turning over in his bunk.

"You mean you'd try to break out of this place, Earl?" Jack asked incredulously, for from his experience, the Leon County jail might be bad, but nobody had to his knowledge ever escaped from the place.

"Nah, nah, nothing like that," Earl said, "I mean I'm setting my mind on what might come if I lose this thing." Jack was astounded at what he had just heard. He had been in trouble with the law often, and being a poor man he had never had the luxury of a high priced lawyer fighting for him. Jack could not imagine how anyone, no matter what they had done, who had a capable attorney could still lose.

"Shorely Earl, you ain't no way expecting to lose this, is you?"

Earl slowly turned over in his bunk with his arm behind his head and said, "I got a snitch on me and they somehow got the gun with my prints all over it. What's a feller to do in a case like that?"

"Damn!" was about all Jack could say as he thought on it for a few minutes. Then the room went silent as they stared at each other deep in their own thoughts. One man facing the possible if not probable end of his life with a rope at the end of it, and the other practically tired of continuing the path of his own.

Jack's head was still pounding and the long awaited telltale reflective twitches and shakes of the tremens were undulating throughout his body. Earl watched the old man thoughtfully and began to realize he was approaching troubled waters. It is difficult for a man, at the depth of his own depression or fear, to see that someone else is in more trouble than yourself but Jack Sanford was approaching those very dire straits.

"Jailer!" Earl shouted out, "This man is in trouble, can we get some medical help in here?" "Jailer?" Within minutes, Jack had been carried out of the cell on a stretcher and Earl had been left on his own.

Before long, inertia having played itself out, he soon returned to the solitude he had thought, before Jack's intervention, that he desperately desired. He was now not so Sir that moping around about something he had no control of anyway was the best way to approach this thing. A little company, even from a new found friend, had not been so terrible after all. In fact, he rather missed it.

39. Floating

The only trouble was that Johnny could not swim and Tony, who was struggling to swim on his own in the wet clothes and in the cold river water, had a difficult choice to make and he had to make it in a hurry. Johnny bobbed like a cork as long as the natural buoyancy of his human body was given any assistance at all in the process; but like most non swimmers, the fear and panic of drowning sets in so fast that they do all the wrong things and sink.

Johnny Caldwell was no exception to the rule. Tony watched with horror as Johnny, just a few feet away from him, submerged below the raging flood tide of the river current and failed to reappear. Tony's instinct for Survival was overridden by his belief that he had a chance to save Johnny and of such reactions, sometimes heroes are made.

With one or two vigorous strokes in that direction, he grabbed Johnny by the collar of his rough homespun shirt and swam for all his might downstream to give him the maximum leverage in the rescue effort, using the momentum of the flood current which was substantial.

At the same time, he made an attempt to angle toward the western bank of the river, but was making little headway in that direction when a large log came floating by within reach. Tony grabbed on to one of the limbs of the floating tree remnant and jerked Johnny over to him with all his might to get his body moving his direction. Then with a feat of superhuman strength that would have made Superman or Mighty Mouse proud, released his grip on the shirt collar and reached across Johnny's body to secure him against the unsteady log.

At the same time, he said, "Easy man, I've got you. Trust me Johnny!" This soothing assurance, given in the time honored way of lifeguards the world over, had the desired effect to still the natural instincts of the drowning in Johnny to fight against even his rescuer. However, he allowed himself to be held securely alongside the floating boat like log as it hurled its way recklessly downstream in the control of the natural current.

The blackness of the night added nothing to help the men in their peril for if they been able to see clearly the derelict trees, stumps and branches of all sizes moiling in the flood waters, their sense of panic would have been even greater. To Johnny and Tony, this did not seem possible. No greater peril could be imagined as they lay in the pitch black of night alongside the huge log bobbing up and down on the surface with the log like two water soaked wharf rats, wondering what hit them.

The Ochlocknee River originates far up in Georgia near Albany and flows southward to cross the Florida border east of Havana. It crosses under the highway that is now US 90 about fifteen miles west of Talla-hassee. This is where the highway connects with the rest of West Florida before it meets the headwaters of Lake Talquin on the way to Quincy. This man-made lake is five or so miles wide and fifteen or twenty miles long. Highway 20 runs east and west below the lake on the way to Hosford and Bristol. Above the bridge, a mile or so north of there, the river is stopped up like a cork by the Talquin Electric Company power dam. That is it had been until the dam had ruptured this day, and the river had unceremoniously dumped Tony and Johnny's Ford into the raging current of an unnatural flood.

Later investigations would reveal that the "cork" had sprung a leak from undetermined causes and twenty miles of lake water will turn any substantial leak into a fissure and then a collapse in a hurry. Regardless of cause, the effects were predictable and the floodwaters raging down the Ochlocknee River valley that morning had swept the previously thought to be impregnable bridge structure downstream like all the other flotsam and jetsam, tree, root, and branches alike. Tony and Johnny had just accidentally received an unfortunate case of terribly bad timing and location to be caught there.

However, after floating downstream at a breakneck pace for what seemed to them like hours, the log was headed for a landfall on a spot on the west side of the new boundaries of the expanded river where the Ochlocknee ordinarily makes a sharp eastern turn for a short stretch before turning back on its southern course.

The slope of the land above that spot was uphill substantially, so the rising river had just moved the shoreline to a higher elevation. This was extremely fortunate, or that's just the way it is sometimes, because the timing was impeccable for these two erstwhile victims. As the log had drifted in its search for a path downstream, it had settled gently against a smooth section of the new bank and had stopped.

At the same time, Tony's feet struck the new bottom of the river and realized he was now able, for the first time since being dumped into the deluge, to stand up on the firm earth. He stepped down on the bottom and his foot found a log or some other standing place, which permitted him to stand and survey the invisible shoreline. He made his way carefully to a place where he could walk out of the water on to dry land.

Johnny was still floating on his back so Tony had to wade back into the water to where he could reach Johnny with his hands to pull him to safety. He shook and shouted Johnny awake from the slumber he had miraculously fallen into which had allowed Johnny to miss most of the fear and anxiety that would ordinarily grip a person deathly afraid of the water. Tony's rescue shout and shake had caused him to come awake in the now shallow water with a start at Tony's command and he sat up like a faux corpse at an Irish wake.

However, even though a river fisherman, Johnny knew the terrain fairly well at least in the daylight hours.

"What in the hell has happened here?" Johnny asked, with the first words out of his mouth.

"I wish I knew Johnny, all I know is we got dumped in the river and this log saved our bacon. Where we are at is anybody's guess but safe, if not sound, we are. Are you all right Johnny? Anything broken or hurt?" Tony asked, standing there shivering in the cold night air.

"Naw, nothing broke, least wise as far as I know.

"No point in hanging out here Johnny, let's get out of this mess and try to make it to some dry ground," Tony said, as he mushed his way through the shallow water and felt his way up the bank in the dark until he found a level spot leading to dry ground. With Johnny right behind him, they flung themselves on a bed of leaves under a canopy of live oaks and collapsed, wet, cold and exhausted, waiting for daylight.

40. Coffee and danish

Aaron was having his morning coffee and danish at the Garden Grill. He was joined that day by his father, who the day before had a meeting with the Board of Trustees where a bridge permit application was being considered on behalf of one of his clients. The Board of Trustees in Florida consists of top elected officials of the state government where all-important decisions were made affecting important public projects, with private contracts attached attract powerful lobbyists and lawyers pushing for or against one side or the other. This was the world that Roland Martin excelled in: the world of persuasive push and political pull.

The radio was softly playing Mood Indigo, by Ellington, in the background as the two lawyers took turns discussing their respective cases in between glances at the headlines, sips of coffee and comment on an occasional article in the *Recorder*.

"We interrupt this broadcast for a news flash!" the announcer said, gaining everyone's attention in the restaurant, including the Martin table.

"Wonder what that's all about?" Aaron said, and Roland cocked his head slightly to hear the very soft sound of the news announcer over the restaurant's background noise.

"Turn that radio up!" somebody yelled out and the waitress dutifully reached over behind the counter holding an assortment of bakery items and turned the volume knob up so that all in the room could easily hear the news flash expected immediately.

"We are sorry to announce, Ladies and Gentlemen, but there has been a disaster at the Dam on the Ochlocknee River. For reasons as yet unknown, the Talquin Electric Dam has ruptured and a veritable torrent of water has been thrown down stream flooding out the Highway 20 Bridge. Numerous automobiles have been submerged or washed away in some cases and rescue efforts are underway as we speak. The number of casualties is unknown but we will keep you posted as we receive further bulletins. We return you now to the regularly scheduled program," the announcer said, and the melodious strains of Mood Indigo were absorbed in the sound of the room as the clientele jabbered away in excited undertones and the waitress turned the knob back to a lesser volume so that the real business of the morning could be resumed, the private conversations of the powerful and the meek of the earth.

Roland Martin said nothing for a few minutes and seemed to Aaron to stare into the void of whatever it was his very active mind was examining. He knew his father well enough not to interrupt him in one of these reveries. But there were limits to this, for even Aaron's patience and respect as he too had other thoughts on his mind, such as the preparation for Earl's defense. He used these rare moments with his Father to extract all the wisdom and experience he could. He thought reflectively for a few more minutes and asked, "Dad is something wrong, you're too quiet this morning just for a news bulletin?" Roland heard the question and seemed to come out of his somnambulistic trance with a start.

"Oh, sorry Aaron, that bulletin stirred something in my memory. Do you remember old man Carlson from Quincy? He owned a good share of the land on the western side of Lake Talquin, wanted to develop it, but Talquin Electric had what they call a Project Area reserved against building below a certain elevation. I forget the level. Well, I represented Talquin Electric in the permitting process, you know, getting it through the Board of Trustees, like today on the Highway 98 Bridge permit application down at Alligator Point, only bigger. Carlson, a tough old bird, personality wise sort of, like your client Bryant, threatened to blow up the damn thing, pardon my pun, if they wouldn't let him develop to where he wanted. He was capable of it too, the old cuss. I was just wondering, that's all?"

"You mean, Dad that Carlson may have sabotaged the Talquin Damn just to get even? I thought I remembered that he got around those restrictions somehow," Aaron asked.

"He did get around them, but it cost him a bundle in legal fees and loads of time. The project still hasn't quite caught on and I'll bet he's hopping mad, mad enough to encourage a little leak to start in that thing," Roland said.

"But wouldn't that damage his own project?" Aaron asked, thinking like the lawyer businessman he was becoming.

"Yeah in the short run, but Talquin Electric will rebuild and the new damn and all the attention will be bound to draw in more folks to build lake places. He's a smart old cuss, that Carlson," Roland said.

"I worry more about the poor souls trapped in that flood, Dad, that's inhospitable territory south of the Highway 20 Bridge, and its winter time too. It wouldn't surprise me if there were a few fatalities. There just might be a wrongful death case or two coming out of that. I wonder if Earl will introduce me to some of those folks if we are so fortunate to get him off. Have you thought any more about his defense Dad, it looks pretty hopeless to me?" Aaron said.

"Don't worry about it Son, you'll find a defense and remember there are no eye witnesses and that so called confession will never hold up. The only thing that worries me is that gun. It had his prints all over it. Wonder if that gun was truly his?" Roland asked.

"Oh it's his all right Dad, why did you think not?" Aaron asked with puzzlement.

"Oh nothing really, just a thought that went through my head, probably nothing to it. You always have "the golden thread argument" Son, Northern District Juries will always listen to an appeal for reasonable doubt. Say, I have to run, that Trustee's meeting will be starting soon and I want to get my points in at the beginning of the session. The Commissioner of Agriculture is sympathetic to my case and he falls asleep pretty easily. He's getting pretty old, you know. Will you join your Mother and me for dinner this weekend?"

"Sir Dad, Betty and I will be there Friday about six."

"Sir Son, see you then," Roland said, as he rose from the now generally called Martin table and left the Garden Grill. Aaron finished his coffee and danish and the latest opinion page in the *Recorder* before leaving for his duties for the remainder of the day.

41. The remnants

Dawn came as it always did that December morning. After the flood the Ochlocknee River Valley south of Highway 20 was transformed into a veritable lake of immense proportions. It wouldn't last long once the volume of Lake Talquin had emptied its contents into the flooding drain way to the sea, but it would be impressive had someone been able to see the whole thing by a flight over that country by plane. That view this morning was confined to highflying birds like fish ospreys and possibly migrating geese. The light appeared gradually and the darkness lifted like a melting blanket of fog. Three shadowy shapes, which would in the presence of light, be revealed as figures of men, made their way cautiously along the river's edge in the early dawn.

There were three of them that morning, looking for a new spot to set up for the day's fishing. The unusually high water would make the chance of a catch improbable but there was nothing else for them to do but try. The three fishermen had come to this particular spot because of the relatively steeper bank stemming the flood surge at this location and acted as a natural barrier to create an eddy where catfish and other edible fish just might be hovering out of the water's surge.

Whether that was true or not, it seemed to these men the best place to try. These were Negro men who lived in the river swamp country where fishing was the main source of food along with hunting the occasional deer, wild hog or turkey they could shoot or sometimes catch or trap.

The lead man paused in his approach to the river as he moved into the little swale in the land that was cut by erosion over time into where a bed of oak leaves seemed to be occupied by two strange objects that didn't quite look like they belonged there

"What's that yonder?" Israel Manley, the lead man asked, pointing ahead to two figures lying prone in the bed of leaves and turning his head to the two men behind him. Hoover and Nooby came along side Israel and stood there with him studying the two unmoving figures in the early light. "That's people there, white folks seem like," Nooby said, and the others nodded their silent agreement.

"Drunk maybe, or caught by the flood?" Hoover Spencer asked, noticing how still the now recognized two men lay, as if dead.

"Let's go see," Israel said, and all three of the Negro men cautiously eased their way down into the swale and paused, waiting in front of the two silent figures as if they expected someone or something to make some sense out of this appearance before them.

Their desires were answered it seemed as Tony came into consciousness and suddenly realized he was freezing cold in his wet clothes and unsheltered location. He looked up for no apparent reason. The three men had made not a sound, since Israel had spotted the sleeping men and called the fishing expedition to a halt. Tony saw the three silent figures standing before him like three sentinels on the dawn watch in a medieval castle, their erect fishing poles standing beside them like lances.

"Hello," Tony said, not having anything particular to say to the three strangers standing before him, but felt he needed to say something in this awkward situation.

"What you want down here, white folks?" Nooby asked, as he stood there staring at the strange phenomenon before him and not knowing what to say either in the mutually awkward moment.

By this time, Johnny had come awake and as he looked up he recognized Nooby Oakley as one of the Negro men employed by Earl Bryant and said,

"Nooby is that you?" Nooby sprung back as though struck, not out of fear of Johnny Caldwell but at the total surprise and astonishment to find his former Boss Man's closest friend laying there wet as a drowned swamp rat at a place no one expected him to be this morning.

"Mr. Johnny, it shore is, what you doing down here in the river swamp this morning?" Nooby asked in equal astonishment. Johnny and Tony raised themselves up and stood shivering cold in the early winter morning air.

"Don't suppose you fellows could stir up a fire so we could dry out of these wet clothes?" Johnny asked hopefully.

"Yas Suh Mr. Johnny," Nooby said, "We'll set one over in the clearing yonder," pointing to a flat more or less open area away from the swale and headed that way quickly with his two helpers.

Any self-respecting Negro, whiskey still hand or not, was practically born knowing how to set a fire on a moment's notice in this fuel abundant territory. Nooby gathered up a stray lightered knot which he split apart by pounding on the edge of a convenient root nearby into fragments ideal for kindling, with some relatively dry leaves and reached into his overalls and pulled out a flint and steel that every man carried on him. You never knew when a fire might be needed and this was just one of those times. Besides, on a cold December morning like this one, the men would have had a fire going soon anyway to warm themselves for fishing whether or not they encountered two white men soaked to the gills down in the deepest part of the Ochlocknee River swamp.

Within a few minutes, Nooby's skillful efforts had a roaring fire going as the two wet and exhausted white men huddled as close as they dared to the blazing and warming flames as the three Negro men stood around waiting to see what would happen next.

"You boys wouldn't have anything to eat, would you Nooby? Come on in here to the fire, its cold this morning," Johnny said hopefully, looking up at the three Negro men hanging back respectfully.

"We got some hoecake and sausage in a pail. If you want any, we'll share some with you, if you want it" Nooby said. He reached his arms out to take the lunch pail handed him by Israel, opened it and handed out some of the food. After that, the three men sat down by the roaring fire in the vacant spaces and warmed their hands and joined in the communal breakfast.

At a time like this, hunger, cold and convenience will override race considerations every time. And this was an illustration of the old southern expression that there is only a half an hour's difference between hoecake and biscuits.

There are no preferred seats by an open woods fire because the smoke follows the wind and eventually one seat is just as uncomfortable as another. In fact, dodging smoke from around an outdoor fire on a cold day is the closest thing to a democracy you will ever find. Everybody has an equal chance to escape the troublesome smoke. The warmth of the fire more than made up the difference, however. Before long, all of the fire sitters, black and white alike, were engaged in the process of eating their breakfast, getting acquainted with each other and listening to the incredible story of the flood and the sunken bridge.

42. Visitation

Ellie finally prevailed on Emily to accompany her on a visit to see Earl in jail. The mood in that place was depressing enough just thinking about it, but to actually go there and see someone you care about was almost an insurmountable emotional obstacle, especially for Earl's daughter. Ellie had come on a weekly basis but so far, Emily had offered support only from a far.

She had found the courage with her Husband's late support to make it to the arraignment but the courthouse was safe and even dignified. Seeing Earl in court and even hugging him in public with his small group of supporters was one thing, but to sit opposite him in an interview room at the jail and discuss things so personal such as his possible fear of death, was another matter altogether. With her Husband's encouragement, who had become quite attached to Ellie living with them, Emily had reluctantly agreed to drive her Mother down from Bainbridge to the jail.

The interview room was small, dark and damp; reeking of the unforgettable smells of aged sweat seeped into everything. The small metal table and metal straight back chairs were positioned together in the center of the room, cold, unpleasant and as lonely as the hearts of the inmates who were permitted visitors there.

Eddie Johnson, a jail guard, led the visitors into the room and they took their seats to wait for Earl's arrival. Eddie left them there as he left the room and headed back into the jail to retrieve his prisoner.

"This is some place," Emily said, not really knowing what to say, but saying anything relieved some of the tension hanging over the room like a black blanket waiting to wrap them up in the despair of the place.

"It shore is," Ellie said, equally aware of the danger the place presented to them emotionally. Before they had very long to wrestle with the demons of their imaginations, the unmistakable sounds of approaching footsteps could be heard coming their way down the dimly lit corridor. The guard and Earl stood just outside the door and the unmistakable sound of the key turning in the old lock announced that

Earl was about to be delivered to them for the precious thirty-minute visit allotted to inmates under inflexible jailhouse rules.

The door opened slowly and Earl walked into the room. When he saw Ellie and Emily, who had silently risen to their feet waiting for him, he moved quickly into the room stretching his arms out which were immediately filled by his family. They rocked back and forth gently absorbing all the emotion that radiated from him in his loneliness and despair like a sardonic melody of grief absorbed into the longing from their caring. Finally, they parted without apparent direction as if the composer had marked that place on the musical score and they stood there looking at each other waiting for the right moment to begin making a symphony of reunited feelings of love again.

"Ellie, Emily, you've come! Bless you," Earl said.

"Dad, are you all right, are they treating you…?" Emily stammered it out trying to hold back the tears. "Yes, child, they ain't harming me, not yet anyhow," Earl said. Words were beyond Ellie's reach as the thought of the "death by hanging" pronouncement by the Judge in Court still reverberated in her memory. It was like a guitar string plucked by a perpetual motion machine stuck on a permanent sour note, so that the burden of the visit had devolved by emotional necessity to the daughter.

She intuitively understood the role thrust upon her and took it without hesitation or need of explanation.

"Dad, have you talked to Mr. Martin, about the case, I mean…..?," Ellie asked hesitatingly, knowing deep down that the question was foolish for she knew that answer to be yes, but she was unable to ask the really important question, such as will he succeed and get him off?

Earl understood the real question too and answered the one that wasn't asked, to the relief of his daughter's hesitation. Ellie stood by dumbstruck, too afraid to speak.

"He thinks we got a chance but truthfully Daughter; Ellie, you need to hear this too; Drucker's going to try to make an end of me and there's that damned gun," Earl said gloomily, and thinking worse. *Hang me, they will, guilty or no, cause somebody got to pay the price for it. Who's going to care for Ellie when I'm done for, that's what I can't ask nobody, family or no, but Emily being here gives me pause,* he thought, not willing to share his deepest thoughts on the matter.

"You have the best lawyer in town, Dad, Hugh checked him out. His Daddy may be better but he's hung up the trial work they say and Aaron's the second best at least, and I'm going to remain hopeful," Emily said, trying to embolden her Father's courage and hopefulness without speaking out loud her true feelings, that it looked just as hopeless to her as it sounded in the shallow courage coming from her father's voice.

"Can we bring you anything, Dad, are you comfortable?"

"No child, it'll be all right, you'll see," Earl said bravely, as the door behind them reverberated by the turning of the rusty lock and Eddie Johnson entered the room announcing that their time was up. The Bryants embraced once more not realizing that the thirty minutes had vanished like a buck deer on opening day and released each other quickly to permit Eddie Johnson to do his duty and return Earl to his cell. They followed them out into the corridor and Ellie resumed the lead and found her voice at last to show Emily the way to the exit from this dismal place.

43. Out of place

"How come you white folks down here is wet as scrub washing in the swamp with no boat or nothing, Mr. Johnny?" Nooby asked, using the preferred formal first name address by black men to the whites they knew, last names being uncomfortable for most Negroes to use by a custom whose origins nobody could remember.

"It's a flood, Nooby, and we got dumped in it, automobile and all at the 20 Bridge, which is gone now, if you was wondering," Johnny Caldwell said, clearing up exactly nothing for Nooby.

Tony saw the blank expression on Nooby and the others' faces and instantly realized they had understood nothing in Johnny's explanation, so he tried to do better. The wood fire was warming him now and the food and was bringing life back in him which unleashed his very active reporter's mind. "Let me introduce myself men, I'm Tony Callaway, news reporter for a Tallahassee newspaper and Johnny offered to bring me down here to Liberty County to interview some of the people who knew Earl Bryant. You may not know it, but Mr. Bryant is on trial for murder of a Federal Revenue Agent down here back in early December this past year. He's being held in jail up in Tallahassee and Johnny here had come up to testify for his release. Well, the Judge wouldn't turn him loose, so I offered to bring Johnny back home and we made it only as far as the Highway 20 Bridge when the flood came. Johnny and I don't know what happened to cause it but we figure the dam on Lake Talquin must have blown out and dumped twenty miles of lake water down this river swamp and swept us with it and here we are!" Tony explained all this to the amazement of the men who didn't even know there was a dam up river since none of them had ever left the river country their entire lives.

"Dam", Israel thought, *That water got to come from somewhere, but what's a dam for and newspaper what?* "You white folks done swum all the way down here in this river swamp, but you is here now, and that's the long and the shorts of it," Israel said as sarcastically as any Negro dared, directly with white people present, that is. In their own conversations and among themselves, sarcasm was regular fare.

"Did any of you know Earl Bryant?" Tony asked, hopefully.

"We all knowed him," Nooby said, and Hoover and Israel nodded their agreement vigorously.

"What kind of a man is Earl Bryant and how did each of you know him?" Tony asked, having to rely on his memory for this record since no note taking was possible under the circumstances.

"We worked for him at de Lagoon Still, that's how," Nooby explained.

"I'm not too familiar with how a still works; maybe you fellows could explain it to me?" Tony asked.

The three men looked at each other nervously, not very ready to speak just yet, and looking for a leader to emerge to show them the way out of this dilemma between loyalty to Earl and the need to escape the present awkward demand that they tell it all. There was a natural distrust of white men by Negroes in Liberty County or anywhere else in the Deep South at that time, especially about something as sensitive as the inner workings of their former employer's illegal whiskey operation. They desperately needed some guidance here or fall back to the natural position taken in such situations and play dumb.

Johnny Caldwell saw the problem immediately and jumped into the breach. "What Mr. Tony means boys, is he needs to know all you know about Mr. Earl and his liquor business and that he's a friend to Mr. Earl and I can vouch for him on that" Johnny said.

Johnny Caldwell was trusted as a reliable man in the river country of Liberty County. As a river fisherman, he had pushed his one-man skiff up and down the Ochlocknee for as long as anyone alive could now remember. Johnny was a simple man, loyal to a fault to friends and cold and hard as steel to those who weren't. The truth was you just knew where you stood with Johnny Caldwell, either way. In addition, he was well known to all the Negroes of the river country if not personally, at least by reputation, and this fact alone assured the three river men that he and his companion could be trusted. If Johnny vouched for you, you were in, so to speak, and he was doing just that this morning for Tony Callaway, "*Tallahassee Recorder*" reporter, who could get exactly nowhere with these men without it.

So far, Tony's plan was working, although he never in a million years would have expected to be sitting here by a roaring wood fire miles down the Ochlocknee River country drying out from a flood soaking.

"We tended the mash fire and hauled stuff in and out the Lagoon," Nooby said.

"You keep referring to the still as the "Lagoon," what or where was that exactly?" Tony asked anyone who would answer.

"Over yonder," Hoover said, pointing over his shoulder to the west.

"But why was it called that?" Tony asked, figuring out that he needed to keep his questions to one subject at a time to reduce confusion.

"Boss man found that old slough where the river been years before and covered it up to hide from prying eyes and he call it the "Lagoon" cause a lagoon it was once," Nooby explained.

"How does a whiskey still work, Nooby?" Tony asked, pleasantly.

"You have to set up the mash barrels for the corn and yeast to make it work. That take three to four day to work for the ferment of mash ready for cooking in the kettle, which cook off to a thumper by a stretch of tube. From there, to the cooling' barrel with the worm in it where the whiskey drips out into a fruit jar or something to catch it in," Nooby explained the process so familiar to him but utterly beyond his ability to put into words that any person unfamiliar, like Tony, would understand.

"Wait a minute, Nooby; let's break that down into little pieces, so a city fellow like me can understand it. What goes into the mash barrel, for example?" Tony asked deferring to Nooby's superior knowledge.

"Okay, the barrels are a regular wood hoop barrel that holds 55 gallons of mash mix. Boss Man used corn meal, white sugar and yeast to make it ferment, capped off with shorts. That mash cooks in itself and makes mash beer, as we calls it, taking the working time. When Boss man says it ready, we pour the mash mix in the copper cooker with a fire under it. The top is capped off with a one gallon wood keg, sealed with dough, in case it blows off with the pressure. A piece of copper tube run from there to the thumper and they calls it the worm," Nooby explained, taking a pause for breath.

Tony jumped in at this point, "What's a thumper, Nooby?"

It's a large keg with another tube running out of it to the cooling barrel. I don't know what it do to the inside but it make a noise like a thumpin' or bumpin' or like that. That's what the name thumper for it is, anyways" Nooby said.

"And what's "the worm", Nooby?" Tony asked, having figured out that the cooking mash is converted to gas with mostly alcohol and that it needed to condense back to liquid in the cooling barrel before it made whiskey you could drink, but he just wanted to learn the meaning of the terminology used by these men.

"The worm is a piece of copper tubing that coil like a snake inside the cooling barrel before it stick out at the spout at the bottom where the whiskey drip out," Nooby explained.

"I see" said Tony, pleasantly enough but understanding very little of it. "Do you suppose you boys could show us where the Lagoon site is? My paper will pay you for your time, since we'd be taking your fishing time?"

"You mean pay with real money, Mister?" Hoover said, with a rising excitement in his voice, since the end of the still operation there had been no work or money coming their way.

"Yes Hoover, and by the way, how'd you get the name Hoover, that seems a strange sort of name. The only person I know of by that name was the President elected in 1929 but you were too old to be named for him by then. Nooby, you must be 20 years old at least, I'd guess", Tony said.

"Yas Suh, that's who I'm called for, but it was hung on me later on. I was named something else by my mammy and pappy. I don't know how that come about, it just stuck on me , shore enough and cain't shake it. But it's all right, one names bout the same as another long as they knows it when the food is cooking, and time come to call me to eat" Nooby explained.

"Yes boys, my paper will pay you each a dollar if you show Johnny and me where that old still site is. "Yas Suh! We can do that, shore," they all said in unison.

"Well, kill this fire boys, and head us on over there. I've been there once or twice but I couldn't find it in the woods from the river side like this," Johnny said, and the men rose to douse the fire and headed single file cross country in the direction of the Lagoon.

44. Mutual concern

Earl sat on his bunk after the women left, deep in his thoughts and with nothing to do really but dwell on his hopeless situation. The tell-tale sound of an approaching guard caught his ear and he paused to wonder who could be here now. The key turned the lock and the door opened to a sight that brought a mixture of anticipation and dread.

The slumping figure of Jack Sanford shuffled into the cell. He was better in a sense because he had left on a stretcher, but worse in another sense because the spirit of life was gone out of him. His head was down on his chest and if his eyes were open as they stared fixedly at nothing. He reached his bunk, sat down on the edge of it, and rolled over facing the wall.

"Jack, is you all right?" Earl asked with real concern for his new friend and cellmate. His question was met by a stony silence, but he could not tell whether Jack was asleep already or just uninterested in conversation. The silent figure began to tremble with the unmistakable tremors reappearing. The hospital had stilled the beast but not killed it.

Earl rose and walked over to where Jack lay, knelt down on the cell floor, put his hand on the trembling man's shoulder, and leaned over to whisper in his ear, as if Jack was having difficulty hearing his normal voice.

"Jack, I'm here, can I get you anything?" Earl said with a genuine concern, realizing he had no goods or services to give, but the gesture was made anyway in the time honored tradition of compassion. This was strange behavior for Earl Bryant, which surprised even him. It was just not his way to be concerned with the suffering of any man and Lord knows, he'd caused enough of it in men like these. He had convinced himself that even though corn whiskey was hard on a man, it was Earl's livelihood and more or less rationalized that most folks are blind to the evil they cause. This is especially true when they have benefited from a dreadful practice long enough to confuse cause and effect.

Jack stirred just enough so that Earl see he was not dead but little more than that. "How's the pain of it, Jack?" No answer. He tried once more, expecting little else than a quiet acknowledgment that he cared. Jack breathed deeply as he lay there shaking on his bunk as though he was a chrysalis struggling to get free from inside a moth's cocoon.

Earl reached down underneath the bunk where Jack's blanket had been rolled and pulled it out. He then spread the coarse wool garment over Jack's trembling body and added what to him seemed to be nonsense words like a mother hen clucking over her chicks. Just when Earl thought Jack was safely asleep and temporarily relieved from the consciousness of the pain, Jack spoke in a clear voice that belied the appearance of his condition.

"It's tolerable Earl and thanks for asking. Been living with dis mess for so long, it's almost friendly like to me" The obvious suffering the old man was going through had a profound effect on Earl, more than he would ever have imagined or been able to contemplate right now with his own troubles, but he was thinking about it.

This was a side of the problem he had never been able to see before. His customers wanted the stuff he made and paid good money for it. Somebody had to make it, so it might as well be him. That had been Earl's attitude for as long as he could remember but seeing the actual effects on someone who had befriended him in his own troubles, gave him pause to consider it thoughtfully. The moment passed just as quickly as it had begun, as the snoring sounds signaled to Earl that for now at least, the talking about this was over.

45. A view

Tony and Johnny followed the three Negro men as they trekked through the woods by some path obviously familiar to them but not to Tony at all. If it were just Tony walking this way, he would have been so lost he might never find his way out of this country. Johnny probably had some idea of where they were, and could find his way out to the highway but probably not to the Lagoon itself.

The trail meandered into ravines, which would be followed for a time, and then abruptly the path would head out onto a relatively flat place with the only common element being the ever-present canopy of trees.

Since it was wintertime, many of the trees had lost their leaves so the sky was visible here and there but the prevalence of evergreen live oak, magnolia and pine trees scattered throughout the forest, left their path covered by a more or less total canopy.

They had walked for at least an hour and Tony was wondering if trusting these strangers had been prudent. But then suddenly, the lead man dropped down into a sunken area in the forest floor and the group following him down, found themselves standing in the unmistakable remains of a destroyed whiskey still.

The place was a mess with the crushed copper-cooking kettle leaning on its side on one side of the floor area and the severed mash and cooling barrels laying around in pieces almost beyond recognition. The remnants of the ingredient inventory had long ago been consumed by swamp rats and other critters, but scraps and fragments of the containers were still discernable beneath the covering of leaves that had fallen or blown into the floor area through the collapsed roof.

Tony surveyed the debris left about the still and could hardly imagine how the description the men had given him of the operational still would have appeared that fateful day when after Frank Stiller had been shot, Earl Bryant had come down to the Lagoon and had his meeting with George Drucker that had led to the supposed confession by Bryant.

"Who else was here the morning of the shooting, Nooby?" Tony asked, looking at the young man across the ruined floor of the still.

"Hub and me and two or three others was working that morning like always, we seen it all," Nooby said.

"Who is Hub, Nooby, I haven't heard that name yet in this deal?" Tony asked.

"Hub work at the still same as me," Nooby said.

"What did you see? You said you saw it all, Nooby?" Tony asked.

"Oh, Mr. Bryant, he come down here, same as usual that day to see bout the day's work and Drucker come right afterwards and they talk. I couldn't hear what they say or nothing but something strange going on, leastwise that what Hub say. Course I ain't heard it myself," Nooby rather pathetically explained.

"So you don't know what was strange about it, huh Nooby, only Hub knows? Where's Hub anyway, any chance we could talk to him?" Tony asked, sensing a story that might be lurking around the edges of what had been presented to the Grand Jury.

"Hub done gone from here, ain't seen him since the day they bust up the still.

"You mean he's truly left this country?"

"Yas Suh, he used to live at the settlement where all us live at, but he gone now and where he gone to, I don't know!" Nooby said, putting a note of finality to the matter.

"How about the rest of you fellows, do you know where Hub lives now or even where he might have run off to?" Tony asked without much expectation of learning anything more about the incident.

"Naw Suh," Israel and Hoover said, more or less in unison, and by the apparent conviction in their manner, Tony was convinced this was a dead end street. It was a nice thought though, and the prospect of uncovering some evidence unknown to prosecutor or defense was tantalizing to the reporter instincts in Tony's head, but without a better lead than this, it was pretty well hopeless.

Better let that one go, he thought. "Well Johnny, you and I better head back to civilization cause with the flood and all, I've lost all interest in learning about the life styles of Liberty County men. If you think you can find the way out of here, or do we need to hire these men as guides?" Tony asked, as he reached in his pocket and pulled out three dollar bills and handed them one each to the three men as promised.

"We won't need no guides from here, Mr. Tony, I can find the way out to Earl's place, and from there it will be easy to make it back out to Taylor's Crossing, and from there you can catch that bus to Tallahassee," Johnny Caldwell said. The three former guides' hearts sank as the chance of earning more cash money to guide these white men back to the highway had just disappeared, like the memory of last night's dream. Tony thanked the three men and he and Johnny headed out of the destroyed still site by a forest trail apparently well known to Johnny on the way north toward the Bryant homestead and for Tony, back home. He would have to uncover the societal effects of the moonshine economy in rural north Florida for his Pulitzer Prize story later on. He had had enough of this river country for one trip.

46. Homecoming

One foot ahead of the other is the way to get on down the road no matter how long the road is. If you worry only about the next ten steps, then the next ten miles will take care of themselves. That was the philosophy of life of Hub Douglas that had always served him well. He had lived this way whether it was getting up each morning to go back to the still at the Lagoon one more day to do the same old job without respite or different reward or, as on this particular day, to strike out for home when there were seemingly endless miles of dirt road still ahead, applied the rule of his life all the same.

Funny, how the routines of life at home, which seemed so restraining those many years ago, didn't seem so terrible now with nothing left for him in Bryant Country. He had started out that morning with determination once the decision had been finally made to go. He had a spring in his youthful step as he trudged along, first over familiar ground from the settlement along the winding river trail that was not much more than a game path in the deep lowlands, and later climbing up a gradually increasing grade until he joined the dirt road south of Taylor's Crossing.

Deep in Liberty County there was no traffic through the Crossing that morning or any morning for that matter. For the last several years, Hub had known nowhere else. He moved along with a steady clip and once he got the stride of it, could probably reach the place he had once called home in a day or so. He wasn't used to this much walking, but he was young and in a few hours, his body would adjust without too much pain.

The place where he was headed may never again be called "home" to Hub for he had left there under unforgettable circumstances years before against the wishes of his entire family as he recalled it this morning returning home. It wasn't one particular act, ridicule, shame or dispute that had forced him to leave, in fact he hadn't been forced to leave at all.

His daddy had begged him not to leave that morning, pulling out all the emotional stops that tug on the heart with such force. But a team of wild horses could not have held him there. The crying of his mother and the desperate begging of his brothers and sisters could not stop him either. It wasn't that he didn't love his family, he loved them dearly in fact, but he just had to go to find a place where Hub could be Hub. He would not fill in the pattern of life somebody else, insisted that he should fill, no matter how well-meaning or caring they had been.

He could imagine and almost see his future as a farm hand, sweating in the hot summer sun, his hands coated by the sticky green tobacco leaf stains, and his back straining and aching in the bent over position of a primer in the long rows of the tobacco fields with no hope of any avenue of escape. He didn't like anything about the thought of it.

The truth was, he just couldn't stand it anymore. It was not that he had thought himself better than the others, far from it, but he just could not see himself sucked irrevocably into the quagmire of being an ordinary farm hand. However, on that fateful morning, he had no plan or dream that made any sense to him as an alternative course either.

He just knew he had to leave that place or he would have been trapped forever. He could not have found the words to articulate his feeling of meaninglessness in the life available to him back then. However, he was conflicted in his thoughts and the desire for change, but was deathly afraid of the uncertainty that lay ahead. He had weighed it all out on the scales of choice, saw what he thought was the tip of the scale, and made the decision in that direction with his feet.

But that was then and this was now and he was headed right back to the beginning of his life story.

"What are they going to say about old Hub is back?" he shouted out to the trees and sand ruts, thinking more and more about the future that lay ahead of him. *"Ain't goin' to be no Christmas candy for you this time, Suh, no celebratin' neither. That's for shore now. They will say, you made your bed, so now you better go lay down in it. Go get back on that road out of here Hub, you like it so much away from here, go try it some more and don't come round here messin' us up when you know you ain't stayin'. What trouble you in, boy? Mr. Martin don't want you kind round here,"* Hub heard those imaginary voices say over and over and over again in a parade of accusations, which he knew how to make better than anyone, but more of it was anticipated as coming from the family he had abandoned.

He was trying to gain the courage to face the accusations that had grown in his mind year after year, and as far as he was concerned, he was guilty as charged. The only real question was what would be the punishment? Would it be ridicule, laughter, shame or banishment that would be thrown at him by the spectators that he imagined in the theatre of his mind?

He had to climb up on that stage with no hope of welcome or applause but rather almost certainly face one of those punishments. Each of the prospects were dreaded now almost as much as the despair of staying in the river settlement that he had felt he had been forced to leave.

What it came down to was that he really had no choice and had decided to throw himself on the mercy of his family and take whatever they decided to dish out and then decide what to do next. As he walked along that lonely road, hour by hour, getting closer and closer to home, he could find little to be hopeful about and much room for despair. He was in effect the prodigal son headed home to face uncertain music from his family.

As each step brought him closer and closer to home, his head was no longer lifted high, his stride was shortened and his feet seemed to be encased in lead as he approached. He had left the unpopulated countryside and passed through one fairly good-sized town by the end of the first day. He had spent the first night as a trespasser in an old abandoned barn set well off the road and slept restlessly in some musty old hay piled over in the corner on the ground floor. At least it was dry and relatively warm.

When he awoke the next morning, he finished the last of the food he had brought along; there was nothing for it but to get up and head on to his destination. By late in that morning, he had climbed a high hill and approached a turn in the road that seemed to turn more to the north than he remembered and a fork headed more east. It seemed the right one to take but he was unsure which was best. It had been too long since he had traveled here and his memory of the country had faded beyond recall.

A solitary black figure was standing by the side of the road watching him up ahead and Hub approached the stranger with caution. Under more pleasant circumstances, a weary traveler like Hub might have considered this location a pretty place, covered by live oaks and grassy slopes and to the stranger ahead, it was probably still considered that way for it was part of the beauty of what people call home. But to Hub, it was just another turn in the road with a difficult choice to make, and little information to make it with.

When he got within hailing distance, Hub called out in as friendly a tone as he could muster to signal to the stranger he was not a threat, "Morning Suh, is you familiar with the road to take to the Martin place over by Ha-vana town?" The man heard the question all right, since Hub was close enough for that, but stood there silent, sizing up the stranger that approached him.

What is you doing out on this road all by yourself? Going somewhere I ain't figured out yet, by that Martin Place talk? The stranger thought.

"Morning to you Suh," the stranger said finally, following the time honored ritual of welcoming strangers on the road unless the way the man held himself or looked, set off warning bells but there were no such signs from this one. Hub approached the stranger cautiously and stopped short at a respectful distance to engage the man in conversation and hopefully learn the right road to take. Hub stood there with arms akimbo and said,

"I'm Hub Douglas from down Liberty County way and got my head set on going toward Mr. Martin's tobacco farm over east yonder somewhere," as he gestured in a sweeping swing of his right arm to cover either fork of the road up ahead.

"I don't know about no Martin place but there is plenty tobacco farming all over this country east of here, but I'm pleased to make your acquaintance on this public road this morning. I is Elbert Newton, Sr.," reaching out his hand certain now that the stranger was not a threat to him.

"Pleased to make yours," Hub said and eagerly grabbed the stranger's hand and pumped it gratefully. With that ritual complete, the two men felt safe enough because they were of the same race at least. They looked at each other waiting to see what would happen next.

"If you don't mind me asking Suh, what you doing up this far from Liberty County? Folks down there is different, people say", Elbert asked.

I ain't shore myself what I is up to and ain't telling no stranger that, Hub thought and in the usual manner of keeping your pain for yourself, he said, "Yas Suh, different they is from most folks but it been a long time and I forget the way to go exactly at this road junction and man was I glad to see you Suh. If you live round here do you know the way to it," Hub asked hopefully, forgetting already that the stranger said he never heard of any Martin place in that direction. But the stranger hadn't forgotten that he didn't know any such farm over that way and explained once again that he didn't know.

"You see Suh, I has lived in this country all my life and know most of the folks round here and I does not know any Martin farm and you asking over and over ain't changing that, you see?" Elbert explained again patiently, as if talking to a little child who just wouldn't pay attention to or understand what he was being told.

"Yas Suh, and I thank you Suh, but if you don't know this road go to the Martin farm," pointing to the road east and not the north fork, "where do that road go to, Suh?" Hub asked, pointing to the eastern fork. His built in sense of direction learned from years in the river swamp country and the little bit of memory he had left of the way to home, told him that the east fork was most likely the right way to go.

"You going back home, ain't you?" The older man perceptively discerned and said accepting that admitting it would be painful to this young man and a terrible attack on his pride. Hub's chin dropped on his chest in an undeniable admission that the older man, Elbert, had seen through him like a magician with a transparent looking glass. The "magician" wisely moved quickly and wisely to asSir the stranger that he meant no harm and understood about such things.

"I left home myself as a young man, Hub Douglas, and found out it ain't all it's cracked up to be, but every man has to find himself wherever he end up. It ain't any shame to admit you still searching for it, and home is always a way station to get there," the wise old man explained. "Your Momma and Daddy still living there and family with them?"

"Yas Suh, Mr. Elbert, they there all right and I expect to find out how me showing up going to fit in that shoe," Hub said with an unusual metaphorical exposure of his inner fears.

"You better give them more credit than that, Hub Douglass. If they loved you once, they still do, unless you hurt somebody or something, even then, good chance they done forgot over that if it's been some time," Elbert said.

"Yas Suh, it weren't nothin' like that, and it has been a long time since I left there. I just uneasy about going back, that's all," Hub said feeling very comfortable now with this wise old man on the road, total stranger or not.

"You worrying more that it calls for Hub, my advice is give your family more chance than that and if it don't work out, you none the worse for trying. Besides, it's the right thing to do and that count for something, I always say!" Elbert Newton pronounced with finality and then turned to the practical business at hand.

The stranger turned facing the eastern fork, as though looking down it would improve the extent of his knowledge, and said, "From this hillside which local people call Shady Rest, the road turn east yonder, go down that hill you can see from here, and crosses the crick at the bottom. From there you climb on up and around till it end up on the highway way over yonder somewhere, maybe five, seven, eight mile or so and they is farming all over there, tobacco too, so that may be the one for you or might not. The other way, end up in Ha'vana town and connect to the same highway out of Georgia from up north, down south to Tallahassee way and them two road forks join up somewhere over east of here. That's the best I can say about it and you has to find your own Martin Place if it down there. I just cain't say about that," Elbert patiently explained once more.

"Very well then, you helped me more than you realize and I appreciates it," Hub said and thanked the man by shaking hands one more time, and having made his decision, took the east fork and left the stranger standing under the grove of oaks just as he had found him there. He had learned nothing about who this stranger Elbert Newton, Sr. really was.

But Elbert had learned plenty about Hub Douglas and that was the way each man needed it to work out. The custom of courtesy to friendly and harmless strangers had been observed and Hub, having received much more than he expected, even if he had not learned as much as he hoped about the road to take, had learned enough to decide and act on it.

He walked faster now, partly because it was down a long hill and partly because he had made up his mind that whatever awaited him at home, bad or worse, it would just have to be. He was through worrying about it. By midafternoon he had made his way east and the memory of his childhood began to fill in the blanks on the previously blank memory screen of the view ahead of him.

There was something about the trees he began to pass, a stream bed in a little ravine that had a familiar look and finally another intersection with a little farm store perched confidently at the corner as if saying, "try and come by here without stopping!"

The Corner store, it must be, cain't be two like this, shore, this it!, This here is Martin's corner and the big house be up there in them trees, You is home!, Hub thought to himself as he came upon the little farm store where the road turned north again on one fork and continued east past the front of the Martin Place.

Hub Douglas was home and from here it was a simple matter of walking past the Martin house and finding the Quarters where his daddy, Mack Douglas, lived with the rest of his family. He could not help himself from getting excited, for even though one side of him feared the reunion, the rest of him longed for it, with a deeply felt longing that only throwing himself on the mercy of his family could satisfy.

He had worried long enough and the time for action was here. It was a matter of minutes before he would discover whether blood was thicker than water as he turned into the Negro Quarters where the farm worker families lived on the Martin Farm. The Douglas cabin stood where it always had been, emoting in his soul that slowly reviving memory that flooded back to the present from childhood. The tears began to stream down his face as he saw one of them standing in the front door looking with astonishment as Hub Douglas, the prodigal son, was returning home.

47. Plans

Aaron had set aside Tuesday morning for thinking. "Hold my calls Anna" was the signal for absolutely no interruptions for her boss and she knew from long experience that with a serious case coming up with a jury trial in two months, that Aaron had to mentally process all he knew about the evidence and the credibility of the witnesses to plan for the defense of his client.

A Grand Jury indictment for first-degree murder of a federal officer was not to be taken lightly with the jurors he knew from experience were likely to be seated in the box. These were good people in this district full of conviction that truth was truth and life was sacrosanct. You did not take a human life in this part of Florida in 1933 without serious consequences. They were convinced, as the prevailing attitude among the good citizens of the broader community that the death penalty for murder was appropriate as a deterrent against violent crimes no matter what the sociologists in New York or Philadelphia might opine on the subject.

So Aaron knew he had to carefully consider his case for the defense and to not rule out recommending a change of plea in exchange for life imprisonment no matter how determined his client was that he was innocent of all charges. His client's belief in his innocence was not strong enough with clearly doubtful defenses, to override Aaron's good judgment.

Appellate longevity in death penalty cases for the future yet unknowable to members of the bar in 1933, was not something for a defendant to even consider. If a jury found you guilty of first degree murder in 1933, a federal judge like Benjamin T. Parker, Jr., would have no difficulty calling for the rope. It would mean his seeing that the sentence was carried out would likely be before the end of the year, barring aggressive appeals which most Defendants could not afford. Public advocacy groups to take on appeals of every single death penalty case all the way to the US Supreme Court, including public candle light vigils right up to the moment of execution, were unheard of in that period.

"Let's see," Aaron began out loud doing his best thinking that way. "What am I up against? A bullet in the wall supposedly matching Earl's gun. Have to have our own expert check that out. Angle of the bullet is suggesting a short man like Earl? Nonsense there's enough reasonable doubt room in that theory to drive a Model T Ford loaded with ten hay bales through.

Knee print at the scene, only means a giant could have made the shot at that angle. The Snitch's testimony and that lame brain confession? I'm going to have to build up evidence proving that he was a snitch.

Nobody likes a snitch. Nobody! Earl is a moonshiner and guilty as hell of that! But he's not charged with making illegal whiskey, thank God! But the big talk testimony will hurt. It goes to motive; especially that revenge angle! That's bad for us, I'm thinking. Sure he didn't do it when it's told that the Federal Man victim killed his pappy and he just forgot about it, right? A man with Earl's reputation, who'll believe that? Strange though that Drucker shows up about the same time as the shooting and he was only the operations man with no real reason to be there that morning. What was his angle? Take over? Get Earl sent to prison and safely out of the way? Possibly? But can I prove it sufficient to raise a reasonable doubt? That rifle, that's my biggest problem. His prints are all over it? Wait a minute, no prints on the trigger guard! How come that? And Drucker said he checked the magazine and found a shell missing. How'd he do that with no prints of his left on it? No evidence Drucker had a gun. Note to file, check with Earl and the crew? What do they recall about this so called confession conversation? Strange that, damaging confession by a man who just committed federal murder and he tells his right hand man in front of the whole Still crew that he had a motive for it? Better get somebody to get down into Liberty County and find those men, wonder if Johnny Caldwell could help on that?"

"That rifle bothers me some, matches Earl's prints all right but why did the damn fool keep the thing with him if guilty of murder with it? He might not have wiped the prints clean; lots of guilty men forget about four or five critical points in the so called perfect crime, but left it right there in his house, didn't he? That's the old "stupid criminal argument" I will be up against however; He can be stupid and guilty; most of them are, right?"

"Can't have Earl testify can I? A moonshiner in the "Prohibition Over Bible Belt"? The WCTU types on the jury, and there'll be plenty of them, would have a hissy fit! Rifling in the barrel matched? That federal expert would find a match in a collapsed bullet buried in a door frame if it was a machine gun bullet fired among thousands at Black Jack Pershing in the Argonne Forest battle field. Definitely have to get our own expert." His verbal dialogue with himself ended for now.

Glancing over the Discovery documents furnished by the US Attorney's office, he wanted to see if he had overlooked anything.

"Let me think now," Aaron summarized in his mind the weak points for his own planning and his own investigation yet to come and for a change of pace, he turned in his chair looking out the window of his office picking up the phone and said, "Anna, Aaron here, has the Recorder come yet? Uh huh, and yea, I'll take that coffee now and Anna hold my calls a while longer will you? Thanks Anna", and he hung up the phone. In less than a minute Anna Devlin came into his office without knocking carrying his favorite cup filled with black coffee and the folded up morning edition of the Recorder. She sat the coffee cup down on his polished mahogany desk and handed Aaron the paper and promptly left the office, recognizing in his look that he needed some more time to unwind from the laborious mental exercise of mapping out his defense in the Bryant Case.

The front page had a story that caught his eye immediately, a byline by his good friend Tony Callaway. He would read Tony's bylines on any subject, but this one set off alarm bells of interest immediately.

"Personal Terror of Flood Victims," the headline read. Aaron quickly read the article and saw that Tony Callaway, Senior writer for the Recorder had both the misfortune and the good luck, depending on how you looked at it, to be caught in the Lake Talquin Dam break flood a few days before. What caught Aaron's eye morer than the good luck of a newspaper writer stumbling into a news and personal interest story involving himself that would be picked up by the wire services and broadcast all over America, was the details in the story about Tony and Johnny Caldwell of all people, stumbling across and being rescued, sort of, by men who had worked in the Bryant Still where his case facts had was evolved.

"Great God, what luck!" shouted Aaron, and in moments Anna Devlin came running into the office thinking somebody had shot the boss through the window, the Capital Building was on fire or some other such disaster the way he was shouting in there.

"What's wrong, Sir, are you hurt?" Anna asked anxiously.

"Heavens no, Anna, quite the reverse, explain later, call Tony Calla-way and make an appointment for lunch. Tell him it's me and nothing is more important today than lunch, not even the Pulitzer Prize Review Committee if he offers up some lame excuse, and you tell him that, Okay, Anna?"

"Yes Mr. Martin, I'll get him, Sir," Anna said catching up with Aar-on's enthusiasm even though she had no idea what he was so excited about. Later that morning she could in vision the two good friends having lunch at the Garden Grill, or she was not Anna Devlin, "girl Friday" and social coordinator extraordinaire.

48. Lunch

The usual lunch crowd had gathered at The Garden Grill starting about 11:30 a. m. that morning. It was a typical American eating place in most respects. It was made unusual only by its location near the State Capital when the session was coming on as it was now, where it hosted lawyers and clients, state workers and friends, an occasional Circuit Judge and friends or Bailiff, lobbyist of all stripes, together or with clients and of course legislators. In other words, this was the place to be at the lunch hour in Tallahassee if your work was a part of the "Courthouse or Legislative ring of power," as it was called, and the concomitant influence over matters political.

The menu was varied and appealed to an array of eclectic tastes but food was an incidental benefit to the many collaborators who met here to conduct business of varying sorts.

The main seating area contained tables for four or less in the usual fashion and the outer perimeter of the interior walls had high backed booths where more private conversations could be conducted. Two special rooms were in the back for meetings of Kiwanis and Rotary on different days of the week of course of which this day was not a club meeting day for either and if you made arrangements ahead of time with Samuel Sorrentino, proprietor, and you had the right connections, one of the back rooms could be reserved for really private conversations even for a couple of people.

The Martin law firm was one of those who were well connected with Sammy Sorrentino and Anna's call to reserve a room for lunch between Tony Callaway and Aaron Martin had been arranged without a hitch. Aaron understood how the system worked and as an extra tip for Sammy would be casually handed to the waiter even before the normal tip. It was just the way things were done at the Garden Grill.

Aaron arrived first and made his way by escort to the back room to prepare for Tony's arrival. He didn't have long to wait. Tony rapped softly on the closed meeting room door and opened it to find his old college roommate and good friend waiting there for him patiently over a cup of coffee.

"Hey Tony, my man, come on in, coffee? I'll have the waiter send back a fresh cup," Aaron said, rising to greet his closest friend in town, grasped his hand in a warm shake and signaled to Fred the waiter who was standing at the door having followed Tony through the crowded restaurant as Sammy had directed.

"You take care of my good friend Aaron Martin, Fred, he's the best and that includes his guests naturally, capeesh?" Sammy had made clear to his headwaiter, Fred Barnes. Fred would never disappoint the boss in these special arrangements especially concerning certain customers. Tony took a seat next to Aaron.

"Tell me about it Tony, this disaster you and Johnny Caldwell had out on the river. How did you manage to be just in the right place to get washed off the bridge and land this important story? "How, Tony?" Aaron good-naturedly asked him.

"You can have that story Aaron, it wasn't worth it, believe me. I thought we weren't going to make it, seriously man," Tony said, "I've never seen that much water raise that fast and in a borrowed car too. You wouldn't believe the crap I took from Dick Powers when he heard about it. It was his brand new car you know, and he may never get over it."

"I'll bet he won't, but tell me Tony, your story said you and Johnny were rescued, sort of, by some of the men working at Earl Bryant's Still, the one that got busted up after his arrest. That really caught my interest," Aaron asked curiously.

"Thought that might just set your ears on fire, Aaron, my good friend," Tony said, smiling all the while. "Seriously Aaron, you might be interested to know the names of two of the Negroes working at the still that morning, the day Frank Stiller was allegedly killed. One of the men was a savior of sorts for Johnny and me. One was Nooby Oakley and another one was named Hub something or other, never got his last name. Oakley says he and Hub saw Bryant come down to the still that morning and Bryant's number two man, Drucker, I believe he said his name was, came down right afterwards and then Drucker left. He couldn't recall whether he had a gun or not either coming or going. This Hub fella supposedly heard what they said and all, but Oakley says he couldn't hear any of it. Of course Oakley has no idea where Hub went and he's long gone from the river settlement where all the Negroes lived who worked for Bryant. The other two men confirmed that as well. Their names, believe it or not, were Israel Manley and Hoover Spencer. That's right, one was actually called Hoover. Said he got the nickname from the former President, which is odd for those folks who can't read and don't have radios, I'll bet ya, in Liberty County, least wise not in the river settlement where those still worker Negroes lived. I figured it more likely came from a vacuum cleaner salesman lost in Liberty County or maybe J. Edgar, but anyway, they're still down there in the deep woods and Johnny can probably find them if that's what you want. He thinks you are God's answer for justice because you're defending his good buddy Earl. You might be able to find Oakley and the boys again, but I'm convinced they don't know where Hub is and don't have anything useful for you. As you know, George Drucker is the key prosecution witness, so this Hub fella seems important to me, at least from a story's perspective. As you know, Aaron, I'm no lawyer, but it might be useful for your case if you could find him, or at least prove that Drucker was on the scene when the still events happened," Tony concluded.

"Yeah, possibly Tony, but that one cuts with two edges, like all good swords do. Putting Drucker at the scene just at the right time fits my theory that he had plenty of reasons to make up that harebrained story about a confession to help him ease Earl Bryant out of the way so he could take over the whiskey business. No sensible Northern District Jury would ordinarily believe Earl would confess to Drucker in front of his whole crew, but confirming his presence at the time with our witnesses too, adds some validity to the charge that he may have been arrogant enough to believe a loyal crew would never turn on him and therefore convince a reluctant jury of the very thing they wouldn't ordinarily believe as their common sense would tell them. It's sort of like the metaphysical argument made by a true believer that there is an invisible cat sitting in the chair and when the skeptical one in the audience runs his hand across the chair and says, "See there's no cat there." The rebuttal argument is, "But don't you see, that just proves the cat is there, because you see, he's invisible." Aaron said, ending on a lighter note.

"I'll have to think about that one," Tony said. "It's a little obtuse even for me."

"And I'll have to think about using Oakley, Manley and Spencer but it's worth a try, considering how bad it looks because of Earl's gun? I'll tell you Tony, that gun evidence bothers me the most. It's hard to explain his prints all over it except none on the trigger guard, and that is strange. I'm telling you straight, Tony, my gut tells me there's something we don't know about that gun," Aaron said.

"And by the way Aaron, the name Drucker rings a memory bell with me. Remember Pete Drucker, our old friend growing up over in Havana, he had an older brother that was always in trouble, didn't he? Wonder if George Drucker is the same guy? Wasn't that part of Pete's story in that silly secret club initiation ritual I thought up back when you, me, Ben Collins and Pete were just kids?" "That's right Tony, I had forgotten completely about that! Where's Pete now, sort of lost touch with him over the years? How time flies and lets you forget even without trying"

"I think he still works at the same hardware and tobacco supply place he started with after school; I know he never went to college. What was the name of that one, Stallworth's or something like that?" Tony quizzed

"Yeah, I think it's still over there, I'll get a hold of him and ask about that brother of his or try another line, maybe. Learn anything else that might help me?" Aaron asked hopefully, but soon saw that he had learned all he was going to get today. Someone as observant and perceptive for news as Tony Callaway didn't miss much and it would have been an insult, sort of, to keep priming that pump when the information well was obviously running dry. With that subject out of the way, the two friends did what friends do everywhere; they enjoyed their time, lunch and other common interests together.

49. Travis

Back in the office, Aaron called Anna Devlin on the office phone and said, "Anna, get a hold of John Travis and tell him I have a job or two for him, all right?"

"Sir, Mr. Martin," Anna said and hung up and then immediately picked up the phone again.

"Number Please," said the operator.

"Sallie," Anna Devlin here, connect me with the Travis Detective Agency out on north Monroe Street, I'd like to speak with John Travis if he's in this afternoon."

"Yes, Ma'am" Miss Devlin, here's your number. You can figure out if he's in or not" Sallie said. The phone rang three or four times in the hole in the wall office of John Travis, former Chief Investigator for The Leon County Sheriff's Office. The office was placed under the bigger than life sign outside, "Travis Detective Agency", designed to draw in the business that seldom ever wandered in off the street anyway.

Inside, a more secretive and quietly competent John Travis, former Cop and the man to go to if you had a really tough investigative job on your hands, picked up the phone in this one-man office, and answered quietly,

"Hello, John Travis here, can I help you?"

"Mr. Travis, Anna Devlin, here's Mr. Martin, Mr. Martin the younger that is, would like you to drop over, if convenient, he has a job or two for you," Anna said.

"Music to my ears, Miss Devlin, you tell Attorney Aaron Martin I'll be right over," Travis said, hanging up the phone and in the same moment, rose from his seat and strode out of his office to drive over to the Martin Law Firm. With the depression in full swing, detective work had been infrequent, if not absent altogether, and the prospect of a paying job from one of the top law firms in Tallahassee was indeed music to his hungry ears.

John Travis had been a good Cop by ordinary standards, working his way up from patrolman to Sergeant in the Patrol Division, then Detective, and finally Chief Investigator for the Leon County Sheriff's Office. He was well on his way to a secure career as Chief Investigator where he could have stayed comfortably until retirement had it not been for Benjamin Bradley.

Ben Bradley was one of those government bureaucrats with connections to the movers and shakers in State Government. Early in his professional life he had learned that it is not what you know that counts, but who you know that counts for everything. He had cultivated this crop with energy and purpose and reaped the harvest in abundant and fruitful political connections. In his job as Finance Chief of the State Board of Conservation he was in charge of budgets and accounting, a veritable rooster in the hen house as far as opportunity for personal gain was concerned.

In that Department, charged by law with the regulation of commercial fishing, oyster harvesting, timber and turpentine production, the political gamesmanship was seething below, above, and on the surface of this regulatory rich environment. The Elected Cabinet selected the Administrator of each department by majority vote, but the Governor

had only one vote. The Cabinet's job was to balance the political for-
tunes of these powerful and often competing interests. Ben was in
the position of shifting funds from one budget to another; and the
decisions he made may have made somebody mad, and somebody else
very glad indeed. Since political appointees of the cabinet come and
go, his steady hand on the Department's finances made him valuable
to each new incumbent to the Department Head's post, regardless of
political party.

The Republican Party had run things in Florida since Reconstruction days until recently but there were changes of personnel from
time to time with the changes of winds, that blew across the political
landscape. It had been a rumor for years that Bradley had managed
to feather his own financial nest in the process. It is axiomatic that
whenever truth and legend conflict about some tale or the other, that
legend generally always prevails.

Then, one election cycle put an unexpected candidate in the Governor's Office. This tipped the political scales in the cabinet that year to
such a degree that Bradley's boss was changed and the new Governor,
full of idealism and rare political courage, had launched an investigation
of the alleged corruption in the Board of Conservation.

The Governor's man for checking on things political in State Government was Louis Drake, The Inspector General, a political appointee
serving at the pleasure of the Governor. The Inspector General given
his marching orders by the newly elected Governor that year decided
to bring in an outsider to do the gumshoe work of the investigation and
that unlucky assignment ended up in the hands of John Travis on loan
from Sheriff Cole's Office, also politically friendly to the new Governor.

John Travis, who was hired supposedly as an outsider and therefore
politically neutral, smoked out the corruption all right. But before
Bradley's guilt could be made public, Bradley, who knew where all

the bodies were buried, managed to head off the disaster by exposing some minor indiscretion John Travis had committed while serving as a Detective in the Sheriff's Office.

The misdeed was minor in the eyes of the police at the time, but major in the eyes of the public if it ever came to the light of day. As it turned out, Bradley had managed to have the fact of Travis's problem leaked into the record that while he was conducting a murder investigation years before, he had managed to use a rubber hose to coerce a confession out of an otherwise guilty suspect.

The man went to Raiford since this was in the days before Gideon v. Wainright when if a Defendant had no money, he got no lawyer; and in the depression there were plenty of those without money, including this one. Without a lawyer, such information of mistreatment was useless but the confession made it to the jury anyway and the man went to prison. He would probably have been found guilty on the rest of the evidence, regardless of whether the confession was used, but this had made the conviction easier.

The only harm done was to the Constitution and to the rights of some possibly innocent future Defendant, an issue not too troubling to the police and prosecutors in those days. It is undeniable that in human affairs there is a tendency, that the means to an otherwise worthy end will, given enough time and selfish human nature, left to its own natural tendency not being able to recognize their own excesses, will destroy the objective sought.

This was just such a case. The terrible injustice as to process in that case notwithstanding, John Travis's career as Chief Investigator for the Leon County Sheriff's Office was over. In the shuffle, Ben Bradley escaped a demotion, and a corruption conviction with the investigation as to his personal graft being effectively killed in the process.

There was nothing left for John to do but quit since he couldn't ever go back to the Sheriff's Office, and he still needed to eat, so he had to take up the only other work he was qualified to do, that of the proverbial "Private Detective."

He had managed to eke out a living watching wives or husbands in juicy divorce cases or interviewing difficult witnesses in an occasional large personal injury case that might come along. However, lucrative, his practice was not. But staying on the good side of the private bar was not only helpful for John's Survival but also essential. That is why he so quickly drove over to Aaron Martin's office the minute after he hung up the phone.

50. Here's what I want

Aaron looked up from a brief he was writing as Anna Devlin led the man into his office and showed him to a seat across the desk from him. If you walked past John Travis in a crowd and didn't know him personally, you would never in a million years pick him out as a private detective, policeman or anything else of any distinction. He was small, possibly slightly over five feet in height, light brown hair color, brown colored eyes and slender. In fact, he was so ordinary looking that he could blend into a crowd and get lost. That was a gift to one in his profession really, where going without being noticed was a plus. His apparent physical strength was misleading too. Growing up, he had been the kind of kid every bully thought he could have for lunch, but regretted later the indigestion, as it were, that came with it, to wit, loose teeth, black eyes and sometimes bloody noses.

In his interrogation techniques honed from thousands of police investigations, he had a confidence beyond appearance that worked to his advantage. He seemed on first impression to be easy to fool or lie to, and many suspects had tried it to their disappointment and utter exasperation. He was all the while reading them like a boOkay, digesting every chapter and playing back verbatim what they told him in such astonishing accuracy, contrasting what they had been telling as truth or their own inconsistency, so that capitulation was the rule rather than the exception, compared to most investigators' experience. He was one of the few really good men at this game who could play the good cop bad cop routine all in the same person. In that sense, he was cost effective to the department because it only took one man to get the job done rather than the usual team of two officers. Those skills are lost to the police establishment now and if a good job came along in the private arena today, they would not be wasted. Aaron's needs this morning were just made to order for John Travis and John needed the work. A match was about to be made.

"Good morning John, are you available, I need somebody with your special skills?" Aaron asked the peripatetic detective.

"You've got my full attention, Aaron," Travis said, in his usual manner of speaking to people without any deference to who they were or better yet as they wanted to be known. For some, this direct approach was a put off because some employers might expect him to grovel, sensing accurately at this particular time that he was desperately in need of work. They may want to have their egos stroked but that was not the way of John Travis.

Aaron, however, was not one of those guys, and he was more interested in results than protocol, knowing already that Travis was his man for this job.

"Hell, John, you must know I've got the unenviable job of defending Earl Bryant, the notorious moonshiner, on that Federal Agent murder charge. I need somebody to go see some black men down in Liberty County who worked for him; and as I've heard it, have bits and pieces of the story to tell. The problem is, John, the men we know about, don't know enough or won't say what they do know and the one of these who knows the important details has vanished."

Aaron explained to Travis the information he had gleaned from Tony Callaway and indirectly from Johnny Caldwell, that Nooby Oakley and friends either didn't know enough or wouldn't say all they knew about the odd meeting that morning between George Drucker, the chief government witness and the accused.

Aaron needed to know what the men actually knew or could be persuaded to testify to, needing the identity and location of this man called "Hub" and a general background check on George Drucker. He told Travis that his boyhood friend who lived in Havana was probably George Drucker's younger brother, giving him the details on how to reach him, but to concentrate on the still workers first.

John Travis got the picture fast, found out how to locate Johnny Caldwell, and made the deal with Aaron for his services, including a generous advance payment for actual expenses and fees.

"Okay, Aaron," John said. "I'll go talk to your Negroes and find out what they know and report back to you before tackling that Drucker part of the assignment."

"Fine John, get back to me in about a week, that's all the time I can give you, the trial's coming up pretty soon and I'm worried about my case? I've got some bad gun evidence against me and I need all the circumstantial evidence to blunt it or Earl's goose is cooked," Aaron explained, rising to shake Travis' hand and walk with him out to the reception area of the office for his departure.

Anna sat there in her chair, busy with everything else, but missing nothing all the while. Aaron handed Travis an envelope he was carrying and said, "Oh yeah, here's a letter from me to Johnny Caldwell. I think he can read, you'll need it to let him know you're on Earl's side. Those

Liberty County men don't trust just anybody. You may have heard of Johnny. He can usually be found hanging out at Salty's down on the river off Highway 20", Aaron said.

"Yeah, I've heard of him and know the place," John said, turned, shook Aaron's hand and promptly left the building.

Aaron watched him go and thought, *If anybody can get to the bottom of this it's that fellow right there. After this part is done, I've got to find out what Drucker was up to!* He then returned to his office and his brief.

51. Mixing and mingling

There was nothing "brief" about the journey John Travis had to make to Liberty County and Bryant Country, but he made it without delay and with the purpose of achieving his aim. He would find out who knew what happened in that aftermath scene following the shooting of Frank Stiller or he was not John Travis, the best private detective in Tallahassee, according to him and some others.

His long experience in interviewing Negro suspects or witnesses told him you needed to gain their respect and to maintain control. The trick to it was to somehow do both. In this case, he had an edge because he felt he had one of their own, so to speak, in Johnny "Down Home" Caldwell. Johnny was as authentic a country man as you would ever want to have on your side in these parts.

Johnny had no telephone, so Anna Devlin had sent word to Johnny through his new buddy Tony Callaway who had connections with people throughout the district that even lawyers could only dream of having. However made, the arrangement had worked and Johnny was ready to be convinced that he should trust this wiry little man sent by the lawyers.

Johnny was sitting on the gallery of Salty's at the time appointed with his chair kicked back and balanced with his brogans on the foot rail when John Travis pulled up in his old Model T. Ford. "You're Johnny Caldwell aren't you?" John Travis began with a standoff approach, not assuming too much familiarity to put Johnny ill at ease. He liked to keep his contacts cool and distant at first to allow some room for movement on both sides. He had found by long experience, that people liked to feel a sense of progress in relationship and never to have it assumed that anything was owed to him before the meeting.

"I is, and who wants to know it?" Johnny said, playing his part in the game to a tee.

"You were told by Mr. Tony Callaway of the "*Tallahassee Recorder*" that a man from Earl Bryant's defense team would be coming here today to see you and I'm that fella, John Travis investigator, Mr. Caldwell," John said, with a broad disarming smile, extending his arm and rather small right hand, offering to shake Johnny's hand. Johnny looked the little man in the eye, found his look to be genuine and took the little man's hand and smiled in acceptance that the connection had been made.

"Let's take a walk Johnny, too many ears hanging around this gallery, Ok?" John said, and the two men walked together down to the fish camp, besides being early in the day, it was deserted this time of year.

"This Nooby Oakley fella, you know him well? He's the key guy in my investigation as I see it." John asked it this way to open the conversation.

"I don't think "well" is the right word, since no white man in Liberty County knows any Negro well, the way you probably said it, Mr. Travis. What I mean is, he ain't going to tell me anything he don't want you or the po'lice to know about anybody or anything such as this Earl Bryant mess, jest cause I ask him. But I know him well enough to talk him into listening to you, if that'll help. Earl Bryant is the only man I care about in this deal, you see," Johnny said. This was good enough for Travis, so he pointed back at the Ford and said, "Well, good man, that'll do it, Johnny, you come with me and show me the way to find that Negro settlement down in Bryant Country and let's see if we get lucky this time and find that fella down there, all right?"

"Yes, Sir, let's do it," Johnny said and the two men climbed into the Ford, pulled out of the front yard at Salty's and headed toward Bryant Country.

They stopped the Ford right at the settlement deep in the river country, got out and headed to the cabin Johnny pointed out as the one that Nooby lived in, knowing full well the men in the settlement would have known ever since they left the paved road that a vehicle was headed their way. There was nobody in the cabin as expected since the natural thing for these men to do when confronted by a motor vehicle this deep in the woods was to head for the river swamp where no vehicle and most men could ever trace them. John Travis had anticipated this reaction so he and Johnny sat in the crude homemade chairs on the front porch and waited. He figured that as soon as Nooby or any of the men saw that Johnny Caldwell was with him that the fear of arrest or worse would disappear and would bring them by natural curiosity out of the swamp country and up to them for a chat.

He had it figured just about right for it wasn't long till a voice came across the clearing and said, "Mr. Johnny, that you?"

"It's me all right, that you, Nooby Oakley?" Johnny asked.

"Who that with you, Mr. Johnny?" Nooby asked from the edge of the clearing still out of sight.

"You can come on up Nooby, this here is Mr. John Travis, what works for Mr. Earl's lawyer. I vouch for him," Johnny said, and in a few seconds after Nooby processed that information, he ambled across the clearing and up to the porch where the two white men were seated.

John Travis rose from his chair and approached the man cautiously, stopping a safe distance from the zone of privacy where strangers are not allowed to invade without threat.

"If you want to help your old boss Earl Bryant, you'll need to talk to me Nooby, I'm the only one that can do it, but I need your help," John Travis said, probing to get a feel of the response in the encounter that may or may not become confrontational. "Let me explain who and what I'm about. I'm trying to get information that will help Earl's lawyer defend him from this charge of murder, would you like to help him or am I wasting both our times?" John asked, taking the direct approach.

"Shore I wants to help Mr. Bryant, he been good to me and the men at the Still," Nooby said indicating his general intention to help his old boss.

"Good, so why don't you tell me what happened that day when Mr. Bryant came down to the still after the shooting," Travis said neutrally.

Nooby started out with a careful recitation of his version of events that he had told to the white men previously, but careful to leave out some of the details, particularly Hub's involvement, or at least what in his mind had grown considerably to be Hub's involvement. The only problem was that John Travis had gleaned enough details from Tony Callaway through Aaron Martin to not let him off that hook that easily, which was one horn of Nooby's dilemma.

"You were friends with this fella, Hub, weren't you Nooby?" John asked cautiously being careful not to press his man too far right at first until he saw which way he was going to jump.

"Yes Suh, me and Hub, we all right," Nooby said, revealing nothing.

"That's great, Nooby, nothing better than friends and I can see you would be loyal to a really close friend, was Hub one like that?" John asked.

The pause and the silence that came with it was deafening for Nooby may have been a young "ignorant" Negro in the eyes of most whites but stupid he was not, and he could see clearly where this was heading, exactly where he was not prepared to go. Finally, he spoke in a meaningless response, "Uh huh, yep, if you say so, Suh."

"What's bothering me Nooby is how Hub heard all about this conversation between Mr. Bryant and you and the other fellas heard nothing. That Still as I heard about it was a small place, you could hear a rat snoring clear cross it, am I wrong, Nooby?" John Travis said, closing the gap a bit. "Besides, even if you couldn't hear what they said, you could see all right, couldn't you?" John said.

"Yes, Suh, we could see plain enough, all right," Nooby said getting off one horn of the dilemma and landing squarely on the other.

"Another thing, Nooby, did you see Mr. Bryant bring in his rifle that morning and hang it up on that rack of pegs on the wall of the Still?" John asked this pointedly shifting the line of attack slightly to throw Nooby off balance.

It worked too, because Nooby was determined most of all to protect his friend Hub Douglas for he had become more convinced than ever that Hub was in on the thing with Drucker. He had seen Hub leave the Still just before Drucker came, had come back just after he arrived and seemed to remember just a little too much of it all. Hub clearing out of the country without so much as a "fare thee well", was more proof of his complicity to Nooby, if he needed it. He didn't need more proof for his convictions by this point, but getting out from under the steely-eyed gaze of this little white man was going to be tougher than he had thought. Nooby thought a long time about that last question and realized he was in deeper than ever; and it was time to take the time honored escape clause used by Negroes in the south in those days, which was to play dumb all of a sudden, trying to live up to the image most white people had of them in the first place. "I don't know Suh, please Suh, I just a simple Negro man down here in the river swamp and remembering them details this long back go beyond my ability, Suh," Nooby said, rolling his eyes in that ignorant man role he had seen played out time and again in difficult situations in white man company in a tight spot.

John Travis was no fool either, and he knew he had his man now. "Just tell me then Nooby, if you can't remember those details, the man who can, this Hub fella. Just tell me where Hub went off to and I'll get the details from him," Travis asked facing Nooby squarely just in case the man would panic and try to run out of the cabin.

"I don't know Suh, where Hub gone to, I ain't seen him since that mornin'," Nooby said.

"Then tell me his last name, Nooby and I'll find him myself," Travis said closing the circle with a final thrust of attack. Nooby couldn't very well pretend not to know Hub's last name, since he had already admitted that Hub was his loyal friend, but telling this stranger, no matter how connected he was to Mr. Bryant, was a risk he was not prepared to take.

If Hub was as deep in this as he thought, then possibly his life was in danger from that Drucker fellow; and Mr. Bryant was not likely to be back in business anyway. Once the trial was over and Bryant was in Raiford or hung, which was more likely, Drucker was probably going to take over the Bryant Country Empire and Hub would be in the cat bird seat, Nooby figured and this white man would be somewhere bothering somebody else besides him.

With that reasoning, he decided there must be a safe way out of this trap he had inadvertently set for himself. He took a little too long to figure it out which was like a neon sign going off all over his head saying "liar, liar, his pants are on fire." "Hub Williams is his name, Suh, and I think he come from out west somewhere, best I remember it," Nooby said unconvincingly. He had already said he had no idea where Hub was from and now he was giving directions on how to find him.

John Travis reached up with his small sinewy white arms gripping Nooby's shoulders and forced him to sit on the floor of the cabin with a bang. "Listen here you worthless piece of shit, you can lie to some Tallahassee newspaper man any day of the week but you can't get away with lying to me! I may look small to you but bigger men than you have thought that and lived to regret it. Do you understand me Nooby?" Travis said with no little threat intended and much threat taken.

"Yes, Suh, I get it," Nooby said.

"That's better Nooby," John said, changing gears once again to the friendly approach. "We understand how it is with friends, Nooby, you feel threatened by me, don't you. Well let me put your mind at rest on that, I'm not here to hurt you Nooby, Mr. Martin was clear about that, "You look after those men," the lawyer told me straight." Nooby was now completely confused. Should he come clean and tell on his friend or stay true and finesse his way out of this.

"You done got it mixed backwards, Suh, yore good side and bad side has done melted and done run down into one pot," Nooby said, and then came clean, well mostly clean anyway. "I left out the part he come from Alabama," Nooby said, splitting the baby so to speak giving Hub some geographical clearance, but pretending that he had given Travis his supposed real name, hoping that no one could figure out exactly where Hub had run off to or back to. The truth of the matter was, Nooby had no idea where Hub had gone off to. Any place was possible, but going home was the least likely place he would have run back to, and to Nooby Oakley, Hub would have avoided going home like the plague.

Believe it or not, he was not going to point this man toward the most likely place to find Hub Douglas, and he had done as much as he could to protect his friend from these white people. His strategy had saved Hub for now, especially if he was right in his suspicion of Hub's involvement with Drucker was correct. This white man could look all over Alabama for Hub Williams and never find him in time to involve him in the mess of this trial. That was as much as Nooby dared to do for Hub and it seemed to have worked.

He stepped back from the conversation as the white men began to figure out what they would do next. In a few minutes, he would ease his way out of the settlement and make himself scarce for the next few weeks. That should not be too hard to do.

John Travis had interrogated some really clever folks in his many years as a policeman and private investigator and he was convinced that this simple Negro man had finally told him the truth. Nobody could withstand the old double whammy of John Travis's good guy, bad guy, routine and he was the victim this time of his own prior success. Round one had gone to Nooby Oakley and time would tell who would be standing at the final bell. He would put out his feelers into Alabama and if necessary, maybe pay another visit to this clever black boy of Liberty County if he was still hanging around the settlement by then.

"And where might we find those other boys, Johnny, the ones that pulled you and Tony Callaway out of the river that night? They might just remember where this Hub Williams ran off to," John Travis said.

"Finding them other fellas ain't likely to be easy," Johnny said, "Leastwise on this here same trip." Johnny was right about that as the rest of the settlement had cleared out on the arrival of the white men and after news of the interview with Nooby Oakley spread quickly around the river swamp country where the former Still workers lived and worked as such stories tended to do, there would be no more interviews on this case with these men.

John Travis had had his one chance with Nooby, the most likely witness with helpful information, and since that encounter had left John with an empty sack, there would be no more produce or fruit on this vine, at this time.

52. Thinking it through

Aaron was buried in preparations for the trial that was due to start the next week. He had gone over the facts as Earl had presented them, and re-read his notes a hundred times from his interview with John Travis. He was disappointed for Sir that John had been unable to turn up any really useful information from the Negroes who worked in Earl's Still and were present when George Drucker had coincidentally arrived just after Earl and the shooting had taken place.

He would have loved to be able to present live witnesses who actually heard the supposed confession and better yet contradicted Drucker's version of it. He had considered at length the timing question and the unsavory background of George Drucker that Travis had turned up in a quick visit up to Havana and a talk with Peter Drucker, his younger brother and Aaron's friend. There was no love lost between those two and that part of the assignment had been quick and easy. The interview in Liberty County had been a bust all right, but the Drucker background stuff had been golden by comparison.

It was true that George Drucker had been a moonshine man since birth and his other work after he had left home had spread a trail of fraud and deceit all across north Florida. It was also suspicious, and not wildly speculative that George Drucker was the most likely successor to the moonshine operations in Liberty County after Earl was safely put away or hanged, but there was no evidence sufficient to prove he was making it only look like Earl was guilty.

If the truth was known, as Aaron saw it this morning taking the critical view necessary for a good defense lawyer, there wasn't much chance Aaron could create a reasonable doubt that this small time crook could actually have pulled off such a seemingly flawless plan to eliminate his competition that had come off without a hitch. No jury in North Florida would believe he was that good to plan it that way and have it come off without a hitch or mistake in some part of it. The reverse of that speculation was more closely like the truth, that he was telling it like it actually happened.

George Drucker would not be a credible witness under normal circumstances but these were not normal circumstances. No matter how unsavory George was, there was no getting around the damaging evidence of the murder weapon. Sir, it was incongruous that Earl's prints were all over the gun stock and barrel but completely clean on the trigger guard and the trigger itself. But the bullet dug out of Earl's front door post did indeed match the rifling in the barrel to make it fairly conclusive that this Prosecution Exhibit 1, the Model 1917 Enfield war Surplus rifle, owned by and found in the possession of Earl Bryant that fateful morning, probably used in the actual battlefields in France in W W I, was the very rifle that had killed Federal Agent Frank Stiller.

Aaron would do his best to suggest to the Jury that George Drucker's timing at the Lagoon that morning was just a little too perfect and that George had everything to gain and not too much to lose. Aaron believed in his heart of hearts that George was not really clever enough to pull it off either and Earl had not helped matters by not very forcefully proclaiming his innocence.

Aaron had followed the conventional wisdom among criminal defense lawyers in not directly asking his client if he did it. If he did and Earl confessed, he could not put him on the stand to testify to the contrary. The general rule is never have your man testify in his own defense and therefore make the Prosecutor prove his case beyond a reasonable doubt because there are just too many ways to screw up on two or three out of fifty details that could convict you even if innocent of the crime. Memory was just too much of an impediment even of the truth. But Aaron had not finally made up his mind on this in the Bryant case and he needed to keep that option open.

Those almost confessions as admissions from Earl to Drucker could be explained away making the Government's case seem silly on those points, but the revenge motive might be strengthened by Earl's testimony that he actually witnessed the killing of his father, Terrell Bryant, which was much stronger than Drucker's admission from Bryant that was a little bit vague as to details.

Also it had been twenty years with many opportunities for Bryant to take out his revenge on Stiller, since Stiller had truly been a thorn in the flesh of Earl Bryant's illegal moonshine activities. But Aaron also did not want to dwell on the illegal whiskey business of his client and his testifying would open the door wide on the history of that business by evidence from his own mouth. All the evidence and his considerable experience was convincing to Aaron that Bryant was not going to testify. This was a difficult case to defend because in his mind Aaron kept meeting himself coming and going on the evidence. But one thing was certain and that was that Judge Parker would commence the trial on time and Aaron Martin, defense lawyer, had better be ready. He would decide before next week whether the coming or the going was the wiser course.

53. Drucker

"Mr. Gilchrist, you may call your next witness," Judge Parker forcefully stated. The attorneys for both sides had laid out in opening statements for the cases they intended to prove or defend. The coroner had testified to the death of Frank Stiller. The U. S. Marshal had testified of his arrest of Earl Bryant, the recovery of the spent bullet, the weapon and established the chain of evidence of the weapon and bullet from the crime scene to the courtroom. The examination of the key witness of the trial was about to begin.

"The Government of the United States, calls George Drucker to testify," Houston Gilchrist said and waited as the Judge's Bailiff walked slowly out of the courtroom into the hallway of the Federal Courthouse to retrieve the witness, where he had been waiting under protective custody. George came slowly and cautiously into the courtroom behind Ervin Floyd, Bailiff, right down the center isle as if he were a nervous bride approaching the bridegroom at the alter in church, not really Sir he was prepared to do this.

There was no bliss, wedded or otherwise, awaiting George Drucker at the end of the aisle, and he had no illusions to the contrary. You could go over a man's testimony so many times he could recite the answers ten times in a row without mistake, but even a hundred such recitals would not take the fear and trepidation out of it. George had been playing a high stakes game known only to him, and his stomach was generating so much acid and adrenalin it was like a stranger within him twisting his insides so tight he was afraid they might split from the strain. He could not quell the turmoil within him by any kind of mind control or relaxation techniques, and could only lock in his feelings with the hope that this had to end someday and only time would heal the painful gnawing within him.

Judge Ben looked down at George as he approached the bar of justice and directed his Bailiff to seat the witness in the witness chair for swearing in, as if Ervin needed any help in this task having performed the same thing thousands of time over the years.

"Swear the witness, Mr. Clerk," the Judge said and Frank Hopkins, Deputy Clerk on duty that day, brought out the leather bound Bible that had been used for that purpose for so many years the leather binding was as cracked and lined as a ninety year old grandmother's face with all the wisdom and experience such a face could signify. This ancient book had an aura about it that conveyed truth in its bearing that only the morally depraved or the faulty of memory could avoid without tremendous risk. Its symbol as a reminder that perjury in Judge Ben Parker's Court or the court of cosmic justice for most Americans in that era could not be committed lightly.

"Do you swear to tell the truth, the whole truth and nothing but the truth, so help you God?" Deputy Clerk, Frank Hopkins, asked as though he not only expected an answer but that the witness, by God, better really means it when he said, "I do." George answered the only way expected, as if anybody in their right mind would even if they intended otherwise, to admit the contrary. Whether he was willing to tell the whole truth or not the trial was now underway.

All the planning and tactics were over and the case of the United States against Earl Bryant relied really on the testimony of this witness, the otherwise dependable assistant to the most notorious moonshiner in the District.

By advance arrangement with the Government, George had not only been given protection by armed guards against any attempts on his life by forces loyal or under the direction of Earl Bryant, now more or less safely restrained in jail, but he had been given immunity from prosecution for any of his own participation in illegal whiskey making activities, which had been by this time, considerable. In other words, he was free to talk about the moonshine operations involving the Defendant and not worry about his own prosecution from any State or Federal authority, which the making of moonshine would ordinarily land you a sizeable sentence in its own right. To talk about it in open court or anywhere else a reliable witness might over hear it, would under normal circumstances, land you in serious trouble.

"Please state your name, address and occupation," Houston Gilchrist asked to get the ball rolling. While this seemed like a harmless enough question, right away George was stuck on the answer for a part of it. He understood the immunity part all right, but the address question was harder than it sounded. He was one of those men who really didn't live anywhere and Houston had forgotten to give him an answer that was safe and easy to state. He couldn't say he was a drifter and that he really didn't live anywhere since that fateful morning of Earl's arrest. That wouldn't sound right to the jurors who all had a place they called home and besides, since he had been under Federal protection, they had moved him around from place to place and he didn't really have an address.

"I'm George Drucker and at present I am unemployed since the Government have shut down the whiskey still business that one time employed me and I have lived from place to place ever since the arrest of Earl Bryant, as I ain't as yet been back to where I was staying at. I ain't got no address as such anymore, anyway, Sir," George said answering truthfully as best he could.

"Then you are a moonshine man by work experience, is that right?" Houston asked.

"Your Honor, I object, he's leading the witness," Aaron rose to his feet and stated his objection vigorously, just to flex his rhetorical muscles and let Houston know that he had to follow the rules of evidence even on preliminary matters.

"I'll allow that question, Mr. Martin, it's a preliminary matter and the witness is understandably uncertain as to his residence and occupation under the circumstances for which he has been given immunity, let's get on with the facts of the case, shall we?" Judge Parker said.

"Exactly what whiskey still business were you involved with, Mr. Drucker, before it was shut down, as you say?" Houston asked the well-practiced question and answer routine they had practiced for hours in the weeks leading up to the trial.

"I was employed by Earl Bryant, of Liberty County as his operations man. That's him seated right over there (pointing to the Defendant's table in the courtroom where Bryant was in fact seated) and I worked for him at his still until the Government shut it down just recently," George said.

Houston by rather deft direct questions, carefully avoiding the leading of the witness, but still more or less led George through the history of his relationship with Earl Bryant. George told the jury how as a young man he had taken a job with the Defendant as an ordinary hand in one of his single whiskey stills and worked his way up in the organization until he found his notch as the man in charge of ordering sugar, corn meal and other supplies to make the large still operation function as smoothly as it did.

Along the way, he was careful to paint a mental picture of Earl Bryant, Defendant, in this charge of murder, as a notorious illegal whiskey operator without saying so in so many words. By the looks on the faces of the jury, made up of honest citizens of the District who had a healthy respect for law and order, however ambivalent they were on the whiskey question, it was obvious this picture was being painted with clarity and color and would leave an indelible imprint on their minds when it came time to decide the fate of the Defendant.

While Earl was not on trial for illegal whiskey making, the fact that he ran this rather large operation under the noses of the Federal and State law officials could not bode very well with the jury, or most of them anyway, on the question of his character and credibility. Aaron Martin furiously made notes during this phase of the testimony to prepare for the cross examination that was to come. It would be his only chance to undermine the Government's very strong case for murder with the murder weapon being traced by fingerprints and circumstantial evidence as being in the hands of the Defendant Earl Bryant on the day of the murder. Judge Parker sustained some objections and overruled others to maintain the flow of evidence but fairly and even handedly protected the rights of the Defendant on trial for his life and allowed justice to proceed.

"On December 5, 1933, in the early morning Mr. Drucker, where were you and why?" Houston asked the witness. George explained to the jury that he had had left his home in Telogia and traveled south toward the Lagoon Site Still by way of the Back River Road to coordinate the shipment of whiskey planned that morning by the Defendant to distribute their inventory of corn whiskey to the network of bootleggers and small time operators all over south Georgia because of the expected push in the Florida territory to wipe out the illegal whiskey trade. As the coordinator of raw material purchases, it had been George's job to arrange for the shipment out of the production areas in Liberty County and this morning he had arrived at the main production site right after breakfast as planned.

"You were asked by Mr. Bryant to come to the still that morning?" Houston asked to be met by a vigorous objection from Aaron Martin for his leading the witness.

"Just ask the witness for the direct facts, Mr. Gilchrist, if you please and don't lead. You know better than that, Sir," Judge Parker said, not even waiting to hear Defense Counsel's explanation for his objection.

"Yes, Sir, your Honor. Mr. Drucker, when you arrived at the main Still site, who was present?" Houston said.

"Earl, Mr. Bryant that is, was already there tending business with the Negroes when I got there, Sir," the witness said.

"Explain to the jury, would you, Mr. Drucker, the layout of the still, you know, size, equipment and the like?"

"Well it's a big room like place under cover of a frame with limbs and such overhead and built up against the wall of the lagoon bank for one wall and sort of open ended for the other. The mash barrels, cooking kettle, thumper and evaporator are spread all around it. Where you come in down some little steps to git into the place there are a rack on the bank wall on your left where Mr. Bryant had his gun and coat rack and in front are the kettles and other stuff I was telling about," George said.

"Now this rack, as you call it, Mr. Drucker, was there anything on it that morning as you came into the still room itself?" Houston asked the witness.

"Yes, Sir, there was Earl's gun hanging on one of them pegs that mornin' and I hung my old coat on one right next to it, cold it were that morning, right nippy with a little frost about the place, coat and glove weather we sometimes say," George said.

"How did you know it was Mr. Bryant's gun?" Gilchrist asked.

"Well, Sir, I have seen it lots of times, that old Enfield military rifle Earl always carried when he was down at the Still," George said.

Houston walked across the Courtroom to the Clerk's table and picked up the alleged murder weapon and brought it to the witness box and handed it to the witness. "Take a look at this rifle, Mr. Drucker, which has been marked for identification as the Government's Exhibit 1. See if you can identify it, take a close look. Is this the rifle you saw hanging on a peg in the still that morning?" Houston asked.

"Yes, Sir, this here is the same one, Mr. Gilchrist," George said, holding the rifle in a long familiar manner.

"How long were you down there at the Still that morning, Mr. Drucker?" Houston asked, setting the stage for the important testimony soon to come that the rifle identified as Earl's had only one shell missing from a normally full magazine.

"I was there quite a spell that morning, Mr. Gilchrist, we had business to attend to," George said.

"Tell the jury what happened next, George," Houston inquired being careful to familiarize the jury with the witness as a person and not with some impersonal or formal "Mr." designation. George responded to this rather open-ended question with his prepared narrative description.

"We tended to business as a normal day about things. But mainly Earl, Mr. Bryant, that is, questioned me about what I seen and heard on my way to the Lagoon that morning," George testified.

"What did he say to you George, about the trip down there, I mean?" Houston asked.

"When I told him I come by way of the Back River Road, he want to know whether I heard a shot up toward his house that morning, he even wondered if I was hard a hearin'," George explained.

"At the time he asked you that, did you know Mr. Stiller, the Federal Agent had been shot?" Houston asked.

"No, Sir, I didn't know that," George said in his most genuine almost incredulous tone of voice.

"Did he tell you what had happened, George?" Houston asked, lobbing the softball question right across the plate.

George waited a second or two for effect and then drove the pitch right back at the mound, "He said there were a shooting at his house and that a Federal Man had been shot dead on his front stoop and more than that, he knew the fella and told me who it were!"

"He knew his name?" Houston asked equally incredulously as if he and George were having this chat for the very first time.

"Yes, Sir, he named the man as Frank Stiller, a Federal Man we all knowed that had been after us for whiskey making down there, for years," George said.

"What did he say about the fellow, George?"

"He said this fella had been a burr under his saddle for years and that the Federal men were bound to think he done it," George explained.

"Did he say anything else about the dead man, George?"

"Yes, Sir, he said I ain't forgotten what that bastard done to me and my family way back when, and who else besides me would have had the brass ones to do this and on my front stoop George," George said. Aaron rose to his feet as fast as he could, "I object, Your Honor, that is not responsive to the question, move to strike that answer" "Sustained," Judge Parker said, and then went on, "The jury will disregard that remark about what somebody had done and the brass whatevers," but the damage had been done as Houston and his witness had planned it.

"Did he say what had been done to his family?" Houston asked expectantly.

"Not right then, Sir, but it was well known that…"

"I object to this whole line of questions, Your Honor, the knowledge of any past event would have to be hearsay, as in learned from somebody else and offered in this court without the benefit or opportunity to cross examine the declarant," Aaron had jumped to his feet and said vigorously, explaining more than necessary to Judge Ben, the elements for a true objection to hearsay statements.

"Your Honor!" Houston stressed equally vigorously, "The witness never got the answer out before that objection."

"He's learning that with you Counselor, it's necessary," Judge Parker said, "Sustained!"

"The Government requests a side bar, your Honor?" Houston said.

"We'll excuse the jury for this one, Bailiff, escort the jury out and we will take our morning recess for now. We'll do this in Chambers, Counselors," Judge Parker said, rising from his seat as the jury filed out of the courtroom.

"All rise," the Bailiff announced as quickly as he could,

ambidextrously, as it were, as he stood by the exit as the jury filed out and remained on the job for courtroom decorum at the same time. The lawyers followed Judge Parker into Chambers and the jail guards stood by the prisoner during the recess.

The Courtroom was all a buzz over the developments in the trial for the prospect of a juicy historical motive for the alleged killing was tantalizing to most of them, especially the small press contingent seated on one side of the courtroom. Tony Callaway was seated in the middle of the collection of mostly local journalists with a few out of town reporters from the larger newspapers around the state, as the word of this trial had been spread over the news wires for weeks now. The end of Prohibition and the increased Federal enforcement of the whiskey laws had given this trial of a small town murderer more than its normal news appeal, with the Federal Agent angle being the major attraction to the out of town journalists for the story. Tony sat back in the pew like bench in the courtroom and reflected on what he had heard so far. His disastrous trip to Liberty County had turned him into a kind of celebrity himself. Tony had written some amazing stories of his and Johnny Caldwell's adventure into the wild and wooly river country, and the wire services had picked it up for substantial national circulation.

He made a point, however, to avoid discussing this side light with his colleagues of the press, but his notoriety had not gone unnoticed by most of the press corps. But what puzzled Tony about the testimony so far, was why Earl Bryant, if he was indeed guilty, would have ever discussed the shooting with his hired man, Drucker. And even assuming he had actually committed the crime and would have been fool enough to practically admit it to someone else, why on earth would he have given Drucker his motive for the killing? It just didn't make sense. This Drucker fellow, according to his friend, Aaron Martin, was an unsavory character and that was well known to Bryant and practically everybody else in the County. Why would Bryant, who by reputation was nobody's fool, ever do that? Tony could not figure it out yet.

"Come in gentlemen," Judge Parker said as he unzipped his uncomfortable black robe,

hung it on a rack placed in his office for that purpose and took his seat in his leather chair behind the massive desk provided by the Government and gestured to the lawyers to take their seats. "Now where are we headed with this testimony Houston?" Judge Parker asked.

"Your Honor, Drucker will testify that it was well known around Liberty County that Terrell Bryant, Earl's father, was shot down by Federal Agents back in 1902 and that Bryant, the Defendant I mean, talked about it all the time," Houston explained.

"Will he testify that Bryant said it to him is what I want to know, Houston?" the Judge said.

"No, Sir, I don't believe he can, Judge," Houston said, hopeful still he could get this important motive testimony into evidence.

"Your Honor," Aaron countered, "This is not admissible evidence, its rumor, that's all! Sir my client told people he was upset about his father's death by Federal Agents way back then, and who wouldn't have been, but that's got nothing to do with this Federal Agent and motive for this crime. Any suggestion by the witness that it is, based on some rumor floating around the county, is pure speculation, hearsay and highly prejudicial. The Circuit Judges in Atlanta would take a dim view of allowing that stuff into evidence, Judge!" Aaron argued, hinting at his likely appeal of a conviction in the case if Judge Ben let this evidence in and he was not able to find a reasonable doubt somewhere hidden in the evidence to persuade the jury for an acquittal.

"I'm not inclined to allow any such speculation into my trial, Houston, Aaron would turn your conviction into a reversal so fast it wouldn't make it past a Motion on the Merits in the Circuit Court of Appeals, but if Bryant told Drucker that Federal Agents had it in for him and had done in his father without naming the victim as the one he believed had done it, I'll allow that much," Judge Parker said gravely.

Split the baby, didn't he, Aaron thought, but was glad at least that he didn't have to argue against a rumor that Frank Stiller had killed Earl's father. Some Federal Agent had killed him for Sir but that was thirty years ago and even Houston Gilchrist, as talented as he was, couldn't sell that bill of goods to a common sense jury like this one. What he had wanted to do, if the judge had let him, would have, in the end, been disastrous to the Government's case on appeal!

"Okay, men, then that's it, we'll go back on the record and you each decide how you want to proceed on this and I'll make the call on each pitch. Play ball!" Judge Parker said laughing and they followed him back into the courtroom.

When the jury returned and Judge Parker explained that he and the lawyers had had some legal matters to resolve, the trial resumed.

"How long did you talk to the Defendant that morning?" Houston asked the witness, staying carefully away from the minefield that the motive testimony had become.

"We must of talked twenty minutes or so, don't know how long it were, don't have no watch, Mr. Gilchrist," George said.

"What else did you talk about and do that morning, George" Houston asked.

"We discussed the shipment that had been scheduled for that morning, and then he went on about the business of running the still, you know, dealing with the Negro hands on supplies and such and I had some time to check on things about the room," George said.

"What kind of things did you check on, George?" Houston asked, waiting for the bombshell to land he had planned so carefully all along.

"I checked on the gun hanging on the wall hoOkay," George said and stopped.

"Why on earth did you do that?" Houston asked, as though it had just occurred to him.

"Well, Sir, after he told me about the shootin' that morning, I naturally was curious about his gun and the timing of the shootin' was about right, you see," George said.

"Did you examine the rifle George?" Houston asked, holding his breath and hoping against hope that George would get it right as they had practiced and not screw it up with some harebrained product the Jury would never buy.

"When Earl was busy over with the Negroes at the far side of the shed, I pulled open the breach and found one shell missing from a full magazine of the Enfield," George said.

"Had you seen this rifle of Mr. Bryant's before?" Houston asked.

"Yes, Sir, like I just said, he carried it everywhere he went, it was one of them Surplus army rifles, a Model 17 Enfield, like they used late in the last war, Sir," George said.

"Did you serve in the last war, George," Houston asked.

"No, Sir, not me, they never caught me, I mean I never was called by the Draft board, leastwise, I never learned of it if they did, Mr. Gilchrist," George said honestly if carelessly.

"What happened next, George?" Houston asked.

"Well, Sir, I finished my business and left the shed and headed on back to the office up north as planned," George said. Houston Gilchrist, winding up his direct testimony with the witness, regretting he had ended on such a weak point in the testimony and mentally kicking himself all the way back to his seat, before saying,

"Your witness, Mr. Martin".

The jury had been watching George Drucker all during his testimony.

He was obviously a key witness for the Government so their attention was riveted on his every word and mannerism. Could they believe this witness who had established a motive of sorts for the shooting, a probable identification of the murder weapon and the important evidence that one shell was missing from the 30-06 rifle's magazine.

It bothered Fred Warner, the tobacco farmer from Quincy that George Drucker had been an employee of the Defendant and so ready to testify against him. He hated the notion of a snitch, which he suspected George Drucker of being. The Judge had admonished the jury several times they were not to discuss the case among themselves and they had followed the instruction but that did not keep them from forming opinions as they went. Fred didn't like this witness but he could not have told you why at the time for he did not know the reason yet himself. The jury was a mixture of people from all over the Northern District of Florida. Since most of the citizens of the region were involved in agriculture to earn a living or worked for businesses that depended on it, several of the jurors either owned farms or worked for farmers. There was a smattering of other tradesmen, state employees, and academic people, including one professor, Dr. Steven Mathewson, a teacher of mathematics at the State Women's College. The Jury seemed to be attentive to the proceedings, which was a good thing for justice given the disputed nature of the evidence in this case and the fact that a man's life was at stake in the outcome. The key to this trial was going to turn on the credibility of George Drucker, plus the tangible evidence of the gun and bullet so the Jurors eagerly waited for the contest of wills that was about to begin on the cross examination of George Drucker.

Aaron slowly rose from his seat and walked around the end of the counsel table and turned his full attention to the older brother of his old school friend Peter Drucker, hardware and tobacco supply clerk from Havana. His client was also acutely attracted to the upcoming encounter because his life literally hung in the balance.

"Mr. Drucker, for a period commencing roughly ten years ago until December the 5th of this past year, you were a faithful and loyal employee of the Defendant Earl Bryant in the business of making whiskey from corn mash in Liberty County, were you not?"

"Yes, Sir," George answered.

"That activity was against the law, was it not?"

"Yes, Sir, it were."

"In addition to that illegal activity, you have a record of convictions for larceny, possession of stolen property, and being drunk and disorderly for which you have served time in this District on various chain gang road construction crews, have you not, Mr. Drucker, and I could go over each and every one of those if your memory has faded any?"

"Yes, Sir, I have that record is true and it won't be necessary for you to spell that out, Sir," George said, beginning to squirm in the witness chair.

"Isn't it true, Mr. Drucker, Sir," Aaron continued boring in on his target with increasing pressure designed to shake the witnesses confidence, "You not only were paid to be loyal to Mr. Bryant, here (pointing behind him to his client), but you were paid to provide information to the Government bringing this prosecution against your regular employer?" Aaron said, with the witness pausing for what seemed like an unusually long time before answering.

George cleared his throat after that pause and answered, "I did my duty to report on the illegal activity Mr. Bryant was engaged in, yes."

"For which you were regularly paid, isn't that correct?," Aaron asked.

"Well, yes, I was paid; it was only fair and hard work too, serving two masters, and keeping it straight in my own mind who I was telling what to," George said jutting out his chin defiantly at Aaron as though lying to one side or the other was a virtue.

"You were what we call a "snitch," were you not, George Drucker?" Aaron asked or more or less stated the obvious.

"I wouldn't call myself that, Sir, no, I never snitched on nobody," George said, trying to avoid what to even him sounded like an indictment in the public mind and he wasn't Sir whether that was legal either.

"Well, now, George, what would you call it when you go to work every day for the man who pays you with good money to do his bidding and be loyal and faithful to him and at the same time you are being paid to feed information to somebody else against that very man you were pledged to be loyal to?" Aaron asked, trying to put George on the spot and hoping he was not swift thinking enough to remind the jury that what his employer was doing all those years was wrong and that "snitching" against illegal activity was a noble thing to do whether it was considered that way by the criminal element in society or not.

But unfortunately, George had been a part of the criminal element of society for so long, he could just not see things through the eyes of the good citizens of the jury so he squirmed and weaseled his way through it, acting exactly like he had been caught in a lie or something worse, just exactly as Aaron had hoped he would do.

"I don't know,.... I expect you might think that....the pay was good and I needed the extra money.... And it was whiskey work we was doing....Yes, Sir, I told on him all right.

Aaron smiled as the tactic seemed to be working as the jury began to look at George as though he should be carefully scrutinized from now on and then changed directions in his cross examination.

Professor Mathewson particularly seemed to cock his head to one side indicating special attention as he listened to George try to avoid the false corner the lawyer had just painted him into.

"You arrived at the Lagoon Still about the same time as Mr. Bryant and came there on foot that morning on the Back River Road from "The Office," as you called it, up north, did you not?" Aaron asked.

"Yes, Sir, I had," George said, still recovering from the successful painting by the lawyer of himself as a lowly "snitch" in the previous round of questions.

"It was one of those quiet, cold, windless days we get in December wasn't it Mr. Drucker?" Aaron asked.

"Yes, Sir it was cold and quiet morning as I remember it," George good naturedly answered not realizing where the cross examination was headed.

"That Back River Road passes within three hundred yards of Mr. Bryant's house, does it not, Sir?"

"Yes, Sir that do," George said, being particularly confident he was safe in this answer.

"When you arrived at the Still that morning right after Mr. Bryant had arrived, you learned for the first time that a Federal Agent had been shot up at Mr. Bryant's house, didn't you Mr. Drucker?" Aaron said.

"Yes, Sir, I learned it then for the first time, indeed I did," George said.

"If you were on the Back River Road at the time the shot was fired that killed the Federal Agent up at Mr. Bryant's house, you would have heard that shot from the distance you say it was, would you not Mr. Drucker?" Aaron asked.

"Yes, Sir, a 30-06 rifle shot would be heard at that range," George said, wondering where these questions were headed.

"Considering the timing of your arrival, right after Mr. Bryant, and the report to you that he had found the dead agent just before he came to the Lagoon that morning, isn't it fair to say that you were on that River Road about the time that shot was fired, George?" Aaron asked, setting the trap for the step George Drucker was about to take into it, based on the information in the Government's witness statements he had carefully reviewed.

"You would think I would have heard it, Yes, Sir," George answered.

"You told Mr. Bryant that morning that you never heard that shot isn't that true George and I remind you are under oath in this Court?" Aaron said and waited for George to step into the trap. George thought about it for as long as he dared and then said,

"I guess I just wasn't listening very well, I don't know why but I never heard it that morning," George said, trying to wiggle off the hook.

Damn, Aaron thought, *slippery rascal ain't he.* What Aaron had hoped was a trap was the contradiction between being that close to Earl's house at the time of the shooting and admitting it was a still and quiet cold December morning and telling Bryant he had heard nothing prior to arriving at the Still that morning. The problem was he didn't have much evidence contrary to his client's guilt and was grasping at any straw he could reach for on his cross-examination. There was really no good reason George did not know about the shot at least as he walked through the quiet woods that morning; but when you boiled it down, it showed no evidence that Earl was not the shooter and Aaron had to let it rest with that on this part of his challenge of George's direct testimony.

George Drucker was an unsavory character by way of his record and his rather tasteless job as a snitch on his employer; but after all, his employer was engaged in illegal moonshine whiskey making and why shouldn't George provide information to the Government to help them put an end to it? That made perfect sense and Aaron could only hope that the prejudice of common men against snitches would count for something. It was odd that Drucker had not heard the rifle shot that morning but that by itself didn't prove anything.

"Your job in the Bryant operation was to keep the flow of the supplies of corn, sugar, yeast and other ingredients in the whiskey making, was it not?" Aaron asked, taking a different tactic in his examination.

"Yes, Sir, it were that," George said, without hesitation, for he had been given full immunity from prosecution and had nothing to fear for any testimony in the case concerning his own illegal activities in the making of whiskey.

"You were a key man in the operation, in fact, Mr. Bryant could not operate his whiskey making without you, is that not true, Mr. Drucker?" Aaron asked.

"Yes, Sir, he needed me to run it," George said with no little pride.

"You knew how to order supplies, how to make the whiskey, who the bootleggers were in your distribution system, in fact you could have run the entire operation if Mr. Bryant was not around to see about those things, could you not, Mr. Drucker?" Aaron asked.

"I suppose I did know everything in the business, Mr. Martin, and I ran things when Earl wasn't available, which weren't often, I might add," George said.

"You could practically take over with Earl out of the way, couldn't you George? Aaron asked. Now George Drucker was a clever fellow but occasionally he would miss things and this was one of those times. He did not quite get the point Aaron was making through him that this murder charge against Bryant was awfully convenient for one who was set up to take over the kingpin's business. He was suggesting this could happen once the king was safely put away somewhere, such as being hung from a murder conviction.

If George was perceived by the jury as an opportunist to take advantage of the fall of Earl Bryant, it wasn't too much further to get them to believe he could have set the whole thing up or at least cast some doubt on Earl's motive to pull this off as a revenge killing, especially since Judge Parker had been so helpful in his evidentiary rulings on that point. When you defend someone for murder, you use every twist and turn in the case that's favorable no matter how much of a long shot. You throw enough stuff up against the wall, sooner or later some of it will stick.

"I suppose, I could run it if Earl was tied up, yeah, shore," George said in a manner that was convincing even though he should not have taken that tone had he been aware of the consequences. This was also one of those times when a lawyer stops short of the final question and saves it for final argument for Aaron could not tell when George might wake up and figure out the point George was making for him and mess it up with an unexpected answer, so he let it rest right there.

"You say you checked the rifle hanging on the wall and found one shell missing, did I hear you correctly Mr. Drucker?" Aaron asked cautiously.

"Yes, Sir, I did that," George said.

"How did you determine that the one shell was missing, Mr. Drucker?" Aaron asked, bothered about something but he was not Sir yet what it was.

"You open up the breach of the Enfield and push down the stripper clip and if a round is missing, the clip will sink. The clip holds five shells and you can add one more if it's tight. His sunk just enough for one round to be missing, that's how" George answered triumphantly.

"For this opening of the breach, you use your hand to grip the end of the bolt and rotate it open, do you not Mr. Drucker?" Aaron asked.

"Yes, Sir, that's how it's done, Sir," George answered. Aaron walked over to the exhibit table, picked up the rifle, Prosecutor's Exhibit 1, carrying it over to the witness box and handed it to George.

"Please show the jury exactly how you did that checking, Mr. Drucker, would you please Sir?" Aaron said.

"All right, Sir, it goes like this," George said as he balanced the rifle in his left hand by the wooden undercarriage and expertly took his right hand, closed it over the knob on the end of the bolt and rotated the bolt open to expose the magazine where the stripper clip was loaded with five cartridges was seated. He then took his right thumb and pushed down on the stripper clip by pressing the top cartridges and the spring action within the clip retracted just the amount of space one missing cartridge would make if the sixth cartridge had been added in the magazine and said, "You see Sir, if there had been six cartridges in the magazine, the stripper clip would not seat any further but this one did, showing me that only five were in it that morning," George said.

Aaron thought about this for a few seconds and wondered why the forensic expert for the Government had found no fingerprints of George's on the murder weapon if George checked it that morning like he said, to learn there was one round less than full like he had just done in the courtroom demonstration. There should have been some of George's prints on the bolt knob, unless he was careful to use his palm only in opening the bolt and definitely his fingerprints on the cartridge casing on the top of the stripper clip, for sure. Somehow this point had escaped the Government lawyers, which they would come to regret terribly.

So Aaron decided to leave it alone for now and wait for the weapons and fingerprint expert to reveal it on cross examination. He would let this delicious little fact just drop into the case at that time after Drucker was safely all through with his explanations rather than allow the witness to come up right now while it was fresh with some unexpected and exculpatory explanation. This might avoid taking away his argument to the Jury that Drucker couldn't have checked for the missing round that morning or he would have left his own fingerprints somewhere at least.

It wasn't the vital bit of evidence to set his client free. He was an experienced enough trial lawyer to not count on some exculpatory explanation raising its ugly head later on but any weakening of the star witnesses' credibility, just by interrupting the flow of it if nothing else, could not help but hurt the Government's case. The truth was, there was another explanation for the missing fingerprints that had not occurred to anybody yet and it might come out eventually in the trial or it might not. It was too early to tell.

"Your Honor, that's all I have for my cross exam of this witness," Aaron said and sat down.

Judge Parker looked at his pocket watch propped up on a little stand on the desk in front of him and said, "It's nearly four thirty, gentlemen, we'll leave it right there until nine o'clock in the morning. Mr. Gilchrist, you can do your re-direct of this witness at that time. Judge Parker rose from his seat as Deputy Clerk, Frank Hopkins, gave the "all rise" and the day's testimony in United States against Bryant was concluded. At this point, it had not occurred to Houston the damage that had just been done to his case, a discovery he was to painfully make a little later on. Besides, it was the end of the day and he was tired.

54. Searching for hope

Ellie Bryant hurried down to the front of the Courtroom to have her precious few minutes with her man before the guards came to take him back to the cells for the night. "Are you all right, Earl that Drucker is trying to…" Ellie started but could not complete the sentence as she sat next to Earl at his counsel's table where they would be left alone for a few minutes as arranged by Aaron with the jail guards.

"Never you mind, Ellie girl, it's all right, they ain't licked me yet!," Earl said, as he tried to reassure her as best he could, though there was no way to erase the anxiety he felt as the testimony of his trusted assistant accumulated in his mind.

"Earl, I… miss you, its…well…." She stammered, being unable to get out any coherent sentence with the weight of the fear she felt for him welling up inside of her intolerably.

"How about you, Ellie, has Emily and that husband of hers made things tolerable for you? I know that Doc Wilson has no use for me before this and especially not now," Earl said, realizing her difficulty talking about his terrible condition and thought he would change the subject to her somewhat, wondering how his wife was faring in that hostile environment.

Ellie rallied and said, "He's all right Earl and done got over the worst of it. Don't you worry about that, you just get out of this mess and come back home where I needs you," Ellie said sincerely.

"I ain't likely to get out of this mess Ellie girl, and that's the God's truth in this business," Earl said, and held her arms between his hands which were limp by her side in the only sharing of affection permitted under these terrible circumstances and noticed the tears begin to stream in rivulets down her cheeks.

"Time's up Mr. Martin, we got to get him out of here," the jail guard said, waiting patiently to the side in deference to the request of the Defense Counsel who he had grown to respect over the years.

"Better wrap it up Earl, you have to go now," Aaron said, and Earl and Ellie hugged each other one final time for that day, looking deep into each other's eyes as if they could find the other's soul hiding deep inside. Then they parted, as commanded, and the jail guards restored the shackles and leg irons mandatory for transport for all felony Defendants in Federal Court trials, and Earl was escorted hobbling out of the courtroom.

In a moment he was gone, and Aaron turned to Ellie and said, "You keep up your spirits now Mrs. Bryant, you have to be the strong one for you and Earl both. Because no matter how he talks, we have to keep up our hopes now, don't we?"

"Yes, Sir," Ellie said, and shook her head contrary to her words. Aaron could tell his words of wisdom were falling on deaf ears at the moment, and he hardly believed them himself; but resolved to try even harder to make tomorrow's testimony something to give her hope and through her eventually preserve some hope to him.

"I have to go now, Mrs. Bryant and prepare for tomorrow's testimony, but are you all right, with a way to get to where you're staying, I mean?" Aaron asked and then nodded his head in understanding as Emily Wilson walked up from the back of the courtroom to greet her mother. There was none of the hostility there that he had heard about in this part of the family, and he was a good enough judge of human character to recognize support when he saw it.

"Mrs. Wilson, I'm Aaron Martin, your father's attorney, I'd recognize you as one of them anywhere. Thank you for standing by the family, it really helps them in this, believe me."

"You don't have to worry Mr. Martin, we're family all right and we'll stand together through this no matter how it may have been before," Emily said.

"I'm reassured by that, Emily, but say, I have to run now, if you'll excuse me," Aaron said and picked up his briefcase and headed out of the courtroom. A trial lawyer's work never ends with adjournment if the case continues tomorrow, and this one was just getting warmed up.

55. Alien appearance

Hobbling down the corridor of the jail was a depressing experience for Earl every time he had to do it and did not get much better once the handcuffs and shackles were removed and he was behind bars. Jack was buried under his blanket in his usual position mitigating the effects of his debilitation with an uncanny ability to drop off to sleep almost anytime he chose.

Earl quietly sat on the edge of his cot, and thought about the day's events and there was nothing in it to bring comfort or cheer. *Here we are again*, he thought, *Jack sleeping to bury his pain and me wide awake to suffer mine. How come he gets off the easy way and I get nailed with the hard one? Ellie, bless her, she tried to cheer me up but damn, there ain't much cheering to be done after that Bastard Drucker tried to rip me a new one today. Ain't it strange that I sit here in this jail accused of killing a man when that Stiller has done his share a killing. My Pap would be whooping it up about now to see him get his deserts. Hell, maybe he is or maybe Hell don't let them folks see out of it. That was always a puzzle, that Hell and Heaven business. Lord knows I done enough to earn the worst of it. Look at that Jack there in the mess he's in, all from drinking that stuff I been makin' and sellin' for years?*

Earl leaned back against the cell wall after rolling the bunk pillow up behind his head, closed his eyes, stretched out his legs and thought about just drifting off to sleep. There must be a way to put the day's events out of his mind. But the day kept running through over and over again like a bad dream that wouldn't go away. Just as soon as it finished one playing on the memory screen inside his head, it would start all over again forcing him to relive every terrifying minute.

The part that bothered him the most never actually made it into evidence, the part about his motive for the shooting the Federal agent. His lawyer had cut that one off at the pass and the prosecutor had not even tried to sneak it in after that recess with the Judge, but Earl could not stop thinking about the charge that he had killed Frank Stiller because Stiller had killed his father Terrell Bryant. It was a plausible theory, for in his mind that was a good motive, as the Prosecutor had been planning to prove. He could remember that scene back in 1913, just like a picture post card of a place you have been to that you keep around the house in a drawer, not so much because it was so vivid, beautiful or real, but that you fear that throwing it away would somehow cause the place to go away, or at least your memory of it to be lost.

He had wanted to shoot the man Stiller that day long ago, with his rear profile in view of his gun sights and close, too. All he had to do to get that sweet revenge was squeeze the trigger slowly, withdrawn and half released. He remembered to breathe as his pappy had taught him to do, to shoot a deer or bear so as to allow the piece to fire without the jerky motion that caused most untrained marksmen to miss whatever the target was. It had been disappointing in a way even back then, before he decided to lower his rifle and pass his chance, since he would have had to shoot the man in the back of the head not full in the face the way Stiller had done his pappy. That would have been a cheaper revenge in a way. It was not that full belly laugh kind of feeling you get when you know you have done it right; and more importantly, when the one on the business end of the rifle knows for a split second that it's coming and can't do anything about it and you get to enjoy it as it happens. There is the fear factor naturally in the mind and more importantly in the eyes of the target when he knows it's over and can't prevent it. It is better yet, when he knows you have done it, even if only for a split second before the shot. How delicious that thought of what he had wanted to do with all the pent up desire a few seconds can stimulate, but could not out carry it out from a practical sense of self preservation.

Those other agents had been closing in and after all, there was freedom to think about. Such a trade off! Worse than disappointing with one side of the self saying yes, do it, and the other side of the self-saying no, don't do it, and no part of the self left to be the judge. There was just one or the other to win out, but always looking back with regret, and at the same time in another sense, in relief. The ambivalence of the memory was oppressive to him this night when he was facing a charge of murdering the very man he so much wanted to kill that day. He just couldn't do it back then, as he had replayed that scene over and over in his mind over the years with no joy in the recall. Safety, yes! Regret, yes! How to ever merge the two and have peace about this was the question?

He wasn't sure at first whether he heard something in his cell, like a jailhouse rat stirring across the darkened room in search of a dinner scrap that so rarely but occasionally was spilled on the cold cell floor, or whether there was some movement by Jack's sleeping form. One quick glance put that notion to rest, as the old man lay motionless on his cot in that sound sleep that only the dead do better. But something had roused him from the haunting memory of his father's assassination, but for the life of him, he could not figure out what it was.

Then he saw it, sitting or possibly standing, he was never really Sir afterwards, an object there anyway, across the cell just behind Jack's sleeping form looking at him. He took it to be that anyway, a figure like that of a man between Jack's form and the cell wall. But that was just it, there was no room for that to be, but there it was all the same. He was Sir afterwards it was not a ghost, for this one had flesh or it looked as though it did. The face of the thing was calm, unmoving but definitely looking at him, Earl Bryant, felony Defendant, prisoner, probably for life until the hangman's noose was to be put an end to it. Earl didn't know whether to call out to the thing, the apparition, ghost, devil in disguise, or angel to him unaware at least, or man? Could it be, this thing was here to bring a message, scare the hell out of him, or him into it, receive something, give something, or something else unexpected entirely, but what? It looked like nothing he had ever seen, man like, yes, but less or maybe more, he was never Sir about that. Maybe it was an invasion into his space, or maybe the world's space or something he was to never know, or possibly not even related to him at all. But those questions would not be resolved by him this night.

No! It was personal to him and of this he was Sir, but in what way? That was the question that demanded an answer, by God! Could it be that or even Him? No way, not the God of the Bible, not here in this place, but what? But there was a familiar quality to the figure but in a way he could not describe or could not place. Was it the memory of a long forgotten experience or a man, possibly? But which man? Which experience? No, more like the memory of a man but distant like a dream that has faded so fast from the reality and vividness of sleep, even though it makes no sense, that evaporates in the consciousness of coming awake.

Just when he had worked up enough courage to do something, anything, the figure moved ever so slightly by a slight turn of the face even more directly at him, if that was possible. It was already pointed at him with those eyes that seemed as though they could find the middle of your being and expose anything that was hidden there, as there always is, that you never want to come out; but the slight motion was undeniable all the same. There was a shiver that ran up the back of his spine as he braced himself for nothing he could imagine, but something was about to happen and of that he was certain. The mouth of the thing then opened and a sound came flowing at him out of it, ever so smoothly and softly as though it was mercury being poured out of a flat beaker onto a glass table top. The sound was like no voice of a human he had ever heard for its tone was flat but almost melodic also, if that was possible; but a voice definitely and he could not describe, but the message of the words was clear yet so enigmatic he could make no sense out of it.

Yet, he was never Sir whether the sound, if you could call it that, was really a sound or just understood like people who know each other so well they don't have to speak, yet the message is clear. But one thing was certain; he would never forget the message as long as he lived, however he had received it.

"There is an end coming to you for which you must face the consequence of its beginning. But not all will find that end as they expect. I bring you greetings from those who care for the most important things and urge that you tarry until the time for your ending has come. I will be in attendance until the time of the end. Look for me!"

The voice then abruptly ended as though sucked out of the air into a vacuum for which there would never be an emptying, a vortex into a void, and a downward spiral into nothingness. And before Earl could open his mouth to respond, if that was what the thing required, it was gone, not like a ghost that you hear tell fades away from sight by degrees, like smoke or vapor that gradually disappears; and not like a live man who must walk, run or duck away from sight; but instead, just suddenly it was gone.

One second it had been there in its flesh, if flesh is what you could call the texture of such a thing, and the next second, not. And Jack remained motionless all the while, sleeping the sleep of the innocent, unavailable for validation, assuring that no one would ever hear of this experience. Certainly no one would believe it, so why bother to tell? Earl was left as alone as maybe he had been all along with no comfort or trust that anything from the real world had been with him, just absorbed in his thoughts on this lonely night in jail.

56. The expert

Houston had decided, after thinking it over back at the office, that George Drucker was more of a liability than an asset so he did not call George back the next morning to repair the limited damage Aaron had inflicted on cross examination and continued his case with his forensics expert.

Houston called for William (Bill) Stevenson, FBI firearms and fingerprint expert, to testify; and after he arrived in the stately old courtroom and was sworn to tell the truth. Houston began with the testimony that would prove, in his mind anyway, that Earl Bryant's gun that had been seized from his home at the time of the arrest, had been the weapon that had fired the fatal bullet that was the cause of death of Frank Stiller.

"Please state your name, address and occupation Mr. Stevenson," Houston said, and Bill Stevenson did so. Then with another leading question permitted on preliminary matters as to the qualifications of the witness, Bill Stevenson lay out with precision a curriculum vitae that would have convinced anyone that he was qualified to give opinions in the field of forensic science related to fingerprints, guns, bullets, muzzle velocity and the matching of bullets to barrels that fired them.

"Your Honor, the Government tenders the witness as an expert in the fields he has stated," Houston said, and sat down to allow the opportunity if not the expectation of an examination by Defense Counsel.

"You may inquire as to the witness's qualifications as an expert to give opinions in the fields stated," Judge Parker said, and the whole courtroom's attention was directed to Aaron. He rose from his seat and walked the pace or two over nearer the witness stand and faced the witness.

"You are an employee of the United States Government in your capacity of an expert witness are you not?" "Yes, Sir, that's my job," Bill Stevenson said.

"In other words, you get paid to testify for the Government in criminal cases, is that correct, Sir?" Aaron asked rhetorically.

"Yes, Sir, in part Sir," the witness said.

"How many times have you testified in criminal proceedings in your career, Mr. Stevenson?"

"Can't say with precision Sir, don't keep a record of that, but a lot."

"Is it fair to say Mr. Stevenson, that in your capacity as an expert in the field of forensic science concerning firearms and fingerprints, that every single one of those times you have been asked to testify by the Government you have reached the conclusion that the Defendant's weapon was the one used by the Defendant in the commission of a crime?" Aaron asked knowing the answer would have to be "yes" for the witness would obviously not be used in a prosecution when the Defendant was to be cleared but it sounded good to make the jury think this witness was a witness for hire and would say whatever the Government wanted him to say.

It was a standard technique for cross examination as to the qualification of the so called in house Government experts which never resulted in their disqualification as experts but was useful to weaken the Government's otherwise fool proof cases, especially when the reasonable doubt defense was about all defense counsel had to offer. This was the case in almost every criminal trial that was brought in State or Federal Court because the Prosecutors didn't waste their time on doubtful cases.

"Yes, Sir, they don't call me to testify if the man is innocent of a crime, nobody would do that," Stevenson said, not realizing how stupid that sounded. It only meant that Houston Gilchrist had a little more work to do to rehabilitate the witness.

"You hold yourself out as an expert in the two fields of fingerprints and firearms. Doesn't that get confusing at times Mr. Stevenson?" Aaron asked, really about through with his cross examination of the witness's qualifications as an expert but the last stupid answer by the witness left a fair chance that something else good for the case might turn up so Aaron took a flyer with the last question.

He was disappointed though as Bill Stevenson had recovered and gave the professional answer he was supposed to, and said, "No, Sir, the confusion ends when the prints turn out to be found on the weapon that matches the bullet that did the killing as it did in this case." That was a "take that" kind of an answer and in a way Aaron had asked for it and got it, in spades.

So much for breaking the rule of never asking a question you don't know the answer to, he thought. "Your Honor, the Defense accepts the witness as qualified in the fields of forensic science concerning weapons and fingerprints." Aaron said knowing from the start it was hopeless to try to disqualify Bill Stevenson as an expert who had testified against him in at least ten criminal trials but he had to make an effort anyway. The results of his cross were mixed but not totally harmful.

Houston rose to his feet after Aaron returned to his seat and continued with his direct case. "Mr. Stevenson did you examine the weapon identified as The Government's Exhibit I for purposes of testing the same for fingerprints?"

"Yes, Sir, I did and found a series of fingerprints around the stock end called the pistol grip, on the barrel and the stock supporting the barrel," the witness said.

"Have you enlarged that series of fingerprints and compared them to any known prints of individuals in the Government's records?" Houston asked, as Bill Stevenson brought out a series of enlarged reproductions on paper charts about four inches by five inches in size that had been previously marked for identification.

"Yes, Sir, they are these documents here, the first ten prints are the ones taken from the weapon as stated and the others are the fingerprints obtained from the US Government files for Earl Bryant, the Defendant in this case. Mr. Bryant apparently applied for exemption from military service in the last war and was required to present his fingerprints in the process."

"Are fingerprints unique to every person, Mr. Stevenson?" Houston asked.

"Yes, Sir, it is well established that everyone has unique immutable fingerprints," the witness explained using technical language that probably no member of the Jury understood. Houston saw the gap created and moved quickly to close it by asking,

"Please explain what you mean by unique and immutable, Mr. Stevenson," Houston said.

"Yes, Sir, every human being on the earth has identifiably different fingerprints and they do not change over the life of the person. The pattern of grooves and ridges are produced in the embryonic process of human development and they never change after birth. We have accumulated a vast record of fingerprints in our Washington, DC, offices of the FBI, such as the ones of Mr. Bryant, the Defendant in this case. If prints are obtained from a crime scene are compared with those on file and a match is made, the identification of the person who left the prints is certain," Bill Stevenson said.

"How is the identification made in general and specifically on the Exhibits presented to you?" Houston asked.

"Yes, Sir, a fingerprint is made of a series of ridges and furrows on the surface of the fingers and thumb. The uniqueness of a fingerprint can be determined by those patterns as well as what we call the minutiae points. These are local ridge characteristics that occur at a ridge break or at its end. For example, in the prints of the Defendant here as shown on Exhibit, was it Number 3, yes, there are thirty six such points I have marked on Mr. Bryant's forefinger print and they correlate exactly to the same thirty six minutiae points on Exhibit 8, the fore finger print from Mr. Bryant's right hand taken from the pistol grip of the weapon, Exhibit 10. I made the same analysis of each of the prints lifted from Exhibit 3 and 1 and they were matched exactly by Mr. Bryant's prints on file. I can tell from the location of the prints lifted from Exhibit 1 that Mr. Bryant held the weapon like this," Bill Stevenson said, holding the weapon in his hands, right hand around the pistol grip and left hand under the stock of the weapon.

"Have you examined the projectile, marked as Exhibit 17, that Marshall Boyle and his team recovered from the door frame directly in line with the estimated path of the shot that killed the victim Frank Stiller as the Coroner testified in this trial?" Houston asked to set the stage for the next piece in the chain of evidence he hoped would throttle and convict Earl Bryant for murder.

"Yes, Sir, I examined it carefully," Stevenson said.

"From your examination of the bullet that was dug out of the door frame at the crime scene, previously identified as Exhibit 17, what tests did you perform to relate it to the weapon, Exhibit 1"? Houston asked.

"I first examined the recovered projectile under a microscope and determined that there was sufficient remnants of helical grooves, called "rifling" that are present on the inside of the barrels of all rifles, made since the Civil War, to make the bullet travel in a straight line, to make an identification. The particular projectile (he lifted the spent bullet from a tray marked as Exhibit 17, and held it up as if examining it) that was recovered in this case, had been dug out of the soft pine wood making up the door frame on the porch door of the Defendant's home after it passing through the body of the deceased man. It had been damaged somewhat but the helical lines were still clearly identifiable on the spent bullet. Then we fired the same rifle into a water tank using the same kind of ammunition that was found in the weapon itself. The water absorbs the shock of the projection and the bullet is recovered without damage. We can then compare the sample round we know was fired through the same barrel to the round the crime scene investigators identified as being used in the crime. We can then make an analysis of the similarities and differences under a set of side by side microscopes with an optical bridge that reveals abutting rounds for the comparison. In every rifle manufactured including this one, there are machined imperfections, scratches, scrapes and other minute nicks that, over time with use, make each barrel unique and microscopically detectable. In this case, the groves or rifling on the undamaged end of the recovered round, matched the pattern of the grooves on the test rounds recovered.

I have produced a photograph of the match and that is the previously marked Exhibit 17. It is possible to reach three conclusions from this type of analysis: identification, exclusion or no conclusion. In this case, I was able to reach the conclusion of identification. In my opinion, the projectile that was recovered from the door frame was fired by the weapon, Exhibit I containing the fingerprints of the Defendant Earl Bryant and none other," Bill Stevenson, concluded emphatically.

"Wait right there Mr. Stevenson, Mr. Martin may have some questions for you," Houston said and sat down.

Houston was confident Bill Stevenson had made his case beyond a reasonable doubt. The bullet that had killed Frank Stiller had been fired by the Model 1917 30-06 surplus military Enfield rifle undisputedly owned by Earl Bryant, recovered from him the day of the shooting. The testimony of the coroner had certainly proved the death by homicide and no matter how much of a blow hard Marshall Boyle had been, the crime scene investigation had shown enough of the location of the place of the shot, the line of the bullet's path, and the recovery of the spent round showed that somebody had made the fatal shot.

Bill Stevenson had established beyond question that the fingerprints of Earl Bryant in the position of holding it for a shot were lifted from the same weapon and that the microscopic grooves in the round came from the weapon used in the crime. However flaky George Drucker's testimony had been, he had identified that the very same rifle was hung up on the pegs at the Lagoon Still the morning of the shooting and that he had examined it that morning and found one round missing from the normally full magazine.

The motive testimony he had wanted to get in was not available to him since he was convinced from Judge parker's signals in Chambers that he would not get it in and an unsuccessful try would do more harm than good; but that "icing on the cake" that had melted was not fatal to his case, he confidently thought.

He could not be sure whether Aaron would call Earl Bryant to testify. Conventional wisdom augured against it. This was an unusual case with so much evidence to convict and with the sentence of a hanging a likely prospect, the Defense may just find it necessary to take the risk. He would just have to wait and see.

Another person in the courtroom was reaching a similar conclusion. Earl listened carefully as the forensics expert drove nail after nail into his pre-prepared and imagined coffin. He sat there slumped in his chair and looked around the courtroom. The Judge sat back in his chair impassively behind the impressive disk watching him and listening to the testimony. The members of the jury sat silent with stony cold faces revealing no sympathy whatever as Earl could determine it. Ellie and Emily sat behind him both weeping softly, but audible to his ear accustomed to picking up slight sounds in the woods, of birds, critters or softly walking feet on forest leaves, much softer than this.

The press corps paused momentarily from their writing, or drawing in some cases, and also watched. He felt the whole world had him under one of those microscopes he had heard about, like the one the forensics expert had testified as using to look at rifle bullets. He felt like the whole world could see inside the secret shell of his soul where the fear of this death thing resided and welled up in him in increasingly uncomfortable proportions.

Then he turned his gaze back to the little man who was testifying and the sight that met his eyes surprised him so much he almost shouted out in the courtroom. Fortunately for him, he was able to suppress that temptation. Standing next to the witness and obviously not noticed by anyone else in the room, was the same figure he had seen the night before in his cell. Afterwards, he could not have told you what the figure was wearing, but there was no doubt in his mind that the specter was the same. Worse yet, the thing began to speak and it seemed that he alone could hear it. "You must tell of these things and only those who matter will accept them", the apparition said, that apparently no one but he could hear. At least, there was no indication they had heard this voice or whatever it was that he had heard. Then just as suddenly, the apparition was gone. It had lived up to its promise, this spectral nightmare. It had not left him and seemed to be watching the proceedings, probably all the time, though it had appeared only to him and now a second time. Quick looks around the room showed that no one else but him saw this thing or heard what it was saying.

The problem for Earl was one of trust. Should he take the advice of that thing, which it most assuredly was urging him to do something, assuming he could figure out what the damn thing was telling him to do? There must be some purpose if it was determined to visit him like this? He decided that if he was not going insane, which was debatable at this point even to him, he might as well give it a name, which would keep it in perspective at least. What to call it, him, and it was clearly male like in appearance? *Clarence, I think I'll call the damn thing Clarence. Sort of reminds me of my Uncle Clarence, Pap's old brother long dead. Nobody will believe me if I ever told it, but I figure I better call him by a name. Hell, maybe it is Uncle Clarence, come back from the great sleep to help. Judgment day ain't come yet, has it? He seems on my side of this mess anyhow. Seem like he is telling me to get up in that box and tell my side of this. Hummn, is that Jury likely to believe anything I say? Mr. Martin says it's too risky but maybe old Clarence know more than he do about what's coming, I wonder,* he thought.

These thoughts had been racing through his mind like wind in a winter squall at the beach; and to Earl it seemed like an hour had passed but he quickly realized it had only been seconds for his lawyer was on his feet ready to take on the expert.

"Mr. Stevenson, your credentials are impressive, Sir, and I'm sure the Jury has listened carefully to what you said, but one or two points in your testimony confused me a bit. For instance, that bullet the Marshall and the crime scene investigators recovered from Mr. Bryant's door frame, it passed through Mr. Stiller and buried itself inside a pine board and ended up in a smashed lump." Aaron held up the projectile between his thumb and forefinger so that the jury could see it clearly. From this, you and your Government microscopes and optical bridges, I think you called them, reached a conclusion that the rifling grooves matched and could be identified as having come from the same gun belonging to Mr. Bryant with his fingerprints on it?" Aaron asked with an incredulous tone in his voice as the lump of a bullet to the naked eye made the conclusion seem clearly incredible.

"Yes, Sir, it matches on all the grooves compared to the test bullet retrieved from the water test I described, it was the same all right," Bill Stevenson said.

"That is another thing that puzzled me Mr. Stevenson, that gun and those fingerprints. You personally examined that rifle and took all the prints from it, didn't you Mr. Stevenson? Aaron asked, closing in for the kill.

"Yes, Sir, we examined it carefully and lifted all of them from it," Stevenson said, wondering where this line of questions was headed. He had been cross examined by Aaron Martin numerous times before and knew he rarely did anything without a plan designed to discredit his testimony, but he thought he was safe on this case, since there were no other prints.

"You found no prints on the trigger or trigger guard but did find prints on the pistol grip of the rifle, did you not?" Aaron asked and then waited for the answer expectantly.

"That's true, there were no prints found there," Stevenson said.

"Marshall Boyle testified, did he not, that the crime scene investigators found the spot where the gunman, whoever it was, knelt behind a stump to steady his aim, supposedly?" Aaron asked.

"Yes, Sir, that he did, Sir," the witness said.

"Marshall Boyle testified, did he not, that Mr. Bryant handed over the rifle without a fight or fuss, this rifle filled with his fingerprints?" Aaron asked.

"Yes, Sir, that he did," the witness said.

"Can you suggest, Mr. Stevenson, how Mr. Bryant, if he was the person shooting this rifle that morning, might manage that, without leaving his fingerprints on the trigger area of this rifle?" Aaron asked, taking a tremendous risk but the evidence against his client made the risk justified, in his opinion.

"I suppose he could have wiped it off but that is only speculation on my part," Bill Stevenson said.

"He wiped the trigger area clean, but left prints all over the barrel and the stock and then presented the thing immediately on his arrest without attempting to hide it or objecting in any way. Does that seem likely to you from your experience in investigating murder weapons for twenty years?" Aaron asked rhetorically.

"No, it doesn't seem likely, but people who commit crimes are not always clever in that way," Stevenson said in rebuttal to the obvious flaw in his theory and the evidence. Houston was sitting on the edge of his seat for he could see his whole case evaporating before his eyes.

"Then one final point maybe you could help us with Mr. Stevenson, Mr. Drucker testified and demonstrated in this trial that he discovered that one round was missing from the full magazine clip by pressing down on it with his fingers after opening the bolt action of Exhibit 1 the morning of the shooting and left the rifle hanging on its peg at the still. How could he have done that and not left any prints of his own? Did Mr. Drucker wipe his own prints off and somehow manage to leave only Mr. Bryant's on Exhibit 1?" Aaron asked.

"I can't explain that Mr. Martin, I truly can't," Bill Stevenson said for the point had seemed contradictory to him, too. The people in the courtroom, lawyers, Judge, Jury and spectators alike, were stunned. Had Aaron Martin, trial lawyer extraordinaire that he was, just demonstrated that lawyer skills can sometime pull off a miracle even for a guilty man? The average person in America thought, if there was enough money available to hire the best, this could happen. It seemed at that moment that in this case, that point had just been made.

"I have no further questions for this witness, Your Honor," Aaron said and sat down with some cautious satisfaction.

Judge Parker at that point, much to the relief of Houston Gilchrist, announced, "We will be in recess for the day, and trial starts again in the morning at 9:30 a.m."

The Clerk shouted, "All Rise", and Judge Parker left the bench.

The press corps scrambled for their phones while the Defendant, his lawyer, and close family supporters, gathered around the Defense table for a little celebration this day, especially enjoying and enhancing the brief time they had each day to greet and cheer up the accused.

Houston Gilchrist and his assistant, Eric Driskoll, on the other hand were in a mood far from that of celebration, as the significance of the job Aaron had done in cross examination gradually sunk in; so they sat there for a few minutes, pretending to gather up their papers before joining the general exodus from the courtroom. For the spectators, parties and lawyers, finally this day's proceedings were over.

57. Search for rebuttal

Houston Gilchrist, like most of the lawyers in town, was a family man and after court would eventually make his way home to the wife and kids. That did not rule out an occasional stop off after work at the Duvall Hotel which was the gathering place for lawyers and the ring of title agents, real estate salesmen, surveyors, appraisers, accountants, a few higher level state employees, and even upper echelon courthouse personnel of the Federal District and State Circuit Courts.

Although Prohibition was soon to be officially over, the bottle club or "speak easy", as they were called in some places, operated in the county, but never in such obvious places as The Duvall. The Hotel operated a restaurant for evening dining but also a coffee shop that was a popular hangout for the Tallahassee professional "in crowd."

The business of government influence, lobbying when the legislature was in session, money making or rumor passing for the rest of the year, was the common fare at The Duvall Coffee Shop. It was true you couldn't get high or drown your disappointments in coffee but the elixir the environment there provided was higher than any bottle club could ever provide.

The British philosopher, Lord Acton, those many years ago had a few things to say about power corrupting public life and while there wasn't much corruption going on in Tallahassee in 1934, at least not that most folks were aware of anyway, the power part was just as prevalent and practiced by those patrons in the coffee shop of the Duvall Hotel, as it had been in any legal pub or salon in British high society in Lord Acton's day.

The habit of just hanging around the people who made government, justice and business run, in that small state capital in that year was a powerful incentive enough and a lot of fun for everybody involved in the process.

In the fall and winter months, called by the locals the "R" months, containing that letter in the name, the only safe time of year to eat Florida oysters. Jake Kitrell, the manager of the Hotel, would arrange to have some of Apalachicola's finest on the half shell available for his regulars, a popular menu item indeed on a late winter afternoon at the Hotel.

But for Houston Gilchrist and Erik Driskoll, this was not the day for coffee, oysters or convivial congeniality; or even a chance to talk a little politics, for they had some serious work to do. Aaron Martin had eviscerated their expert witness with some skillful cross examination, but the impact of the developments was even worse to Houston because that hole in his case that was now so glaringly obvious once you heard Drucker and Stevenson together. He had missed that completely.

Dan Fernell, as the United States Attorney for the District, was not one of those prosecuting attorney administrators who hung around the trial to check up on his assistants; but he would know about the goof up before sun down tonight. Of that, Houston Gilchrist was certain.

He only had an hour or two at most to come up with a recovery plan, or he would be looking for a job teaching trial practice in some second tier law school in Alabama, or somewhere else, before the year was out.

Houston reached his office with Erick right behind him and Driskoll closed the door without even a hint or gesture from the lead prosecuting attorney. "Sit down Erick; we have our work cut out for us. How could we have missed that hole in our case?" Houston asked rhetorically.

"Yeah, looking back on it, it seems obvious, you could drive a truck through it," Driskoll said, running the day's testimony over and over in his mind looking for ways out of the blind alley they seemed to have driven into.

"Think man; find me a way out of this. Let's go over that damn sorry ass, George Drucker's, testimony again. Did you keep notes on the direct?" Houston asked, relying on his assistant trial attorney to pull up notes of that detail, since he had to concentrate on the questions and answers as they happened.

"Let me see, Houston," Erick flipped over the ringed notebook he kept his trial notes in. "There was something that occurred to me when you had Drucker testify about his arrival at the still that morning…what was that part about his coat…hung it on the same rack as the gun… and there was something else he said on direct…just in passing…. Didn't make any sense at the time or rather didn't mean anything then…here it is, "it was coat and glove weather, we sometimes say," that country talking way he has is almost disarming at times. If you don't listen closely enough," Erick said with a smile.

"I don't get it, Erick, what's that…wait, it was cold, December, right, frost on the ground, old coat he said, mackinaw, was it, he hung on that rack next to Bryant's rifle, could he have… no, that would be too easy Erick, wouldn't it?" Houston said warming to the suggestion his young assistant had made almost accidentally, and who for himself had not gotten the full significance yet.

That's the way it is with knowledge sometimes, the facts are there all along, and all you need is the inspiration. The "ah ha" moment is when you can make innocent and meaningless facts connect together in a flash that no one noticed before. "He had on gloves, Erick!" Houston said, so loud he was almost shouting. Then it dawned on Erick at that moment the same point. If Drucker was only in the Lagoon Still for twenty minutes, he probably never took his gloves off and if he didn't, he handled the rifle to check for the missing round and naturally left no prints.

That suddenly made the whole thing crystal clear. Now all they had to do was see if George Drucker could get the same point without them telling him to remember it. Preparing a witness was one thing, but putting words in his mouth, which he would be glad to testify to on a crucial point like this was beyond the pale.

Winning was everything in sports, business and life but these men were sworn to uphold the law and punish those who broke, it not deliberately break it themselves. Besides that, it was unethical as well as criminal to suborn perjury. A man like Drucker would damn well say whatever they needed him to say, even under oath, but the office of the United States Attorney could not prompt him to say it and that much was certain.

At that propitious moment, the phone rang with Dan Fernell checking in after the news of the day's disaster had just reached him over at the Duvall Coffee Shop. Fortunately for Houston, the timing could not have been better. As he talked to Dan and explained how he had everything under control and was ready to snatch victory back from the jaws of defeat, he gave the high sign to his assistant who left the office to round up what they hoped would be their final and star witness tomorrow in Judge Parker's Court.

58. That elusive quality

The lights burned late into the night at the Recorder as Tony Callaway pecked away at his typewriter composing the lead story for the next day's edition. There was talk of little else in Tallahassee these days and the "Recorder's" readers expected to have a new twist come out of this trial every day and the local newspaper was the only source of daily news in those prosaic days before television.

It was news when the Government's case seemed to be teetering on the brink of disaster in a high profile case. The cross examination of Bill Stevenson would be the centerpiece of the story. Naturally Tony enjoyed writing about the success of his old college chum, Aaron Martin, whose star seemed to be definitely on the rise in legal circles from this turn of events. *But what should the angle of the story be*, he thought as he pondered the various approaches, *prosecutor screws up, Defendant has a glimmer of hope, is any Federal Agent safe in Liberty County again?*

Then it came to him, he would paint a picture of the trial's progress and Bryant's chances ebbing and flowing like approaching storms.

"STORM CLOUDS THREATEN AND SUBSIDE FOR LIBERTY COUNTY'S MAN ON TRIAL," would be the headline followed in Tony's inimical style of writing, by the following text:

"Just when the Defendant's chances seemed about to sink as the approaching winds of storm threatened to overwhelm his strained defenses, Earl Bryant, notorious moonshiner from Liberty County, Defendant on trial for murder of a Federal Agent here in our fair city, seemed to find new life today as Tallahassee's rising legal star, Aaron Martin, pulled off a brilliant cross examination of the Government's star forensic witness who had to admit in Judge Parker's Court today that it didn't make sense how the Government's undercover witness could have checked the alleged murder weapon and left no fingerprints in the critical magazine and trigger guard area of the rifle. George Drucker had testified that he had checked the Defendant's rifle that day at the whiskey still immediately following the shooting and found one round missing, even demonstrating for the jury how he had done it. The only problem for the prosecution was that none of Drucker's prints were found on the rifle. The courtroom was all a buzz on that revelation as Judge Parker recessed the trial for the day. All will not be well in the Offices of the United States Attorney tonight as the prosecution team scrambles to find a way to repair the damage. The clouds of despair that seemed to be welling up over the Defendant's horizon were suddenly swept away like a northeaster in winter by the brilliant light of the cross-examination success. It's too early to predict an outcome for this thriller of a legal battle because of the typical roller coaster effect that reigns supreme in most closely contested cases, so stay tuned for tomorrow's developments.

From there, Tony would fill in the rest of his allotted column inches with details of the trial in gradually increasing insignificance until even the most interested spectator tired of the story, like most casual readers of news stories who never make it to the "Please See-Storm, Page 7" for the rest of the story and move on to the sports page or other lighter fare of the Recorder for that day's print entertainment. If he hurried, he could make Dick Powers' deadline for tomorrow's edition.

Meanwhile, in another part of town, Aaron and his father sat in Aaron's office pondering his good fortune. Rarely does a hole in the prosecutor's case turn up in such a startling and obvious manner. Roland was cautious though, and from his years of experience in criminal trials he knew it was too early to be getting over confident. There was too much that could go wrong.

Their big decision was whether to put Earl Bryant on the stand. The moonshine evidence was undeniable and Earl's risk for a future prosecution for illegal whiskey making, even from a confession in open court on cross examination by the Government, seemed a minor concern in relative terms with the hangman's noose swinging figuratively over their heads as they discussed the matter.

"If he testifies the jury will hear him say he never shot the guy, won't they?" Roland asked his son.

"You know I never asked him that directly Dad, conventional wisdom is against it," Aaron said.

"But Son, you will only get one chance, and that rule doesn't apply if he testifies. Maybe you better get out there to the jail tonight and find out before we waste any more time considering whether he should testify or not. What do you think, Son?" Roland asked, deferring to his Son, who as trial Counsel had to be the one to decide. It was his case.

"I can't get my mind around this yet. If Earl denies he did it and tries to account for all his movements that morning, and we could use Ellie in support it although she can't account for the entire morning, it's a lot to ask a jury to accept. It would still come down to whether the Jury would believe a moonshiner, as well as the risk of that business about motive seeping into their minds. I don't know yet, Dad, it just seems too risky," Aaron said, really struggling with the decision.

"Houston will wind up in the morning, probably with some of the support cast involved in the arrest; and maybe that boy, Browning, was that his name? That kid that was standing on the steps with Stiller when the fella got shot. That would be a dramatic ending to his case. He has to do something to take the pressure off the failure of the expert witness. For once, we don't have to use our expert. He would only confirm our client's fingerprints on the murder weapon and that just piles on the proof, better avoid that like the plague, I'm thinking. So you better get on out to the Jail tonight cause it will be decision time for Sir about noon tomorrow, if the Government suddenly rests its case. Are you ready with your final argument in case you decide not to put on a case?" Roland asked.

"Yeah, Dad, I've had the outline done since before the trial but as you well know, the evidence rarely comes in exactly like you expect. I agree it's time to put the critical question to our client," Aaron said.

Another conference was going on at the Leon County Jail of which Aaron and Roland Martin were unaware. Johnny Caldwell had managed to make his way by bus into Tallahassee and had been sitting in the back of the courtroom for several days unnoticed by anyone. Friends stand by each other even in the darkest hours and this friendship was one of those that were not an exception to the rule.

In more normal times, visitors at the jail could not just drop in any old time they felt like it and must confine themselves to weekend daylight hours for visiting but Eldon Strickland, County Sheriff, had been admonished indirectly by Magistrate Stillman Henry at the bail hearing and word had gotten back from the Prosecutor that no harm was to come to Bryant during custody.

"You treat that prisoner with kid gloves, Dickey," Sheriff Strickland had said to his head man at the jail; and when Johnny Caldwell showed up after visiting hours asking for a visit with his friend, Officer Tooms had made an exception and showed Johnny into the visiting room and brought Earl there shortly afterwards.

At this hour, the two old friends had the room to themselves uninterrupted for a time, though Eddie Johnson, jail guard, stood watch through a bulletproof glass window in full view of the prisoner and visitor, if not in full hearing. Actually Eddie could hear nothing of the conversation but he made mental notes of all that seemed to be going on by the way the pair interacted and stood ready on a moment's notice to charge into the room if any undue movement or potentially harmful collaboration occurred within his watchful sight.

"You saw the thing again, Earl, and right there in that Court House?" Johnny asked, after Earl had related the strange experience he had had in his cell the night before and in the courtroom that day. "Yeah and the damdest thing was, I could see this here Clarence, that's the name I give him, named him for my Pap's old dead brother who he looks like some. That ghost, Johnny, and it may even be Clarence who it was for all I know. Figured I better call him something. He was standing right there in full sight, to me anyhow and low and behold Clarence speaks out at me. Only, I'm the only one that kin hear him or see him and that thing tells me I better tell what happened to the court and the ones what matter will believe it or something like that," Earl confided to his friend.

"I know, Earl, I was there and heard or saw none of it. Damn, Earl, I've hear tell of ghosts before but ain't never heard nor seen one myself. But this Clarence, as you call him, he shore acts like he's real enough and talking pretty good sense. Maybe it was your old dead Uncle Clarence come back from the dead to help out. You know I ain't never asked you if you done killed that Federal Man, I mean," Johnny asked, not sure whether he wanted to hear the answer for he had no doubt that Earl Bryant would tell him.

At that moment, and before Earl could finish thinking it over and give an answer, the visiting room door was suddenly opened and Eddie Johnson followed by Aaron Martin came into the room.

"You have to go now, Mr. Caldwell, the prisoner's lawyer has come. The lawyer takes precedence over just visiting, you hear? Come on now, you can leave with me, Mr. Caldwell," Eddie Johnson said, working his transition magic as Aaron winked collaboratively at his client and said farewell to Johnny, making a special effort to show his appreciation for his support of Earl.

"Thought it went fairly well today, but there are rocks and shoals still ahead, Earl, how you doing, hanging in there?" Aaron said, starting off the interview on a positive note before he got around to the serious business of the direct question of the night. There would only be one question that now mattered, and he wanted Earl to be ready for it when it came so that he could make an accurate and wise decision about his testimony in his own defense.

"Yes, Sir, could be better, naturally, but you shore lit into that gun man today, I felt damn good about that!" Earl said, not hiding the show of enthusiasm he genuinely felt.

"That did go well, we were lucky Gilchrist didn't have him better prepared for that. It was clear to me afterwards that they had no idea that hole was in their case. I'd like you to think I anticipated that but I can't claim credit for it. It was a fishing expedition I was on all right, but it couldn't hurt our case even if he had an explanation. I could not figure out before why Drucker left no fingerprints on your gun if he checked it out as he said he did. Bill Stevenson apparently didn't either. Do you have an explanation for that Earl?" Aaron asked his client seated across from him behind the small metal table that served as magazine display or writing table for visitors at the jail.

It was an preliminary or lead up scene to the main act of the play so Aaron watched his client's body language carefully for any sign of his being uncomfortable with the questions or reluctance to answer forth-rightly. He could see no such signs as Earl answered almost immediately.

"Can't say as I can, Mr. Martin. He was right in one way, I always carried a full clip, you could never tell when the Federal bastards might pull a raid on the place, but that clip were full cause I never fired my rifle that mornin'," Earl said, looking his lawyer right squarely in the eyes with an unmistakable sign, from his lawyer's perspective at least, that he was telling the truth.

If he could answer that way in court, the case for him testifying would be easy. But what about the rest of it, Aaron thought.

"What jury would believe you, Earl Bryant, the most notorious moonshiner in north Florida and how would you answer questions about your illegal whiskey making, assuming I couldn't convince Judge Ben to keep those questions out.

"Won't bother me none," Earl said, "Spending a few months or a year or two in jail or even Raiford for making whiskey is nothing compared to hanging."

"Well now," Aaron said, "You must have figured out by now that I'm trying to decide whether to have you testify. I would not even consider it unless they find a way to fill that hole in the Prosecutor's case on Drucker's fingerprints on your gun for without that turn today, your goose was about cooked, speaking only from your lawyer's experience in watching juries."

"Yes, Sir, that were plain about then," Earl said.

"Why don't you start over from the beginning Earl and tell me everything you did that morning. In fact, let me not beat around the bush anymore and ask you direct like, Earl, did you shoot Frank Stiller in the back in front of your house last December 5th at 6:00AM in the morning? I need to know that, if it's true." Aaron asked him, boring with his eyes into the very soul of his client and trying his best to see if he could detect any hesitation or other signs of a less than sincere answer.

"No, Sir, I did not shoot Frank Stiller that morning, and did not even want to shoot Frank Stiller that morning because I was not anywhere close enough to shoot that Bastard!" Earl said with such force of conviction that Aaron was convinced his client was innocent of the crime.

"How about that story George Drucker wanted to tell about your Daddy being killed by the same agent, but Judge Ben wouldn't let him, any truth to that, I really need to know Earl?" Aaron asked expectantly and waited for the other shoe to drop that Earl's honesty held in his hand. That would about make or break his decision as to whether to allow his client to take the stand.

"He killed Pappy all right and I watched him do it. He shot that poor old fella right square in the face; even after that he had dropped his gun and give up, pleading for his life. It was an execution is what it was and that bastard said so on the spot. I would have shot him right then and the good Lord knows I had a bead on him, but those other Federal men were closing in on me and I had to choose between revenge and death. Those Bastards would have shot me shore, right then and there. I guess I wanted to live bad enough so I slipped out while the slipping was good but I shore left the re-venge behind in doing it," Earl confessed, and the shame he felt right then for not having taken the chance, when he had it, so affected his demeanor that Aaron was Sir beyond certain that his client was telling him the truth. But that Sir gave Earl a motive to kill Stiller the next safe chance he got, like this one, and the risk of that coming into evidence was more than he was prepared to take.

"That's an incredible story Earl, but we can't let you testify. Gilchrist would eat you alive on cross and the jury might just believe you did finally get your revenge last December 5th, after all. I'm sorry Earl, we just can't risk it," Aaron said, reaching out to grip both arms of his client to let him know, what he wasn't sure, whether it would be welcome or not but felt the need to touch the hardened old man facing the trial for his life. Earl thought about what his lawyer had said, shook his head ever so gently and said,

"I feel like I got to tell that Jury I didn't do it," Earl said.

"They have to prove the case Earl, don't forget that, but let's sleep on it and wait and see how it goes tomorrow. We'll decide then," Aaron said. Earl nodded his acknowledgement, if not agreement, and Aaron rang the buzzer on the visiting room wall. In a flash, Eddie Johnson was there to show him out. He had been observing this bizarre scene on his night watch at the Leon County Jail just outside the bullet and soundproof glass window.

59. Chambers

Judge Parker called for a conference of attorneys in Chambers before the start of the next morning's testimony to get an idea of the length of the case. Trial calendars are jealously guarded by Federal Judges, for their time is a precious commodity. The problem was always that the witness's testimony tended to run longer than the attorney calling him or her expected, because just like any other predicted events involving human activity, the unforeseen development was difficult to control. The lawyer on direct examination, like Houston Gilchrist had done in this case, would overlook some tidbit of evidence the witness could provide and that extra question would take opposing counsel that much longer on cross examination and then re-direct to cure the damage done on cross and then re-cross until the Judge tired of it and put a stop to the extra questions.

That circumstance was about to rear its head in the Bryant case this morning for Houston had called George Drucker on direct examination and released him for the cross exam that revealed the terrible hole in the Government's case and now Judge Parker and Aaron were about to learn that the Government wanted to call Drucker back as an additional witness. This was highly unusual but not unheard of in these cases.

"Good morning Gentlemen, I wanted to hear from you Houston just how long you plan to go on with this case My schedule is very much set for the month and I'm getting concerned about how long this is going to go on?" Judge Parker said, asking and lecturing both sides all at the same time.

"Your Honor, after yesterday's cross examination, we feel we need to recall Mr. Drucker to the stand to clear up an inconsistency that has developed in the case and after we finish with Him, I have one more witness, the young man, Clyde Browning, who witnessed the shooting and arrest and then the Government will rest its case in chief," Houston said positively and sat back waiting for the objection from Defense Counsel and Bench, ready with his rebuttal. It was imperative that he get Drucker back on that stand and have him explain about those gloves or he could lose this thing. Dan Fernell, U.S. Attorney, would have none of that or at least him, if he did.

"Your Honor, I object to this unusual procedure. The witness already testified and has been cross-examined by me. If they wanted to put him back on the stand on re-direct, they could have done that yesterday, but I believe he excused the witness and my cross examination is prejudiced by having to piece meal it this way. Mr. Gilchrist has had overnight to think about the hole in his case this witness left him and his expert and now he wants to try to pull his iron out of the fire. You shouldn't let him do it. We do have a schedule as Your Honor so ably pointed out to us this morning and this case needs to be moved along," Aaron argued, pulling out all the stops he could think of before stopping for a breath.

"Your Honor," Houston protested, but Judge Ben held up his hand for him to stop and said, "Now Gentlemen, you can make your arguments in Court for the record but I am inclined to allow the witness to testify again. As I recalled, I called an end to yesterday's proceedings and Houston was never presented the chance to call Drucker to bolster up his expert so to speak. At least that is the way I remember it but we can check with the shorthand writer when we are back in session. "How much longer will you need, Houston for this and the other fellow?" Judge Ben asked.

"I can wrap this up by noon today if we get started right away," Houston said.

"And you Aaron, how much of a case will you have," Judge Parker asked, trying determinedly to get a handle on the expected length of trial.

"We don't know yet, Your Honor, whether we will put on a case or not. If anything, Mr. Bryant will testify and we should be done with all evidence by close of business tonight," Aaron said, much to the surprise of Houston Gilchrist, who could count on the fingers of one hand in his twenty years of prosecuting Federal criminal cases that the Defendant actually testified, it was just considered too risky. But in this crazy case, anything could happen.

"All right then, Counsel, we will go back in there and get this matter on the record. It's beginning to look to me like we will wrap up the case tomorrow come hell or high water. You guys can make your arguments to the Jury after that, and we can move on to that big civil case I have on the docket while the Jury deliberates. This is a death penalty case so I expect a rather long deliberation given the way the evidence has gone so far. See you in Court, Counsel," Judge Parker said and they were excused to head back in the courtroom.

60. Back in court

"Objection, Your Honor, Mr. Gilchrist has already called and rested on this witness, I've cross examined him on the full extent of his testimony and he created a problem for Mr. Gilchrist with his own expert witness. He couldn't think of a remedy for it on the spot and did not have any re-direct questions for the expert. He had already finished with this man, Drucker. It's unfair to the Defendant to give the Government overnight to think it over and find some "recollection" in the witness' memory that he didn't have while testifying yesterday. Isn't it odd that the Government feels it needs to bring rebuttal for its own side of this case? The problem he created with that wasn't apparent to them until I exposed it on the cross examination of their expert. We just want the truth to come out, Your Honor, not some truncated version of it so these people can try to win, regardless of the truth," Aaron argued for dramatic effect.

Aaron having had a few minutes to think of the best argument to make on the record and did get a subtle dig in at the witness in the presence of the Jury, preparing them to be cautious about believing this new "recollection" that was bound to come, knowing how Judge Parker was likely to rule anyway. The statement about the restored recollection not available in Drucker's memory the day before was true enough but that truth was not likely to be exposed to the light of day.

"Your Honor," Houston interjected, "We checked with the shorthand writer and she confirms that you recessed the trial for the day after Mr. Martin concluded his cross examination and we really had no chance to recall the witness right then."

"I'm inclined to agree with that last point Mr. Gilchrist and Mr. Martin you can make whatever arguments you have on the witness' overnight "recollection" in your closing statement to the Jury," Judge Ben said, trying maybe unsuccessfully to avoid commenting on the evidence and overruled the objection for the record.

"The Government recalls George Drucker to the stand," Houston said, and the Bailiff hurriedly went out to get him in the corridor where he was being guarded, for protection naturally, by two underlings on "The Great One's team of marshals.

George nervously took his seat on the witness chair, for he was still not Sir in his own mind how much of the truth he had told and to whom. That is the trouble with lying, you forget details and can't remember which ones were made up and which ones actually happened, or which lie you told to which person. But he was into this now and had to do his best to pull through it. He dreaded the thought of having to go on the run if Earl Bryant was acquitted. Earl's memory was long and he could not be accused, based on his pattern in the past, of letting somebody get away with something that hurt him.

"You will recall Mr. Drucker, that you remain under oath to tell the truth, the whole truth and nothing but the truth," Judge Parker reminded the witness, as if presaging the perjury that was Sir to be forthcoming, if Aaron's forecast of the testimony whatever it was to be, turned out to be true.

Houston cautiously and deliberately approached the witness chair and began his questioning. "George, what were you wearing the morning of December 5th, the day of the shooting?"

"I had on my old coat that I wore on cold days like that one," George said parceling out the evidence as though it were not rehearsed.

"Did you wear a hat that morning George," Houston asked, taking his revelation as to clothing piece by piece as though this was terribly important.

"Your Honor, I object, what possible relevance could a hat, coat or clothes have to this case?" Aaron explained the objection cautiously knowing full well there was about to be some very critical relevance by this testimony. Houston had had an overnight to plan his repair of the hole the cross examination of Bill Stevenson had created in his case; and what he was observing was a layer by layer fabric being constructed all over that very hole, and Counsel must be given some latitude to construct it.

"Overruled," Judge Ben said without waiting for a defense of the question and said, "Mr. Gilchrist has to be permitted to show the background and foundation for his evidence, but if he doesn't show it soon, I will reconsider my ruling, you may proceed Mr. Gilchrist."

"You may answer, George," Houston said. "I had an old cap, a wool one I think, it were cold that morning, Sir," George said.

"Was it cold in the Lagoon, George?" Houston asked, setting up the grandstand where the spectators were going to see the main act.

"Yes, Sir, even with the kettle fires lit up, but it were early that morning and the kettle firs was low yet," George testified.

"Did you wear any protection from the cold on your hands, George?" Houston asked as the main act made its way to the stage. Aaron sunk in his seat, realizing what was about to come as he thought:

Damn, he's going to say he had on gloves and left them on and that's how they plan to get him out of this jam. Bet they had to spend all night thinking that one up, and of course, Drucker will say anything they need him to. I bet that was a delicate operation, asking without telling him. Houston is a good man and he would never suborn perjury, not deliberately. But I don't put it past him, good man or not, to let Drucker come up with it on his own, however long it would take for the revelation to materialize. Old Dan Fernell would ream him a new one if he lost this case, or if he cooked up this testimony for the "recollection" of the witness and got caught doing it.

"Yes, Sir, I had on gloves that morning," George said.

"Did you take them off when you took off your coat and hung it on the rack next to Earl's gun?" Houston asked, less carefully now for this part of the rehearsed testimony had gone smoothly in practice and his confidence level was high.

"No, Sir, I knew I weren't going to be there for long and it were cold that early morning, as I done said, and there was always some heavy lifting to be done down there," George said.

"Did you still have the gloves on when you found time to check that rifle for the number of bullets?" Houston asked, with a broad smile on the inside of his face carefully camouflaged by a stoical external demeanor.

"Yes, Sir," George answered. Then wanting to make Sir the Jury was awake and clever enough to get the point that was obvious to everyone else in the courtroom, he asked,

"So George, when you cradled Mr. Bryant's rifle in your left hand, opened the breach and pushed your right thumb down into the chamber and found room in the stripper clip for one more round, you had gloves on all that time?" Houston asked almost by now rhetorically.

"Yes, Sir, I had them gloves on the whole time that morning, Mr. Gilchrist.

Erick Driskoll sat at counsel table beaming as though he had just been anointed a star for good behavior in Sunday School, just discovered he had graduated first in his law school class, or just been told by his fiancé that she would marry him, that made it possible after all to repair the hole in their case.

"You sit right there George, I'm Sir my learned opposing counsel will have a few questions for you on this," Houston said, beaming with confidence and not to mention pleasure at this turn of events. George waited anxiously as Aaron rose to his feet and approached the witness box.

George's side of the lawyers might be confident, maybe over confident to his mind, but he alone knew where he was vulnerable and even though he was not a praying man, there was some of that going on right now inside his mind. This lawyer just had better leave that rifle business alone. They could chew on the bone of these fingerprints and his dressing habits all they wanted to but they had to stay away from the meat of his main lie that there were two guns in the Lagoon that morning.

He sat there silent, if not calmly, and anxiously waited for that other shoe to drop. A conviction for perjury was one thing but he would get out someday and Earl Bryant was young enough to come and get him, so avoiding this and lying to help convict Earl was the something else that just had to be.

61. The battle continues

"You were sworn to tell the truth and the whole truth, before your testimony yesterday, was you not Mr. Drucker," Aaron began somewhat sarcastically.

"Yes, Sir" George said in response. You never told Mr. Gilchrist about those gloves till last night, did you?" Aaron asked in violation of the practical rule for cross-examination of not asking a question you don't know the answer to.

"No, Sir, not till then, Sir," George said positively. This really hadn't been much of a risk on Aaron's part because if he had told them, Houston would have used it yesterday. In fact, a nervous second year law student in a trial practice class would have picked up on that and used it.

The only mystery was whether it was true and how long, if it were not true, it had taken George to come up with it. This was Aaron's burning desire to know for in that lay the secret to breaking him down on this unlikely story. Earl really didn't remember one way or the other and none of the Negro Lagoon workers who saw it all could be found, so there was no help from either source.

It was a pity the Still men could not be found because they rarely missed anything going on around them, especially concerning the whites in command of them like Earl Bryant and even George Drucker in the Bryant Lagoon operation.

"The weather was cold enough for gloves in December, here in Florida?" Aaron asked, not sure where this would get him.

"Yes, Sir, it is cold down in them woods, frost on the ground and all that," George answered.

"That Lagoon as you call it, it had six copper kettles and all six were fired up with hickory smoke fires by the time you got down there, correct Mr. Drucker?" Aaron asked, demonstrating to the jury his grasp of the details of the evidence trying to suggest that the glove story was a stretch; necessary for George's lie all right, but a stretch nonetheless.

"Well there was fire in the place all right but not much yet, being we was getting ready to ship product out that morning," George offered, trying to duck the dilemma his earlier testimony had created. This gave another little fact he had omitted to mention before, a practice he was coming around to with a relish.

"Wasn't it a bit unusual to keep your gloves on that long Mr. Drucker?" Aaron asked with pure unbelief veritably dripping from his tone.

"No, Sir, it were cold that morning and I weren't planning to stay long no how," George said. Then Aaron took the gamble he had to take and asked the question that was to lead him to the heart of the matter,

"Mr. Drucker, you met with Mr. Gilchrist and Mr. Driskoll last night to prepare your testimony for today on this glove business didn't you?" Aaron asked.

"Yes, Sir, they called me in last night," George answered truthfully.

"You met for several hours didn't you?" Aaron asked.

"I don't know how long it were, Mr. Martin, being I ain't got a watch but it was some time that," George answered.

"Who suggested that you were wearing gloves, you or the Government lawyers?" Aaron asked and sat back as though waiting for an explosion.

"I did, I guess," George answered.

"You were asked, were you not (and Aaron was really out on a limb here not having a clue as to what had transpired between them) how your fingerprints were not on the inside of that rifle, weren't you, and someone suggested you were wearing gloves then, isn't that the way it happened?"

"No, Sir, well, Yes, Sir," George sputtered not Sir how to answer and in his confusion getting it backwards, intending to say "yes" as to fingerprints and "no" as to gloves and doing the opposite.

"Your Honor, objection to that question. It's a compound question which could not be answered with a single yes or no, and the witness is naturally confused. We move to strike the answer," Houston said, wishing he could have anticipated that question and objected before it was asked and George gave that ambiguous answer that the Jury could take either way and that ambiguity is what you don't want if you are the Prosecutor, and have a beyond a reasonable doubt standard to meet. George was making this extremely difficult for Houston.

"Sustained," Judge Parker ruled and again instructed the Jury to disregard the question and the answer, whatever good that ever does.

"You were asked why no prints right?" Aaron asked and George answered clearly and without confusion,

"Yes."

Then Aaron decided to change tactics since the witness was now ready for the second half of the compound question. "It took quite a while for you to come up with that little bit of recall that you were wearing gloves, did it not Mr. Drucker, even in a quiet room with the Government lawyers and no interruptions?" Aaron asked with the unbelievable question tone at the end of his statement as though anyone would recall something that important and not take all night to do it. Aaron knew, just from what he had learned today, that if they went over this small bit of evidence for two hours or even an hour, that Houston and Erick had had to pull it out of the witness, which told him that the knowledge wasn't there in the first place and George Drucker was lying big time about this.

"It had been some months ago and I ain't truthfully thought about it much but I was wearing gloves that morning and kept them on the whole time I were down there," George said with conviction in his tone that had finally settled into his feelings on what had to be said to make this work.

Aaron had to admit to himself that he had gotten about all he was going to get out of this witness and better save the rest for argument. It wasn't where he had wanted it to be such as where things were left at that glorious moment after the expert's testimony but at least he had the argument that if George Drucker really had gloves on that morning it would not take two hours for Houston Gilchrist to wiggle it out of him.

The laymen on the Jury would not appreciate the finer ethical point that hampered the Government's lawyer as Aaron or any other lawyer did and that difficulty was about all he needed to try to paint a picture of a reasonable doubt.

"That's all I have for this witness Your Honor," Aaron said with a heavy emphasis on the "this" and made his way back next to Earl at the Defense table. *Now bring on the kid and let's get this mess over with*, he thought.

"Please state you name and address, Sir," Houston said as Clyde Browning settled into the witness chair after being sworn to tell the truth.

"My name is Clyde Browning and I reside at Mrs. Ruston's Boarding House out on East Tennessee Street here in Tallahassee," Clyde answered. As Houston took Clyde through the preliminaries and started down the road with his story to Liberty County, Earl sat glumly in his seat thinking over everything that had transpired:

That damn Drucker is going to get me yet. How can we get around that gun and them fingerprints. For the life of me I can't remember about them gloves. Maybe he had um and maybe he didn't. That Drucker would take all night to cook up that story or any story them lawyers told him they needed. Speaking of cooking, I'm thinking my goose is about cooked if anything are. Just as Earl was running this over and over in his mind and Clyde Browning was answering Houston's questions by telling his hair raising tale about how he and Frank Stiller were standing there innocent, or at least they felt safe as policemen ever feel in making an arrest, like this one, on the front door step of Earl and Ellie Bryant's house deep in the woods of Liberty County, when suddenly a slight motion caught Earl's eye.

This time Clarence was standing just to his left between him and the Prosecutor's table and looking directly at him with those eyes that bore into you. Earl had noticed no movement or shapes in the courtroom prior to seeing the figure out of the corner of his eye. He was just suddenly there. If Clarence was a ghost in the traditional conception that people had about such things, and if it really was his Uncle Clarence, then this coming and going quality was perfectly understandable.

As a member of a country church where paying attention to "familiar spirits" was heartily condemned, Earl was a little resistant to the apparition as probably sinful and to be avoided. However the dire straits he found himself in had weakened this resolve to resist such images. Earl made a more careful assessment of the little ghost, angel, Uncle Clarence or whatever it was. No matter how much he knew to distrust such things, he didn't have Ellie's good common sense judgment to help him resist the image. He could recall later that Clarence was about four feet tall; wearing a nondescript set of workman clothes of a type he had never seen before. His feet, if there really were feet on this figure, were inside what he recalled later as brogan shoes that farm hands and tradesmen of that age wore. The material aspect of this figure were so real that Earl could not ignore him even though he was the only one in the courtroom, or anywhere else for that matter who could see or hear him. When Clarence spoke, the words were not so much audible as they were understood, regardless of their lack of form or sound. It was clear to Earl that Clarence was speaking to him, however, and he was prepared to listen. Naturally this meant that Earl could not pay attention to both so he didn't hear a word of Clyde Browning's testimony.

"You must understand that things are stacked against you unless you speak out for the truth", the apparition said. Earl looked straight at Clarence and wondered whether that since he was the only one in the room who could see or hear the thing, that maybe he could speak to it and clear up some of the confusion. But speaking right now was a little bit of a problem with the trial going on. He decided to try whispering.

"Say, you there, Clarence, I call you, can you hear me?" Earl whispered just slightly under his breath. Aaron heard him, even though it was soft and he was concentrating at the time on the testimony of Clyde Browning, looked sideways briefly and signaled Earl with a downward gesture of his hand held flat and returned his attention to the witness.

The ghost Clarence nodded his head in response and spoke ever so softly to Earl and if not heard audibly, Earl could see the words forming in his own mind, as though he thought them.

"I can hear you, Oh troubled one, as I have heard all along in this trial stacked against you. The witness Drucker is lying about his gloves and the gun, too, for there were two of them, his and yours. You must take the risk and tell your story. The jury will believe you if you tell it as if you are convinced. Your lawyer will not agree but he must listen to the one who pays him no matter what he may tell you. His judgment is against this, but you must not listen if you want to live."

And then just as suddenly as he had appeared, Clarence was gone. Earl was stunned, confused and uncertain what he must do.

"Where were you standing when the shot was fired?" Houston asked the young witness.

"Right on the front steps of Mr. Bryant's porch, right next to Mr. Stiller," Clyde said.

"What happened next?" Houston asked, opening up the witness to explain in his own words a description of the shooting. Houston had chosen to end his case with this account from this very believable and sympathetic witness. He was young, innocent looking in appearance and manner, and by telling the personal story of his involvement as almost a victim would permit the jurors to vicariously visit the horror and suddenness of the crime.

Houston would win this case now, if at all, on the totality of the fingerprint evidence, the circumstantial evidence developed by the coroner, crime scene investigators, and the credibility of George Drucker. It would turn on his suggestion as to motive, opportunity and the means of carrying out the crime. Also critical to the outcome would be whether the Jury would accept the explanation of the gloves as obliterating the fingerprint evidence Drucker had to have left, if his story of the missing round was to have been believed.

It had not occurred to anyone that even if George had never touched the weapon after the alleged shot from it, there was no real reason why there should be any of Earl's fingerprints on the knob on the bolt activator since a palm does not leave prints, and he did not have to use his fingers inside the chamber. But since the expert had stumbled like a fool into the trap set by the clever cross-examination which had left such an indelible imprint on every one's thinking in the courtroom, and most likely the Jury's who counted most of all, Houston had had no choice but throw George right into the breach with his glove story.

Houston was thinking that unless there truly was a God in Heaven in favor of justice with a *deus ex machina* ready for the occasion, he might just lose this case after all. Little known to him, no possibility of that was working in the mind of the frightened and confused Defendant just as Clyde was winding up his story of the crime.

"I quickly looked at Mr. Stiller lying there, apparently dead as a doorknob and ran like hell, if you pardon my language, Your Honor, I was scared and I'll admit it," Clyde explained, and everyone could see that this was the truth, the whole truth, and nothing but the truth on this moment in the witnesses' testimony.

"What did you do next, Clyde?" Houston asked.

"Well, Sir as I was running away as fast as I could go, it suddenly occurred to me that the keys to our truck were back there in Mr. Stiller's pocket. I could either run or walk all the way back to Tallahassee or I could turn around and go back for those keys and risk getting shot myself and join Mr. Stiller's body on that front step. The last thing in this world I wanted to do was go back there but walking to get help from the middle of Liberty County just seemed ridiculous. I thought about it for a second and went back. Fortunately, I never got shot. Mr. Stiller's body was still there and dead, or so it seemed to me, and I got back and out of there as fast as my fingers and feet would pick up those keys and carry me," Clyde said.

"Your Witness, Counsel," Houston, said.

There comes a time in every trial lawyer's experience when he sees a witness that is simply telling the truth and the urge to get up there and poke some hole or the other in the story is nearly irresistible, but the urge must be resisted. The medical profession, following the Dictum of Hippocrates tries to never do harm to the patient. Conventional wisdom would have dictated that the same maxim apply to lawyers, who should never try to do harm to their cases on cross-examination of good witnesses for the opponent, but sometimes wisdom is set aside by a trial lawyer. Call it hunch, insight, or error, but in this case, Aaron felt he had to ask something to avoid leaving this mood of the obvious victimhood of Frank Stiller hanging over the courtroom with the fingerprints and gloves like the Sword of Damocles. Aaron approached Clyde Browning delicately and artfully, and said, "Mr. Browning, how long have you been in Federal service?

"Not long, Sir, I think it's been two to three years," Clyde answered thoughtfully as he was being put at ease by the gentle nature of the question.

"You had some special training for this job, I presume?" Aaron asked, being fairly familiar that the training of Federal Revenue Service Agents at the time was more on the job and not formal classroom or academy training like the FBI and some other more long standing police agencies.

"They assigned me to Mr. Stiller and I followed him around for a spell, you know learning as I went," Clyde said.

"You had plenty of these encounters over that two to three years, where there was shooting and people got shot nearby, right?" Aaron asked almost rhetorically, realizing fully that most policemen of all stripes go their entire careers without ever drawing a gun, and although he really didn't know about Clyde's experience in this regard, he was fairly safe in asking the question this way.

"Oh no, Sir, this was the only time and I Sir hope it will be the last," Clyde said enthusiastically to a murmur of chuckles across the courtroom.

"You never got involved in a crime scene investigation, collected evidence or did any of that before, right?" Aaron asked.

"No, Sir, never did," he said.

"You were just accompanying Frank Stiller on this visit to Mr.

Bryant's homestead down there in Liberty County and happened to be standing next to him when he got shot, right?" Aaron asked, standing just inside the line of objectionable questions bordering on argument. Houston noted the line and kept his seat, but was ready should Aaron ever cross it.

"You didn't see the person who made the shot did you, Clyde?" Aaron asked it this way wanting to keep his attitude toward this boy more personal in the eyes of the Jury. His fight was not with Clyde Browning. "What you testified to here today is all you know about that shot, isn't it, Clyde?" Aaron asked, wrapping up all he had wanted to accomplish with this witness, which wasn't much.

Aaron ended his cross-examination and notified the Court of it and returned to his seat.

Houston stood up and said the magic words, at least magic in the mind of the Honorable Benjamin T. Parker, Jr., ever mindful of his busy court docket, "The Government rests its case, your Honor.

Judge Ben took the good news and being the experienced trial judge that he was, was already pretty much expecting this time to be about right, turned to Aaron and said, "Mr. Martin, are you ready to proceed with the case for the Defense?"

Aaron rose, looked at his client who was gesturing frantically to him by his side, and said, "Could I have a few moments Your Honor?" Judge Parker looked at the clock at the back of the Courtroom and saw that it was approaching four o'clock, noticed the frantic nature of the Defendant trying to say something to his lawyer and exercised judicial discretion that only Federal Judges appointed under the Constitution for life, if not in some of their eyes by God, and announced a recess for the day.

Judge Parker rose to the accompaniment of the herald of the "All rise" and almost everyone left the courtroom. This included the Prosecution team, appreciative of the extra time to get ready to start preparing for final arguments that had to come very soon, sometime tomorrow. It also included the press, also appreciative because of print deadlines looming oppressively near, and the spectators, having satiated their voyeuristic cravings for another day.

The usual cloister of family and well-wishers, including Johnny Caldwell, friend for life of the Defendant, waited respectfully to allow Aaron and Earl to confer privately with their lawyer-client thing before smothering Earl with comfort and support, with well wishes and genuine or not so genuine, expressions of confidence as to how the case was going.

In most of their minds, the case was won since none of them believed Drucker's testimony for a minute. They also were thinking, did not the Defendant still have his case to put on? This logic was missing the premise that the obvious benefit of having Earl testify and say he didn't do it was offset, fatally so in the mind of Aaron Martin, by the motive testimony that was bound to get into evidence in the process.

The family, lay sympathizers and even Earl were not able to see this problem with their logic or their emotions. Aaron dismissed perfunctorily the matter of Earl's request that he testify but in deference to his client's determined resistance to this sage advice, he agreed to come out to the jail later and go over it again.

As the attorney client conference broke up, the cloud of well-wishers descended over Earl like a rare dense fog at a summer picnic down by the river. There was nothing for anybody to see in it, but its presence presented its own comfort as they touched each other by embrace and other expressions for the comfort starved Defendant.

The jail guards stood their distance and sensed that extra time was needed today, and even these paragons of civic virtue, in the face of these most serious criminal allegation against the Defendant, found a little sympathy for the plight of this fellow human being no matter what he was accused of doing and allowed the time limit to extend. The affection of the supporters was contagious at least for now.

62. In search of a strategy

Aaron was troubled after he left the Court and headed back to his office. Earl wanted desperately to testify in his own defense, to just stand up and tell that Jury that he never shot anybody and not even his old nemesis Frank Stiller. Every time Aaron ran that scenario through his mind he had visions of Houston Gilchrist exposing the motive for the crime in such vivid fashion that the Jury was bound to think he did it. But what was he to do?

He personally believed his client was innocent but he was biased as all lawyers are. Wasn't it his job to make those objective judgments because the clients could never see beyond their emotions? But what if Earl insisted? He needed advice on that and Dad was just the one to give it. As Aaron walked down the hall and turned into the reception area of the firm, he was relieved to find Anna Devlin seated on station, busy with answering the phones and such, and as soon as she took a breath, he said emphatically, "Anna, find Dad wherever he is, I need to see him immediately!" He's here Mr. Martin, back in his office, you head on down there and I'll tell him you're in, O.K.?" Anna said, and dialed Mr. Martin Sr., on the office intercom to give him the alert that something serious was on Aaron's, mind today.

"What's up, how's the trial going?" Roland Martin said, as Aaron came in. He plopped down in the leather client chair opposite his father.

"You know Dad, this is one of those cases that could go either way but I think we have a strong, and I repeat, a strong case of reasonable doubt. As I told you yesterday, I asked the magic question and I am convinced Earl Bryant may be a notorious moonshine man but he is not one guilty of murder. Hell, I even believe him when he says he didn't do it, period," Aaron said, with exasperation in his voice.

"Then what's your problem Aaron, that's a rare position to be in, in a criminal case?" Roland asked, truly puzzled. He had tried hundreds of these cases in his career and usually the guy did it, and the only good cases for the defense is when there is some doubt on the evidence that can be made to sound reasonable, not the act itself.

"Dad, the guy wants to testify and say he didn't do it, in fact I think he is going to demand it. I've never seen anything like this. I've explained all the reasons against it but he's determined. I promised to come out to the jail tonight and give him one more shot at me. My problem is that he has a motive that would convince a philanthropist, do-gooder, he's guilty. You know the type, one that believes anyone charged with a crime is not guilty because society made him do it, or some other sociological bull shit like that.

I've managed to keep motive out of the evidence so far, but if he testifies, he's fair game and Houston will eat him for lunch," Aaron said.

"I see," Roland said, "What's the motive?"

"He witnessed the execution of his moonshiner father, Terrell Bryant, back in 1913, by the same guy, Frank Stiller. He says the guy shot his father in the face as he begged for mercy, that Earl had his gun trained on him, but didn't shoot because the other Federal Agents were closing in and he got cold feet.

The rumors of this have been floating around Liberty County ever since. George Drucker, that snitch probably killed Stiller himself to set Earl up for this, and then take over his liquor empire, if you want my thinking on that. Talk about motive, Houston's hearsay evidence was so weak on that, that Judge Parker wouldn't let it in.

But if Earl stands up on his hind legs and denies he killed him, the relevance of that event which he will have to admit if he testifies, will be glaring. I couldn't put him on the stand to lie about it not even if he wanted to, but I think Earl wants to tell the whole thing anyway. It beats anything I've ever seen in a criminal case!" Aaron explained, desperately looking to his wise old father for help.

Roland sat back in his chair deep in thought and didn't say anything for a while. Aaron knew his father well enough that when he did this, not to interrupt him. This was a crisis in attorney-client relations in a case and he needed help, badly!

"It is a problem, naturally, and his life may be at stake, but it's his life, Aaron. Your job is to defend as well as you can and it sounds like you've done that. Something is driving our client to do this and all the reasoning and experience in the world is not going to shake him. I suggest you tell him you won't do it, and if he insists that you will withdraw. You should also bring his wife in for the meeting. She has a stake in this, too. Isn't she staying in town for the trial? Aaron nodded. Take Anna with you, you need a witness if this should go wrong. If he backs down, then you may have saved him; but if he won't, no lawyer in this town will take his case right now.

Judge Parker will delay the trial. However, because Earl has assets, he can't appoint a new attorney. You can't let him go into this alone. So if he doesn't take your bluff, then back down gracefully and try the damn thing the very best that you can. Tell him you had a change of heart, but don't do it until all else fails. We can't leave an innocent man to face the gallows without a fight, even if we lose. Your reputation as a trial lawyer will be damaged if you go with this defense and lose. Doing the right thing will overcome that. But you would have done the right thing for your client, giving him the benefit of all your experience, and when he rejects your advice, you do it anyway. That's the way it's supposed to work. So you and Anna get out there and you convince him. I'm proud of you Son," Roland concluded.

Aaron thought about it for a short while, and agreed with the plan and he and Anna Devlin went first to have some dinner and then head to the jail. Roland said he would explain this to Aaron's wife, so not to worry her about how that might look in town. That was comforting to his young partner who had too much to think about this evening.

63. Jail doings

The Leon County jail was busy that evening and the pattern of allowing visitors to this one particular prisoner at all hours of the day or night was making him into a celebrity of sorts among the other inmates. When Aaron and Anna arrived about seven o'clock, they found that they were not the first visitors for the evening. Eddie Johnson showed the lawyer and secretary into the visiting room to join a visit already in progress. Ellie Bryant and Emily Wilson were engaged in an intimate personal visitation with the prisoner and Aaron asked them to stay for a while. He and Anna greeted the family warmly and allowed this comfort giving to continue as long as possible.

Earl needed this just as much as he needed legal preparation in Aaron's view, for there was to be no courtroom testimony by this group, if he had his way about such things. After a bit, he suggested to Emily that she wait out in the lobby area of the jail for he had some trial preparation matters to discuss with her Dad. He asked Ellie to stay, because he wanted her to hear his advice that Earl was not to testify. From there, Aaron and Ellie followed Eddie Johnson back to Earl's cell for this delicate and critical conference.

"Look folks, I know Earl wants to tell his side of things to the

Jury but the risks are just too great. We have an excellent chance to get an outright acquittal or at worst a hung jury, which isn't half bad in a murder case. I believe that the Prosecutor will be merciless on cross-examination, Using every bit of that awful episode from 1913 will be pulled out of you Earl, and that will be a gift of a motive all wrapped up with a bow, ready for delivery, just like Christmas, Earl, can't you see that?" Aaron pleaded with his clients.

Earl listened to his lawyer and saw he meant it for the best. But the lawyer couldn't understand that he had the straight scoop from the ghost, Clarence, on this, and there was no way he was he going to tell the lawyer about Clarence. He had been told by the little man to tell his story, which was the God's truth anyhow, and by damn he was going to tell it. *I didn't shoot that Federal Agent Stiller and no jury would believe that liar George Drucker with that stupid story about having gloves on inside the Lagoon, with all them kettles fired up, December cold or not for God's sake*, he thought. "I aim to tell it Mr. Martin, and I'm decided on it. Ellie, you tell him," Earl said forcefully.

"That's right Mr. Martin, he's set on it," Ellie said.

"Well, I was afraid of that folks and here is my position, I'm your lawyer and I decide what evidence is put on in my case. You can fire me if you want to but no lawyer in this town will take you on if you insist on this "tomfool" notion of yours. Maybe Judge Parker will give you time to find somebody else but I doubt it. He has to approve me withdrawing in the middle of a trial and that is unlikely. It will be legal suicide, in my opinion, to take that chance. So if you insist on it, I'm withdrawing. You think it over and let me know in the morning in Court. Try to see it my way folks, if you do this thing and get convicted, and I represent you in it, I will never live down the shame of it, can't you see that?" Aaron pleaded. "Ellie, you say that Earl came into the house that morning after the shot was over, where had he been, do you know?"

JOHN E. WOODBERY

"He had been to the Lagoon, like he always did on shipment days and came back in time for breakfast. He acted Surprised, if not shocked, when I told him that there was a dead man on the front stoop. If he had shot that fella he would' a knowed it," Ellie argued.

"Can't you see Ellie, and Earl, that just fits into the Government's case? It gives the Jury a reason to believe the opposite that Earl went out that morning just in time to shoot Stiller and come back in and acted Surprised over it. Your bias would be showing like flags on the Fourth of July, Ellie," Aaron argued.

"Well how did he know that feller was coming, answer me that, Sir?" Ellie argued and she had a point there, because there was no way in the jury's mind that Earl would have known the raid was on that morning.

"It won't help Ellie, I know you are desperate to help; but it won't take much speculation for the Jury to conclude that Earl came back about the time the Federal Agents showed up at the house and it doesn't take long for a country man to fire off a shot. That kid skedaddled afterwards like any sensible person would have, and Earl simply had time to circle around the house and come in the back way as if nothing had happened. No, it's too risky and I won't do it," Aaron said, carrying out the plan he and his father had worked out. Anna dutifully made notes of the conversation to protect her boss from any ethical complaints later on in case Earl had been hung for a murder conviction that was not Aaron's fault.

But of course, Earl and Ellie knew none of this, and the pressure on them was enormous. Aaron's only hope was that the threat of losing his lawyer would be enough for Earl to abandon this damn fool notion of his and wake up to accept the force of his lawyer's efforts to represent him to his very best ability, which to his mind meant to talk him out of the nonsense of testifying. Earl was strangely calm in the midst of this emotional storm and Ellie; in her loyal and faithful position of a devoted wife to the man she loved, stood by him and managed somehow to hide the currents that were raging like a river inside her feelings on this decision.

"All right Mr. Martin, we'll think it over and let you know in the mornin' but I plan to tell my story 'less something changes my mind on it befo' Court, g'night Sir. Ask that jail man to leave Ellie and me alone for a bit to talk this over and we'll discuss it with you in the mornin'," Earl said.

Aaron signaled to the ever diligent Eddie Johnson that he and Miss Devlin were leaving. They left the jail visiting room, walking out in a way to avoid Emily in the waiting room area. As he left the visiting room he glanced back in time to observe Ellie and Earl embracing and getting to the heart of the matter in the few minutes left to them for this visit. The talking done, Ellie was escorted out of the room and Earl back to his cell. She caught up with Emily and they left the building together. Earl had some heavy thinking to do this night of nights.

The room was dark and Jack was sleeping as usual as Earl was returned by Johnson to his cell. Earl sat on his bunk and stared into the night mulling over the decision he had to make.

Can't do this without my lawyer, but if I don't tell my side of this, I'm sunk. That's a hell of a damn mess if there ever was one. Must choose somehow. Where is you Clarence when I needs you. Help me out here, won't you, he thought.

At that point, Jack Sanford rolled over and waked up from his deep sleep. "That you Earl"

"Who in the hell do you think it is, Jack," Earl said, that ghost ain't seen fit to show up tonight has it?"

"What ghost, you crazy or something Earl?" Jack asked incredulously.

"Oh, I ain't told you about Clarence, have I?" Earl said, not realizing until too late that he had never discussed this apparition with his cellmate.

"Clarence? What Clarence, you better explain yourself, Earl, folks'll think you are crazy," Jack said in wonderment.

"Well, maybe I am, but you see Jack, the other night when you was sleeping, I had a visitor in the cell, a little man, ghost or something and he spoke to me. He also appeared again in that courtroom and spoke again, but I'm the only one that sees or hears him. However he's speaking to me all right and telling me I need to tell my story in the trial and that the Jury will believe me. My lawyer is dead set against it, and in fact tonight he threatened to quit If I don't give up on this thing about testifying," Earl said.

"Damn, Earl, you seen a ghost right in this here cell, that spoke regular words at you?" Jack asked skeptically. Most country people in the County really believed there were ghosts, but none of them had ever actually seen one. That never changed the common conception that there was a spirit world of some kind.

"You ought to listen to your lawyer, Earl, he knows best and leave them ghosts alone, that's my advice to you," Jack said.

"You may be right, Jack," I'll sleep on it," Earl said and without another word, turned over and drifted off to sleep.

Jack shook his head at what he had just heard and wondered if somehow Earl had been dreaming or something else strange was happening. Seeing or feeling the effects of what were believed to be ghosts, or at least hearing about them was one thing, but talking to the things and having them give you advice on what to do, that was something else again and he was having no part of it. He had seen enough apparitions in his many drunken reveries to distrust every one of them. It was the only sane thing to do. He, too, turned over on his cot and soon the room was quiet except for the snores of sleeping prisoners rumbling throughout the cellblock. The little man hovered above the cots, waiting for his next opportunity to help or harm the man on trial for his life. It was just too soon to tell which one it would be.

64. He is persistent

The ride to the courthouse was in reality a short one that morning but for Earl, it seemed like an eternity. The car was traveling at normal speed, but the conception of time for Earl Bryant had stood still. He had slept and dreamed but was no closer to a decision than he had been the night before. Maybe his lawyer and his cellmate friend were right and he should abandon this damn fool notion; but that vision or whatever it was, was so clear, he was afraid to let it go.

Ellie would back him either way, she was loyal to a fault and he loved her for it. *What must I truly do?* He thought and looked up in the front seat and right there between the two officers or inside them or where ever the damn thing decided to be visible, Clarence was back, looking at him with those penetrating eyes that spoke volumes of sincerity to him.

He knew a lying man's look when he saw it, and this one of Clarence's was not one of them. The bullet proof screen that separated the front seat of the jailer's car looked like a mirror this time with Clarence's figure projected on it like one of those newfangled moving picture screens, but at the same time, it was three dimensional and as on every other appearance, also seemingly real. The little close set eyes were black as coal bricks but alive with light as though on fire. Then the voice came again which he heard as audibly as if the school teacher of his youthful past was standing in front of the one room school room, and speaking to the entire room of school kids of all ages with the clarity and projection of an orator. Earl was certain by now that the voice was real, but equally as certain that no one but him could hear or see Clarence as he appeared and spoke.

"Time is short for you my threatened one and today you must choose to act. You may choose life or you may choose death, for death is the prescription the doctor of time has prescribed for you if your courage fails you. You can listen to him and follow the lead of those you trust, but he does not know as I know what is best. Tell and they will believe; withhold and they will reject you. I ask you to speak to those on the Jury Will you do it?" Clarence spoke looking right at him and the message had settled in the will of the man on trial. He had decided, and that was final.

Seeing that, Clarence was suddenly gone, and the glass partition was as translucent as before and the jail men never once turned to look in the back seat or even noticed that there had been such a monumental disturbance. Earl rode silent for the remainder of the short trip that was taking a forever in his troubled, but now settled mind.

65. Practically the last day

The courtroom filled to capacity was electric with excitement among the packed seating areas. This was to be the end of the trial and no one who could justify in his own mind one more day off from work or in the case of the press corps and the supporters of the Defendant, no one could pry themselves away from this day.

Aaron sat quietly at the Defendant's table, waiting with uncertainty the arrival of his client from the jail. Would he testify? The word had somehow gotten out in the community that he might and few didn't want to miss that. Aaron's job was to be prepared either way. In doing this, he had little sleep the night before going over and over in his mind how he would argue the case if Earl decided to testify. A trial lawyer never gets a night off during trial because when the bell sounds, he has to come into the middle of the ring and answer his opponent, blow for blow. The doors on the side of the courtroom opened, Earl was led into the courtroom and unshackled from his restraints to take his seat next to his lawyer.

Aaron took one look at Earl and knew without asking that the fool was going to testify. "Well, apparently you have made your decision, Earl; must I tell the judge I am withdrawing?" Aaron asked, expending the last remnant of his ammunition and said nothing further waiting for the response.

Earl turned his head to the left, faced his lawyer, and said, "Mr. Martin, you do what you must do and I will do what I must do. If you must quit on me, then so be it." Aaron took one last serious look at his client, rose to his feet and stopped.

"All right, Earl, you win. If you insist on committing legal suicide like this, I will not abandon you. We go to trial!" Earl heard the words like a shot that had been fired and had struck home, but the sound had not seemed to reach him yet. Then the gravity of Aaron's words struck him like a billowing curtain of fog. He was in the bank, covered by it but not Sir where he was because he couldn't see clearly yet, or at least not understand it.

"You mean, you ain't quittin' on me after all? Earl asked, in unbelief.

"That's right Earl, I'm with you to the end. Right or wrong, wise or stupid, I throw my reputation into that pit with you and only one dog is coming out, win or lose.

"Damn," Earl said under his breath as the all rise was sounded and Judge Parker came flowing into the courtroom, seeming to presage a dark specter himself, and took his seat.

"Mr. Martin, the Government has rested, call your first witness. The entire audience waited with baited breath to hear what Aaron would say. If his client testified, this would be one of the most exciting criminal trials in north Florida legal history. If not, then it would be business as usual with the tired old reasonable doubt arguments played over and over again by the Defense like a 78 rpm record that had been played so many times that the scratches were louder than the recorded sound.

"The Defense calls, Mr. Earl Bryant," Aaron said and Earl rose from his seat and walked to the witness box. The audience was audibly stirred by the announcement as the tittering and whispering echoed throughout the courtroom only to be silenced by Judge Parker's gavel and command to be quiet on pain of eviction from the room. Earl was sworn in and Aaron began the perilous journey, in his mind at least, toward oblivion.

"Please state your name and residence, Mr. Bryant," Aaron asked.

"My name is Earl Younger Bryant and I live at Bryant Country in Liberty County," he said. Aaron let the unspecific locale reference stand and proceeded with his questions.

"Where did you spend the night on December 4th, this past year?" I spent it at home in bed with my wife Ellie down at home," he said.

"What time did you rise the morning of December 5th, 1933," Aaron asked his client.

"I woke at five o'clock in the morning," he said.

"What did you do on rising, after the usual dressing, etc.?" Aaron asked him.

"I went direct to my place of business down by the river," Earl said.

"How long did you stay there?" Aaron asked.

"Thirty minutes, jest long enough to check on the finish up of the night shift work and return home in time for breakfast around six o'clock," Earl explained.

"When you arrived home, what did you do?" Aaron asked.

"I came in the back way and found Ellie to see about some breakfast?" Aaron asked.

"Did she say or do anything unusual that morning on your return?" he asked.

"Yes, Sir, she said they were a dead man on our front door stoop and I had better go and see about it" Earl said.

"What did you do and see?" Aaron asked, trying to get to the important point that was looming like a tidal wave about to crash against the seashore.

"I went out front and shore enough found a dead man lying on the stoop, just like she said," Earl explained.

"Did you recognize this man?" Aaron asked, trying to deal with the obvious that was Sir to open Earl to a vicious cross examination as he had expected on the matter of motive, but there was really no way to avoid it so he might as well face it head on.

"Yes, Sir, I could see his face turned sideways like and I recognized him as the Federal man, Stiller," Earl said.

"Mr. Bryant, did you on December 5th 1933, shoot the man Frank Stiller you found dead on your door step before returning home to breakfast?" Aaron asked, giving Earl the clearest chance to convincingly deny the murder.

"No, Sir, I never shot anybody that morning or any other time, Mr. Martin," Earl said with as much conviction as he could give it.

"What did you do next?" Aaron asked.

"I talked it over with Ellie, and I went to work back at the Lagoon," Earl said.

"Did you have a telephone?" Aaron asked, giving the jury an explanation why he had no way to report this incident.

"No, Sir, we ain't got one of them modern devices, Sir," Earl said.

"How far is it out of the woods to the nearest phone?" Aaron asked.

"Ten, maybe fifteen miles," Earl answered.

"Why did you go to work and not go out up the road and get help?" Aaron asked.

"I figured this here Federal man was dead and I couldn't help him with nothin'; and since he had been chasing me and my business for years, I figure the po'lice would think I done it, so I went to work where they knew where to find me and let things take their course. There weren't no reason to hide from it," Earl said.

"Your witness," Aaron said.

Houston Gilchrist could not believe his good fortune. This was better than Christmas morning, as a child with a stocking full of goodies just waiting at the foot of the stairs to be plucked. He must have been living right he thought, or Aaron Martin had clean lost his marbles. He hardly knew where to begin; the legal pickings were so full on the bush, he was afraid he would fill his basket before he got them all.

He approached the witness who strangely did not seem afraid or even nervous and it appeared as though he fully expected to be acquitted and wasn't worrying about the disaster that was about to befall him. Figuratively licking his chops, Houston began. "Mr. Bryant, you left home shortly about five o'clock on the morning of December 5th 1933, did you not?" Houston asked, setting up the witness with what was about to come. You went to your "business" you say, that would be an illegal whiskey still, would it not?" Houston asked, getting his licks in early.

"I went to my business, yes," Earl answered dodging the admission nicely.

"You stayed there for a short time and returned home just after six o'clock, right?" he asked.

"Yes, Sir," Earl said, limiting his answers to the minimal response as Aaron had instructed him.

"You have been sitting in this courtroom in this trial and heard the Coroner testify that Mr. Stiller died about six o'clock, didn't you Mr. Bryant?" Houston asked.

"Yes, Sir, I heard him say that," Earl responded.

"That gave you time to go out of your house, wait for the Federal men to come and take your time to shoot one and return home as though Surprised, didn't you?" Houston asked and was met by an immediate objection from Aaron, as it being argumentative, but the jury got the point even though Judge Parker sustained the objection.

Houston hammered away at the opportunity Earl had to plan and execute the shot. That the weapon he had with him that had his fingerprints on it and no one else's. That there was the lack of any recall of Mr. Drucker having on gloves that morning and that it was indeed a cold winter December morning. In his questioning, and Earl's answers, there were plenty of opportunities that Earl could not deny being a notorious moonshiner with a terrible reputation for illegal activities of that kind before turning to the motive matter.

"You knew Frank Stiller well enough to recognize him because he had been after you for years in your illegal whiskey making business, didn't you?" Houston said, opening a new salvo that was designed to crush the witness under an avalanche of admissions as to motive for the murder.

"He had been after me, yes," Earl answered truthfully.

"In fact, you had a special reason to dislike this man didn't you?" Houston asked and waited for the explosion that would flatten his opposition.

"I did not like this man," Earl answered, pulling back from the edge of the cliff ever so gingerly, "But I did not shoot him!"

"Isn't it true, Mr. Bryant that in 1913, you witnessed this same Federal Agent, Frank Stiller, shoot your own father, another illegal whiskey making man, isn't that right, Sir?" Houston asked almost certain that he knew the answer to come unless the witness would outright lie and add perjury to his legal troubles.

"Yes, Sir, I seen him do that in 1913, that is true," Earl answered truthfully to the total surprise of his antagonist.

"You had every reason then to kill this same man that had killed your own father and you never forgot it did you?" Houston asked, closing in for the kill.

"I did not like the man. He did shoot my old pappy, but I never got the chance to shoot him. He was already dead when I got home," Earl said.

Houston was satisfied with this, he had his motive, he had established the man's terrible reputation. Having the tangible evidence of the gun, the bullet, and fingerprints, with even a rebuttal to the one weakness in his case that the gloves gave a plausible explanation; even though from a shaky witness as to credibility, that no prints of the witness, George Drucker, were on the murder weapon, was enough.

"I've finished with this witness, Your Honor," Houston said and sat down with much satisfaction.

Aaron rose to re-direct a few questions at the witness, although it seemed hopeless to him at this point. Every fear he had had about Earl testifying had proved true. Since motive had been clearly established, he decided to leave that alone. A detailed explanation by Earl as to how he had meant to take his revenge back in 1913 for the execution style slaying of his father but abandoned the chance to shoot Stiller out of fear of arrest would have had such a devastating effect on the jury that it would literally sink the ship of Defense, even without a cross-examination. And with it, they might figuratively lynch him on the spot and not wait for the deliberations.

He asked a few clarifying questions, got one final denial from his client and sat down. The witness was excused. The only thing left to do was to have Ellie testify that Earl had acted Surprised that morning when she told him about the body, but that really wasn't going to sell well to a jury. Any wife would say that unless she hated her husband and Ellie clearly didn't hate Earl. Ellie did the best impression of the genuine article of truth she could, but her acerbic nature just came out vividly on the cross-examination that followed.

"You have been married to Earl Bryant for many years and no one else, is that right Mrs. Bryant?" Houston asked rather politely.

"Yes, Sir," Ellie answered.

"You do consider yourself loyal to your husband, Mrs. Bryant?" Houston asked.

"Yes, Sir," she replied.

"You would do anything to help him as that faithful and loyal wife, isn't that true, Mrs. Bryant?" Houston asked, baiting the trap. She didn't fall for it.

"I would not lie for him, if that is what you are driving at, Sir!" Ellie stated with such conviction that the Jury was impressed. You could see the smiles flittering across their faces as each Juror thought, *he asked for that!*

Houston took it in stride as he was aware of the gamble, but things were going so well, he thought it was worth the risk. For his recovery, Houston took a flyer with the next question. "When Earl came in for breakfast at six o'clock that morning and before you told him about the dead man on your front door step, breakfast wasn't ready yet, was it?"

"No," Ellie said without explanation.

"So he didn't need to wash up yet, did he, by then, I mean?" Houston asked.

"No, Sir, breakfast weren't ready yet, but he said he needed to wash up anyways," Ellie said.

Houston was puzzled by that answer so he followed up just out of curiosity.

"Why wash up then?"

"He washed always when he comes in, just in case something was on his hands," Ellie explained enigmatically.

"You mean in case he had been shooting at something?" Houston asked, speculatively.

"Oh no, Sir, nothing like that," Ellie said.

"How do you know?" Houston asked, figuring he had nothing to lose at this point. "Whenever he fired that thing, it smelled and it didn't smell that time so I'm sure he hadn't fired it that mornin'," Ellie explained. Houston finished his cross examination, not seeing anything particularly by that answer since he figured the jury would expect her to cover for her husband anyway and he felt he had covered enough ground with this witness.

On re-direct Aaron, did his best to give Ellie a chance to unequivocally state that she believed her husband would not lie for him and that the Jury should believe her. All in all she had been a credible witness but probably not strong enough, with the expectation that a wife would twist the truth a little to save her husband without outright lying, and to cover up the harm that Earl testifying had caused the defense of his life.

It was basically over except for the arguments and the Jury was soon to get the case. The arguments were long and emotional with the evidence picked apart by the Defense and immortalized by the Prosecution. Houston hammered the circumstantial evidence home pointing ever so directly at guilt.

Aaron tried to paint George Drucker as unbelievable as a witness with every reason to lie about the gloves. Without the gloves, the absence of prints in the bullet chamber made George's testimony unbelievable. He painted George as waiting in the wings, just waiting to take over the empire after Earl was found guilty of a crime Earl never committed. Drucker had the same time opportunity to make the shot but Aaron lacked the direct evidence or any witnesses to contradict him on the glove story. Earl certainly hadn't acted guilty, he argued. He kept the supposed murder weapon with him for the Marshalls to find without a fight or any attempt to hide it. No criminal mind would have done that. But in the end it came down to the fingerprints and the matched rifling grooves on bullet and barrel.

How to explain that phenomenal coincidence if Earl was innocent, Houston argued in rebuttal. It was hopeless for the Defense, every spectator was thinking. Even Aaron couldn't suppress the depressing conclusion that he had presided over the conviction of an innocent man. How could he live with himself being responsible for that? But for the Prosecution, it was like the melody in a song called "he did it", intertwined with the harmony blending nicely in as the circumstantial evidence of the strongest testimony in support of motive, anyone on the local scene had ever seen.

Houston was magnificent in his summation building a crescendo of eloquence that could hardly lead anywhere but a unanimous vote for conviction. Eloquence can only go so far but both lawyers were well equipped in that department.

In spite of Aaron's vanishing confidence, he valiantly made the most of his arguments. All the while, the little man figure that had seductively enticed Earl into this fatal blunder, stood by in that place or was it time in which he resided, invisible to all, with the ever so slight smile of contentment on his face.

Earl would never see his "Uncle Clarence" again.

Judge Parker read the instructions to the Jury and by four o'clock, they had the case. The courtroom was cleared and the long wait was to begin with deliberations to start first thing tomorrow. Aaron and the Bryant supporters conferred briefly, hugging each other where that personal longing was appropriate, just standing by for the others. He returned to his office to lick his wounds. He was in no mood for dinner or social contact.

Houston on the other hand was in a celebratory mood and took Erick Driskoll and another assistant with him to dinner at the Duvall Hotel.

The usual crowd was there and much congratulating was going around as Houston basked in the glow of a seeming victory to come in a day or so. This was a hanging case and no jury would take that lightly, no matter how convincing the evidence. It was a circumstantial evidence case for Sir with no eye witness to the crime, except the undeniable fingerprints resting ever so carelessly on the stock and parts of the supposed murder weapon that the Defendant never even bothered to hide. He would leave it there and start thinking about his next case, as soon as the applause died down, that is.

66. Deadline

The press contingent made a mad rush for the available phones in nearby pay booths where quarters jingled, as editors across the state frantically took down copy by shorthand for filling in column inches stingily reserved for the latest on the Moonshiner Trial as it had come to be known.

Tony Callaway was heavily invested in the story by now and while a few inches of newsprint may suffice for the Times Union, The Tampa Tribune or St. Pete Times on the beginning of jury deliberations, the Recorder's readers demanded much more. It was four in the afternoon and Tony's deadline for the presses was about suppertime. There would be no time for Tony to eat until that deadline was met, as he ran quickly over to the newsroom of the paper.

He thought over the day's events for a few minutes as he sat in front of his "Iron Mike", as he called his manual antiquated typewriter, a Royal, with its black frame and ornamental scrollwork. He typed away and the staccato sounds of an accomplished typist transferring the power of these fingers to the impressions on the paper beat a familiar rhythm that resonated throughout the newsroom. His would be the lead story for tomorrow's early edition and it had to be good. The copy writer's continual dilemma is how to convey news to inform the reader, but to confine its essence to only the few early paragraphs that most readers would devote to a story even a spectacular one like The Moonshiner Trial. Tony began with a dynamic lead:

"The moon may be shining across the forests of Liberty County tonight but the "Moonshiner" on trial for his life for the murder of Frank Stiller, star Federal Agent in the whiskey wars, can see none of it from the confines of the Leon County Jail."

Tony went on to describe the sudden turn of events in the trial and the totally unexpected testimony of the Defendant.

"It was unheard of for a man on trial for his life to have the courage and even the audacity to get up on his hind legs in a witness box and say that he just didn't do it. What was his lawyer thinking to let him do this crazy thing? However, the Constitution only prevents the state from compelling a Defendant to testify against himself and allows the assistance of counsel for his Defense; but nowhere does the Constitution prevent a person from testifying in his own defense if he insists on doing that, no matter how unwise that course of action. The lawyer for such a man can only persuade not compel. This writer is convinced the Defendant in this case made his own decision to expose himself to that terrible risk. Time will tell who was right, for the attorney client privilege seals away the answer to that question for all time, unless Mr. Bryant decides to reveal it. Even with his death by hanging, the privilege remains."

Tony thereby concluded his story, being sympathetic for the impossible position of his friend Aaron Martin. If Bryant were convicted, Aaron would go down in legal history, locally anyway, as the lawyer who let his client do this damn fool thing. None of the local bar would ever believe the client had the courage to do this on his own, and Aaron would suffer mightily in reputation.

Tony had finished his story just in time for the seven o'clock deadline imposed without variation by Dick Powers, Editor of the paper. He pulled the sheets from his Iron Mike and read them over for final editing. *That will have to do,* he thought and rose from his chair, walked across the room to Powers' office and handed in the finished product. Dick looked it over quickly, nodded and dropped it into the hopper for typesetting just in time for the press run for tomorrow.

"Not bad, Tony," Dick said, with an unusual compliment for him. Then the two men walked out of the newsroom to go their separate ways for the evening. With colleagues who knew and respected each other's talents, such words are rarely necessary. This was just one of those times. The Jury was expected to take at least a couple of days to decide, for after all, a man's life was at stake. There would be a time then for not only reporting but reflecting on whether justice was served in an uncertain and often cruel world. The opinions on that would always vary.

67. Curious boarders

The feeling of relief in certain other quarters of the City that evening was only slowly making itself felt. This trial had been an emotional ordeal for George Drucker as he struggled to keep his stories straight. Using tales he had been telling as an undercover man before the shooting and with even more difficulty, ever since that night at Salty's Place on the Ochlocknee River, when he had told the federal agent what he knew about the shooting. At each step along the way, the story had been embellished just a little and George had had a hard time keeping up with its own growth in the telling. George had been safely kept at a low cost boarding house in the southern part of the City out on the way out to Wakulla County on the Old Crawfordville Highway.

Mrs. Gibson, who ran the place, occasionally would take on boarders for the Government in special cases where the witness was under some kind of police protection, like George Drucker was in this case; but the usual residents at "The House", as most of them called it, were itinerant salesmen, railroad construction workers, seasonal farm hands, and even a few lower paid workers that came into the Capital for the annual Legislative session.

They were on the whole, a friendly, loquacious sort that loved to sit around in the parlor or out on the gallery, if it wasn't too hot or too cold, and shoot the breeze until bedtime. Tonight George was in an expansive mood as the dread of the trial that had hung over his head like a dark cloud was slowly lifting, as he sat there and listened to Earl cut his own throat by taking the witness stand in his own defense. He remained cautious because the verdict was still to come.

He had stuck the dagger in Earl's back and Earl himself could try to reach back and pull it out, but the jury was the only one who could drive it home and finish the King of Bryant Country once and for all. Only when he heard the magic words, "guilty as charged" followed by the celestially enshrined words Sure to then follow, "I sentence you Earl Bryant to be hanged by the neck until dead!" would he be able to finally breath free air again.

Tonight the gallery crew was jovial and full of talk about their jobs, the rumors that the Florida State College for Women would someday receive a few male students and maybe even bring a decent football team to this town, the quality of the Apalachicola oysters this winter, and the speculation when the amendment making whiskey legal again would be ratified by enough of the states to open up the saloons again.

To George's relief, there was no talk about the trial or more importantly, his role in it. These were hard workingmen and having an
interest in current events, and especially reading the newspaper was
a low priority item with them.

George leaned his chair back against the wall on the front porch
of the boarding house, closed his eyes and let the jaw jaw of the conversation flow around him like the gentle lapping of waves around
a fishing boat used to do on Lake Talquin on a Saturday afternoon
speckled perch outing in the dead of winter. But that was before the
dam burst last month and ended everybody's fun for a few years ahead
because there was not even any discussion about reconstructing the
dam and who knew how long it would take the river to refill it, if they
did rebuild the thing.

He tried to relax and get the trial completely out of his mind, at least
for the evening, so that he could get some sleep. But try as he might,
he could not get rid of all of his anxiety. Earl Bryant was safely locked
away in that jail and if everything the Prosecutors had told him was
true of how badly it had gone for Earl in the last day of the trial, he
shouldn't have any worries.

But he was too wrapped up in the what- if's to really relax just yet.
In half an hour, he had absorbed enough local color from the gallery
gang for his liking and excused himself and went up to his room for
bed. He didn't know what he would do tomorrow, for the testimony
was over and waiting around was all there was left to do.

The meal that night had been filling and even delicious. One thing you
could say for Mrs. Gibson, she might be fat and ugly, but she could sure
cook. He lay on his back in bed with the spread and blanket pulled up to
his bearded chin to cut off the chilled, unheated air He thought about how
he might get his empire started once the King was gone for good, but until
that Jury had finished him off, such planning was only a wasteful luxury.

In a few minutes, George was asleep and the crazy dreams he had been having were Sure to come again, with their nonsense scenarios he couldn't remember for five minutes after waking anyway. The nightlights winked out in the boarding house room-by-room as man after man finally called it quits for the night. All was quiet now and the steady but irregular snoring could be heard reverberating throughout the place. It was like each instrument in an orchestra as it warmed up trying to find its tune, sounding fine by itself, but together with the other instruments, an inharmonious mess. That is if anybody were awake to hear it.

68. Deliberations

The Jury arrived the next day at Judge Parker's Courtroom at the appointed hour quite anxious to get on with the deliberations that were in store. They gathered in the jury room where Ervin Floyd, Bailiff' had brought in coffee and donuts from one of the shops not far away on Monroe Street. They had become familiar with each other by now, by name at least, as juries are bound to do with the terrible task ahead of them and having lived this case for several days.

The very thought of considering the guilt or innocence of a fellow human being, for which Judge Ben Parker might impose the death penalty by hanging, was abhorrent to some of the members and necessary in the minds of others. Each one of them had promised Houston Gilchrist on the voir dire examination that if they found from the evidence proof beyond a reasonable doubt of the guilt of the Defendant, they would do their duty and convict. At nine thirty, Ervin came in to escort the Jury into court where they each took the same seat in the jury box they had used since the beginning of the trial.

"Good morning, Ladies and gentlemen," Judge Parker said, as everyone was seated after his arrival. "Today you people will have the awesome responsibility to decide the guilt or innocence of the Defendant, Mr. Earl Bryant. Your first job upon retiring to the jury room will be to select a foreman whose job it will be to preside over your deliberations. There is no power in this office. Let me assure you that each person's vote carries the same weight and authority as each of the others. Your decision must be based on the evidence presented here in this courtroom during this trial and you must all agree before you can announce a verdict.

Mr. Floyd, my Bailiff, will stay in touch and tend to your needs. I will now read to you my prepared instructions which alone will be your guide on the law that applies, except the good common sense and intelligence the Good Lord has bestowed on each of you by birth and most of you, I sincerely hope all of you, have fully developed by life's experiences ever since."

With that, Judge Parker read the standard jury instructions for a case of this kind and the Jury was excused, whereupon he announced an indefinite recess except for call to counsel, and the trial was essentially over. The lawyers had agreed to stay in their offices in case of an early verdict but no one expected it in this case. The trouble with that maxim is that you can never tell what twelve tried and true jurors will do when they get their hands, as it were, around the evidence. It is an awesome responsibility, especially in a murder case, but the American jury, by and large, fairly dispensed justice without pride or prejudice.

Earl was permitted to stay for a while to visit with Ellie, Emily and even Dr. Wilson who had driven down from Bainbridge with them for this moment. He was concerned about Emily's reaction to a guilty verdict based on what he had heard about the way things had gone. Earl had never been a person you would want to touch, wrap up to in a bear hug or even sit down with to talk about the day, important things, or just nothing. But this day was different, in fact more different than any he or he and Ellie, for that matter, had ever experienced.

Earl's competent lawyer had threatened to quit his defense if he chose to disregard his advice that to do so would be foolish if not crazy to testify. Earl had bull headedly thrown caution to the winds, listened to the very clear words, coming from "Uncle Clarence", and had been proved the fool his lawyer predicted he would become. The only ones supporting him, who knew about the visions, were Johnny Caldwell and his cellmate Jack Sanford. Neither had been able to persuade him to abandon the foolish notion that he testify.

He had been no match for the cross examination of the federal prosecutor, and just as Aaron had predicted, the testimony about his decision not to shoot Frank Stiller back in 1913 came across just exactly the opposite of what Earl had hoped. What Earl had considered restraint back then, and his remembering it over time had eliminated the urge for revenge from his mind. But the average person on hearing him tell it would naturally take it as an offer of proof of the latest crime, where the same man had been gunned down by somebody and the Jury was very likely now to think it was him.

It couldn't be helped now, however, and what was done was done. His family was kind enough in their pain and frustration not to heap the blame on him that he richly deserved. They just touched and hugged him in a community of tears.

"It'll be all right Earl; you just wait and see. It's not over yet, we can trust this Jury, these good people, they'll see the truth, you wait," Ellie said with as much comfort as love can bring. She continued, "You know we'll stand with you through thick and thin." These words of probably false security and comfort; and although sincerely delivered, had a hollow ring to Earl. He was strong and resilient, and his faith in the truth and himself would just have to see him through this time of crisis. The jail guards in charge of transporting him back and forth for the trial had gradually come to respect him in an odd sort of way and bent over backwards to give him the maximum allowable time with his family. Today more than others, this seemed appropriate to them. But eventually, even they had their duty to do, and the dreaded handcuffs and shackles were clamped on once again and he was off to his depressing cell.

Old Jack was still there and tonight he just might indulge his cell-mate in some heart to heart talk about things. Soon after Earl was taken away, the others left the courtroom. The room lights were turned down to conserve electricity as the depression was still going strong, or would it be better to say still going weak. Even the mighty Federal Government had restraints.

But things would be lively in the other part of the courthouse where the Jury began to talk about the case. Lively was a good description for the discussions in the jury room. Ervin Floyd had kept the coffee pot plugged in and the donuts handy. Judge Parker's last words were still ringing in their ears, "If every one of you find from all the evidence presented beyond and to the exclusion of a reasonable doubt, that Earl Bryant, with malice aforethought, that is that he intended to act and commit the act of homicide against and causing the death of one Frank Stiller in the Northern District of Florida, you must return a verdict of guilty. If every one of you agrees that any of the elements of the crime Earl Bryant is accused of are not proven to that same standard of proof, beyond and to the exclusion of a reasonable doubt, you must return a verdict of not guilty. If you cannot all agree, then you must try very hard to do so, one way or the other or let my Bailiff, Mr. Floyd, know and I will give you further instructions. First you must pick a Foreman who will lead the deliberations and make all the presentations back to me at the appropriate time. Good luck, ladies and gentlemen." With those final instructions they were ushered into the jury room where the real work of the trial was to begin.

Every trial lawyer with much jury trial experience thinks he can predict before the trial is over which juror will be voted the foreman. There is something in the eyes or is it body language that gives it away, that way the person carries himself or herself sends out a signal as if there was an electric sign flashing letters across the forehead with the words "Pick Me" for everyone to see. This Jury was no different. The range of skill, location, and temperament was spread across the pool as the members had been drawn from across the District.

The out of town jurors had been put up in the hotel with strict instructions every day from Judge Parker that they were not to discuss this case until now. That had been a heavy burden for most of them as thinking about events you observe, literally cries out to be shared, tested or examined and the sense of relief now that they could finally talk about the case they had absorbed without comment for these many days was palpable.

There was Fred Warner, tobacco farmer from Quincy, who was a very practical man whose sense of right and wrong had been instilled in him by a religious upbringing that sounded well in an innate sense of the moral.

Orien Preston, the State Historical Society librarian, was quiet and reflective, keeping most thoughts to himself, as librarians are prone to do. He defers greatly to the needs and wishes of the library customers, as it were, and giving out the aura of a wise know it all sort of person. Neither lawyer had any idea how the man would be as a juror except they both secretly believed he would not be the foreman.

Howard Gray, state employee in the records section of the Secretary of Agriculture's office, was a get through the day and come home to his real life interests of fishing, hunting and family, not necessarily in that order, sort of guy, who was basically bored by this whole process.

Elliot Barnes, twenty-eight year old farm hand from Marianna, lacked much formal education, but had practical common sense for one so young in life experiences.

Eldon Williams, auto mechanic from Greensboro, was a bit ornery from time to time in his moods as the problem of the moment presented itself, like rusted motor mount bolts when the job was due to be delivered late in the day.

Elizabeth Hardy, sixth grade schoolteacher from Crawfordville, was small and diminutive and had little to say about things contrary to what you might expect for a schoolteacher.

Roger Farris, Madison druggist, was a quiet, intelligent and a reflective man, suited well for his pill counting and powder mixing, done mostly alone in the lab in the back of the small drugstore on Main Street, Madison. He was smart and quiet, but not likely to be voted as leader by the group.

Fred Smith, oyster shucker from Apalachicola, was a rough and tumble but shrewd sort of guy, given to much profanity when the little unexpected disturbances popped up in his work on the oyster piles, which was often.

Victor Katansky, newly naturalized US Citizen out of Russia, a postal clerk from Chairs, somehow managed to escape the preemptory challenges by Houston, possibly because he failed to disclose in the jury selection process, for very personal reasons, that he had escaped Communist Russia. This was not because he had been a lover of freedom, which he was, but because he had an abiding resentment of power exercised by those over him in the government bureaucracy. He had served in the Civil Service as a munitions inspector and was constantly in trouble with the bureau that employed him, constantly registering complaints and was close to being arrested from time to time. No self-respecting prosecutor would knowingly have allowed such a man on his Jury. As luck would have it, he was seated too deep in the jury pool and Houston had used up his last challenge on a cop hater, before Victor had made his way, by the process of elimination, to the jury box.

Frances Drake, sales clerk from Tallahassee working in a jewelry store, was a calm submissive type that any lawyer would allow to serve and this case was no exception to that rule of juror stereotype conventional wisdom.

Archibald Kline, barrel maker from Chipley was a cautious contemplative man and he likewise was a lawyer's dream pick. From the Defendant's perspective he would examine the evidence and understand the heavy burden of proof issue more suited to his natural love of freedom. For the prosecution, he would track the evidence and see how all the elements fit together to make his case.

Dr. Steven Mathewson, mathematics professor over at the women's college here in Tallahassee rounded out the twelve. He was an intellectual's intellectual, fond of abstractions that made sense only to other academicians, but having the hard discipline of thinking, such a profession required.

Aaron had debated long and hard with himself whether to use his last challenge when Dr. Mathewson made it to the box, but liked the man who he assessed as fair and smart enough to really keep track of and sort out the evidence, which is about all a defense lawyer can hope for in a murder case. Dr. Mathewson like most intellectuals would likely weigh carefully the imposition of the death penalty and Aaron had a hunch he would be reluctant to impose it. He was Aaron's prediction for foreman. Houston made the same choice, though the two opposing lawyers never discuss such thoughts during the heat of battle.

Judge Parker had excused the two alternates just before they were given jury instructions. A more diverse group you would never expect to find in one small room to decide the fate of Earl Bryant on the charge of premeditated murder. Ervin Floyd reminded the Jury that they were to contact him if they had questions, but to get to work and try to do as much as they possibly could without bothering the Judge.

69. How could a party help?

Roland and Marian Martin sat quietly as they made their way through the evening meal without much enthusiasm for the spread of delicious food Annie had prepared as usual. Annie made several trips into and out of the dining room, not because she really needed to tend to things but because she sensed the family was in deep worry about something. She loved the Martin family so much that she could not bear it when they were depressed or disappointed about something. Staying busy was her way of just being a part of things, even if she was helpless to do anything about whatever it was that troubled them. If it was important enough to rise from the depths of just worrying to actual conversation, she would learn about whatever it was soon enough without asking. She knew her place in the household and had no desire to push the limits of her inclusion. They literally picked at their food with both of them deep in thought.

"Roland," Marian said as she raised her eyes from where they had been gazing purposelessly at her food.

"Yes, Dear?" Roland asked duplicating the movement and fixing his gaze at her.

"It's going badly, isn't it?" Marian said.

"Afraid so, Dear. Aaron had no choice but to put the old man on the stand yesterday even though he knew it would be a disaster. We had talked about it the night before, and Aaron at my suggestion even threatened to quit the case if he testified but it didn't do any good. Something was driving the old man, but where to is my question, the gallows?" Roland asked rhetorically.

"Well, I suppose it's in God's hands now, Aaron's done everything he could possibly have done. I was just wondering, do you suppose that after it's over and if it goes badly for Mr. Bryant, we could have Aaron and Sue with a few friends over here for a quiet Saturday? You know, a social occasion of sorts but not formal or a celebration because it wouldn't be right if he loses, but he ought to know his people are supporting him," Marian said, searching for the right approach to the tugging of her Mother's heart that something needed to be done other than to just ignore him at this critical time.

"I don't know, Marian, Aaron would see through that in a minute, he's too smart to be manipulated like that," Roland said questioningly.

"Roland Martin, I am not suggesting we manipulate anybody, least of all our Son. He needs to have people around and get this thing out in the open so the healing can start, I'm convinced of that!" Marian said forcefully.

Annie busied herself removing the dinner plates without a word as if she could soak up the angst that emanated from the pair's conversation. Roland looked at Marian thoughtfully, pitching aside his immediate reaction to her motherly suggestion, to see if there might be some wisdom seeping through the veil that his methodical and logical approach to problem solving draped over his wife's aesthetic and sometimes emotional consideration of things. He had been a lawyer too long to overlook another's suggestion, just because he had not thought of it first.

"Maybe just a few close friends. Who would you suggest we invite, Marian?" Roland asked.

"I was thinking that we would limit it to Ben and Sally Collins and Tony Callaway, and maybe that other friend from law school with Aaron, what was his name?" "Nelson, I think" Roland said.

Then Marian suggested, "How about Peter Drucker from Havana, those boys were all very close growing up, or would that be touchy because his brother was the key witness for the prosecution?"

"I think we better leave Pete out this time Marian, the connection to Aaron's loss is just too close. Course if the Jury acquits or is dead-locked, we could turn it into a celebration from the "wake" it sounds like you're planning," Roland said.

"All right Roland, I'll get together with Annie and plan a barbeque for the next Saturday after the verdict comes in, unless it's a Friday then we'll skip a week. I'll let you break it to Aaron, Mr. Politician. And a second thought, you better have Mack clean up the barbeque pit and get that stuff ready, but you know all that. This will be good Dear, I'm glad you saw it my way in the end," Marian said. As if on cue, Annie brought in the coffee service and a small and tasty dessert tray, to the perfect end of the evening meal.

She knew her timing better than anyone and without having said a word, she had kept the mood of the evening on an even keel and the family vessels seemed to be headed for smooth sailing after all. It would have been presumptuous for her to smile, but she radiated internally a glow of satisfaction that the worry that had gripped her dining room, like an evil omen at the start of the meal, had been released like the evil spirit it truly was. She resolved that the Saturday party would not suffer from the lack of the finest food known to the Martin kitchen and that was saying something indeed.

70. In search of consensus

"Well, let's get it over with folks," said Howard Gray, "Anybody want to volunteer to lead this mess?" "Pardon me Howard, but deciding whether or not to take another human being's life is not a "mess" as you call it," Fred Warner said, being offended slightly by Howard's lack of sensitivity.

"Gentlemen! Ladies! Let's not get into it with each other as we have some important work to do here and we do need to get started. It's the hardest part of any task, you know, getting started" Dr. Mathewson said.

"I think you ought to do it Doctor Mathewson, I've noticed that you've been paying close attention to the evidence," Roger Farrens, the Madison druggist, said.

"Hell yeah, do it, Doc," Fred Smith chimed in cheerfully.

"Makes no difference to me folks who ever does it, Let's just get on with it," Eldon Williams said.

"Does anyone else want to be considered, we could hold a vote, democratically, that is," Doctor Mathewson suggested. The room was silent as it became apparent that the Earl Bryant Murder Trial Jury had just selected its foreman.

"All in favor that Doc Mathewson takes the lead, say aye?" Orien Preston said and a unanimous chorus acclaimed his election.

"All right, then that's settled. I suggest we just take a vote on the verdict, with three options, guilty, not guilty or undecided. You know just to see how we're split up, if at all; and if it's not unanimous, which I suspect it's not, we can discuss the evidence until a consensus develops. As Fred said, a man's life may be at stake and none of us want to take that lightly, all right?" Mathewson said and looked around the room at all of the faces to see no objections.

They were just beginning, but the process at least was off to a start.

Where it was headed, no one yet knew. Erik started for openers, "all those who believe the Government has proved its case beyond a reasonable doubt that Earl Bryant is guilty of killing Frank Stiller, the Federal Revenue Agent, with malice aforethought as Judge Parker explained it to us, please raise your hands?" Howard Gray, Eldon Williams, Arch Kline and Fred Smith all raised their hands.

"I count that as four. Orien will you agree to be our counter, just to double check me on that part of the procedure? We don't want any mistakes in this." Mathewson said. Preston nodded his agreement and made three columns on his note pad and added the figure four under the heading of guilty. He put a number one on the row to indicate the first vote and listed the jurors so voting.

"All those in favor of innocent by the same standard, please raise your hands?" Steven said. Only Elizabeth Hardy and Victor Katansky raised their hands and Steven noted the number two, which Orien Preston noted and identified on his pad. "That's two against and four for guilty so far, do the rest of you vote undecided, and if so, please raise your hands?" Steven asked. The remaining jurors, six in number, all raised their hands with all so far having voted.

"Okay, then we have our work cut out for us, why don't any of the six of you that care to, tell us the parts of the evidence that troubles you?" Steven said.

"I'll start it," Fred Warner said, "The part that troubles me is the fingerprint evidence, or more accurately, the lack of it. If Bryant shot that rifle that same morning he was arrested, he had to have put his fingerprints on the trigger guard and there was none. How they were missing is my question?"

"That's easy Fred, Drucker had the gloves on that morning and he testified that he opened the rifle to check out the number of bullets, he rubbed them off, that's all," Howard Gray said.

"I'm bothered by that George Drucker, he was a little too slick for me and I don't trust him," Elizabeth Hardy, one of the dissenters, said.

"Those guys were up to their eyeballs in breaking the law. There's no honor among thieves, you know," Fred Smith said rather too loudly.

"Remember, Fred, Mr. Bryant is not charged with stealing or whiskey making and we have to look at the evidence that was presented and base our decision that way," Steven reminded the jurors, staying in the undecided camp for now.

"I voted undecided just for starting, but I must confess that when Mr. Bryant testified that he had witnessed the victim shoot his Father back in 1913, and said he did not have a chance to shoot him that morning, the only thought I had was that he had every reason in the world to shoot the man. I'm leaning toward guilt now myself," young Elliot Barnes said, previously one of the undecided.

"Yeah, that was persuasive to me too," Roger Farrens said, seeming to join those in favor of guilt.

"The part that makes the most sense to me folks is that there is no doubt from the evidence presented by the Government's expert that the bullet that killed Stiller came from the rifle that the Defendant had in his possession the morning of the crime. It had his prints on it and there you have it. No other explanation necessary, I'm coming over to the side of guilty," Orien Preston, said softly, as if reluctant to speak out what was else may be on his mind.

Frances Drake nodded her head silently in agreement, which the rest noted.

"But it's a man's life at stake, and what if you are all wrong and there is some explanation we don't have. If we vote him guilty and the Judge sentences him to hang and we were wrong, I couldn't live with that," Fred Warner said. He was deeply troubled with the thought of being in effect, the eternal judge for another man's soul. His faith had taught him that all choices he could make ended with death. In the meantime that was God's prerogative but he knew he had agreed in serving here that if he was convinced of guilt he had to live up to his responsibility.

"Who else could have done it with the means, opportunity and motive other than Bryant?" Professor Mathewson asked rhetorically, himself also coming around to the side of those leaning toward guilt. "Remember Fred, the legal standard we are operating under is "reasonable doubt," not absolute certainty. No one will ever know that, except God and unfortunately he is not able to vote on this. We are the ones stuck with this responsibility. As I understood Judge Parker's instructions, we must find a doubt for which reason exists, that is, something in the evidence that points toward it as a rational man would see it," Steven explained.

Elizabeth could sense that she was one of the two holdouts along with Victor, the Russian, as the jurors had taken to calling him. Victor didn't mind that for he stated he loved "Mother Russia" as he fondly called his homeland to anyone who would listen.

The debate among the tentative, undecided jurors raged on for several hours, if debate was what you might call it. All six of them, with the possible exception of Fred Warner, were leaning if not going over to the other side.

Steven wisely avoided an up or down vote, for he suspected that the need of a consensus required more than a simple confrontation as to decision. That cheapened it in his mind for having to decide. One might act because he had to make a choice, but that nagging uncertainty that you were not quite fully Sure you wanted to go on record in favor of taking another man's life, just wouldn't go away easily.

He looked into the eyes of Elizabeth, Fred and Victor and could sense that even if they voted again, these three would probably dig their heels in and say no. It was just going to take more time. He also suspected Fred Warner, was a religious man, not that the others weren't, but he was the only one who openly talked about his faith, and said he needed some time to pray about this decision and that would have to be tonight.

This day was not going to end with a verdict of guilty, he was certain of it. *If you looked at the evidence,* he thought, *there was really not much of an argument in Earl's favor. He had stood up there or sat in the witness chair and said he didn't do it with conviction, which undoubtedly had taken a lot of courage. But that motive he confessed to, seemed to rob him of the very moral strength his denial might otherwise have provided,* Dr. Mathewson thought.

The consensus was developing that Houston Gilchrist had proven his case but Steven was not going to push it to another vote just yet. *Just let it develop for a while,* he thought.

"I say he did it folks. That gun, them prints, and he even said he didn't have time to or something like that, which to me is as good as saying he wanted to do it," Howard Gray argued, ready to end this thing and go fishing. He was anxious to have this trial behind him so he could catch the speckled perch that were biting in Lake Jackson.

"Right on, I'm with you Howard," Eldon Williams chimed in.

"Wait a minute Howard, Eldon, and the rest of you," Frances Drake said, "The man said he didn't do it. But that comment about not having enough time could go either way and it didn't rise to any confession in my book. I would never vote guilty on the strength of that!"

"Naturally he would deny it, what do you expect him to do, confess it right there on the stand?" Orien Preston said quietly, having come around to the side of the guilty voters but he would not be swayed by an irrational argument like that. During this "debate" the original group of six drifted back and forth but Steven sensed they would eventually come down on the side of a conviction.

The lunch break found the Jury still undecided and Ervin Floyd brought in food for them keeping away the temptations of contact with outsiders. Steven called a halt to the deliberations as they enjoyed the noonday meal, and they all talked about anything but the evidence. However it never left their minds.

When the hour was over, Ervin came in with some help from some of the ladies in the Clerk's office and cleared away the remnants of the meal and left. Steven called the Jury back together, after the time to wash up and tend to personal hygiene was done.

"Ladies and Gentlemen, let's get back to work; any thoughts any would like to make that came to you during lunch?"

"Yeah," Fred Warner said, "I am also troubled a little bit that those gloves of George Drucker's that supposedly wiped away Mr. Bryant's fingerprints, didn't show up until after the Prosecution expert got caught by the Defense lawyer. Drucker never mentioned them before, as I recall."

"Not completely true folks," Roger Farrens, the druggist from Madison said, "Don't you remember that when he testified about when he came into the whiskey still it was cold. He was talking about the gun rack where he hung up his coat and he made almost an offhand comment, as I remember it, something about "coat and glove weather. I didn't connect it at the time, but he did mention gloves before any of this other stuff came up," he added.

"That's right," Steven said, "I had forgotten that Roger, it was consistent."

"And another thing," Fred Smith said, "Remember that he said, and speaking of confessing, that he asked Drucker who else but him would have the brass ones to do it; and pardon my French ladies, but you all know what part of the male anatomy he was talking about."

"Wait a minute Fred," we can't use that statement as evidence, remember Judge Parker sustained the objection of Mr. Martin and instructed us to disregard that comment. They took a break and we never heard anything further about that," Steven Mathewson said, applying his careful analytical brain and good memory to the problem, always trying to be fair.

Right, strike it right out, and we're supposed to forget about it, Fred thought. He wasn't the only one thinking of that comment that had been indelibly burned into their brains, so to speak.

The comments, questions, and arguments went on for the remainder of the afternoon. Those in favor of a guilty verdict early in the day had remained as convinced as ever. The undecided, except for Fred Warner, pretty much had come over to the guilty side at least as far as their leaning was concerned.

Elizabeth Hardy, who had voted not guilty that morning, was wavering though she had not spoken of her change of heart to anyone. Elizabeth was a strong believer in family loyalty, and she had sensed that in Ellie Bryant. It was hard for Elizabeth to imagine that Ellie's testimony could be questioned that Earl had truly acted surprised when she first told him about the dead man. That was a powerful reason in her mind to hang on to the idea of a reasonable doubt, for she admitted to herself that the rest of the evidence Sure made it look like that he did it with a clear purpose.

Victor was rock steady against conviction because he just didn't like the idea of a government doing anything to a person, and even though he admitted to himself that Bryant had probably killed the Federal Agent, he was one of those jurors who would have to be leaned on to vote yes and that time had not yet come.

Fred Warner had to pray and reflect before he could make a decision, and Steven figured that now was the time to recess for the day. He sent a message to Ervin Floyd that the Jury needed a break for the night and after consultation with the Judge, they were brought back into court and instructed once again not to discuss the case with anyone being released for the night to home or hotel as applicable. The deliberations had been fair and work was getting done. The magic process of the American jury system of justice, for right or for wrong was working as it was supposed to work.

71. Is it a winner?

The newsroom at the Recorder was full of reporters and staff people talking about the trial. The sudden turn of events with the Defendant's surprise testimony in the last day of trial had made the national wire services and drawn the tremendous interest of the national press. Not many major papers had reporters on the scene, after all Tallahassee was too far away from Washington, D.C. and New York for that, but these major news organizations had a way of tapping local press representatives in the northern part of the state.

Tony, as the lead writer for the Recorder on this story, was getting bylines across the country, either directly or indirectly through the Associated Press News Service that all major papers relied upon for stories. Many newsmen thought this case may very well make a national reputation for the local boy made good for his stellar news writing on this story. His involvement in the flood incident, as it related to the trial, didn't hurt to spice up the story and attract even more than normal interest. Tony tried his best to keep his ego under control, but this turn of events presented that as a terrific challenge. "Thanks," "You're too kind", and the usual platitudes that fend off the affection, much of which in his case was genuine, didn't work so well in the news fraternity.

In this environment of the outside press, the words were more cutting with jealousies expressed without reservation. These guys really thought they were the only ones who had the perspective to see the actual truth about a story so that the reader could understand it and each one sincerely believed no one but them could really write adequately to paint with word pictures the landscape news events made across the societal canvas. So when one of their own was in the limelight, there was only grudging respect as a tolerance to another professional. The use of words can be a powerful elixir to the writer, which he is so fond of once created, that while music tastes may vary from one consumer to the other, the news writer thinks he alone will make the top of the popular charts. For the life of him, he can't understand why any sane person would see it differently.

Tony broke away from the pack of hangers on in the newsroom hoping some of the magic would rub off on them for future stories. He made his way to his news desk to compose another by-line for tomorrow's edition and possibly national circulation.

Those who have achieved fame seldom see the principle at work that permeates the entire American competitive environment, that once you achieve one level of accomplishment, the benefit is multiplied geometrically. Once in, you are in it big time at the next cycle. However it works, Tony had a deadline to meet for tomorrow's edition. His usual practice was to get away from the hubbub of collegial repartee and think for a time about the news event before trying to write his copy. For Tony, writing was easy once you figured out what you were trying to say. That was the hard part.

He had an emotional attachment to the story because his good friend, Aaron Martin, looked like he might be losing his big case, because his client was foolish enough to disobey conventional wisdom and testify in his own defense, even against his attorney's advice. He was also involved in the story by his terrible experience in the Lake Talquin flood episode with Johnny Caldwell, friend of the Defendant. He had actually met some of the participants in the story.

Unfortunately for Aaron's client, the people he had met in the flood disaster, they had firsthand knowledge of some of the events related to the crime, but had disappeared from the scene, if not the earth, ever since. He thought that strange and longed to be able to find Hub Douglass, Nooby Oakley, Israel Manley, and Hoover Spencer to see if they possibly had anything to say about the murder weapon, the checking for missing bullets or the conversations that went on between Earl Bryant and George Drucker.

Tony, at the time he had met these men, had no idea what the issues would be in the trial and did not ask the right question to get to the bottom of this mystery. He had been kicking himself about that ever since. Somehow, he sensed that Earl Bryant may be innocent of the crime but he had to agree with his colleagues in the press that it looked like he was going to be convicted, whether innocent or not.

Even if an occasional guilty party goes free, the prospect that an innocent man is convicted, much less put to death, is so abhorrent to the average American that the procedural rules that are enforced and called technicalities are carefully if not liberally construed by the average jury in favor of findings of innocence.

As he thought about the case, the genesis of a story for tomorrow's edition slowly came to him. He decided to take a bold approach and claim that Bryant was innocent. The copy he dropped off in Dick Powers' copy slot that went to press that night, read as follows:

THE INNOCENT DO NOT ALWAYS GO FREE
By Tony Callaway, *Recorder* Reporter
Throw caution to the winds, take the easy road, follow the general

sentiment and convict the man, guilty or not. The trial of Earl Bryant in the United States District Court is winding down with an apparent conviction for the notorious Moonshiner for premeditated murder about to happen. Contrary to all expectations, and probably the advice of counsel, Earl Bryant took the witness stand today and testified in his own defense. Unfortunately, the end result of his providing a likely motive for the crime that would not have been available without it will probably bring a guilty verdict and possibly the hangman's noose for a man this reporter believes is actually innocent of the charge of murder. It may very well all be in the hands of Judge Benjamin T. Parker, Jr., as to whether the rope will stretch. Your *Recorder* Reporter actually had the privilege to interview some of the witnesses to the aftermath of the crime, although the issues had not been framed sufficiently for your reporter to ferret out the truth of the relationship between George Drucker, the witness, and Earl Bryant, the accused. Those witnesses are now gone with the wind and Bryant had been left with the Hobson's choice to testify and deny the crime he did not commit, or not testify and leave the witness Drucker standing alone on the table of truth. If any reader knows the whereabouts of any of the potential witnesses, please bring forth the information and give freedom a chance to vindicate him. Earl Bryant may have had every reason to kill the Federal Agent, Frank Stiller, but the largely circumstantial evidence presented, should not justify his conviction in this case. Earl Bryant may be guilty of making illegal whiskey or making unwise choices of when to speak or forever hold his peace, but in this writer's opinion, the evidence presented at trial does not justify conviction. Witnesses, please come forward so that Lady Justice who is blind to race, color or choice of occupation may be truly served in this case.

Tony was satisfied with his work that night and thought that he had made a strike out in favor of freedom, truth, and the American way. His heart was sick about what he feared would actually happen tomorrow.

72. The second day

The entire group made it to the jury deliberation room on time the next morning; eager to start what they all felt was the end of deliberations and the doorway to go home. A genial greeting all around met each member or groups of members as they came in, helped themselves to morning coffee and donuts faithfully provided by the representatives of the Judge.

Steven Mathewson called the group to order, as it were, so that deliberations could begin once again.

"I think we made significant strides yesterday folks but our work is not done until we have a consensus over this verdict, which I don't see just yet," Steven said, getting the ball rolling for day two of deliberations.

"Why don't we take another vote?" Eldon Williams said, having announced for a guilty verdict at the opening and believed, as many did privately, that they were close to reaching it.

"Yeah, I'm for that too," Howard Gray said, eager as ever to get this business over with.

"I'm not so Sure we're ready for that people, let's not force anyone to take a firm and fast position until all the views are expressed," Steven persuaded.

"Yeah, I'm as ready as the next guy to get this thing over with but Doc has a point," Roger Farrens, the Madison druggist agreed.

"I'd like to hear from some of those who think Mr. Bryant is innocent, your reasons for it, that kind of thing, or at least those who are genuinely in doubt," Fred Warner said. Fred had spent a restless evening after having driven his Truck back to Quincy for the night, not being from far enough away to merit hotel accommodations. He was troubled with sending any human being to the gallows and had prayed long into the evening seeking guidance in accordance with his good faith. The only answers he had thought he heard from his prayers were that he should listen carefully to the others before deciding to send this man to the gallows.

Victor Katansky, the Russian immigrant, had said nothing through the proceedings, but he had voted with the not guilty contingent on the first round and had heard nothing from the others to change his mind. He was so adamant that anything a government did was wrong, based on his painful experiences in Communist Russia before he escaped to the west. He felt like he just needed to oppose this one, even though even he had to admit that the government of the United States was totally different from the one at home. Irrational or not, he was sticking with his opposition for now and was saying nothing.

"How about it then, some of you undecided jurors, care to express your concerns or reasons why you think we should not vote out a guilty verdict?" Erick said, hoping to bypass the demand for a vote and engage some of those concerned about the evidence to speak their minds.

"What bothered me before and kept me in doubt was the timing of the whole thing. How did Earl Bryant know his old enemy would be there that morning in a way to set up out there in the woods and wait to shoot him? Then within minutes of the shot, he turns up acting Surprised," Frances Drake said.

"Well, which way are you now leaning Frances?" Orien Preston asked, having kept up with the leanings as expressed during deliberations. He had Frances Drake down as undecided, then nodding agreement for guilt on the argument from the hard evidence and now sounding ambiguous as all get out. He wasn't Sure where to put her now.

"I just don't know, is what I'm saying, and it's not strong enough to convict yet to my way of thinking. Take the wife's testimony, she sounded very believable to me and I place great weight on loyalty," Frances said.

"Remember, though," Arch Kline said, "Loyalty cuts two ways and she could be lying about that Surprise business just to protect her old man."

"I can't believe she would get up on that stand and tell a big lie. Family trust is important to me," Elizabeth Hardy said, speaking out for the very first time.

"You don't get the point Elizabeth, the man's life; her man's life is on the line. She'd say anything to get him off," Howard Gray, argued.

"Show me any inconsistency in her testimony, any hint that she wasn't telling the truth and I will re-consider," Elizabeth said looking confidently around the room and convinced no one could do that.

"Interesting challenge," Roger Farrens said and stopped for a minute or two thinking back on her testimony at the end of the trial. Then he did a double take and said, "Wait a minute, I think you are on to something with that question Elizabeth, consider this," Roger Farrens said.

"Remember when she testified, she said her husband had washed up even though breakfast wasn't ready yet because he always washed up in case something was on his hands. The government lawyer than asked her if she meant he had been shooting at something, trying to trap her, I think. And she said something about he hadn't shot the gun because it didn't smell that time and it always did when he shot it and brought it home. She didn't have to say that to answer his question unless his point was bothering her somewhat or she was covering up, which is what I suspect." Roger continued, "What I mean is that part was strange, because if the only gun we've seen in this case was the one that shot Frank Stiller and Bryant brought it home, after he had been down at the still where Drucker identified it as having one shell missing from the spring clip. It had to have been smelling to her sensitive nose just a little while later, if she could always tell about such things as she claimed. And another point, why did she bring up that hand washing thing too. Nobody had asked her about that. I think it was one of those slips that fellow Freud over in Europe keeps writing about," Roger said.

"Fred who?" Fred Smith the oyster shucker chimed in, having not a clue who the noted German psychiatrist was.

"Sigmund Freud, not Fred anybody. He is a famous psychiatrist from Europe who has a theory that what's true in your life has a way of slipping out even when you're trying to hide it or cover it up. Like Ellie Bryant was doing with that gun smell story. It just didn't wash folks and there's your inconsistency," Roger said emphatically"

"You mean, if she was covering up for him with that story that he acted surprised when she told him there was a dead man on their front steps, when he wasn't surprised at all because he knew it already and she knew it too, she might accidentally let it slip out some other way?" Elizabeth Hardy said, beginning to question for the first time the veracity of Ellie Bryant.

If she couldn't trust Ellie Bryant to believe the part about the smelling gun or more accurately the absence of smell when they all knew pretty much for certain that the old rifle had just been fired, then she couldn't accept the other more important part that he wasn't Surprised at all. She was fast becoming a convert to those who saw that the evidence actually introduced at trial pretty much conclusively pointed toward a guilty verdict.

What the decision was coming down to was whether this notorious whiskey still operator and his loyal wife could get up in this court and convince these twelve jurors that just by their saying so, the cumulative effect of the gun, the opportunity, the dead man, the motive of revenge, the fingerprints and the matching bullet and barrel should be disregarded.

Like it or not in some parts of the room, a consensus was emerging even if it had taken all day. No one had noticed or bothered to explain how Earl had known Frank Stiller and young Elliot Browning were headed to his house that fateful morning in order to have time to plan such a shooting, get into position, make the killing shot and get away. It seems no one had pointed that significant fact out to them.

In the end, the Jury only had what it had heard and seen and no one could blame them for reaching the decision they were about to make. Steven Mathewson saw his moment had arrived and decided to put the matter to a one at a time vote.

"Ladies and Gentlemen, I think we are at the place where everyone of you must commit to a decision. We've discussed the evidence and arguments fairly. If there is no objection I will go around the room and each person will say how they vote and why if you care to," Erick said, and seeing no objections he began by pointing to Fred Warner.

"It was a hard decision for me folks but after thinking it over and praying about it, I have to vote that he did it, guilty!" Fred said.

Elizabeth Hardy expressed her agreement after she had gotten over the hurdle of Ellie Bryant's loyalty to her husband, and the apparent inconsistency in her testimony was enough for her. "Guilty," Elizabeth said without further elaboration.

"I am unchanged and vote guilty," Howard Gray said.

"Me too," Eldon Williams said.

"I think I already gave my reasons, but I vote guilty too," Roger Farrens said.

Victor Katansky remained sullen and silent. "I'll go along with the others, guilty," Frances Drake said.

Elliot Barnes and Fred Smith said, "guilty" almost together as the momentum accelerated toward what had probably been the inevitable result when Earl Bryant took the witness stand and admitted that he had a darn good reason to shoot his old nemesis and gain revenge from the 1913 killing of his father.

Orien Preston who had been furiously taking notes, looked up from his unofficial scribing, looked each member of the Jury in the eyes one at a time and calmly said in his best most gentle librarian's tone,

"I'm voting guilty and by my counting all have done so except you Mr. Foreman and Mr. Katansky, who have not expressed any opinions or arguments of any kind so far in these proceedings."

"That is true, Orien, and thank you for tabulating everyone's reactions. You have provided a valuable service here indeed. I have thought this over carefully, the tangible evidence of the fingerprints, the gun that the forensics expert unquestionably matched with the fatal bullet, the denials of Mr. Bryant and the somewhat questionable alibi of sorts by Mrs. Bryant. The one persuasive thing to me was the motive for the shooting. I am puzzled somewhat why Mr. Bryant ever testified. We would never have heard about that motive if he hadn't and for me that would have left a reasonable doubt. But I can't get around that most pressing motive to kill. He had opportunity and the tangible evidence pretty much wraps it up for me. I vote guilty," Steven Mathewson, PhD said.

"Well now, that leaves only one, Katansky, the silent one," Erick said beginning to bring the subtle pressure on the one hold out to make a decision. If he was a true hold out and was going to dig in his heels even to hang the jury as the lawyers called it, that was one thing but if he just could not make up his mind that was something else. The pressure really started to build now that Victor was the only one who would not commit except to say not guilty on that very first vote.

"Come on, Victor, let's get this over with," Howard Gray said rather forcefully as in his mind he could already imagine himself tomorrow on Lake Jackson in his fishing boat waiting for a big one to strike.

"Yeah, Victor, this has gone on long enough. If you have a reason say so but if you're just being stubborn then I've had damn about enough of that!" Fred Smith said as if he were talking his oyster pile mates into quitting early for the week so they could go hunting or go to the beach for a long weekend.

Victor sat silent. One by one the others joined in until the pressure on the Russian was unbearable.

Where these commissars get their impertinence? They never see injustice like I have or they have another think comik' someday. But what this whiskey man is to me to take such abuse, he thought.

"All right then! If you want to send innocent man to gallows in this country, then do it! Victor Katansky will not stand in way. That fool tell his story and sink with it, so it seem! Guilty, me vote too!"

"Then it's unanimous at last, are we all agreed? Any objections, or I will send word to the Judge," Steve announced and seeing or hearing none, went to the door, rapped his knuckles against it to rouse Ervin Floyd from his early nap in the station chair outside in the hall, and the trial of Earl Bryant for murder was all over but the announcing.

The final chapter was going to be written in the mind and heart of the Honorable Benjamin T. Parker, Jr., where he must decide whether this case merited the death penalty or something less. At that time, in Federal Jurisprudence, it was totally up to him to impose sentence. And impose it he would once he decided just what that sentence was going to be. The reading of the verdict would come tomorrow and the lives of many would be affected by the outcome; not just that of the Defendant Earl Bryant.

73. News

The decision the Bryant Jury had reached had indeed taken most of the second day. Judge Parker, when he was interrupted by Ervin Floyd with the message of a decision, looked at his wall clock and decided it was too late in the day to summons the lawyers for the reading of the verdict. The press would want to be there to get the full flavor of the dramatic moment but Judge Parker didn't care about their convenience that much and would let the press fend for itself.

"Ervin, get on the phone to Martin and Gilchrist, or their offices at least, and let them know our Jury has reached a verdict. I expect them to be in my Court tomorrow morning at 9:30 a.m. for the reading of the verdict. You know the rest to do, with notice out to the jail for the prisoner to be delivered here in time as usual."

"Yes, Sir," Ervin said, and turned to leave the Judge's Chambers and spread the word as directed and to others he thought would love to get a heads up and a favorable seat by an early arrival time.

Tony was finishing up his story on the trial for tomorrow's edition when the phone rang. He stopped his typing momentarily and picked up the phone, continuing to re-read his copy, checking for content and errors and answered, "Hello, Callaway here" he said impatiently.

It was his contact Ervin from the Court who said, "Tony, Ervin, can't talk long, but we have a verdict. Judge will read it tomorrow morning at 9:30 a.m., I'm on my way to call the lawyers, thought you would want to know, bye," Ervin said in a hurry and hung up the phone without time for a response expected or given, as good friends will often do. It was enough for Tony and the story he had been writing now needed major revisions. This was the premiere news event for tomorrow's edition and by the time it hit the streets and newsstands no one would ever figure out that he had a heads up from what had to have been an inside source. He was too good of a news reporter to compromise a source like the Judge's Bailiff, but this was a risk worth taking. He held the phone to his ear for a few seconds longer as if assimilating the full impact of what he had just heard, then hung it up and returned to his typewriter.

He ripped out the draft that was practically finished and threw it into the wastebasket. He leaned back in his chair, propping himself at a precarious angle where he did his best thinking, and summoning all his memories of the events leading up to and during the trial, dove into the recesses of his mind where the amazing sea of creativity floats words across the Surface like lily pads waiting for just the right geometric pattern to be formed by the prevailing winds. Then in an amazing burst of energy, by a process that no scientist will ever discover or metaphysicians ever understand, the story came together in his mind just as clearly and definitely as if the "Master Writer in the Sky" had stroked the keys of a celestial keyboard and typed it out for him to see and transcribe.

Like all good writers, once they know what they wanted to say, usually as this time by inspiration, the composition and execution came easy.

Tony loaded a fresh sheet of paper in the old Royal upright and the story for tomorrow began to show itself across the page, as the keys imprinted the magic words on paper across the platen. Not Pulitzer caliber maybe, but he was satisfied for this evening.

Anna Devlin took Ervin's call and quickly passed the word to Aaron back in his office. He called his Dad over at the Legislature and the men agreed to meet for dinner and speculate together about the probable result. Every lawyer sweating out a jury verdict is tempted to speculate on the length of time the Jury took as influenced by the reactions he thought he saw on their faces and by body language during the trial to make a reliable prediction. It is rarely accurate but they do it anyway. Aaron planned to call Ellie so the family could be there for support, and stop by the jail one more time before bedtime for a visit to prepare his client for the worst eventuality.

Houston Gilchrist was handed a note as he was watching a line up through a one-way mirror at the jail. He quietly unfolded it, read the simple words "We have a verdict 9:30 a.m. tomorrow sharp," crumpled it up and mentioned to Erick Driskoll to finish up here. He then left the viewing room. Even experienced prosecutors like Houston could not avoid the temptation to return to his office and speculate over the likely result.

Like all rumors, especially when true, it takes little time for them to spread. A call to the jail, the word about the courthouse carelessly dropped, contacts with staff in attorneys' offices; or a change in the excitement level in a news room even though not mentioned to anyone intentionally, sets in motion a network of dissemination of news worthy events that is magical to behold.

By dinner time in Tallahassee tonight, the whole world, or at least those that mattered or cared, seemed to know that the Bryant murder case verdict was about to be announced tomorrow morning in Court. Family and friends, those who enjoyed these things simply for the excitement, the very few given to schaden freude about town or simply the curious, would be attracted to the courthouse tomorrow like bees to their honeycombs.

Anyone who thought he would show up early to get a good seat had better get up with the birds or be prepared to wait in line. It would be first come first seated and no favoritism would be granted or tolerated. It was truly a newsworthy day coming tomorrow in Judge Parker's Court.

74. The verdict

Aaron called Ellie in Bainbridge before heading over to the jail to be with Earl one more time before the verdict was read. She agreed that the family would be in Court tomorrow morning to give Earl all the support possible from those who loved him.

As Aaron waited in the visiting room, he thought back on his representation of Earl Bryant in the case. The Magistrate's hearing and his loss of the argument for bail, his agonizing hours of interviewing Earl and Ellie to pull out facts they might have known but were unable to recall, Johnny Caldwell and the reports of John Travis of the missing Negro witnesses that might have made such a difference, all ran together in a mesmerizing memory of melodrama.

The fateful decision to put Earl on the stand after learning the sad truth about the 1913 revenge killing that never happened, but had the effect of making the Defendant look like he damn well pulled it off this time, reverberated in his mind and memory with a pathos that was unbearable to one accustomed to victory in court.

In his thinking it through the conclusion was inevitable. He had lost this one and no amount of speculating about two days of deliberation or occasional winks and nods from some of the jurors during the trial would soften the inevitable blow. He felt that he had lost his case and now he had to prepare his client for the blow that was about to land tomorrow morning.

Earl was led into the visiting room by his jailer, leaving him released from his restraints and allowed to take his seat across the little table from Aaron. The jailer left.

"Well Earl, the Jury has reached a verdict and tomorrow morning you will hear it. Are you ready for this Earl?"

"Yes, Sir, I'm ready for whatever it turns out to be," Earl said.

"You realize, don't you, Earl that you may be convicted of the charges?" Aaron said, looking into the heart of the man by reading his eyes to see what he really felt. What he thought he saw was one brave and courageous client ready to face whatever the verdict might bring.

Earl hung his head ever so slightly as if he was finally speaking out the despair he undoubtedly was feeling and said, "How do I do that, face it I mean, they could kill me, right?" Earl asked, finally transparent.

"I have to believe Judge Parker is a fair man. I knew his father well as a boy growing up and him somewhat, but he will do his duty. The law says that a life for a life is within his discretion. A good federal man, in the world's eyes at least, was shot down in innocence. There has to be a balance, a payback in some cosmic sense to make justice mean anything Earl," Aaron continued, "But don't give up Earl, because we will appeal this verdict; and I will not rest as long as there is a narrow chance to find those damn missing witnesses. I get the feeling that there is some undiscovered truth about that meeting you had with George Drucker that morning. If we find that new evidence, we'll open this thing wide open again and get to the truth, so help me God!" Aaron said, with all the conviction he could muster. He meant it too.

"I was so wrong to listen to that feller but he seemed so real, I couldn't believe he would lie to me when he said I had to tell my side of this," Earl said enigmatically.

"What feller… sa…id what and wh….en?" Aaron sputtered.

"It weren't nothin', Mr. Martin, only some apparition I kept having in this here jail, in court and, hell he was everywhere, it seemed," Earl said, with his explanation making no sense to Aaron whatever.

"You better calm down, or I better calm down and have you explain that in plain English Earl. What in the hell are you talking about?" Aaron heatedly said.

"I called him my Uncle Clarence. He, or it, were a ghost, like a visitation; but more than that, the damn thing was real as it could be, but unreal all at the same time. I mean, his flesh, if that were what it was, was as real as yourn or mine but the trouble was, no body but me could see him or hear him," Earl explained.

"Where?" Aaron asked.

"Right here, in this here jail house, or my cell anyway but not even old Jack could see or hear the damn thing, but I Sure could. He spoke plain as day to me, here, in court and in the Sheriff's car even, over and over again, that I had to tell it, my side of things, I mean."

"Are you telling me, Earl Bryant that you took the words of a damn ghost, apparition, vision or hallucination which is more likely, over the advice of your lawyer who even threatened to quit over it. Then you stubbornly testified and got yourself convicted or are about to be anyway?" Aaron threw back his arms in a "I can't believe this" sort of gesture; and all the angst, disappointment and the burden of guilt he had been feeling was somehow lifted or made more bearable.

If it had not been so serious, with such potentially deadly conse-quences, he would have found it hilariously funny. His client listened to a ghost or some other imaginary thing and takes the stand against my best legal advice and gets convicted? That took the cake as far as Aaron was concerned. In a way, the load of guilt was taken off his shoulders freeing him to fight for his client's life without reservation or respite, unclouded by the limitations of his own failing that might have muddied the water in the process.

"LoOkay, Earl, that was a damn fool thing to do but it's done. Unfortunately that is not a legal error. It is close to insanity, but Mr. McNaughton's defense won't help us now. I never have heard of a plea of insanity asserted after a trial is practically over. We will do the best we can on the appeal and work like hell for finding new evidence before they can hang you, if that is what the verdict is, OK? What I want to know is, will you stand up there tomorrow on your hind legs and take whatever comes like the man you truly are and not let that prosecutor see you cave in on me, OK?"

"No, Sir, I ain't giving in to no silly cave-in as you say, I'll look that Jury in the eyes and that Judge, too, and take it like a man, you'll see Mr. Martin. And I want you to know that this was entirely my fault and none of yours. I want to thank you, Mr. Martin. You did the best that could a been done, excepting for my stupidity and stubbornness. I don't hold no blame on you for that, you hear?" Earl said; and then did a totally unexpected thing for a rough and tumble back country man, reaching out and hugged his lawyer in a veritable bear hug, like none Aaron had ever experienced.

After the initial shock, Aaron responded with a hug of his own, becoming two new friends for life, however short that might turn out to be. They had developed an instant personal bond with each other in that moment. They parted, looking each other in the eye and said nothing further, for it had all been said for this night. Tomorrow, for whatever desperate events were to unfold, was to be another day.

75. Here it is

The sun came up on schedule that morning and cast its early shadows across the lawn of the Federal Courthouse building, sitting a block off Monroe Street on East Park Avenue. It was still in the middle of winter and the Mocking Birds had not started their sweet song of spring just yet. The grass, on the limited lawn around the old building, was its normal brown color ever since the first killing frost back in November last year. Not long after the birds would have begun their serenade to another fine spring day that morning, the crowds no one in particular had summoned, but the word had gotten out regardless; made their way in an eager rush for available seats to hear the announcement that would control the fate of Earl Bryant on trial for the murder of Frank Stiller.

The armed guards assigned by "The Great One" at the direction of Judge Ben stood by to maintain order and to settle any claims for preference in this rush to the gold in the form of choice seats in the heavy pew-like bench seats in the courtroom.

The first one to arrive was Tony Callaway who was taking no chances after the tip he had received from his old buddy Ervin Floyd, and his good common sense that told him that if he didn't get up at the crack of dawn, he would probably not get a seat. He wanted to be able to see the faces of the Defense Team, the Jury and the Judge. To do that would take some creative selecting of his seat, considering how many folks would be there that morning clamoring for a seat of any kind that would take some quick thinking and deft maneuvering.

Since Tony was a bachelor, he could get out as early as he pleased without ruffling the home front feathers. There were none to ruffle. Tony figured he could sit behind the table of Houston Gilchrist, back a couple of rows, so as not to make it look like he was favoring that side of the dispute, see the faces of Earl and Aaron, Judge Parker and every one of the twelve jurors. He would explain that to Aaron after the trial, and of course he would understand, if Aaron didn't figure it out first on his own. He had made his way through the US Marshall's check points; and took his seat as he had planned, just ahead of the courtroom being deluged with spectators and other interested parties seeking their own special points of advantage.

The competitive nature of the press corps was no exception. Tony recognized the guy from the Associated Press news service in town on this special assignment. The wire reports would be incorporated in part in news stories in print all across America, as well as men from newspapers across the Southern US, and especially Florida.

The likely conviction of probably the last moonshiner before Prohibition was over in a famous murder case. This was big news on this fair day and the brotherhood of the press were convened for the performance with pen in hand and coins in copious quantities at the ready for the available pay phones to spill the news across America.

The last of the spectators in Judge Parker's Court took the remaining

seats in a catch as catch can manner, and the place was filled up in
no time. Johnny Caldwell, that faithful stalwart from friendship and
home, took his place as close as possible to be close to Earl on that side
of the courtroom, but rather far back as a late arriver.

Aaron arrived soon after with Ellie Bryant, Emily and Dr. Hugh in
tow, to take his seat at the Defense Counsel's table and pointed out for
them to take the reserved seats for the immediate family right behind
him. Noticing Johnny in the courtroom further back, he signaled him
to come forward and had the people in the reserved row make room
for the Defendant's close friend.

Expecting the worst as he was, Aaron especially wanted supporters
of his client to be within reach when the moment arrived, as Earl would
naturally be devastated. The deputies had not brought the Defendant
into the courtroom yet, but they had to be only moments away because
Judge Parker was about to make his entrance as indicated by the restless
movement of the court personnel; and nothing was going to happen
in the Court without the presence of the Defendant. This is one time
when the Defendant could not be late, because things could not start
without him.

The room was warm that morning from the old reliable boiler in
the basement; and even if it had not been up to snuff, this unusual
crowd would have heated the place up anyway just by their cumulative
body heat. It was a somber mood the crowd was in, undergirded by a
vein of excitement that ran through the place because of the expected
verdict. The chatter among the spectators was about nothing else as
they speculated on the outcome and commented to each other their
opinions on the upcoming verdict. If you could have taken one of those
polls that politicians would in the future be fond of taking, the pulse
of the place would have predicted a guilty verdict.

Houston Gilchrist and his sidekick, Erick Driskoll, calmly sat side by side chatting softly as they, too, nervously but confidently expected a favorable verdict for the prosecution. The room grew silent as the side door to the cavernous courtroom opened slowly and Earl Bryant, prisoner and Defendant on trial for his life, was led hobbled and cuffed into the courtroom and over to his counsel's table where the deputies in charge of the transport freed his constraints, allowing him to take his seat next to his lawyer. They left the courtroom immediately.

Justice is depicted in the traditional symbol of that statue of a lady holding scales that balance truth and falsity, freedom and punishment, with a blindfold across her eyes to symbolize that who you are means nothing; and that the law, which is based on the morals handed down by God, means everything. In the traditional depiction of the lady, the scales are evenly balanced to be tipped either direction based on the quality and weight of the evidence leading to a just result. However, in a criminal trial, because freedom which to Americans is so precious, the scales must be tipped to a greater degree than a slightly greater than even balance, before punishment can be meted out under the standard of proof of beyond and to the exclusion of a reasonable doubt.

But since every metaphor eventually breaks down if you stretch it too far, the balanced scales will have to do nicely for image purposes. Unlike some trials in the criminal courts, where the sides are uneven due to the weight and public purse of the government in its role as protector of the people, the poor Defendant often was not represented by counsel or is poorly represented to great disadvantage. There would come a day in America when every person accused of a crime that would take away his liberty would be given a lawyer capable of defending him in court but this was not that day.

This case was an exception to normal, because Earl could afford to have the best lawyer in the District and he had chosen the Martin firm, which had ably defended him. But if the outcome came as the public and the lawyers in the trial expected, the result was about the same. The trial had been conducted fairly by Judge Parker and the outcome was where it belonged in the American system of justice, in the hands of twelve citizens, sometimes the peers of the Defendant.

That is only an ideal and in this case, Earl saw few of his peers on this panel, due to the strange nature of his lifestyle back home in Liberty County. Actually there were a farmer, tradesman, educators, sales clerks, day laborers and the like in the Jury. None just like Earl for sure but common folks nonetheless.

The tension in the room was building almost to the breaking point and with an impeccable sense of timing, the doors to Judge Parker's Chambers opened, and he strode into his courtroom to the cry of "All Rise" by the Deputy Clerk on duty today. There had been a drawing of straws that morning to see who would get this duty and Frank Hopkins, thereafter called "Lucky Hopkins" by the staff, had drawn the shortest straw.

"Good morning Ladies and Gentlemen, please be seated, counsel are we ready?" Judge Parker said, acknowledging their agreement, and turning to his Bailiff, Ervin Floyd and said, "Ervin, bring in the Jury." The twelve filed into their seats and took them. Any critical observer to this scene, while watching the faces of the twelve as they came in and took their seats, would have noticed a variety of expressions.

Some like Howard Gray, Eldon Williams, Archibald Kline and Fred Smith looked eager for the process to end. Others of the more serious and reflective members like Roger Farrens, Orien Preston and Steven Mathewson seemed absorbed with the seriousness of the charge and the terrible burden they felt for having made a decision that could take another human being's life.

Elliot Barnes, even though a young man, showed a resignation that had settled on him once he had, made his decision based solely on the evidence. Elizabeth Hardy sat soberly with a sad expression that none could miss. Frances Drake showed nothing. Fred Warner kept his eyes closed, which some observers later thought an indication that he was asleep. Actually he was quietly praying that the decision he had reached was the one God wanted to be the outcome in this trial.

Finally on the back row furthest away from Judge Parker, Victor Katansky sat hunched over in the appearance of one grimly committed to the decision, but very doubtful that the right thing had been done. Houston Gilchrist later told Erick Driskoll that he thought the Jury would be split eleven to one based on the stubborn mien that Victor Katansky demonstrated. Of course, he was wrong as lawyers often are in such things.

"Dr. Mathewson, I believe you are the elected foreman of this Jury, has the Jury reached a verdict?" Judge Parker asked resolutely, almost rhetorically since he knew very well they had.

"We have your honor," Steven Mathewson said soberly, almost with pathos in his tone.

"Please hand the verdict to the Clerk, Sir" the Judge said, and Erik handed the form of the jury verdict he had filled out back in the jury room over to Frank Hopkins who handed it up to Judge Parker on the bench. Judge Parker gravely unfolded the form, read it silently and handed it back to Frank.

"Will the Defendant please rise? The Clerk will read the verdict," Judge Parker solemnly intoned. Aaron and Earl stood on their feet and faced the Judge's bench. Frank Hopkins looked at the written jury verdict form, cleared his throat and read,

"We the Jury find the Defendant, Earl Bryant, guilty of the charge of murder in the first degree," and sat down. The sound of the reading of the verdict struck Earl like a hammer, even though he fully expected it, and he sagged ever so slightly back on his heels before recovering, without showing any expression on his face. In the professional manner of losing attorneys everywhere, Aaron similarly showed no visible effects of the result, immediately running through his mind the legal steps available to him.

However, inside of Earl Bryant where his will, determination and emotions dwelled, it was a different matter. He had been aware from the beginning that there was a substantial risk he would be at this very spot. Although deep down inside of him, since he knew he was innocent of everything except glad that the shooting had occurred, he had somehow felt that things would work out right. He was aware of the power that the judicial system had over him, but he was also aware of a higher power with more control than this Judge and Jury might even imagine.

That thought gave him some comfort, though at this point, not a lot. He had been convinced that when "Uncle Clarence" told him that if he told his side of the story, everything would work out. It seemed to him now that he had been deceived by that spirit. It was becoming clearer to him by the minute that it was a demon spirit out to sink rather than save him. *Looking back at it, that weren't no angel that were talking at me and I should a knowed it. The other kind is out there too and damned if I didn't forget that,* he thought.

The Judge was droning on about something as Earl later remembered it but he neither heard nor understood what was being said. What was being said was that the Honorable Benjamin T. Parker, Jr., was announcing a time and date when he would pronounce sentence in this case, for he had the awesome responsibility to decide whether a hanging would occur. He thanked and permanently excused the jurors from future service on this term of the Court and having pronounced the Court to be in recess, with the "all rise" announced as Judge Parker left the bench. The day's proceedings were over!

The courtroom cleared except for the family and few supporters of Earl Bryant who somberly gathered around him at Counsel's table, giving aid and comfort to their crest-fallen loved one, if that was at all possible.

Ellie's arms interlocked with her husband's and rocked gently with him exchanging their mutual grief, as if giving and receiving of the same emotion could somehow do the impossible and relieve the pain of it. It never quite works that way, but the effort is the thing that relieves and the hearts emptying their display of shared emotions somehow works through the moment that must be endured.

"It'll be all right Earl, just you wait and see" Ellie said through her tears, not believing a word of it.

"Thanky Girl, you know it ain't so, but you saying it helps anyways," Earl whispered back.

Emily clung to them both and her supportive husband, Dr. Hugh, stood by at a respectful distance, not being one to show an intimate touch where none was called for. He was committed to stand by his wife and if she would love and support this old sinner then he would keep his mouth shut and hold up the rest of the responsibility at home for right now. His patients at Riverside Hospital may have to wait a few days, for his primary duty was being with Emily Wilson wherever she wanted to be.

Johnny Caldwell, that remaining supporter of the now convicted Defendant, stood also a short distance away, just being there. His mouth was silent, but his mind was far from inactive. His old friend, Earl Bryant, convicted or not by this make shift jury as he saw it, was facing the ultimate penalty for something he believed he never did and that fact made him angry. *That damn Drucker, that lying bastard has gone and got Earl convicted and it ain't right. Them damn Negroes that seen it all, down at the Lagoon anyways, scattered to the four winds and left the man to*

take this.He gave them sorry bastards a job all them years and now look
at them, gone with no thank you, them low life cowards them are! Wait
till I get out of this here Court and get back home, I'll find them bastards,
shore as shootin, he thought, but not really convinced that he could ever
find the chaff that the very wind of fear had been driven hopelessly away.

Aaron told the little group that Judge Parker was a fair man and he
would weigh this matter carefully; and that even if the worst happened,
being careful not to actually use the words "hanging" for that would
be a cross too heavy for even love to bear at this moment, he would
appeal. Because Earl who had been denied bail would have to stay in
jail for now, there would be no more immediate serious consequence
to Earl than he had already faced and has become accustomed.

Not convincing anyone of anything, with grief having the run of the
moment, Aaron withdrew a short distance away to allow the last dregs
of that draught to be consumed with loved ones before the jail guards
standing by would come in and return Earl to his cell. In ten minutes
or so, the moment arrived for all of them saw that this clinging would
only prolong the suffering. Aaron therefore signaled to the jail men,
and they took him away. After final discussions about the sentencing
to come up in a month, every one left for home or other destinations.

76. Cellmates to the end

That late afternoon in the jail when Earl was returned, Jack was out
with his turn in the exercise yard, so he settled into the lonely place
with only his worst thoughts for company. Earl sat on the jail cot with
his elbows on his knees and head drooped in dejection. His life had
been a struggle from those childhood days until adulthood, when he
had followed in the footsteps of his old Daddy in the whiskey business.

The trials of desperately avoiding the law culminating in the horrible experience of witnessing the execution of his father; and the terrible choice he had to make between revenge and personal safety, had made an indelible mark on him. It had toughened him beyond imagining and the iron clad determination he had thrown into developing his empire had erased whatever soft edges there had once been, when this same young man that Ellie had fallen in love with so many years ago. And now he had thrown it all away in a sense by making some terrible choices. The hiring of the no good George Drucker was one, and the decision to listen to the advice of that ghost against the advice of everyone, including Old Jack here in the jail, was the other from which he could not forgive himself. Usually that resolve is expressed in terms of forever, but in his case, forever seemed only a few months away.

The worst thing was not that he would be hanged but that he would go to his grave knowing that he was innocent. The stories would be told for many years after he was dead and gone that old Earl Bryant got his revenge, but paid too heavy a price for it. In the middle of this thinking, which did not make its way into recognizable words even inside his head, but only pictures, like they say the animals get, and everybody calls it thinking, when suddenly his despair was interrupted by Jack's return from the exercise yard.

Word of the conviction had made its way to the jail by one of the returning guards; and like rumors and news spreads everywhere, it was all over the jail in no time so Jack was aware of it when he got back to his cell. He took one look at Earl seated all dejected on his cot and paused for a minute to decide just exactly what to say. *Well now, ain't this a sorry picture for you. All convicted and maybe facing the rope or at least the big house for life. My little trouble seems like nothing, a tear in this here jail compared to that. The man needs me, I'm figuring, but for exactly what, I ain't sure. Better say something anyhow, cain't ignore it,* he thought as he reached the end of his pause that demanded that he speak.

"I heard the news, Earl, it's all over this place, and I'm dreadful sorry for you. There ain't nothing I can do but say that," Jack said, as sincerely and sympathetically as he could make it.

"Thanky, Jack, you don't have to say nothin', it's all been said. The wife and daughter, my lawyer, they done their best to cheer me up, but it ain't workin', not yet anyways. That damn ghost thing I called my Uncle Clarence, he done me in, Jack. It weren't no Uncle Clarence or Uncle anything else, I think it were one of them demon things the old church people like to talk about. It shore weren't no angel from Heaven and that's certain," Earl said, by way of a confession, since he had argued with his new found friend on this very point the night before he had testified.

Even though he had been back to the jail since that fateful day, he had not discussed the spirit thing any more with Jack, and Jack, as friend, had not brought it up since the trial could have gone the other way and Earl might have been right. But now it was different.

"My advice Earl, is to let this thing play itself out. You got a lawyer and he'll fight for you. The Judge has to decide the punishment and it will be a heavy burden for even him, you wait and see. I ain't much of a praying man but that would seem to be worth trying about now," Jack said with a heartfelt conviction."

"Would you pray for me Jack, praying man or not, I ain't quite up to it yet?" Earl pleaded with his friend. Jack thought about it for only a few seconds and said,

"Well, I reckon we better kneel down right here by the cots," Jack said, as he took the position he had heard about people taking when they were serious about asking the Man Upstairs, as the country people called Him. Earl hastily joined him, being highly motivated for once in his long life. "Dear God," Jack began, "We beseech you Holy Father up there in Heaven, wherever that is, cause none of us knows, but no matter, reach out your powerful arm to this your servants, Jack Sanford and Earl Bryant, two genuine sinners in desperate need here in this man's jail house. My new friend Earl here has, as you know, been found guilty of a murder he claims he did not commit. I don't know whether he did or not, since I were not there at the time; but you were if the Saints of your Church has any grain of the gospel truth as they claim, we humbly repent of our misgivings and beg of Your Mighty Self to release the burden we bear at this time. If the man is innocent of these charges, then set him free somehow. We can't figure how you would do that about now, but that's what we mean when we say "God knows" about some desperate time or thing. Beyond that there is hardly anything we dare say about it. For this, we ask your pardon and for your help. This we ask in the name of Your Son, the Lord Jesus the Christ of Cavalry, Amen," Jack concluded and Earl joined him in an accompanying Amen. That was about all he could think of to say.

He then thanked his rising friend and they both returned to their cots for a night that just might resemble a restful sleep for once in a long while. To the extent that happened and the snores of the two men soon joined together in an inharmonious duet, that part of the prayer at least was answered.

77. A heavy burden

Judge Parker left his chambers that evening after the trial was concluded with verdict in hand. That ended things for the Jury, the spectators, the press, the lawyers for now and courtroom personnel. He left his office by a back door and got into his automobile for the short ride home. Marilyn would, as always, have dinner ready shortly after he arrived at home after work; and for this day, he was relieved to be away from his office with the ominous duty the Jury had just cast upon him.

He could not set the matter aside in his thoughts, not even for an evening, because a man's life was at stake. There had been so few prosecutions for first degree murder in his court, he could never get used to the idea. He turned his relatively new 1930 Studebaker Commander into the side driveway, parking it inside the garage, a separate outbuilding behind the old mansion.

He walked from the outbuilding into his back yard landscaped in a classic English Garden, by way of a meandering path into the back of the house. Marilyn was in the kitchen as always supervising the preparation of the evening meal, although the actual cooking and serving was done by their maid and housekeeper, Allie Johnson.

Marilyn saw him coming in from the garage and knew her man well enough to sense that he was especially burdened with something tonight. *It had to be the trial*, she thought.

She commented to Allie, who was practically a member of the family, that, "Something special is on his mind tonight!" Allie at first did a double take for it was not normal for her mistress to talk about intimate things between she and her husband which was the first thought that went through her young and romantically inclined mind, but as soon as she saw Mrs. Parker's face, she could see that she had misunderstood. It must be something of a more serious nature. Allie also looked at Judge Ben's face as he came into the kitchen and this confirmed it. There was indeed something on his mind and it wasn't directed toward later in the bedroom upstairs.

"Hello Honey, Allie," Judge Ben said and made his way through the kitchen and into the front of the house where he maintained a private study. As a Federal Judge, he did not need an office at home for he usually prided himself that he could leave all that at the courthouse; but he did have a study with many of his favorite books, an ornate leather covered desk and a black chair that when you sat in it, swallowed you up with its curved wing like headrest and soft leather cushion and arm rest. The desk was cleared of any papers and Allie kept the leather top oiled so that it shone when light would reflect on it. Ben sat in his chair with his long legs under the desk and leaned his elbows on the surface supporting his prominent jaw in a position of pure contemplation.

Thoughts of the trial and the awesome responsibility he had been handed by the Jury's verdict, occupied his every thought. *When that trial started, I really thought Aaron Martin would get him off. That warrant I signed back in December was at best an iffy proposition as to probable cause with that harebrained story by that Drucker fellow. Hell it wasn't much better at trial when that forensics expert for the government was embarrassed on cross about the missing prints. Then Houston resurrected his case with Drucker's sudden recall about the gloves. I bet that was a delicate operation to plant that idea in the witness's head without suborning perjury. No wonder it took him a couple of hours to ethically permit him to introduce it as evidence. He and that young Driskoll, wow! But even with that, they were going to lose it anyhow until Bryant testified. From Houston's perspective, that pulled victory from the jaws of defeat. How that all came about is a mystery to me and I'll bet it was against counsel's orders, that's certain. But that doesn't solve my problem. The Jury has gone and convicted him anyway and I have to treat that as established fact, not what I would have done in a bench trial. The dilemma for me, dear soul of mine, is do I impose sentence on the conviction as made or compromise because I think the evidence was soft and give something less than the ultimate penalty? That is my struggle!*

Marilyn came into the room and interrupted his deep thoughts by placing her hands on both shoulders standing directly behind him and leaned over the side of the chair and kissed him gently on the right cheek.

"Dear, hard day at the office?" she innocently asked, knowing full well that the trial of Earl Bryant had been concluded today.

"Hard is understatement Marilyn; but unfortunately I can't leave it there, the burden's too heavy and it follows me around like a dark cloud," Ben said looking up at her beautiful face as she smiled empathetically at him, letting him know that she was aware of his burden.

"Care to talk about it, or would you like me to stay out of this business?" Marilyn said.

"Oh I don't know Dear, there is no way to share the load for this; it's the penalty phase of the case that is the hardest. The Jury has the easy part, just guilty or not guilty, I have the hard part, its hang him or imprison him. That's my dilemma, Dear," Ben said.

"Why a dilemma, Dear?," she asked.

"Because as I heard the evidence and it was not a strong case of direct evidence for conviction. I know that circumstantial evidence can sustain a conviction, but I'm struggling with giving the death penalty in the face of that. It was a conviction for premeditated murder with ample motive, opportunity and means for it, especially after the Defendant testified. I never would have had him do that!" Ben said soberly.

This was about as far as he was willing to discuss the case, for after all, it was his job as Federal Judge and he had no right to involve his dear wife in that terrible burden. He probably had said too much as it was. Besides, he was almost certain there would be an appeal and there was always a chance that something would turn up. There was no getting around it, only he had this burden. So he would carry out his judicial duty whether a heavy load emotionally or not, but not tonight.

"Why don't we shelve this for now, Marilyn and have dinner, I will deal with my problem back at Court where it belongs, but I do appreciate how you understood I was struggling with something. I love you for it," Ben said, rising from his seat and took Marilyn in his strong arms and kissed her full on the mouth as a kind of foretelling of what was probably ahead for them later in the evening. As it would turn out, Allie's first reaction had not been far off.

78. The sentence imposed

It was early spring by the time for the sentencing hearing had arrived and the windows to the old Federal Courthouse had been left ajar to let in some of the fresh spring air. Spring is the time of renewal or rejuvenation of nature kept dormant by the hard cold frosty winter and released every year at this time as the eternal reminder that life goes on and was never really dead, as it always seems to be in the short run.

The sentencing of Earl Bryant that year was destined; it seems, to be a contradiction or movement in the reverse of nature's eternal longing. Nothing the Judge would say or do could bring about a renewal in the life of Earl Bryant. He was found guilty and would either spend the rest of his life in prison or dangle from a rope until dead. It seemed sacrosanct to think it but he half way longed for the end of it all rather than to sit day after day, year after year in a lonely cell destitute of any of life's little pleasure.

He would never see a spring day down on the river or the dogwoods flowering throughout some deep forest glade ever again. The sound of the coonhounds, Red and Old Blue mournfully sending their tree bark signal that a sow or he coon was run to ground or up a big live oak would be a slowly vanishing memory for little or late. His beloved

Ellie and daughter Emily would visit him for a while but even they would tire of the frequency he would desire or worse yet, the ending of it all by the dangling from a gallows would put a stop to it all anyway.

The mocking birds outside the courthouse wailed their cheerful or mournful songs in their inimical imitations of many other bird sounds, depending on the mood the hearer was in, in a floating of sorrowful sound this morning on the waves of the courtroom air. Sorrow was the mood of the Defense side of the room and resignation on the other. Each lawyer had done his duty and even Houston was not thrilled with the idea of a hanging coming from this case. An execution sentence never ever did, really, an awful process and those inevitable appeals that drug on and on and on tired him just to think about it.

The date for the sentencing arrived with the old courtroom again bulging at the seams. The press was there in droves looking for the chance to put some new twist on the story and give their paper that certain edge to set it apart from the rest.

Tony was no different in that he had joined in the unofficial competition among regional and national journalists to make his mark with this story. Long forgotten was his idealistic or at least romantic notion of writing a Pulitzer Prize piece on the social effects of the end of Prohibition in the northern Florida back country as epitomized in the arrest, trial, and conviction of the old whiskey man, Earl Bryant. It was replaced by the expedient need to write daily stories to satisfy the circulation demands of his editor and maybe just maybe catch the attention of the national wire services.

Most of all, he felt sadly for his college friend, Aaron Martin, who had put so much in the defense of his client, only to see his chances flushed down the drain with that idiotic insistence of his client to defend himself. The family of Earl was back again and well positioned to be close to him in case his nerves failed him, with the possible sentence of at least life in prison, or worse yet, death by hanging. That latter prospect was too terrible for them to even contemplate. They refused to even think about it.

Earl was in place having been delivered, possibly for the last time by the jail guards who had gotten somewhat attached to the old man by now. They felt no rancor or hard feelings toward him as a convicted felon, as he had become "one of them" in a limited manner of speaking.

Aaron conferred with Earl by whispering instructions detailing exactly what he should expect at the hearing. Judge Parker strode into the courtroom from chambers with his black judicial robe flowing behind him like the wings of a deadly specter announcing by its flight a veritable dooms day for the Defendant. The standing room only crowd having been drawn to their feet by the herald of the clerk on duty with the "all rise," returned to their seats on the Judge's prompt command.

"Good morning ladies and gentlemen, this court on the docket of The United States v. Earl Bryant is in session. I am here today to pass sentence on the Defendant Earl Bryant found guilty on the charge of murder in the first degree by a duly constituted Jury of this Court. Will the Defendant please rise and face the Court," Judge Parker commanded.

Aaron and Earl rose and stood side-by-side facing the Judge. *Will he or won't he, that is the question soon to be answered,* thought Aaron as he stood next to Earl showing no fear or anticipation on his face.

I have dreaded this here moment and do not know if these old legs will hold me up if the rope falls on round my neck. Please Dear God, let me not fall into that weakness no matter what this man's court wants to do to my sorry self, Earl thought and prayed in the seconds of uncertainty left to him which was about to end.

"On the finding of the Jury of this Court, it is my duty to pass sentence," Judge Parker began. "The taking of a human life is a terrible thing whether the Defendant has done it or the Court must do it to carry out justice. I cannot take lightly this responsibility that the law has thrust upon me. The man Frank Stiller was a human being, too, and he leaves family and friends that are victims to his killing just as much as he was, though inflicting a different sort of pain. The Stiller family's fate is not final like his was for they have to live with the loss and grief for the rest of their lives. But you, Sir, have taken that man's life and by the finding of the Jury I must take that as established fact. It is not my place to substitute my judgment on the facts as to your motive, opportunity, and the means to commit the crime of murder. They have taken that luxury from me. It is with no pleasure that this Court must pass sentence in this case. I have carefully considered the circumstances bearing on punishment and have concluded and do now impose the sentence of death by hanging in accordance with the law of the United States to which you are subject.

The United States Marshall will carry out sentence six months from this date to permit whatever appeals you and your lawyer may decide to make to be brought to a higher court. But appealing to the highest court of all, if all that fails you, on your behalf I ask that God have mercy on your soul. This Court will be in recess," Judge Benjamin T. Parker, Jr., said as he rose and departed and concluded this phase of the case before him.

The decision announced came as a hammer blow to the courtroom, but especially to Earl and his family. Although they knew this was always possible, no one had dared to really think much about it. But think about it now they must. The all-familiar scene of grief and comfort was played out once again as they clung to each other in utter disbelief. There would be words of comfort and words of hope, but none would have much resonance with him. In his mind, life was over, it being only a matter of time. Brave talk of appeals or sticking by you to the end and such were really wasted words at this point. Grief had to play its part, and for this tightly knit family group this day it was playing like an orchestra with full sound and representation of every instrument of sorrow.

79. The invitation

"Dad, I wouldn't feel right about a party this soon after the loss last week, I'm hurting over that mess. Parading around pretending it doesn't hurt is not my style," Aaron said as he looked over his paper at his insistent father who was trying his third approach to persuading his determined son.

Marian was right, he had to get Aaron past the emotions he was feeling and forcing himself to see people socially was as close to getting back on the horse after a fall as he could imagine. But his stubborn, but principled, son was no easy assignment in overcoming his opposition. He hadn't yet talked to Sue about it and out of respect for his partner and son, would never dream about using his wife to get him to change his mind. How to get him to agree to come? That was the question that had preoccupied his leisure time thinking, and as yet was unanswered. When he was at the office, the demands of the practice were too great to spend any time on it, but as they sipped coffee after lunch at the Garden Grill, he was freed up to ponder his next approach.

Aaron had returned his nose to the Recorder catching up on the latest coverage of the sentencing hearing. The interest and comments around town on this trial were unavoidable.

Roland could not help himself as he sat there with Aaron; thinking of any possible solution to this problem was unavoidable. *This is a tougher nut to crack than I thought. Let me see, how would I persuade a legislator from my party, whose side had just been crushed in the final vote before the legislature, to come to a fundraiser for my party? That would be tougher, admittedly, but doable. I would get one of the winners in on the defeat to suggest it to him as a token of his courage to come out and face it so the public could not see him licking his wounds, sulking over in a corner somewhere. He would listen to him but never to me. That just might do it,* he thought.

Say Aaron, I'm about finished here, you finish your paper, I have some errands to run, see you back at the firm," Roland said confident his inspiration just might work. Aaron didn't even look up but nodded his acknowledgment to the plan.

When Roland got back to his office, he picked up the phone, heard the proverbial "Number Please" from Mrs. French, or one of the sound likes at the telephone company, and spoke the number of Houston Gilchrist to the operator.

"Hello, Houston here," he said, already busy in preparing for his next case, a tax evasion prosecution of a Perry timber company executive who somehow managed to omit his company's substantial dividends from his personal tax returns for five years before he got caught.

"Houston, Roland Martin, how are you?"

"Fine, fine, Roland, what can I do for you?"

"Personal favor Houston, but by the way, great win in the Bryant case even if my partner had to take it on the chin," Houston said.

"That had to be tough on Aaron, Roland, never could figure why old man Bryant decided to take the stand; did him in, I'm thinking. My opinion only, however. Aaron had me on the ropes after Bill Stevenson and I missed that angle on the prints. Quite frankly, I thought Aaron had us there; but you said a personal favor, glad to help if I can," Houston said, good naturedly as one professional to another neither bragging nor condescending in tone.

"Marian wants to have a get together over at the farm to sort of cheer Aaron up, you know with a few friends, giving him a chance to stick his nose out into the public, gradual like. He took that loss pretty hard. And you know there will be an appeal. There has to be in a death case, so you haven't heard the last of the Bryant case yet," Roland said.

There was a silence on the line for just a few seconds as several possibilities ran through Houston's mind, the most likely one that Roland wanted the prosecutor to show up at the party. That had to be avoided at all costs.

"You don't want me over there do you, that is not my idea of bringing cheer to the guy," Houston said. Roland laughed and said,

"Oh no, my God that was the most probable favor you could imagine with my set up and quite frankly, I never thought of that. However, asking the "enemy" to come to a social function to honor Aaron would be a bit much, but we would always love to have you come, some other time, perhaps" Roland said, still chuckling.

"My favor is a solution to a problem, for you see Houston, Marian is determined to have this thing and Aaron is just being stubborn or principled and refusing to come. Somehow he feels it would be unfair to his client to be attending a barbeque at the farm while he sits over in the jail waiting to be transported to prison and the hangman later," Roland said, gently leading up to the favor not yet expressed.

"What can I possibly do Roland, you name it?" He said.

"If you could call Aaron, you know on some minor matter dealing with the wind up of the case and let it drop that you understand his Dad is holding a barbeque with a few friends over at the farm. He'll acknowledge it and say he isn't going, or you can pull that out of him; and then you suggest that the best way for Aaron to get this thing behind him is to get out of himself and show his friends that life goes on. That small step would be a symbol of his coming out after the big loss, you know like a badge of courage he could get pinned on his battle jacket. A social event would make it easier when he has to face the ladies at the church or the Chamber of Commerce Board meeting coming up next month. Or, that he should carry the flag, win or lose, if he is to stay in practice in this town. That sort of thing. He'll have to attend those other events and this coming out in a friendly surrounding will make it easier. He may just take that advice from you but never from me, what do you think Houston?"

"Makes sense to me, Sir, I'll drop over at the Garden Grill, I see him in there every day or so and just ease my way in for a little friendly advice," Houston said, smiling.

"I owe you one, Houston" he said.

"Don't mention it, Roland," Houston said and after a "see ya," he hung up the phone. Mrs. French, not being very busy that day at the phone exchange had violated the company policy about eaves dropping and listened in to the call. It was harmless enough; for she would never use the information only enjoy the voyeuristic pleasures of it for the moment.

The gambit worked later in the week as Houston with unimaginable psychological acumen, built a bridge for Aaron that could cross over the troubled waters of the confusing and conflicted motives in his mind of duty, loyalty, family, and pride. Aaron called his Mother and gave her the good news and the event was scheduled for the next Saturday afternoon at the farm. The other guests would need no such persuasion.

80. The farm

It was a fine spring day at the Martin Farm with the sun out, making things bright and cheerful yet in April, not hot enough to be uncomfortable. Most regular travelers to Florida who don't have to be there on business, follow the axiom of never after April in Florida. With the heat and humidity of the steamy summers, it is wise advice indeed. The new plant growth of spring was abundant everywhere.

The Martin Farm house was really more than just a farmhouse with its two stories and a wide wrap around front porch on the southern side ground level and a small portico in the center off the upstairs area where the bedrooms were located. The house was constructed of a wood exterior with the siding boards nailed horizontally in a lap strake style painted a glorious white. The roof was held up by a series of vertically fluted columns across the front, where the front porch, painted gray, was also supported and capped off with graceful ionic capitals that gave the old structure, and it was extremely old, a graceful and stately appearance.

The shrubbery surrounding the front porch was an interlocking hedge in the English style. The house sat well back from the road and was reached by driveways coming from the corner where the road to Havana joined the road connecting with the main highway to Talla-hassee, and also from the east bound road where Roland Martin could reach his major fields of endeavor, the State Legislature and the Courts.

It was an ideal location for Roland and Marian, for they both loved country living with access to the social life in Tallahassee only twenty miles or so away. Aaron had been raised there as a boy delving into the typical pursuits of boys on the farm in those early years. These included hunting, fishing and playing about the fields and forests with his friends in Robin Hood reenactments, war and other games.

Behind the house was the Martin farm consisting of shade tobacco fields, curing barns and the small houses where the farm workers lived year round. Roland had been a pioneer of sorts in the growing of shade grown tobacco to produce some of the finest leaf grown anywhere to make the wrappers on cigars. This was before he had learned the trade of law-yering and perfected it in the Legislative arena. He kept the tobacco farm for tradition sake even though he no longer needed the income from it.

The guests began to arrive around three o'clock that Saturday after-noon. Ben and Sally Collins were the first, probably because they were the closest friends of Aaron and his wife Sue. Ben was also a shade tobacco farmer over northeast of Havana near the small settlement called Hinson. Ben's grandfather had been a large plantation owner before the Civil war, but had lost much of it due to sickness, Yankee raiders, fires and the other effects of the conflict as had everyone else in the county.

Ben had managed to hang on to the remnant of the place that had been called Kingston in the antebellum glory days of the old south. Ben had also developed a business in packing and grading the leaf for local growers for resale, as well as contracts made to finance the crops, or independently as the market would bear He also had connections with one of the larger cigar manufacturers down in Tampa.

Sally had grown up with Ben in the same area and they had some-how managed to find each other and raise a brood of four all their own. As boys, Ben, Tony Callaway, Aaron and Peter Drucker had been friends for life. A series of events had cemented their relationship into a lifelong personal relationship.

Tony Callaway was not far behind in his arrival. He drove over from the capital where he had finished his writing assignments for the weekend edition at the Recorder. Roland was walking out of the back of the old house with Marian in tow as they heard the guests begin to drive up and park.

"Hello folks," Roland shouted out as he saw Tony and Ben with Sally warmly greeting each other. "Where are Aaron and Sue?" Sally asked, looking around, but not seeing them.

"They'll be here soon," Roland said, "I had to work really hard on my dear Son to get him over here after the trial turned out so badly. He's a little embarrassed, I fear. Maybe you folks could cheer him up?" Roland said, as Marian glared at her husband for being so frank about such a sensitive family matter.

"Hell, he has nothing to be ashamed about, Mr. Martin, a jury found the guy guilty not Aaron, didn't they?" Ben said.

"I know Ben, but Aaron feels badly all the same," Roland said. "Look there they come now," Tony said, pointing to the highway heading east toward Tallahassee. Sure enough, the sleek black Ford sedan came down the highway and slowly turned into the long drive as if hesitant, or lost, but he could not be lost with this old place indelibly burned into the memories of his experience.

Aaron parked the car alongside the house under a covered overhang at the side entrance on the parallel tire sized two track concrete driveway that ran along the east side of the house and stopping and parking it in the rear by the garage. He and Sue got out and walked slowly up to the front where Roland was holding his social court.

"Listen up everybody, I have an announcement," Roland said immediately catching everyone's attention.

"As you all know, the great state of Utah, on December 6, 1933, was the 36th and the last required state to ratify the repeal of Prohibition on the manufacture, sale, and transportation of intoxicating liquors, except where prohibited by individual state laws. It has taken the great state of Florida until this very week to remove its own restriction against that use, manufacture, and importation of that stuff. As most of you know, I have been personally ambivalent on the whiskey question. The dangers of excessive consumption of alcohol are well known and most of you also know that the only whiskey available in this state, until now has been of the illegal variety.

The war that has been going on between our Federal and State agencies with the purveyors of those products led to the very tragedy that our Son, Aaron, was thrust into its middle. As my partner and the legal professional that I know him to be, we can freely discuss this question with him even though the private and privileged matters between our client and his attorneys must remain unavailable to you."

Roland was warming to the occasion and began to elucidate the finer points on the question of whiskey drinking which for those who knew him, everyone at this party fell into that category, expected to be entertaining.

"My friends in the legislature, and there are many of them on both sides of this question, were well acquainted with my position on the bill that just passed, making the use of alcohol and the sale thereof under strict regulations, legal in this state. I was asked often where I stood on the whiskey question, in committee hearings. As I told them loudly and often in answer to the question, do you favor the legal drinking of whiskey? I said, if by the legal drinking of whiskey you mean the excessive consumption that leads to drunkenness, loss of livelihood or freedom or worse and the neglect, harm and abandonment of families, the excessive fighting that often accompanies its consumption and the awful headaches that hang over into the next day, I sure am against the drinking of whiskey. But if you consider the warm glow that one gets on a cold morning on a fox or deer hunt around a common campfire from a flask passed around the group, the fellowship that relaxed and jovial friends can share with each other in front of a warm hearth in the safety of home, office, or restaurant, the conversation freed from the inhibitions of fear and anxiety allowing people to express themselves without restraint; and the expectation that friends and colleagues will have some means to share with each other in these ways on social occasions, I am in favor of the drinking of whiskey."

They all laughed as Roland had risen to the occasion dramatically and caused them all, including Aaron and Sue, to enjoy the performance without any reflection on Aaron's terrible legal result even though the subject was inextricably interwoven with the subject. Roland was of the opinion that instead of dancing around the subject with Aaron in attendance, a direct approach would free him up to talk about it and relax. Most of all he needed to relax.

"Now, my friends, in celebration of my recent legislative victory, I have arranged to have some sample products, now legal for the first time, available for your pleasure. Will you follow me?" Roland said, and with Marian under his arm headed around to the back yard where the barbecue and a make shift bar was set up under the shade of pecan trees that were leafing out in the early spring sunlight.

Just at that point, a car horn honked and they all turned around to see with much surprise, Peter Drucker and his girlfriend Mary Alice Leven drive up in an older Ford Model T roadster refurbished and in mint condition.

"Pete's here, Aaron shouted" and all heads turned in surprise. When they got out of the cars, the old friends embraced each other warmly. They had not been sure that Pete would be here, because of the terrible impact his brother George had had on Aaron's case. Marian had not invited him for she and Roland had discussed it and decided against it for that very reason. So who had done it, was the unasked question of the hour?

Peter Drucker had been a boyhood friend of Aaron, Tony and Ben's. However his inability or lack of interest in getting more of an education or his choice of work as a clerk in hardware and tobacco supply business, after a tour of itinerant railroad crew work, had by practical necessity separated the childhood friends somewhat.

But Ben was a tobacco man through and through and had been a customer of the business known as Stallworth's in the early days and had stayed in touch with Pete. They enjoyed many of the same hobbies and interests such as hunting and fishing, especially the running of foxhounds and enjoying the music the pack of dogs could make in the pursuit of the wiley gray fox, had kept them as fast friends. Besides, there was something in the pasts of Ben and Pete that careers, education or circumstances could not erase.

The others knew all about this bond between the two men, so no discussion or speculation was ever necessary. Ben was the answer to the question of who did it, the inviting that is. After a moment to reflect Tony and then Aaron and Ben, smiling in a know it all look of smugness, moved on to the more important things of the moment to celebrate the loosening of corks and tongues.

The drinks were passed around and contrary to what you might have expected for this "wake," the subject of the trial and Aaron's great loss never even came up. Annie came out to the party and announced that the barbeque was served inside in the house on the inside on the spacious back porch where tables and chairs were all set up to catch the afternoon spring breezes.

The food prepared by Annie along with the serving help on the outside barbeque and was delicious. It was done that way to make for a relaxing and enjoyable evening.

Old Mack was in charge of the coals and his expertise as the builder and tender of coal fires in the tobacco curing process was exceeded by no one, and naturally he would be chosen for this important chore. Also, the boys had all known Mack on many camping trips and hunting parties where he had brewed river coffee in five-gallon lard cans on campfires built wherever the camp was set. He had quite a hand as a cook too, for his squirrel purlieu, a concoction of squirrel meat and rice highly seasoned with pepper, was legendary at fall hunting camp cookouts.

After a thirty minutes or so, Annie called out to Mack to bring some more barbeque, but the noise of the party was so loud and Mack was getting hard of hearing anyway there was no response.

Annie started to walk outside to tell him when Aaron rose and said; "I'll go Annie, besides it's too heavy a cask for old Mack to be carrying at his age. Tony, want to lend me a hand?" Aaron said, as he rose to go out to the pit with Tony right behind him. They reached the pit area out back and found Mack stirring the coals coaxing the last bit of heat from them as the cooking of the barbeque was winding down.

"Hey Mack, how goes it?" Tony, who really liked the old Negro who had been so much a part of his boyhood, was sad to see the old man getting old. "Yas Suh, I's fine, these old bones they holding up pretty good Mr. Tony, how is you, Suh?" Mack said, smiling broadly.

"Great "Tony said, and asked, "You're about out of fire there Mack, got any more coal?" "Shore enough, Suh, we got them, I'm calling Hub to bring some more," Mack said and signaled to his helper standing near the back door to bring another bag of charcoal from the garage. Aaron and Tony picked up the heavy metal basket that Mack used as a grill and started carrying it in toward the house loaded with well-done barbeque meat. They took a few steps and suddenly Aaron stopped almost dropping the basket.

"What's wrong Aaron?" Tony asked, truly puzzled why his friend had stopped suddenly. *What did Mack say just now, calling Hub? Hub? Mack is a Douglas, right, and Hub, could it be? No way, no chance, not the Hub Douglas, the mysterious disappearing Still hand of Earl Bryant's who just might….. his freedom? How could I have missed this before? Sir, Old Mack had a son that ran off as a boy, Hub!*

Aaron turned slowly, set his end of the basket of barbeque meat down on the ground, nodded to Tony to do the same and gave him a sign to follow as he walked over to Mack and stopped.

"Now Mack, be truthful with me, has your son Hub, the one that ran off many years ago, just recently returned home?" Aaron asked. Old Mack, having no idea why his boss's son had such interest in this, looked up and said, innocently,

"Shore now, he come back jest before Christmas, why you asking bout my Hub Mr. Aaron?" Mack said.

"I'll explain later Mack, Tony, come on," Aaron said and walked rapidly over by the house with Tony right behind him to catch up with Hub loading coal out of a large bin into a sack to carry it over to the fire as his father had requested,. Tony Callaway, being smarter than the average guy, was quick on the uptake and from his own experience down on the river disaster and the interviews with the other still hands, knew instinctively what Aaron had in mind.

"Hub, I doubt if you remember me, you left here at such an early age, but I remember you vaguely. Your Pop says you just returned home, that true?" Yas, Suh, I been gone too long and jest come back before Christmas," Hub said.

"Now Hub, did you come here from Liberty County, working for Mr. Bryant in his business down there?" Aaron asked bluntly. Hub stopped a minute from his coal loading and thought about it long and hard before answering. *What tree is these white folk barking up? Is I in trouble? They shore interested in me all of a sudden like. Cain't see what for though. Usually best to be careful round white folks, they got strange business sometimes. How they know about my boss man? This strange!*

"I don't know about no Liberty County business, but I do knows Mr. Earl, Yas Suh, I worked for him before I come home," Hub said.

"It has to be the same guy, Aaron," Tony said getting excited himself, seeing a scoop of a story emerging in front of him.

"Let me explain Hub. Mr. Bryant was convicted of murder for the shooting of a Federal Agent on the front steps of his house deep in the woods of Liberty County. By a set of strange circumstances, I ended up in the river country with Mr. Johnny Caldwell and met some of the other men who worked at the Lagoon. Do you know Nooby Oakley, Hoover Spencer and Israel Manley, they worked there as well?" Yas Suh, I knows them, we worked the Still for Mr. Bryant, is I in trouble bout that?" Hub asked.

"No Hub, you are not in trouble about anything," Aaron explained, "In fact you might help us to set Mr. Earl free," Aaron said, grabbing Hub by both arms and led him over to a bench by one of the large pecan trees in the back yard.

"Sit here Hub, we have to talk?" Aaron said, sitting beside Hub with Tony standing alongside. All thought of the barbeque basket was forgotten as the two men looked at the treasure that had just been uncovered in front of their eyes. Mack, understanding nothing that was going on, realized instinctively that it must be very important by the way these white men were acting, so he went over to the basket, lifted it up easily, even for a man his age, and carried it into the kitchen where Annie waited for it impatiently.

The party inside continued on with no awareness that a breakthrough had been accidentally achieved in the recently concluded murder case. Time would tell whether it was a true breach or just a little crevice in the damn that had been holding back the truth. If you found a field with a treasure hidden within and you knew it, you would pay a great price for that field, the old Biblical saying went. Aaron and Tony had just discovered such a field, and the next assignment would be to see exactly what the treasure was and how much of a price would have to be paid to purchase it. The potential reward was immeasurable.

81. Treasure is where you find it

"It's like this, Hub, the Federal man was up at the Bryant House about breakfast time expecting to catch Mr. Earl at home and knocked on the front porch screen door to talk to him. But he wasn't home, you see. While he was standing there talking to Mrs. Bryant, a rifle cracked and the agent fell dead. The other Federal man ran like hell and made it back to Tallahassee to get help. In the meantime, Mr. Earl came home for breakfast, Ellie told him the agent had been shot dead on his front step and then went on down to the Still to tend to the day's business, just like nothing had happened, or at least acting like nothing had happened," Aaron explained to Hub giving him the big picture.

"Uh huh," Hub said without more comment.

"Yeah, you see, Hub," Tony said, picking up the story as he had learned it, "Mr. Earl's man, George Drucker, came down to work at the Lagoon that morning and found Mr. Earl down there like on a normal day. They apparently had a chit chat about the shooting with each one being a bit coy, you know, not admitting they knew anything, understand?"

"Yas, Suh, I gets it," Hub said, "I was there that mornin' when Mr. George he come on into the Lagoon, excepting I seen him before that."

"You what?" Aaron asked excitedly. "Yas Suh, Mr. Earl, he sent me out to finish up with the sugar counting out in the shed and that's when I seen Mr. George comin' in," Hub said.

"What did you see, exactly Hub and where?" Tony asked, picking up the thread quickly.

"Uh huh, I was standing out by the sugar shack, we calls it, that cause that where the sugar stored at; and Mr. George, he come slipping down from cross the woods with that rifle he carry sometimes, but he actin funny," Hub said, pausing to see how this news was received.

"How funny, Hub?" Aaron asked.

Hub could sense that what he was telling was safe for him and said, "Well, he stop up on that hill over de Lagoon and seem like he was checking that rifle about something. I drop what I was doing and run on back to the Still and get there before he do," Hub looked first at Tony and then at Aaron and back and forth as though waiting for an explosion.

"Yes, go on, Hub, very interesting, what happened next?" Aaron asked as though he were offering an open ended question to a witness in court for the benefit of the jury; but in this case, unlike most of his where the witness was being presented to prove known facts to him, he had no idea where this witness's testimony was headed.

"I watched him as he come into de Lagoon and hung That rifle of his right next to Mr. Earl's on That peg rack and they begin to talk back and forth bout something made no sense to me then, which I couldn't hear anyways and after a while, Mr. George he leave and take That rifle with him," Hub said.

"Which rifle did he take, Hub, and this is very important?" Tony asked eagerly anticipating they were about to uncover some vital information to break the case wide open.

"I don't know, Suh, they looked the same to me. Alls I know was he left and I ain't seen him no more," Hub said plainly. Aaron's was quickly running this new information through his legal mind, analyzing whether it rose to the standard to force a new trial.

It certainly is newly discovered evidence and not reasonably available to me before or during the trial. If believed, it could change the outcome. The problem is whether an all white jury would ever believe this guy, an illiterate black man trying to help his old boss, that there really were two guns that morning. I might get a new trial with this and lose all over again. Houston would call Earl as a witness, already waived the 5th

*Amendment privilege, damn it, and a new jury might just convict him
all over again. Might avoid the rope though and that would be worth it
but it just isn't enough. Have to have more.*

"Do you know where Mr. George went when he left, Hub?" Aaron
asked, fishing for more. "No Suh, back to what Mr. Earl and them called
the office I reckon, but truth is, I don't know," Hub said.

"Where did Mr. George live at, Hub?" Tony probed, looking for
leads like the curious news reporter he was, is trained to do.

"I here tell he rent a room or house or something up near Telogia
way," Hub said.

"You've been very helpful Hub, more than you know," Aaron said
warmly, feeling like grabbing Hub and hugging him in appreciation
but that might have been carrying gratitude a little far. They talked a
while longer and Hub was allowed to go back to his fire and Tony and
Aaron conferred on the way back inside to the remains of the party.

Finally, Aaron felt he had something worthy of celebrating.

"This is going to be another job for John Travis and maybe a means
for his redemption," Aaron said and Tony nodded in agreement both
of them thinking about that second gun which had to be somewhere,
as the two friends made their way back into the house to join the
others. They had begun to wonder in their absence why, after Mack
had brought in the barbeque, it had taken so long just to get some more
barbeque, where Tony and Aaron were.

82. Redemption day

John Travis was sitting in his small office on the following Monday
morning with his feet propped up on his old desk, wondering about
where his next case would ever come from when the phone rang. "Hello,

Travis here," he said, and Aaron hurriedly asked that he come over immediately to his office to talk about the Bryant case. John had no problem with motivation and looking up to the ceiling after he hung up, he blew out his withheld breath in a whoosh.

"That was a prayer I was just making, wasn't it? Thank you Lord!" and rose from his seat, somehow managing not to fall over backwards in his enthusiasm, and headed out of the office on his way to the Martin Law Firm building.

Aaron quickly filled John Travis in on what he had learned from Hub Douglass about the second gun and said, "I have to find that rifle, John. Without it it's an uphill battle to force a new trial. I have to try it regardless, but finding that weapon would Sure be nice. If we get lucky and find it and even luckier if George Drucker got careless and didn't wipe off the prints, that would really be something!"

"You got a point there Boss and I see what you need from me, find where he lived, that should be easy enough, but then find the gun. That will be the challenge. You said Hub heard he lived in Telogia in a rented place? I'll have that located by sundown tomorrow. The gun and the prints, well, we will have to see," John said cautiously.

"You use any means you need, just find me that gun!" Aaron directed bluntly.

"Ok Boss, you got it, and as to those "means," you'll never hear about any that will not be due to put in the church bulletin next Sunday, but you can make book on getting results this time. I lost those boys last time and now that we got the main man, Hub, I won't fail you again and you've got my word on that!" John said with all the conviction that his heart eager for redemption could muster.

He drove his pickup truck to Hosford on Highway 20 and made his way south on Highway 65 to the little settlement of Telogia. It wasn't much of a place in 1934 with a few buildings at the intersection of

Highway 67 that meanders up from Carrabelle down on the coast. He pulled his truck into the one gas station in town and had the attendant check his oil and fill his tank.

The young local man leaned against the rear fender as he filled the tank in the rear of the Ford, and John engaged him in some talk that was bound to smoke out the information he was looking for without alerting everybody in town as to his purpose. "I haven't been down here for several years now, hunting improved over in the Appalach?" John asked, breaking the ice, as the saying goes, expecting that talk about hunting or fishing would be as safe down here as the weather or football is everywhere else. He used the slang name for the Apalachicola National Forest to tip off the local that he was familiar with his subject matter.

"Yeah, pretty damn good, got my buck last year, but only a six point," the local said. "Don't throw that one out man, I bet he ate good, huh?" John said adapting his language

to that of most locals.

"Yeah, my wife can barbeque a deer rib better than anybody in these here parts, Mister," the local said. "Who you hunt with Mister, maybe I know them?" *A gift from the Lord, that is*, John thought and said,

"As I said, haven't been into the Appalach in a few years, my old hunting buddy got too busy, fact is I lost touch with him over the years, have you seen old George lately?"

"George? Oh you must mean George Drucker, worked over in Bryant Country, he ain't been around here since Christmas, don't know where he went off to, Mister," the local said.

Bingo! John thought. "Does he still have a place round here, I used to see him at a place out east of here I think it was or maybe west, but I lost track of where it was exactly. Do you know the way out there, most guys that work in service stations, they know where everybody lives is my experience?" John asked with a puzzled almost indifferent tone, though purposefully complimentary to the man not wanting to attract much attention to his interest in Drucker's location.

"You was right the first time Mister, its east. You follow 67 east till it turn south on you, about two miles out of town, and he lives, or used to anyway, at the old Smith place Like I say, nobody seen him since Christmas," the local said.

"This Smith place is it on the left or the right as you go out there, I might just drive over and leave a note for Old George, just in case he shows up. Can't hunt till fall anyhow, but long as I'm out here might as well try," John said and watched the man carefully to see if he was suspicious at all. He wasn't.

"You turn to the left at the mail box and I think it still has Smith on it, If I ain't mistaken," the local said, as he finished filling the tank and moved around John to lift the hood and check the oil. John patiently waited. "You're about ¾ quart low, you can wait if you want to, Mister," the local said.

"Thanks, I don't want to over fill it," John said as he paid the man the bill for the gas he had pumped into his tank and climbed into the front and turned the Ford around to go east on Highway 67. He watched the local man through his rearview mirror just to be Sure he didn't look puzzled or in any way alerted to the masterful piece of detective work he had just surreptitiously conducted.

The local man's directions were excellent and just about two miles on the odometer John slowed down just past a creek or little stream where the road turned south. Almost immediately on the left was the old mail box sitting on top of an almost rotten four by four with the faded, but clearly legible, name "Smith" on its sides.

The road from the highway was a two lane sand rut road and made its way northeast through a dense scrub forest for about forty yards and pulled into what appeared to be a small white frame house covered with kudzu vines with almost no grounds around it, and certainly not a manicured lawn. No one appeared to be home and no dogs came running as sentinels to guard the place as you usually find if the place is occupied though empty at the moment.

John had a litany of excuses of why he was out there just in case the local man had steered him wrong; such as his Fuller Brush or Encyclopedia salesman routine for which he always kept the appropriate samples in his truck, just in case. He had been rejected more times in his "sales" business than a genuine drummer and had absolutely no concerns over it. It was "thank you Ma'am, sorry to have bothered you" or some such "excuse me please" statement suitable to the personality type he encountered. But today he didn't need I, for the place was empty, unlived in and probably had been that way since December 5th, if he was any judge.

He parked his Ford right in front of the old house finding no need to hide, got out and walked around the house to case the place. Although locked, entry was no barrier to someone with his skills of entry. A pocketknife slid under a latch here, a carelessly left window unlocked there or if all else failed, a rock to take out a glass pain anywhere in the building allowing him to reach the inside lock on the old wood frame post, and anchor style windows found on most buildings in those days.

One pass around the building was sufficient when John found one of the back windows slightly ajar, a telltale sign of an easy entry port. He was not concerned about legality, for he was not working for the Sheriff anymore, and one's constitutional right to be free from an illegal or unreasonable search and seizure without warrant meant absolutely nothing, since he was here at the bequest of a private party. His only exposure was a misdemeanor trespass charge if he got caught.

John Travis was not going to get caught and his target being deep in the woods completely out of sight from the public highway, was as good as an ample insurance policy right after an auto accident. The Martin lawyers and their considerable legal skills and wealth were his insurance policy for this; but besides there was nobody here in the first place.

John put on his tight fitting latex gloves, though not available to the general public, he had several sets he had ordered out of a Chicago hospital some years back that always came in handy to be Sure he left no fingerprints on one of these clandestine entries. He lifted the poorly fitting window with some difficulty but managed to raise it high enough, with his athletic ability to vault his small frame into the building's interior.

The room was, in all probability, a bedroom although bare of anything except a good coating of dust. That meant his footsteps would leave a trail across the floor but he would take extra pains to clean them up before leaving. It was a one-story wood frame building with a typical center hall and opposite rooms, with a kitchen on the back just next to an outside porch.

He walked back there first and took a look out into the meager yard and saw nothing remarkable. A few utensils, like pots and pans, lay in stacks next to the sink, still dirty with the remnants of the last meal and almost crusty black by now with mold growing on the remaining organic matter, quickly now returning by entropy to its constituent elements in nature.

John searched the place methodically, including a thorough search of the closets, chests of drawers and other places where a gun might have been stashed. He did not really expect it to be this easy, so he continued the search, room by room, finding nothing in the house of interest. There were no notes of confession either in some of the scattered papers in a small desk in the front room that might have been suitable for a parlor or sitting room, but he checked anyway.

He was Sure he was in the right place though for he saw some old unopened mail scattered about addressed to Mr. George Drucker, Highway 67. Rural Route 57, Telogia, Florida. He looked through several of them before picking up a couple that bore a postmark just prior to December 5, 1933, and stuffed them in his pockets.

Next he started in the front room and carefully examined the floor for any sign that the planks that made up the floor in the house had in recent years been scratched, replaced by a different color wood from the rest or any sign that entry under the house had been breached through the floor. There was no such sign in any of the rooms. Neither was there any access to the space above the ceiling but he carefully checked just the same.

Then, satisfied George Drucker had hidden no weapon in the house, he carefully cleaned up his dust labeled footprints with an old cloth he had brought along for that purpose. Confident that within a few days a fresh coat would cover the floor again hiding all evidence of his trespass, not that he cared very much anyway.

Outside again, he went around the house once more and when he noticed a crawlspace underneath, made entry and crawled around with his flashlight, finding nothing here either, and exited the crawlspace the same way he came in. Next he circled around the little house again and noticed that a trail meandered more or less southeast from the back of the house and followed it. It wasn't much of a trail but it obviously led somewhere.

The trail, such as it was, was a sand rut closed in upon by myrtle bushes, saw tooth palmettos and wild grasses overhung with a leafy canopy forest. As he followed the trail for a while, possibly forty or fifty yards, he noticed a smell recognizable by all human beings, the smell of an outhouse. It was placed sixty yards or so from the main house probably for that purpose, to keep the odors away.

The tradeoff was the comfort of pleasant air at home versus the inconvenience of a hike to the outhouse in inclement weather. But north Florida rains usually didn't last long and even if you had to go, you could hold it until the rain let up or just get wet once in a while.

This outhouse was quite different than most, having room for the seat and door swinging out so that a minimum amount of lumber was used for this necessary construction. There was a sizeable stream nearby behind the structure, which wasn't a very good idea health wise, but in this case the choice may have been all right anyway because the stream was fast flowing up on a little plateau above the outhouse and paralleled the structure and probably staying clear and clean regardless.

The structure had a two seater, side-by-side design, with privacy built in for double occupancy purposes. It also had a little room on the side, which on first impression looked almost like a tool shed, but there was no apparent reason to put tools this far away from the house.

He never figured out what was the purpose of the room, for it was empty of contents anyway. The roof over the outhouse and "tool room" structure was more than the typical lean-to roof with overhang and porch you often found in the typical country outhouses. It had a ridge running from back to front that did cover a little porch where you could wait your turn, if it was raining at the time. The shingles covering the porch in a manner, revealed, as you looked at it from the front, as though there was a space for a small amount of storage above the rooms' ceilings.

Not that it was designed that way for there would be no reason to store anything up there normally, but space enough for it. He went inside the "tool shed" portion and checked the floor carefully as he had done in the main house for any signs of recent entry there and found nothing. He then looked carefully at the ceiling and shined his flashlight on each board, checking for the same. He finished this fruitless search and was turning to go check the smelly outhouse side when he caught out of the corner of his peripheral vision, a large wood rat scurrying across the back of the shed floor and disappear.

That's strange, he thought, *I checked that area of the floor and that was a stud horse rat, he can't disappear through a solid wood floor unless he's got his heavenly body already and I didn't think rats…no matter, better check again.*

John walked the few steps to the back of the room where the rat had disappeared and spotted a hole in the floor he had somehow missed before. It was indeed large enough for a large wood rat to squeeze into and under a little bench that cast a dark shadow over it, plus a piece of burlap was over to the side which had probably covered it up until the big fellow scurried into it.

So much for careful inspection, John Travis, expert private investigator, he thought. He reached his fingers inside the opening and gave it a tug and low and behold, a trap door of sorts, apparently hinged underneath at a normal joint in the floor pattern, opened up revealing a deep cave of sorts underneath the floor of the shed on the back. He shined his flashlight down into the hole and spotted a pile of burlap over in the corner.

He climbed down the make shift ladder into the hole and crawled over to the pile. Moving the burlap aside, he spotted it, a long crate with a hinged gate across the top. "Well, well, well, what have we here?" he said out loud and whistled with a little spurt of excitement, even for a methodical professional expert investigator like himself.

He examined the box carefully without touching it. The gate was especially tight fitting he could see and questioned whether he could open it without tools, so he decided to wrap it up in the cloth he had brought along just in case he was fortunate to find the weapon, and snake it out of the hole, up the ladder to the floor of the shed for a better light.

His visual inspection in the better light of the shed revealed everything he had suspected when he examined it by his flashlight beam down in the rat hole, as he would ever call it, when he would tell this story time and again.

He decided not to open the crate, for fear of the loss of the evidence, but if he were a betting man, which he wasn't, he would have bet the family farm that inside that crate was an identical Model 1917 Enfield Surplus army rifle, like the one introduced as evidence in the trial. Whether there were prints of Earl Bryant on it was hard to say at this point, but if there were, he could imagine the freedom bell ringing all over Liberty County in a few days.

He carefully hoisted the cloth-covered crate to his right shoulder and headed back up the narrow trail to the house, truck, road and hopefully destiny. What ever happened to Earl Bryant for the future, the reputation of John Travis investigator, would be made. This was truly redemption day.

83. Look what we have here

"What could be so urgent and why have you dragged me over here, Aaron? I start trial tomorrow in that tax evasion case and I really don't have the time, unless you have started to get your share of white collar criminals lately." Houston Gilchrist said good naturedly, having no idea what this was all about.

John Travis, having returned from his mission glowing with pride and practically certain he had found the missing rifle. However, he could not open the box and prove it because the evidence had to be preserved in case a controversy developed over the means whereby the piece was discovered, or to convince Judge Parker of the need for a new trial.

Also, there was too much of a risk that in satisfying his curiosity and calming his natural anxiety, he just might damage the prints he was Sure would be found on it; or that there was some deep significance to the way the case was to be opened and defeat the whole purpose of his otherwise successful demonstration of his investigative skills.

Aaron was ecstatic on learning of the results and carefully and methodically drilled John over every detail of his trip. He agreed with John Travis that it was too risky to open the case even though knowing for Sure would make his case more convincing with Houston but that couldn't be helped. Before calling Houston or even telling Earl, he had driven over to the farm with John and reduced Hub Douglas' story to words, that when Hub's country accent was properly translated into normal English, could be employed in an Affidavit to submit with a Motion, if necessary, to Judge Parker for a new trial. All this just in case Houston wanted to make life difficult for him.

His Dad had a typewriter in his home office so it was no trouble to prepare the thing in final form for Hub's mark, suitably witnessed by John Travis. Then with affidavit in hand and the report of John Travis at the ready, including the "gun case" itself, sitting in his conference room, Aaron was ready to make his pitch for the freedom of Earl Bryant to the Federal Prosecutor.

"First take a look at this affidavit, Houston, we finally located one of the missing witnesses, a man who was at the scene that morning when my client supposedly confessed to this crime," Aaron said, handing over the original affidavit which explained how Hub had witnessed George Drucker fiddling with a rifle identical to the murder weapon outside the Still that morning, hang it up alongside Earl Bryant's and leave with one of them shortly afterwards.

Houston's adrenalin level started to rise as he saw immediately the significance of the two nearly identical rifles. All the controversy in the trial over how Earl's fingerprints were clearly on the murder weapon, how Drucker's were not, even though he had at first testified that he checked the action to confirm one round had been fired or at least was missing. He later had to come up with that somewhat dubious story about having gloves on at the time. This had been probably fatal to his case, until the fool had taken the stand, against all odds and advice, and gotten himself convicted after all.

And now here was some evidence that called all that into some doubt though not too much yet, in his quick opinion to justify a new trial.

"Our theory, Houston, is that Drucker is your killer. He wanted to take over the moonshine operation of his Boss and saw this as a way to kill the Federal Agent and blame it on Bryant. He fired the fatal shot with the murder weapon, brought it to the Still, hung it up on the rack alongside Earl's identical rifle, engaged him in a conversation extracting a revenge motive confession out of him, as close as he could that is, and then left with Earl's rifle, leaving the murder weapon behind for Earl to put his own prints on.

He had on gloves that morning all right to avoid leaving any incriminating evidence on the murder weapon. He just forgot about the gloves or was reluctant to mention it in case somebody got suspicious of him and that we will probably never know. It took you two hours to pull that glove story out of him, not because you had to create it out of whole cloth, which is what I first thought, but because George was too nervous to talk about the rest of the story, you see?"

Houston shook his head with pure puzzlement, *How desperate was his opponent in the case to really push this implausible story? Did he really think George Drucker was smart enough to pull this off?*

"Now Aaron, you cross examined George Drucker and I'll admit for a country boy, he is a cut above the average. But to pull this elaborate scheme off, he would have to top the charts on brains and that he hasn't. There are just too many holes, Aaron. What if Earl had spotted the rifle, or seen him make the switch, it would never have worked. What if Earl didn't bring a rifle that morning, what would he have done then?" Houston asked, really not convinced that Aaron had anything yet, if this was all he had.

"You're right, of course, Houston. It was full of risks, but consider this; that if he couldn't put the frame on Earl, he would have eliminated a real nemesis to the Still operation and even though he could never get credit for it, it would make things safer for him as an employee of the Still. He was pretty Sure no one had seen him make the shot and the natural attention would be directed at the king pen not the peon," Aaron argued, warming to the alternative hypotheses he was creating on the wing, as he flew by trying to decide when exactly to drop the bomb shell on his colleague.

He wanted to prime Houston sufficiently, so that when he produced the rifle box he would have no choice but to follow through on a thorough investigation.

"Think about it Houston, take your prosecutor's hat off for a minute, if that's possible, and consider these questions that I know you had before the trial began. Why did Bryant stay in Liberty County, if guilty as charged? Why take the murder weapon back to his own house rather than bury it so deep in the woods that not even a Texas groundhog could dig it up? He had to know that the Feds would come and get the body of their agent and then look in the house with a warrant at the ready? He asked rhetorically.

You got a point there my friend, I never understood his conduct throughout this mess and that testifying in his own defense, unheard-of!

"All right Aaron, you have my attention. I am interested in justice, you know, not just notches on my legal gun barrel. What else do you have? You wouldn't bring me over here just on this, a hypothesis and an affidavit from an illiterate black Still hand probably loyal to his old Boss to a fault, would you? What jury, or Judge for that matter, would believe him? You must have something else, tell me this is not all of it Aaron? I mean, the man is headed for the gallows, you know?

"Take it easy Houston, there is more, believe me. John go get the case. Houston's jaw dropped when he heard that, for visions of a gun case sitting in the next office was dancing in his head, as though it had been projected on a movie screen in full color. John left the room and Houston and Aaron locked eyes with Houston's in shock and Aaron's in joy on the verge of ecstasy.

"You didn't find the other gun, too, did you Aaron? Houston asked incredulously.

"We did that, Houston and there it is," Aaron said as John Travis came into the conference room carrying the crate still wrapped up in the protective blanket. John sat the box on the table and unwrapped it, exposing the tightly fitted and under hinged door that ran the length of the box.

"Have you opened it and the gun is in there?" Houston asked, expecting to hear that they had.

"No we haven't Houston and we don't know for certain the gun is even in there, but it's the right size and John here found it under the floor of a shed next to an outhouse at a place over in Telogia where George Drucker was renting, see we took some of his mail from the little desk showing you that it came from his place, not some stranger's.

"Wait a minute Aaron, didn't our witness say that he had gloves on before he came into the Still that morning and said he had them on all along. Even if this is the other rifle, what proof was there that it was even in the Still that morning, except for your doubtful eye witness, much less that it has his prints on it?" Houston said, rising to the occasion as a forensics expert as well as a legal one.

"Good point Houston, but if I'm right and the other gun is in there it will have Earl Bryant's prints on it because he put them there bringing it down to the Still and hanging it up on that rack. There would be no way for George Drucker to have a rifle in his possession with Earl Bryant's fingerprints on it that would not force a new trial. The Drucker prints would be just icing on the cake. We didn't open it because we did not want to contaminate the evidence of the crate," Aaron said, confident finally that there were no holes in his analysis. The proof would be in the pudding, or more accurately, in or on the gun; the gun with prints were either in there or it wasn't and Earl Bryant's freedom depended totally on it.

Houston recovered from his shock enough to think it all through and said, "I suggest that you bring this over to see Bill Stevenson with me and let him dust the crate for prints and see what's inside. I won't even ask how you found this thing or got it out of there once you found it. Your investigator is not a government witness and you are not bound by the constitution for illegal searches and seizures; but it is probably Drucker's property and a few misdemeanors were probably committed in the obtaining of it, but that is the least of my worries. If you're right and the gun with Drucker's fingerprints is in there, your man will walk and we then have the task of trying to make Drucker talk.

"Where is he by the way?" Aaron asked. "I don't know but "The Great One" will find him soon enough. He can run, but he can't hide, forever, anyway," Houston said.

Fortunately for the curiosity of all of them, Bill Stevenson was in town and in his office, working in the lab on the evidence of one of the other prosecutors. After a brief explanation, Stevenson dusted the crate and found no fingerprints except some smudged prints of poor quality. This was not helpful and everyone in the room had expected that George still had his gloves on that morning when the case was brought out to the under floor cavern, from where ever he had it stored or hidden where John Travis had accidentally found it, with the help of the fortuitous wood rat.

The material the crate was made of was fairly new, unpainted and put together very well by someone skilled with woodworking within a few months of last December, Bill Stevenson estimated. He carefully pried opened the narrow hatch cover and shined his flash light down inside and there it was, a Model 1917 Enfield military rifle, identical to the murder weapon. Bill studied the gun inside the crate for a few minutes as the others held their collective breaths.

"That is one tight fit," Bill said as he tried wearing latex gloves to lift the end of the rifle out from the narrow opening and with careful maneuvering, he was able to just squeeze the gun out of the case by rotating it slightly at several points as the bolt action handle just cleared the narrow opening.

Once clear, he lifted the weapon out and laid it on an examining table where he quickly dusted it for prints. There were many of them on the wooden stock, barrel support, barrel, bolt-action lever and pistol grip. Just whose they matched could not be determined without a careful analysis later. He signed the property receipt and the lawyers and John Travis left him alone to do his usual thorough job and report back to Houston and the others, once his analysis was complete.

84. The whole truth and nothing but . . .

Aaron was having coffee in his office with his partner and father Roland Martin when the buzzer rang on his desk.

"Yes, Anna, who is it?" Aaron asked his intercom.

"You won't believe this but it's the Man himself with Mr. Gilchrist over here in person," Anna Devlin said, not hiding the excitement in her voice as she gazed at the beaming faces of Houston Gilchrist and Dan Fernell, United States Attorney for the Northern District of Florida.

"Show them back here Anna, we'll meet in the conference room, Dad and I, OK?" Aaron said and rose to his feet signaling for Roland to follow him into the conference room. By the time they got there, Fernell and Gilchrist were shown in and after pleasantries and coffee, Dan Fernell, cleared his throat and began.

"Aaron, Roland, it's a rare thing when one of our juries convicts someone of murder or anything else for that matter and gets it wrong, but this is one of those rare times. The advantage of being a prosecutor and being proved wrong is that everybody wins because justice is served. Personal victories are overrated in this business, I've always said," Fernell pontificated, as though he really thought these two experienced trial attorneys believed that bull shit even for a minute, or if they ever actually had said that if anyone except their consciences had actually overheard him.

"We have the lab results from the rifle your man found on the rented property of our former witness George Drucker. I emphasize the word former because he is now the target of our own investigation for the murder of Frank Stiller, as soon as we find him, that is. The sucker apparently skipped town as soon as the verdict was announced, but we will find him and that is a given. Marshall Boyle is on his trail as we speak with all points bulletins and the hue and cry crossing the land, as it were. But never mind that, the prints on the Model 1917 bolt action surplus Enfield military rifle matched those of your client's and our notorious, and too clever by half for his own good, George Drucker," Fernell said.

"Hot damn!" Aaron exclaimed, not able to restrain himself to that degree, but then paused for a minute and said, "But the gloves and the lack of prints on the box, why cover that up and leave the others planted all over the evidence? Aaron wondered out loud.

"Stevenson has a theory on that, Aaron, but it doesn't matter "why" anymore, Drucker's goose is cooked, no matter what the explanation. He can't explain how his prints got on the rifle along with Bryant's without making the switch as your man, Hub Douglas, says. Without the gun, that testimony was problematical but with it, it is golden. But Bill thinks that the fit was so tight, he couldn't get it in the box without rotating it back and forth as it slid just so into the box opening. He probably couldn't do that with his thick gloves on and took them off to fit it in the box, never figuring anyone would ever check. That's the way with planning the perfect crime, you can get the major things right but some of the details always trip you up. It's those things you never think of, or in this case, the unanticipated ones, that just turn up. He was too cheap or too lazy to get another crate made and too certain he could safely get that rifle out and use it for hunting again someday, once the coast was clear. It almost was.

Bill doubts Drucker built the box himself, it was too tightly constructed with very close tolerances, typical of a very gifted carpenter and probably miscalculated the opening when he gave the carpenter the dimensions, or perhaps the carpenter screwed it up. Either way, it's the best explanation we can come up with," Houston said.

"Do I take it that after this development, the government will join me in a motion for a new trial and a motion to dismiss all charges, with prejudice, expunging the record once and for all of all charges?" Aaron asked almost rhetorically, for he could not imagine it happening any other way. He was right. This case was over all except for the shouting.

The hardest thing for Aaron would be not shouting to his good friend Tony Callaway how this revelation came about. But there was a case going forward against the real culprit and he would do nothing to jeopardize that effort. He also had to protect his star investigator from a charge of trespass on some Telogia residence owned by someone named Smith by a nervous Liberty County Prosecuting Attorney trying to make a name for himself.

85. Final chance

It was a dark rainy spring night in Tallahassee but especially dark in the cell where Jack and Earl were confined. Earl had been brooding over the fate that was now his. He raised himself up on one elbow and faced the cell wall in a deep pathos of despair. Yes he could face the end if he had to, and had to, it seemed he did.

Jack woke somehow in the midst of it, though no noise had interrupted Earl's deep brooding. "Earl," Jack softly spoke to his friend sensing, that he had been awakened just in time before the downward spiral his self-condemnation was taking him, or would leave him irretrievably spent into emotional exhaustion with consequences beyond imagining.

Later generations of physicians would call it a crisis, a breakdown, or some other metaphor to explain a mental illness they were unable to cure, only to give names for it as though that somehow made it understandable or manageable.

Earl said nothing and later on when asked about it, Jack was never Sure whether he even heard him. Earl was busy, however, for the terrible three-dimensional image had returned, haunting him unmercifully. There was no spatial room for the thing to appear for the space between Earl's head and the cell wall was only a foot or so; but in the world of the phenomenal or the world where spirits dwell, neither space nor imagination is a limitation.

It was to Earl's tortured mind, like he was peering into a vortex that showed the entire full image of the creature, and at the same time seemed to be sucking him into the maw of its funnel like world, beckoning to him without sign or direction. "Come hither oh tortured one, come hither to the place that awaits you." He heard no words this time, yet the effect was the same, luring him into he knew not what, one final chance being offered, as it were, to escape the dreaded future that awaited him somehow.

Jack had risen to his feet and leaned over Earl's reclining form and shook him, first gently as though this were the time for polite persuasion, and then harder and harder as he saw that his friend was trapped in an awful struggle with existence itself; more than life or death, far more than that with consequences unimaginable to the living yet seductive from the dead.

End it right here once and for all, he was in effect being told. It was a struggle for existence itself and his eternal fate hung in the balance, like some gigantic bar of life on a teetering razor of a blade with eternal life and destruction waiting to be tipped one way or the other in the balance.

Earl saw for once in the continuum that had been his life that he had a fateful choice to make. One-way led to death as he perceived his chances, and the other to a fate possibly worse than death, but with an allure that it was an ending or something else or was it?

He thought back on the teachings from his child hood of that magic garden in the distant past where a similar fateful choice had to be made. Choose knowledge and then decide what is true, the thing said to his eternal parents and they had chosen knowledge, forever doomed to be unable to say what was true and good.

And here he was in a garden of his own with a similar truth being offered as though he could determine it. He had fallen for it once; he would not do so again.

In the end, he thought, *what are true are what are good, no matter what comes by me or happen to me, and by God they may have the power to kill the likes of me, but they cain't say what are the truth in this, and I by God stand by that, come hell or high water. I've seen my share of the high water and I guess I better go face the other one.*

At that precise moment, the light in the darkened hallway came on and Eddie Johnson came striding noisily down the aisle clanging his cell keys along the iron bars as was his custom just to wake every prisoner up on the way, since his sleep had been interrupted too.

"Earl, you got company!" Eddie, yelled at this odd hour for visitors, the other cell occupants wakened by it all thought. In that instant, or probably when Earl had made his decision just before, the ghost image had disappeared, and from all chances it seemed, Earl would not be bothered by the phenomenon again. In minutes he was in the visitation room getting the good news from his lawyer that he would be let go tomorrow with this hell he had been experiencing vanishing all of a sudden like a morning fog lifting off a duck pond with the advent of the sun's rays.

What he would do with the rest of the life that had seemingly, miraculously been returned to him, was a question for the ages, but he would begin that tomorrow. For tonight he could only celebrate in his soul where the victory over the evil spirit had been won. The release had been just the icing on the cake.

86. Earl's Retreat

The release had been sweet, and the swirl of activity the next day in court was exciting and raised his spirits to euphoria. But nothing compared with the sweet reunion with Ellie, Emily and even Dr. Hugh, as the full realization of the narrow escape dawned on them. The sky had the night before been a red sky in the lore of ancient seaman of the ages but these landed people knew none of such omens.

They embraced in a gripping and clinging that seemed it would never end, with each one hoping that was so. But eventually the emotion of the moment was spent and the time for home going was now. The profuse thanks for the lawyer, the apologies for the lack of trust, the confessions of bad judgment or was it lack of faith in the God of their fathers that resonated in the will of their souls. The press people, including Tony, begged for interviews, for this was a news story for the ages, but there would be time for that someday, but not now.

Home is where the heart lives, and Earl and Ellie longed to be immersed in it, deep in the heart of Bryant Country. Just to sit around the yard or the front screened porch and play with Red and Blue and reminisce over the tragedy of the shooting, the terrible fear of arrest, the horror of the jail, the torment of the devils, and the reality of trial and verdict for days at a time. The realization of a lifetime together that had been mercifully granted them.

The day or so after the return home, Ellie brought iced tea to the front porch where Earl and Johnny Caldwell were holding court with each other.

"Sit a spell, Ellie girl?" Earl said, but she had no time for that now as the demands of the pleasures of routine were calling her, just like a Siren to the ancient Greeks of poetry and legend, although she had never heard of such things.

She returned into her house with its dusting and sorting, before cooking routines were due and that too would now be fun. Everything about life was suddenly fun to her although she knew this kind of excitement would not last.

Johnny rocked his rocker gently and spit into the spittoon handy by the heel expertly as though that angle shot had been practiced all his life, though it was new every morning as this one was.

"Well now, this here mess is over. When will you start the Still up again?" Johnny asked, rocking and occasionally spitting to the rhythm of an imaginary melody.

"Aint going to do it Johnny, done with that," Earl answered.

Johnny thought he heard those very words from Earl but he wasn't really sure. Was he dreaming?

"Say what?" Johnny asked incredulously.

"Yep, done thought it over and I ain't starting nothing up and that's final!" he said emphatically.

"Why in hell not, Earl? The federal men will have backed off for a few years at least and you alone has the brains and the guts to do it again! If you don't mind me saying so", Johnny pleaded.

"It ain't a matter of cain't and it ain't a matter of risk. It is a matter of what's right. In all them years of making the whiskey and selling it too, I never thought for a minute what it done to them people, like my friend Jack in that there jailhouse, or worse yet, what it done to me, the indifference to that suffering and all. It came clear to me in that last night in jail with that "Clarence" thing and, he weren't no uncle neither. I found that out the hard way. He was trying to kill me, and I don't mean my body and this life in it. It was eternal business he was after. He was out to get me, and get me he damn near did, one way or the other. But that's done for now, I'm through with it!" Earl said.

Johnny was dumb struck, but sensed he lacked the experience to understand the level that Earl was thinking on so left it alone. What Earl would do with the rest of his life, he could not imagine. The old whiskey King Pin, being anything else; but he was a friend for life and if that was what his friend wanted, he was all for it.

"Reckon Ellie could scramble up some of them eggs, I'm suddenly hungry," Johnny said as he rocked on to the beat of that silent melody.

"Shore, Ellie ain't forgot how to scramble eggs and breaking them eggs is what a fella has to do sometime if he wants to make one of them omelets," Earl said.

"Shore now," Johnny said. The rockers kept up their rhythmic cadence. Meanwhile the smell of frying bacon wafted from the kitchen up through the whole house as though Ellie had read their minds this beautiful morning and maybe she had.

Epilogue

It was the summer of 1956, and on Lake Talquin that summer as every summer, it was hot and humid, but the view across the lake now long restored after the break in 1933 had emptied the huge body of water in a few days, was cooling to the sensation, if only by illusion. The Democratic convention that year had nominated Adlai Stevenson of Illinois, probably by acclamation, but the losing presidential candidate against the General in 52 had left the Democrats desperate for some new blood on the ticket as his Vice Presidential running mate. Mr. Stevenson had taken the coward's way out and had thrown the choice for his running mate to the Convention for debate, vote, and selection on television before the world. The contest on the convention floor had pitted the young charismatic Senator John Kennedy from Massachusetts against the dull as a post Southern Senator from Tennessee, Estes Kefauver against each other in this brand new medium for national politics, television.

Southern strength or youthful appeal from the northeast, that was the real question to be battled out in the hearts and minds of the delegates that summer. Most homes did not have television, it was still a novelty and not yet the staple for home entertainment as it would later become.

But Ben and Sally Collins, a successful tobacco grower and their family of four children were an exception among the farm families that had recreation properties around the vast lake. They had a television set with the one channel available in those days and that was from nearby Tallahassee.

The property Ben and Sally's lake house was on was right on the water with a view of the dam to the south. The Collins property was surrounded by land owned by Ben, who always had been a shrewd investor in real estate. He had picked up about fifteen hundred acres nearby just for the delinquent taxes because the sandy black jack oak property was good for nothing useful, except running fox hounds against the wily gay fox that was native to north Florida and plentiful in the area surrounding the lake.

But even the little grays could be chased quite a distance by the July foxhounds that Ben loved to run. Many such excursions to retrieve them on extended hunts had given Ben Collins, the opportunity to meet the man himself, Earl Bryant, former moonshine king pin of legend who lived just south of the Collins property across the county border in Liberty County.

The Collins family spent the summers at the lake and Ben commuted, as it were, up to the farm near Havana every day, approximately twenty miles away as the crows fly. The kids and Sally enjoyed the lake with its swimming, boating and fishing as entertainment all summer long.

One summer evening, Ben announced that he had invited a Mr. Earl Bryant to come for dinner that Friday. One of his sons more interested in the dogs, hunting and fishing had been down to the Bryant place on one of the searches for the missing July fox hounds with Ben but he had never met the man. On television that day, the convention was winding down as the Senator from Massachusetts had lost on a floor fight to the old hand from Tennessee and the ticket was destined to end the same way in November against President Eisenhower for his second term, but that was only the future. The summer with its fun was for now.

Mr. Bryant's car arrived midafternoon and the kids ran out to greet him eager for any change being a welcome diversion. The hounds lounging around the yard put up a false bravado, as if protecting the house and grounds from a threatened invader but it was only show as the dogs and everyone else knew.

Since it was a Saturday, Ben was there to greet him and since he was a guest, no fishing trip was planned or allowed today. Mrs. Bryant for some reason could not come that day.

"Earl, meet my family. This is Sally and my four kids, Ben Jr., Mary Alice, Elizabeth and Eddie, the baby. Say hello to Mr. Bryant, kids," Ben said, and obediently gave their manners as Sally had trained them.

Ben and Earl walked around the grounds of the property sampling the scuppernong grapes from the arbor. Ben pointed out the Julys one by one, as if they were people entitled to the respect of an introduction or had qualities everybody should recognize or would want to hear about, which wasn't actually true, but nobody questioned Ben Collins on his domain.

Earl could appreciate that as he had, too, at one time, seen life through such lenses, so he tolerated the presumption. After a half hour or so, they came into the relative coolness of the modest, but spacious house and into to the screen porch on the lakefront where Earl and Ben took their seats. The children gathered together around, without the necessity of a word being spoken in that regard.

"Children, Mr. Bryant owns a good deal of property down south of here and manages his timber operations now. I asked Mr. Bryant to bring some of his home movies that he made of the wild deer and turkeys down on his place, is that right, Earl?," Ben asked.

"Yes, Suh, I brung it, this movie camera and screen. If you give me a minute, I'll set it up right here," Earl said, and Ben directed Ben, Jr., to help Mr. Bryant with his equipment, Ben, Jr, being somewhat talented that way.

The movie equipment was finally ready, the lights were turned off and the movie films began with reel after reel of close up pictures of deer of all ages and wild turkey by the droves dancing across the screen. The kids enjoyed the movie for a time and had endless questions. Finally, Sally asked innocently, "Mr. Bryant, with all that game on your place, what would happen if somebody slipped in there to hunt without permission?"

Earl thought about it for a minute, thinking back to an earlier time when he would have given no thought to taking his rifle and putting the intruder down or scaring the hell out of him, at least. Come to think of it, no one would have been fool enough in those days to even risk it with the reputation Earl Bryant had as whiskey king pin and a self-enforcer of law and his rights, at least in Bryant Country. But that was then and this is now, he thought and said,

"Every man has to decide what he wants to do with his life, Mrs. Collins, and I ain't the one to decide that for him, not for some skinny deer and wild turkeys. I think I has learned that much, ma'am, if nothing else.

The End

JOHN E. WOODBERY

www.ingramcontent.com/pod-product-compliance
Lightning Source LLC
Chambersburg PA
CBHW051936020726
47501CB00001B/146